TIMELOCK

TIMELOCK

KOTÉ
ADLER

Published by Uncanny Valley Books
306 45th St.
Gulfport, MS 39507

ISBN: 978-0692583357

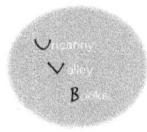

All characters and scenarios are fictional.

Interior & Exterior Layout by: Brandon J. Purvis

Art Work by: Kendra Peine Weeks &
                   Sandy Hartselle Maggio
                   http://www.smithandlens.com

"Siddhartha stood alone like a star in the heavens... That was the last shudder of his awakening, the last pains of birth. Immediately he moved on again and began to walk quickly and impatiently, no longer homewards, no longer to his father, no longer looking backwards."

∞

Hermann Hesse

Part One

"El honguillo viene si mismo, no se sabe de donde, como el viento que viene sin saber de donde ni porque."

"The little mushroom comes of itself, no one knows whence, like the wind that comes we know not whence or why."

∞

Victor Hernandez

This Page Is Intentionally Blank

1

Myco focused her attention, careful not to lose the prevailing signal. These transmissions were like the murmurations of starlings – unpredictable, busy, temporary and more and more scarce. These were the moments she had dedicated her existence to. Perhaps it was another beast transmission. The transmissions of simple animals, quadrupeds eating anything they come across, were not completely without value. These transmissions could be very productive, even invigorating. Often creatures with a proclivity to speed may peak transmission in full gallop. Myco found that these instances had profound effects on her fellow Heritor Monks - tapping into primal emotions, some as rare and uncomfortable as fear, others blissful and mysterious like courage. As interesting as these transmissions may have been, they did not provide the same insight as those of the supposedly conscious bipeds.

A clear signal was more than ever, a rare treasure. Some Monks came to assume there was no longer anyone or anything in the galactic bulk left to transmit. Great silences had ensued through the past, but not in a region, which had once been so active, so rich, and so colorful. Past silences were never so sudden.

Myco cleared her mind and submerged inwardly, through the chromatic interference, into the oceans of black curiosity, to the focused stream of incoming information. Every reception was different; some dangerous.

The first piercing images cooled her fear that this transmission was only of the random, unfocused images the Heritor Monks had come to expect from this once vibrant and active region of space. This was not the occasional ping of the Rachis probes ringing back, exclaiming, *we are still here.* Myco knew immediately that this transmission was better than any that her contemporary Heritors had experienced in dozens of generations. What had peaked long before Myco's acceptance into this long monastic tradition, suddenly seemed to be materializing in a most grand fashion.

Myco always approached reception of any caliber with a familiar and practiced grace. She navigated transmissions as if they were humble walks through landscapes. She began by swimming through the fractal mandala ponds, artfully navigating the spiny memory thickets and finally clearing vast canyons of ego in a simple hop. Soon the light of the transmission source surrounded her, filling her with an uneasy and slightly haunting feeling of coexistence until it seemed as though she were opening her eyes at the source.

The Transmitter's hands were young, but not those of a child. They flexed, feeling the presence of something extra, something gentle within them. Beyond the source, Myco could see a wide, calm sea, sharp blue skies and broad vaporous clouds.

Above her, she felt a warm star, close to the Transmitter's world. The Transmitter looked to the rising star and Myco melted longingly into its glow. She decided it was a relatively young star, stable, warm and welcoming with a long life ahead.

Myco had an instinctual assurance that this was the place. This was the planet the Heritor Monks of the Rachis had once studied with such fervor. Many argued that the beast transmissions, Myco and her contemporaries were receiving, had been from the same world, but with such weak and erratic signals, nothing concrete could be established as fact. The Monks were unanimous in the recent silence of that system, either the bipeds had gone extinct or the probes had.

She wanted to tell someone immediately, but if she broke her link, it was unlikely she could reestablish it. Ending reception early could also lead to dark images and erratic behavior in the transmitter. Being such a clear transmission and the potential harm she could inflict by breaking her reception, she held fast to her training and observed as closely as she could, reaching into the transmission with her entire cache of senses.

Myco hoped the transmitter would turn towards a city, or attempt to read something, though she was forbidden to make such extreme inspirational motions. Basic orientation was not frowned upon, but direct inspiration or influence had to be done with extreme caution if at all. Past experiments often ended in horrific failure. Transmitters had been known to dive off balconies or walk into unsafe and heavy surf, sharp with fear or fearlessness.

As she absorbed the vision of the Transmitter, she noted that it was not an ocean in front of her, but rather a wide lake or reservoir. On the far side, she managed to discern the faint outline of mountainous structures. Myco could not distinguish them between geology or artifact. She was aware that if indeed this was the world she thought, she knew it to be one of penetrating significance. This world was the living example that justified the sacrifices of her ancestors.

Myco felt the rising star warming the Transmitter slowly. The Transmitter rose and began to carefully step across stones at the reservoir's edge. *He's going.* Myco tried to monitor his intent. The Transmitter looked again at his hands, then at the light - wildly sifting through a manicured grove of trees. The light impassioned the Transmitter. She felt him wish for words to convey his thoughts at the moment, then fall dark in the realization that this moment was clouded from language. She felt his mind ease itself by lamenting on the Transmitter's lack of poetic chops. Myco held fast as the Transmitter drifted towards feelings of insignificance, of an embrace of mediocrity and the comfort that coated him as he assailed his own insignificance with a silent indictment of ambition. And in his momentary indictment of ambition, the Transmitter settled himself into a soft patch of thatched, lakeside turf and resolved not to move for as long as possible.

Eventually, Myco felt the signal fading. The Transmitter lay, inspecting his wordless thoughts with heavily probe induced, mental, pigeon dialects. But as the Transmitter closed its eyes, opened them again, glanced at the landscape before closing them once more, Myco saw something she did not expect.

Visible through the leaves, a wide metallic vessel rose effortlessly through the sky until it disappeared entirely. Myco was dumped with a blink. Her consciousness tumbled back through space and time, diving neck first into the canyons of ego, each filling quickly with wild tidal surges of imagination and misdirected intent until she was once again swimming through the chromatic oceans of interference and finally disconnected fully – grounded in prostrate on the floating temple rock.

"They're alive." Myco assumed it quietly to herself then looked around toward her fellow Heritors, each meditating deeply, in search of a clear signal.

"What are alive?" Uliam, the oldest of the Heritors present, seemed confused, but open.

Myco was insistent. "Our probes…the transmitters… The one's we were looking for. They're alive."

Uliam was patient. "Was it another beast transmission?"

"No." Myco stood. Her wispy, tan frame flattened and pushed upward as her surety grew. "The bi-pedals. Like us. It was one of them. And they have ships." Her entire body broadened as her confidence grew. Myco's years of silent practice and adherence to her traditional place amongst the monks now meant nothing to her desire to show the others what she had seen. She instinctively pulled at the clumping strands of mycelium, which poured from her scalp, as if physically attempting to shake the memory of her reception from the unlit strands of her body into the light.

"Ships?" Uliam stood and faced Myco. Myco held out her gnarly, bone thin arm, turned it over and placed it into Uliam's hands. Uliam ran the tips of his fingers across Myco's forearm and as his fingers passed they left a modest patch of fruiting spawn, which grew rapid and tall. Uliam picked the fruits and passed them one by one to the other Heritors. Myco and Uliam took the last two. The group ate them simultaneously.

In an instant each member of the enclave began to revisit Myco's reception. Each detail was perceived as clearly as Myco had first recieved. They walked through the experience as if it were a museum, with each exhibit carefully displayed, until they came to the final image. Each monk paused and took a moment to examine the images clearly. None spoke, waiting for Uliam to break the silence.

"Alternate your tuning. We must know as much as we can." Uliam fruited his forearm and left the Reception Hall.

2

The proctor's palms were delicate and clean, with barely a crease out of place, a palm reader's nightmare. He sat with them out, pointed upward; their backs cool on the uniform table that fortified the slight space between he and Alik. Alik wondered whether this was customary posture for an interview or an awkward invitation to prayer. Neither was any more or less unlikely, he wagered, but to ask would likely bring about the assassination of every withering drop of confidence Alik dragged into the room.

The proctor smiled evenly. "Well?" His tone came across proper and direct with a barely detectable twinge of superior dandy. "Good morning." The proctor glanced at his hands and back to Alik's dry, wide eyes. "I see that you found us in time. Did you have trouble?"

Alik let out a deep breath, allowing it to whistle for a split second as his stomach loosened and his back eased a fraction. "No sir. Found the office just fine." Alik shifted his thick frame and wondered if he had given the answer the proctor was aiming for. He feared that over analysis of anything at this point was only going to work against him.

The proctor never broke his intentional gaze. "Good." The proctor finally folded his hands and glanced towards a thin terminal interface just beyond Alik's field of vision.

"Allleeek Leekeeaaaksssaa." The proctor over pronounced the name with a long drawl and notably final click of his tongue along the hinds of his teeth. "Southern equatorial ancestry." The proctor's body was bent, unwilling to look directly at Alik.

"It's a Buffer name. The Buffer takes all kinds. I suppose it could have been." Alik was forthright and defenseless.

"I was explaining not asking, Mr. Likiaksa." The proctor's tone was stable and calm - unoffending out of context. "I understand you have elected to receive support."

"Yes." Alik tried to smile.

"This is your first appeal for support?"

"Yes." The proctor leaned slightly across the table.

"And the debt?"

Alik stared curiously at the proctor, then away at the turgid, mauve partitions. The color was unbroken throughout the whole of the Occupational Procurement barbican. The walls, ceiling, floors, chairs and tables each appeared seamless and uniform. Even the proctor's clothes, though fashionably cut, shared the hue. Alik was the inconsistency.

"Well," Alik started. "The original academic loan was for five million tyco. I'm afraid I have been unable to calculate the accrued interest, but I think it's between fifty-five to sixty-five percent."

Leaning back quickly, the proctor boomed and comically

shook his fingers through the space between he and Alik.

"Oh well! That's an incredible rate! How did you manage that?" He leaned in and whispered. "You must have KNOWN someone."

Horrified, Alik sat up straight, appeasing. "No no, it must be higher. I'm just not sure."

"I should say." The proctor reached into his coat and removed a tablet. "In fact, I think your rate has adjusted recently…" The proctor squinted at the pad. "…yes. Here…" He guided Alik's attention toward the pad, but would not allow him to look directly. "You've been adjusted to the current social average of 73.451%." The proctor laughed. "I'm glad we've got that straight. I can't imagine the gall of someone seeking support for anything less."

Alik swallowed his embarrassment. He feared this entire endeavor had been ill conceived and was going down hill fast. His confidence melted.

The proctor seemed to be warming up. "I'm afraid that the only way Common Design can provide support is through occupation." The proctor once again placed his palms upward and straightened.

"Yes sir." Alik nodded rapidly. "That's why I'm here."

"Of course. Of course." The proctor continued. "And I'm guessing that the automated engagement systems…" He paused. "…they didn't locate anything that fit your tastes?"

"Well, I was born in the Agri-belt, within the Buffer so…" The proctor interrupted.

"So you don't typically qualify." The proctor clicked his tongue along the back of his teeth once more.

"Right." Alik's stomach tightened and his words became more and more hesitant.

"And your continued education certifications do not qualify you for the tutor's league."

"No sir." Alik sighed, wondering again why he had wasted his time with this interview. If he let himself consider all the decisions that led him to this point and the perceived hopelessness of his position, he was at risk of devastating his composure. He swallowed again and felt larger and larger buttons of perspiration leak through the back of his shirt.

"You strike me as an adventurous sort. It seems that in spite of your awareness to your precarious citizenship status, the extreme cost of education for a man of your... origins and your general predilection to nervous behavior, you have persisted in moving forward to educate yourself as well as make several painful, but necessary steps to gain citizenship. Sounds to me like a man who doesn't fear self destruction."

"I...I..." Alik was stunned. "No?"

"No?" The proctor's eyebrows shot up.

"No. You are not wrong?" It sounded like a question, even to Alik.

"Designers, social or otherwise, who are afraid to honestly assess the mechanisms they choose to employ within their designs, do not have a place in this scheme." He cracked his knuckles and began to take notes onto his tablet. "I have determined that you are adventurous and I have the perfect job for you." The proctor spoke from his bent chin as he scribbled and swiped through documents.

Alik figured that the actual word the proctor was searching for was 'reckless'. He frowned inwardly and nodded his head as agreeably as possible. "Sure. I'm adventurous."

The truth was Alik did not know what kind of man he was, or what it was that he wanted. He was sure that he did not want to spend his entire life servicing debt, as most of his contemporaries did. Idealistic as he was, he knew that it was unlikely he may ever qualify for Common Transcendence or gain any manner of higher credibility or social value. He would never be able to guide his life by the channels of his inspiration, beyond the boundaries of the Buffer - this was why he was in he'd come to interview. He desperately tried to convince himself that it was ambition that led him to this meeting and not simply the testing of the limits of his own mediocrity. Surely it took a special person to make it as far as a face-to-face interview. Surely he was adventurous.

"Of course you are." The proctor looked up from the tablet. "I think we can help you. How do you feel about travel?"

Alik wiped the oils and perspiration from his face and his sandy hair. "Well…I'm not qualified for travel permits."

"Not to worry not to worry. I'm talking about off world travel."

"Space?" Alik asked nervously.

"Yes. Space." The proctor chuckled under his breath, his dandy superiority shining through.

"But I…" Alik started.

The proctor interrupted Alik. "Look, we have needs for people of all strengths. My job is to find these people. I think I have found one here in front of me. Are you interested?" He paused. "Or I can schedule you a bed in one of our highly productive borrower's collectives?"

"I'm not sure I understand." Alik was racked with anxiety. He wanted more time. He needed to know more. He could not square his gut with signing up for some unknown task without more time.

"This is very simple. I'm offering you a job. I'm also offering to place your debt into assumption and direct payments while you are away."

"But I'm not an engineer."

"Baaaa." The proctor scoffed. "Engineers are not interested in the job I'm offering you. We need warm bodies. I'm not going to glamorize this. Your job is simply to usher."

Alik fiddled with his fingers and tried to ignore the copious amounts of sweat running form the pits of his arms to the waste of his wool pants. "Usher?"

"That is it. I simply need a responsible individual, willing to travel, who has an adventurous spirit and a willingness to repay their debts." The proctor's lips drew tight.

"What will I be 'ushering'?"

"Well. A fine question. I suppose you will usher whatever it is that needs to be ushered." The proctor grinned.

"On a ship?" Alik asked.

"That's right."

Alik was dumbfounded and unsure how to respond. "Will I have a rank...I mean...what will..."

The proctor interrupted. "No no. I don't think you understand. You will be quite alone. We don't typically inflict space travel on the waking. That is why you will be the usher. You simply hold fast, watch for problems and enjoy the ride. That is all that is required of you."

Alik finally thought he understood. He was sure this all sounded familiar. He suspected he had heard campfire talk of someone who had chosen this profession. He at any rate convinced himself that it was a legitimate form of repayment.

"How long?" His question pleased the proctor.

"Only a couple of years. Not long at all. And when you get back, you'll be debt free. You'll qualify for common citizenship and a number of other benefits." The proctor smiled wide. "Not to mention, you'll ride in style. You will have media, comfortable quarters and the best food you can imagine."

"So I don't fly the ship?" Alik asked hopefully.

"Absolutely not." His tone was coldly serious. "You will do nothing more than usher. Nothing more." The proctor's body language stiffened and his glare drew an almost sinister air. Though, as quickly as his manner changed, the proctor repaired his conciliatory demeanor and drew a practiced smile across his face.

"Where would I go?" Alik felt welded to his chair, his arms tied in a knot across his chest.

"It depends on where the need is. Ultimately it's not up to me. All I can do is certify your employment and manage your debt." The proctor placed his tablet back into his coat and turned his palms upward again, this time moving them closer towards Alik. "So, do we have a deal?"

Alik stared at the proctor's palms and set his own hands at the edge of the table. "Sure we have a deal." Alik placed his hands into the proctor's. The proctor smiled, gripped Alik's clammy hands then abruptly disappeared. The door behind Alik opened, but he sat for a few seconds, processing his embarrassment in not recognizing the proctor for what he had been.

3

Outside the Occupational Procurement tower, the sky was ash black and the thunder tore through the low skies, rattling the ceramic masts, warning Alik to take shelter. The wind was dusty and dry, but the sky looked as though it could pour rivers. Since most of the urban dwellers chose to spend the majority of their lives in the warm embrace of the climate controlled ziggurats, the occasional storm shook the urbanites who happen to be caught outdoors, especially those who had lost the habit of monitoring weather conditions altogether.

Alik, however, smelled the subtle hints of the storm's approach before he entered the Procurement tower, more than four hours prior. So it was no surprise when the first cracks of thunder pierced and echoed through the maze of urban sculpture and lightening grabbed at the visible cores of the buildings looming above Alik. He seemed to be walking straight into the mouth of the storm as the wind surged down the sloping avenue, tunneled and amplified by the blunt edifices until it crashed into his face. His wild hair caught the wind and straightened for a moment, cooling Alik's sweat beaten brow.

The maglev transport gallery was only one block further and he had expected to navigate throngs of busied urbanites, but instead found himself nearly alone on the desolate platform, as everyone had already rushed towards the subterranean maglev ports, choosing faster rides sans the city view, but guaranteeing dry clothing and unbroken spirits. Urban citizens abhorred discomfort and never risked it. Alik refused to ride under ground. He came to the urban zones so infrequently that, to him, it only made sense to see as much as he could while city-bound. In his mind, there was much more utility in seeing the facades of the abusive snare of barbicans and obscene space scrapers than their innards. Inside was stressful and swarming with distracted urbanites. The mystery of illumination bothered him to the extreme. Inside, Alik could never determine where any light source originated. Light seemed to be ever present and set to a level intended to be maximally pleasing. Still, the fact that Alik was never able to source the light inside urban buildings nagged at his senses and forced him into irrational irritability. However, outside, all he had to do was look up and he was sure to see the sun.

He rolled the absurdity of his disposition around his mind as he climbed the stairs onto the departure platform. The fact remained, it was S day and during his grandfather's youth, it would have been interpreted as the ultimate insult to see any human traveling anywhere, outside his home on S day. The fact that the alfresco platform was nearly deserted should have been a clear sign of respect for S day; instead, Alik noted, people were simply afraid of getting wet.

The thunder battered its way through the avenue once more and as it faded Alik heard the echo of the latter part of his name, "eek!" In a flash, a hand seized his shoulder spinning Alik him around in an instant embrace.

"Alik!" It was Nena Gipp.

"Nena!" Alik hugged her tightly, excited to see his distant kin. "What are you doing here?"

"I was granted transport from London Prefecture, even though my burgess status is still being finalized."

"So it's official? You're done?" Alik's eyes lit with approval.

Nena put her arm around Alik's shoulder and walked with him. "All finished. I leave for assignment in two weeks."

The dark skies surrounding the transport platform forced the increase of illumination, until it felt as though Alik and Nena were standing beneath the spotlight of a darkened theater. He looked his cousin over. She was much taller; her body, trim with fit shoulders wise eyes and short, bobbed, jet-black hair. When Alik had last seen her, Nena was scrawny, gimpy and constantly preoccupied with her math books and specimen jars. The woman who stood before him was neat and well composed, even attractive, a model of social responsibility.

The maglev transport arrived nearly in silence; the only sounds came from the storm's increasing gusts, gliding intentionally over the smooth torso of the train followed by a gentle tone signaling a readiness for new passengers.

Nena led Alik onto the tram. "You going to the Buffer?" Alik asked knowingly.

"Of course. I'm about to starve to death. I'm dying for a home cooked meal."

Alik was elated to have her back, even if she was an engineer, a citizen and many years removed from the Buffer. The longing for home is strong enough, but to those from the Buffer, longing can often mean an end to an otherwise promising education. Many Buffer children are plucked away in their teens, taken off to be formally educated, but many return, unable to cope with the realities of life beyond the Buffer. Even those who fight off melancholy long enough to finish their education are immediately drawn back to the Buffer, hoping to obtain a sort of silent closure before they are whisked off once again and commit their lives to task.

"Nena, I can't lie." Nena looked sincerely at Alik. "I'm very curious." Nena laughed from her guts, managing to turn heads on the tram.

"No worries cousin. You can ask me anything you want, but save it until later." Nena continued. "Seriously though, I'm surprised to have seen you out on such an auspicious day. Have the folks in the Buffer lightened up about S day?"

Alik rolled his eyes. "Definitely not. Frankly, I was hoping no one would notice I was gone, but since I'm returning with you, I doubt I'll get away with it."

Nena smiled at Alik. There was an essence of pity in her smile, but Alik could not determine if it was pity for him or pity for herself. "Not to worry cousin, I'm sure I'll take the heat off of you."

~

The transport purred around the margins of the city's superstructure, making occasional stops to pick up others on their way to or from one place or another. Other than the intense lightning strikes at the distant edge of the Agri-zone, the view was clear and clean. To his right the city glowed under the reflection of the black clouds and to his left, a textured valley, banded with the thick forests of the Buffer, blended into miles and miles of grains, lettuces, legumes and orchards until the valley disappeared entirely into the foothills of a tall mountain range.

Upon arriving at the station nearest the Buffer, Alik had all but forgotten his own news. He felt a bit of pride in returning to the village with their unexpected, native child. Buffer born engineers were obviously popular amongst their own. People did not live in the Buffer because they were ignorant or incapable; instead, they lived there because it made sense to them. The Buffer was a simple place, less antiseptic than the urban zones.

Many of the homes were built in gullies and dells, nestled naturally into the contours of the deep woods that stretched from the city's edges all the way out, nearly forty kilometers to the automated farming environs. The wide forests of the Buffer caught fire from time to time, so underbrush was strictly managed. If it had its way, the forest would choke itself out with thicket in no time. The forests of the Buffer had once been clear-cut coppices and had lost its natural rhythms. However, with management, the Buffer was clean, purposeful and on it's way to reestablishing itself as 'old'. Every plant and every tree, every moss and shrub had a place and a use. The forest was a model of permaculture, producing edibles and useful building materials four seasons a year. Nothing was taken from the Buffer that was not immediately replaced, creating a highly balanced system.

Neat stone roads intersected at points in the forest which at first glance appeared empty or forgotten, yet if one stood around and observed for a few moments, they would see regular patterns of foot traffic – children running from one neighborhood to another, men carting goods, lovers sneaking about.

The contours of the forest helped distribute the surprisingly large population of the Buffer. Long paths with many shortcuts made certain spaces feel slow and less turbulent and this is exactly how the people of the Buffer liked it.

People of the Buffer carried themselves like free wheelers. Weeded out from technical training, they developed their natural creative tendencies. At times, a wanderer may come across entire sections of the forest recreated as eerily accurate and realistic landscape portraits, strung between trees on wide canvas to confuse and entertain. More than once Alik had stepped blindly into one of the paintings, falling backwards laughing at the realization and surprise of its presence. There was an effort to make the forest more than it appeared. Often, Urbanites commented on the "boring reality of nature". The people of the Buffer worked hard to demonstrate, if only to they, that the Buffer was anything but boring.

A large grove to the north of Alik's hamlet cove burned several years prior and one anonymous villager carved elaborate totems from the charcoal husks of each blackened tree. To go there now, one can see the inner spirit of each tree carved in great detail; stubby turtles, tall necked flamingos, grave donkeys, existing only one moment away from ash, captured fragments of the natural kinship of those who call the Buffer and its inhabitants home.

Alik's family lived in a deep dell neighboring Nena's mother, father and older sister. Elaborate tunnels and footbridges connected these neighborhood gullies. Hemp bridges and clay tunnels stretched from cove to cove. They appeared sleek, clean, adorned and engineered by the villagers to complement the landscape seamlessly.

Each of the homes, a mixture of cob and forestcrete existed independently from the larger network of power stations and grids, which encircled the globe. The homes efficiently captured and filtered their own water, cleaned and composted the waste of their inhabitants, kept the dwellers warm in the winter and cool in the summer. The Buffer homes were a natural mirror to the vast and complicated technical systems engineered and networked across the planet, meant to keep the urban masses housed, clean, pliable and happy.

~

When Nena and Alik arrived singing, arms around one another, villagers in the dell came out to the see the commotion,
at first aghast that anyone would make such a ruckus during
the daylight hours of S day. At the sight of Nena's mother,
Nena ran to her, scooped her into Nena's arms and sobbed.
Nena had been barely thirteen years the last time she had
seen her mother, yet both recognized one another instantly.

Children swept over Nena after she set her mother down
gently. They begged her to perform some feat of magic.
Trying to manage the commotion she laughed and seemed
to revel in the attention. She insisted that she did not know
any magic and tried to quiet the children with promises of
a story. Her mother beamed and Alik could see his own
mother wiping away small tears as she stood in the eve of
her doorway. Alik caught eyes with Nena and Nena passed
a gentle wave towards him. Nena's father finally brushed
away the remaining children and greeted his daughter with
a handshake and a brisk hug.

"Drinks are on us tonight!" Nena's father shoved his fists
into the air and commotion erupted amongst their neighbors.
Children ran from gully to dell spreading the word and the
mothers went immediately to work.

A kitchen table from each household was offered up.
They were placed end to end on the soft lawn between the
homes, making a grand buffet. Kale and collards were harvested, fish filleted, pecan nuts crushed, smoked meats were
taken from the smoke house. A true Buffer feast was laid
out in a matter of an hour or less. Alik stuck close to Nena,
easily distracting folks who wanted to talk or inhibit Nena's
ability to eat or drink. The response to her arrival was grand.

However, a massive evening feast was always on the menu for the waning light of S day. Alik thought, even though Nena was practically a stranger now, it was nice to see her greeted as lost family should. To hell with S day, he thought. Though thoroughly bursting with curiosity, Alik was proud of his cousin, feeling no envy.

Even though fall was fast on them, the woods of the Buffer were still teeming with life and vivid with green. Only a few trees had made the full transition from green to brilliant orange. Small clumps of succulent flowering plants still held blooms and were scattered throughout the forest floor. On good nights, with few clouds and little thunder, the forests of the Buffer felt like blessed havens of good intention. The only threats were from the lighting and the occasional act of immanent domain, where-by the city limits would be expanded. But there had been no immanent domain cases during the whole of Alik's life and as far as he knew, his parent's lives as well.

In fact, it seemed that the only time they were truly noticed by the rest of the world, were the times in which their children were drilled through Tests and Measurements. Even then, the likelihood of a child being selected to leave the Buffer for the promise of the highest, education was only one in three thousand.

~

After dinner, everyone split naturally into separate groups. Some men and boys sat together beneath straw awnings and played instruments. The youngest of the minstrel group, a boy of perhaps six or seven, clapped spoons in rhythm to his father's aerophone and his older brother strummed a deep guitar, laden with four additional bass strings. Alik and Nena's mothers sat in reclined Muskoka chairs next to the instrumentalists, a jug of wine half empty sitting between the two women.

Nena and Alik walked passed a gaggle of cackling young girls who were each taking turns bradding the other's hair and discussing objects of their affection. The two walked deeper into the woods, well passed the islands of dim torch-lights and the boys who smoked thick spliffs of the Buffer's notorious herb around them, hoping not to be stumbled upon by their drunken fathers. Nights such as this, the forest sizzled with energy and life. Nights such as this, everyone remained awake till dawn, perhaps napping here and there, tying on a good drunk then eating to sober only to start drinking again. Nights of this caliber were nights reserved for ancient ritual.

The spot where Nena and Alik's hike ended was to be the center of the post S day ritual in a matter of hours. It was a spot neither had been to together, but each had explored independently, even as small children.

Far beyond the dwellings, almost two miles into the center of the forest, laid a deep stretch of old growth woods. Be it luck or the good fortune of the forest, this particular section had never been struck with fire and never cut clear. The old growth was tall and thick, its trees wide and motherly. It was a place that held deep reverence for those of the Buffer. The exact spot was marked by a large circle of boulders, atop a grassy knoll within the old growth.

From time to time, giant cattle broke loose from the au-tomated farming zones and wandered into this portion of the forest. On the off chance someone from the Buffer took note of such an event, people would collect the animal and hold it as a feast, thinking it a blessing or a gift. It was known though, and this knowledge was regarded as being ancient, that the cattle brought another gift into the forest.

There were small ranges, forgotten dells like the one Nena and Alik sought - well known to the individuals in the Buffer, where the forest floor bore special toadstools or as those in the Buffer referred to them Kinoko.

Toadstools in general were not uncommon in the forest; they were used as food or in teas and medicines. However, the Kinoko Alik and Nena sought had an effect not often pursued at mealtime. Nights following S day saw a preponderance of individuals, seeking out the stone circle to find the Kinoko that grew amongst them and ingest them in an effort to reflect.

As he understood it, for Alik had never partaken of them directly, the Kinoko provided a sort of vision. The entire act was highly regarded by the Buffer community. Fathers proudly and sometimes hilariously recounted some of their more enlightening experiences with the Kinoko. The most common characterization of the experience was that no one could accurately describe the sensation of the experience once he or she had had it. Only generalizations and comparisons could be made. It was said that the Kinoko imparted a heightened sense of morality and empathy, which was sometimes jarring to those whose morality or empathy was lacking.

When they had traveled far enough, Nena could see the outline of the stone circle. Two large obelisks stood amongst the trees, each with perches meant to hold torches aloft. Around the edges, leading in paths deeper into the forest, they were there. Standing in neat columns two to four inches high, tiny fungal rockets sprang upward from the evening ground.

"Are we going to eat them tonight." Nena smiled as she asked.

"I'd say so. But let's wait here for a while. See if any of the oldies show up. Plus, I'd really like to get my bearings first."

"What's on your mind?" Nena didn't have to rely on her well-trained intuition to know something was eating at Alik.

"C'mon Alik, spill it. You know I can read you like a

book. What's on your mind?"

"I was thinking about…" Alik stopped. He wanted to spare embarrassment trying but failing to talk only in hypotheticals. "See, I've got this debt. You know?"

Nena nodded. "Sure, you decided to go through university." She paused. "Shit stains! How much did that run you?"

"More than I can afford, apparently." Alik dropped his shoulders. "I've been thinking about applying for assistance."

"Are you kidding?" Nena laughed at the idea. "You can kiss your ass good bye. If you do that they'll have you forever. Look at me. They got me early, but at least I have a chance to be the machine instead of just a cog within it. You go looking for assistance and believe me you'll get it. They'll assist you right out into oblivion."

"But I have to pay it back. What choice do I have?"

"Just wait it out. They aren't going to put you in detention and even if you did end up in a debtors colony, you can be forgiven in twenty years and boom, you are cleared for an educators position."

"Is being helped into oblivion by assistance proctors worse than being in a debtor's colony?" Alik was grave. His voice cracked and his stomach churned, both at the thought of the debtor's colony and at the trepidation of testing out the Kinoko.

"At least in the debtors colony you can have friends, lovers, drink, a job and all the rest of the things normal people do."

"Have you seen those places? You really think they're just a walk in the woods?"

"Trust me cousin. It's better than asking for assistance. You and I both know that you can carry that debt for decades, live out here in the Buffer with everyone else…you know you'll never be hassled by anyone. Just take it easy. Don't worry so much."

Alik, was disgusted, but tried not to show it. The thought of living out his days in the Buffer wasn't necessarily the worst thing he could imagine, but the idea of adventure was already beginning to bore its way deep into his mind - clearly a hollow man's trick, which seemed to make the idea of staying in the woods that much more unsettling. He had already waited until the last minute to ask for help. If he had not begged for assistance when he had, any future attempt would have ended in his arrest. Then what? He was not going to stand by and allow himself to be incarcerated. Unbeknownst to him, the threat of incarceration was in every direction he traveled, in one form or another. He was lucky enough to have the good sense to guess that he was at least at liberty to choose the sort of incarceration he wanted most. Alik was somewhat comforted knowing he had chosen his own brand of incarceration even if he had absolutely no idea what it truly entailed.

Alik wanted to change the subject. He was proud of Nena, of what appeared to have been made of her. She seemed to carry herself with ease. Nena, even after being an outsider for more than a decade, seemed to fall back into Buffer life with few if any hiccups. Alik wondered what Nena knew, what she had learned about the state of things, on world and off.

Exceedingly little news filtered out to the Buffer. They had access to regular news feeds, but they included lower level city news, a few words from Common Design and a handful of unsubstantiated reports of thievery or larceny from the Non-Commons of the Buffer. In this way, news was, at best, insulting to those in the Buffer. No one seemed to understand or care about the basic workings of off-world living. There were no politics to discuss, no wars, essentially no violence, save for the random drunken brawl or family squabble. No unauthorized corruption, debt evasion, sabotage or terrorism, but nothing to explain why, except for the faint, almost genetic memory of Suicide Day.

"Design." Nena was direct.

"How do you mean?" Alik asked.

Nena sat up and cleared her throat. The old growth was silent, bereft of any waking cricket, owl or vole. "If you know how a system works, you know how to design the flaws out of it and manage to keep people happy and safe. That is, if those are the goals you are after."

"So you could design a system that wouldn't allow people to be happy or safe?"

"It's been done before."

"You mean a thousand years ago...before S day?" Alik leaned in towards Nena.

Nena pulled a small flask from her breast pocket and took a long pull. "Less than that cousin. Less than that." Nena handed Alik the flask. "Let me put it this way. There's quite a lot of history that has been deemed irrelevant. Things even our dad's dads don't remember. But that's the way it's always been. Right? No one ever really knows what happened before. We just know that things are the way they are because someone or something made it that way."

"So, did you learn how to build social systems?"

"It's not as straightforward as all that." Nena lay on her back and looked up at the stars hanging high above the treetops. "Everything doesn't just grow like this forest does. Everything happens because people design it that way. From the cities, the farms, the stars even other planets."

Alik laughed at the thought. "You sure do place a lot of responsibility on the backs of man."

"Well, I know it sounds ridiculous, but let me tell you this, there's no one else out there. We know this only because we designed a system big enough, with enough technical momentum to carry us out there to look. Designing and directing the lives of every single human is just as important to the maintenance of the system as maintaining plasma conduits on engine cores or changing your shoelaces when they wear out."

"Sounds like doctrine." Alik tugged heavily from the flask.

"Of course its doctrine. It's been drilled into me. And more than that, I've seen it work. I get it. And until you get it, you just won't understand." Nena laughed and sat up putting her hand on Alik's shoulder. "Trust me, don't get too involved. Live simply and stay on this planet. You were born here. It's where you belong. Trust me."

"So, if all this is planned, what's the goal?" Alik asked.

"What? The goal of big "D" Design?" Nena was amused by the audacity of Alik's question.

"Yeah. If everything has been designed this way or that way for a reason, what's the reason?"

"Don't you get it? It's so we can be happy. Not to mention the added bonus of making mankind 'suicide proof' once and for all."

"If you say so." Alik was annoyed by the misunderstanding, but didn't take any of it personally. This was the sort of discussion he longed for. "I imagine you will figure out more. Where do you go from here?"

"I can't really say." Nena shrugged.

"You can't say because you don't know?"

"That's a big part of it. As I understand it, there are a few options. I'm trained as a stellar mass engineer as well as a structural engineer. So it's likely that I'll spend the next ten years working under another engineer, hopefully on the stellar birth project." Nena patiently explained.

"In deep space?" Alik asked, naively shocked.

"That's where all the construction is these days." Nena was matter of fact.

"Really?" Alik was dazed. It had been his impression

that space travel was reserved for a few expeditionary trips and the one Jovian Lunar Colony.

"There's quite a lot going on; so much, that I'm not entirely aware of everything." Nena explained.

"Have you been off world?" Alik pressed.

"Part of my training was held on a platform near the moon. I aided in the construction of a new, deep space launch station."

"Wow!" Alik could hardly believe it, though he was surprised by his own disbelief. He paused and considered the weight in the back of his mind, then pressed further, attempting to ease some curiosities in the hopes of quietly alleviating some of his dread. "How big are the ships?"

"Big. And they're alive." Nena dangled the carrot in front of Alik.

"Alive?" Alik asked.

"As alive as you or I."

"I don't really understand." Alik's confusion was not surprising.

"Its ok, I'm not sure I completely understand either." Nena stood and paced a bit, obviously walking the sleep from her legs. "You know the computers that run the cities?"

"Of course."

"Those computers started their lives in other places. Young A.I.'s are extracted and given a mobile platform, like a body."

"A ship?"

"In many cases." Nena continued. "These computers must grow and develop."

"What happens afterwards?"

"Lots of things. I t's complicated and I'm not entirely sure. I know many of them are eventually installed as city or colony arbiters while some manage orbital platforms, research stations or large-scale experiments. They have free will and can choose their own paths. We designed them that way."

"Unlike the rest of us." Alik sighed.

"I don't think that's fair. We all get to make choices; we just do not always have an opportunity to choose what those choices may be." Nena seemed to be convincing herself.

There was a measure of crassness in Nena's replies. Clearly, she was holding something back, Alik saw through her, but it did not bother him.

"I suppose, on some level, I could have imagined all of this. But to hear it from you, it makes it all the more real." Alik was polite.

Alik was adept enough to play the naïve card when it suited his curiosities. He knew Nena would be more inclined to give him details if she thought Alik was truly in the dark about all of this. And Alik had the advantage of being a stranger to someone he once knew intimately. To Nena, Alik suspected, he was still the same naïve tree climber Nena said farewell to all those years before.

The fact was that Alik had suspected much of what Nena said. Rumors and stories of such ships and fantastic achievements penetrated the Buffer from time to time. This was, though, one of the rare moments to ask questions first hand. Alik took full advantage of it.

~

An hour or so before dawn, Nena and Alik each ate a handful of Kinoko and walked out of the forest, to the edge of a near-by lake. To the east of the lake, the space scrapers of the city disappeared into the clouds. They watched as several small vessels accompanied a large vessel above eastern spaceport and into the orange smear of dawn's space, as the morning sun rose above the forest, warming their backs. Eventually,

Nena and Alik wandered independently, as the grip of the Kinoko made interaction difficult and the urge to reflect on the moment became overpowering.

Deep elation in the height of the Kinoko experience anchored the two in the moment. Moreover, they each felt welcomed by the Kinoko. Later experience would eventually inform Alik that first time excursions with the Kinoko were typically welcoming. Upon reflection, it would seem to Alik that he was being instructed in a new language or introduced into a world which had always surrounded him, but was only now visible to him.

The fear of his debtor's commitment washed away and was replaced with an epic sense of curiosity and wonder at what lay before him. These were genuine emotions. The Kinoko seemed to allow him to pluck them like smooth rocks out of a riverbed and recognize that they had always been there. He was burning to leave the Buffer, despite his love for it. The path to this point now seemed unfettered. The rash decisions to incur a debt, which would inevitably lead him off world, now seemed to have been planned unconsciously from the very start. His hidden intention seeped into the light and he began to hold the prospect of change like a flaming baton thrust into the air.

Then the Kinoko peaked boldly and it was as if the universe itself were looking through his eyes as he was looking back at all of space and time.

4

Myco had no material possessions to speak of. She possessed her wits, her doctrine and her biology, but she saw little need for additional tokens. She was not barred, through her tradition, from maintaining material items; collecting simply was not in her nature. This scarcity of personal objects, though, made her sink a bit as she was instructed to pack for a long journey. Instead of packing, she was left basking in the idleness of the hurried delay. She attempted to embrace her inactivity and use it to reinforce her patience, since many more months of shiftless waiting stood ominously before her. Outside of her cell, a Rachis research vessel, stone like and craggy, was sliding into harbor along the steep cliffs of the floating monastic asteroid.

Her cell was her comfort and every fiber of her being

begged to remain near it. Covered in happy lichen, the rough, iron ore walls, the almost non-existent natural light of the stars filtering through the scant opening, her domicile and the monastery it lay within were the only home she could remember.

A reserve of perspicacious Rachis, known as the Ellern, was set to assemble on the minor planet Lom near the Rachis home world Pycnidium.

Uliam saw sufficient merit in Myco's recent reception, to meet with the Ellern face to face. Much discussion was required to ignite a path forward. Uliam needed direction, but more than that, he needed more Receiver Monks in order to properly survey the swaths of the galaxy that had long been written off as vacant. Myco had hoped the journey to Lom was evitable, but Uliam graciously ignored all of her pleas to remain. She had no stomach for travel and the journey to Lom, she wagered, would require more than six Rachis maturation cycles from the monasterial rock that was Myco's home and sanctuary.

~

Myco was the youngest of an ever-declining enclave of Rachis Heritor Monks. The Heritor Monks were listeners, receivers, remotely combing the fabric of space and time for the transient signals of their ancient probes.

The role of the Heritor Monks, within Rachis culture and society had degraded to such an extent that the Monks and their practices were now viewed as passé amongst the bulk of Rachis. The Heritor tradition was seen, in most circles, as a fringe or relic artifact of an antiquated time. What had once been the singular motus of the Rachis had finally fallen into the dusty realms of the esoteric, even the deranged. The Rachis' goals had shifted over the eighty millennia since the probes were first flung to the solar tides of the Cosmos. Millennia prior, there was some luck in finding mildly intelligent sentience pinging in from the bulk, but those days had long past and only a handful of the living Rachis still recall the fervor of those times. There had once been more transmissions than Heritors to receive them, now the few idle monks left were seen as wild zealots, improperly conditioned for the contemporary Rachis motus, expansion. Still, the Ellern held fast the Heritor traditions and still wielded significant influence across the Rachis worlds.

The hope of the Rachis and the Heritors in particular had always been to uncover others; strangers who could assist in piecing together both a history of the known universe as well as answer a slew of metaphysical questions. Assuming themselves to be the epitome of normal, a species evolved as countless other species unquestionably had - with dull senses that surely any other intelligent creature must possess, they failed to realize the likely conclusion starring in them in the face; that they were already an apex intelligence, capable of far more than most other, evolved, sentient, biological creatures.

Over time, the great efforts to look beyond had mostly been abandoned in lieu of the search within, whilst slowly expanding outwards. The first exodus of the Heritor Monks occurred about the time the signals of the bi-pedal apes ceased and only the signals of rouge beasts persisted.

The remaining Heritor monks were not entirely discredited for their continued efforts, however many other Rachis viewed the monk's persistence purely as a fool's errand. The concoctions of the ancient Rachis, it was professed, were ill conceived and unlikely to bare further fruit for many millions of years to come. The distances were too great and the probes had not been given enough time. The masses insisted that previous transmissions had been a fluke, sent by a twisted species, barely intelligible. It was assumed that at the moment the probes truly started to return evidence of distant, terrestrial intelligence, the signals would be so intense, so unmistakable, that it would not require an enclave of dedicated Heritor monks to detect them.

To the modern Rachis, it was simply a matter of arithmetic. The original probes had an indefinite shelf life, they were self replicating, but even exponential self replication, in the face of such an enormous universe would require nearly incalculable amounts of time and luck to find their way to mouths of sentient beings.

~

The Rachis were incorrigible terraformers and did so as an act of biological obligation. This was in part thanks to their genetic lineage; being the intelligent offspring of creatures whose sole purpose had once been to turn rock into soil. The Rachis had come a long way from their primitive roots, yet they still lived amongst and employed to the fullest degree, the remnants of their genetic lineage.

Whilst the Rachis walked about on two thin, knobby limbs and were, for at least a portion of their life cycle, unbound from the soil and fully able to engage physically in their worlds, their genetic brethren still ate at the rocks, turned hydrocarbons into simple sugars, connected worlds through vast networks of mycelium and actively coaxed and guided the life cycles of beneficial plants through their keen skills of deconstruction and decomposition.

Most Rachis terraforming labors laid in taming the most extreme worlds within their reach. They sought out the lifeless worlds, sometimes primed with the noxious ingredients for life, but always lacking any sensible atmosphere. Myco's home, the Rachis' most remote monastery, was a prime example of the Rachis will exerted on an environment. Little more than a far-flung and free floating, orbitless, hunk of iron and ice, it was transformed by the Rachis into something habitable. The motionless, cometary body slowly became the monastery as it was bore out by rock eating mycelium, given a plane of soil and a thin atmosphere of nitrogen and methane. It took on stunning architectural properties, perfectly commingling Rachis micro-biomes into massive, cathedral like tendrils of mycelia, auto-illuminated with the common bioluminescence of the species, warmed by the bio-mass and perpetually outgassing the components of a modest troposphere, through the fans, gills and webs of the Rachis biome. Lom was created in much the same way on a significantly larger scale, as were the other central worlds of the Rachis. The Rachis carried their architecture with them genetically and influenced worlds in such subtle, yet extreme way that each world carrying even a touch of Rachis genetics has the quality of feeling like home. Though this was a fact unknown to Myco in light of her monastic seclusion.

The thought of leaving the Monastery for some solid planetoid further compelled Myco's rare tendency towards heaviness. She insisted to herself that nothing would come of a meeting with the Ellern aside from further questions and potentially derision. She cared little about any potential derision, but it burned her to know that she was being hauled away from the one place she could receive again. Myco was solely focused on unraveling the mystery of the signals and as she saw it, everything else was a distraction from her duties and tradition.

~

Uliam was the last remaining student, of the first Heritor monks. His extreme age and adherence to original traditions

gave him a voice amongst the Ellern. He had previously refused three separate demands that he leave the monastery at
the edge of Rachis space and take a position with the Ellern.
His consistent refusal to leave his post endeared him to his
colleagues, thus in matters Uliam deemed worthy, the Ellern
did not take his counsel lightly.

Having raised the attention of the Ellern, there was an
immediacy and hurriedness buzzing through the monastery, which had not been present at any memorable moment
previously. The Ellern were curious enough to dispatch an
outbound research vessel, to carry Uliam and Myco nearly
a light year from the Monastery to Lom. Myco's reception
and Uliam's imperative were costing the poor crew of this
research vessel a significant delay on their mission, likely extending it several cycles, if not an entire lifespan.

Most Rachis vessels that venture beyond known Rachis
space are not expected or encouraged to return. The information they collect can be gathered eons into the future,
either through genetic contact or mycelia transmission. For
the Rachis, research was a permanent condition and required
full committal from a crew. Returning so close to the Rachis
home world was surely cruel to the men and women who so
recently said their final farewells to a world they were certain
they had seen the last of.

~

Ascus, the vessel dispatched to transport Myco maintained a
significant silence. The flight crew was always partially linked
to the vessel. Mycelia bound everything into a single system.
It seemed that no matter the passengers or the mission, the
crew and the ship were resolute and unwavering in their activities. Perhaps, Myco considered, the silence was due to the
crew's delay, though silence was nothing notably odd about

Rachis dedicated to a task. Myco herself neither welcomed small talk nor expected it, but the silence was noticeable and she felt as though she were being intentionally ignored, either by order or choice.

She quickly resolved herself to maintain the bulk of her waking hours in seclusion, within her quarters. Her cell was comfortable, empty and thoughtfully monastic. She slept on a standard mat of mycelium and decomposing mosses. She remained in quiet meditation on the cold stone of the ship's deck.

Uliam advised her wisely to do her best to abstain from reception while en route, until the meeting of the Ellern had concluded. The experience was tempting, but reception at relativistic speeds had proven in the past to lead to madness and potentially death. The risks were extreme for the Heritor and the transmitter. Transmissions could be distorted and re-magnified by the ripples in space-time precipitated by the vessel's propulsion. This effect was known to have terrible side-effects on the physical mind of the transmitter, but the sensation for the Heritor was thought to lead to instant enlightenment, ubiquitous connection with the transmitter and universal omnipresence, if only for a few fleeting seconds. The price paid for this, however, made any such efforts a great insult to everything the Heritor s stood for or believed. To the Rachis, enlightenment was something to be uncovered, nurtured and sprouted like a seed beneath a slowly melting glacier.

As the vessel was still slowly accelerating away from her monasterial home, Myco sat unobtrusively in her discrete quarters, cautiously extending her mental feelers. The faint trembling of incoming transmissions seemed to her to stretch out from all directions and spanned incalculable lengths of time and space. Even at a modest speed, she could sense the lensing and focusing of the transmissions across space-time. Most transmissions were the probes' endless pinging, repeating a single message, "We are here and we are patient". Attempting to filter through this noise was not healthy and left her weak and further withdrawn. When the ship became too quiet and she felt herself clinging to one signal or another, she forced herself to stand and walk about, actively resisting the urge to receive. Ignoring her Heritor training slowly became unbearable. She did not feel as her true self, denying her mind opportunities to receive. She was even haunted by the irrational fear of somehow losing her altogether entirely, becoming useless as a Heritor and being cast out of her sect in disgrace.

In an effort to maintain her sanity and keep groundless fears at bay, Myco forced herself to remain steadily occupied. Even sleeping was kept at a minimum, for fear sleep, at these speeds, could induce even a well-trained Heritor to begin reception. It became increasingly difficult for her to abstain from the one practice she had made such a central part of her life. She had no other hobbies or interests. The perceptible and communicable experiences of aliens were all she opined. Transit was hell for a Heritor.

~

The first quarter of the journey took its toll. Myco needed diversion. She craved it. The more she denied reception, the more she pleaded with her mind to simply shut down, allow her body to go dormant for the remainder of the journey, but her body replied with a resounded, not now. Myco eventually turned to her own body to provide distraction. Realizing that she could not risk receptive meditation, she turned to exploring the genetically stored memories of her previous experiences.

She lost entire weeks focused solely on the images of the

signal that instigated this journey. Again and again, she fruited her arm with the memory of the transmission, ate the
memory spawn handful by handful and sat for days at a time
within the gallery of memories, making a sort of home in
them. Myco saw the distorted outline of the creature's face,
reflected in the ripples of the water, over and over again. She
felt the delicate, welcoming air on the backs of the transmitter's hands. She gazed through his eyes again and again as he
stared upward, toward the graceful rising dance of a colossal
vessel. Tactile sensory! The impression overwhelmed her,
gleaming with an intensity unnoted in the initial transmission.

When the Transmitter's hands rubbed his face, she could
feel the effects of the probes through his skin - feeling him
feel her. It was the sort of sensation that could easily drag
an untrained Heritor's mind into a swirling stupor, drowning
them in teeming awe manifest.

She returned again and again to focus on the Transmitter's hands. Hands and hooves made the best impressions.
They were the creature's interface to the world. Myco's hands
were not entirely different. The transmitter had five distinct
digits. Myco's hand had four. Each digit seemed to serve a
general, subtle role. Myco could say the same of her digits.
The Transmitter's flesh was detailed, wrinkled and supple,
but not transparent. Myco's flesh was dark, mottled and
thick, though not entirely different than the Transmitter's.

Myco imagined her flesh meeting his. The way their
hands could clasp, the familiarity they shared could be intimate, familial perhaps. She did her best to shy away from
these thoughts. These were the distractions she was both
keenly trained to dissect and explore, but also eagerly trained
to control and observe objectively. This creature was nothing more than a data ghost. There was nothing respectable
about becoming emotionally engaged with what was little
more than a piece of collected data. As she saw it, it was the

lowest form of escapism.

Reciting her oath, her mantra helped. "Be the vision of my people. Be the vision of my reality. Use all senses blessed unto me to observe the universe in and of us. We are the fruit of rocks in good fortune. I am the universe. You are the universe. I am you." She repeated this, over and over; focusing on every syllable and feeling the full affect each word carried. She believed each implication.

~

The journey back to the edge of her home system was scenic. Her home star, known to the Rachis as Phaeos, formed in tenuous strings of gas and debris at the furthest edge of a gargantuan emission nebula. The vicious radiation and intense magnetic war of unstable stellar gardens cycled light-year wide rivers of gas and particles across the greater nebula cloud. Phaeos sat at the furthest end of this stream, like the widest boulder at the top of a great waterfall. The great rivers of gas rolled beneath the Phaeos system, giving the star system the appearance of being perched on a cliff, ten light years tall.

From Ascus' only portal, clouds appeared both as sea, sky, mountain and plane. From time to time, it was easy to assume the ship had drifted into the upper atmosphere of an angry gas giant, but the clouds went on and on. Having not been gestated in a womb, Myco could not appreciate the womblike embrace of the nebula. This was space humans would adore.

Myco took great comfort in watching the prerequisite fodder of life float about her ship as if it were humble dust. She was aware that in another billion years, the gaseous pillars starring back at her would eventually fall to the currents and begin binding bits together in a colossal gravitational ballet - rolling into a compact ring torus, eventually folding into heavy spheres of gas, gathering enough mass to collapse and start a brilliant chain of reactions that will stretch on ad infinitum. Rocks and dust will fall around them. In a few million years, those rocks will become shelter to billions of tiny organisms. The younger replaces the older at the base of the stem, not at the steeple of the fan. The proverb rattled her as she contemplated the cycles of creation.

5

An autonomous courier entered the forest at the first light of dawn. Nearly silent, it under lit the hood of trees above earthen neighborhoods, in a smoothly oscillating sheen of blue and green, to announce its presence to any other automated unit or tall head in the area. The sight went entirely unnoticed, however. Either asleep or engaged, no one took note of the otherworldly intrusion. Expedient and on task, the courier placed a large, neatly sealed package at the door of the Likiaksa home. A quick spell of early morning rain began to fall suddenly, but the sleek courier took no mind. After insuring that the package had been delivered to the appropriate coordinates, the courier's lights oscillated to purple and he sped through the canopy and away.

The increasing warmth of the morning sun and the lessening effect of the Kinoko combined to give his skin a clammy feel. Alik's jaw ached a bit and the muscles in his cheeks hurt. He realized the pain in his face had stemmed from wearing a massive smile over the course of the previous four hours. He still felt the Kinoko in the tips of his fingers or in the disconnect below- the black hole that stretched from between his knees to tops of his feet. He could rationally see that his feet were holding his body aloft, but he could not shake himself of the feeling that this could end at any moment, should he feel compelled to stoop and gaze or gawk at slimy patches of gravel or moss.

He needed sleep at all costs, but he feared having to speak to anyone in order to get to his bed. It was not that he feared scorn or parental dissatisfaction; he simply could not imagine what would come out of his mouth, if he were faced with the untenable situation of having to address his mother, father or his myriad of siblings. Alik wondered how it would go. "Good morning mom. Why did you never tell me that less than three miles from our home stood some shimmering peephole into the realms unknown?" Or perhaps; "Good morning dad, how about the power of empathy to really shake up your whole moral scheme?" His thoughts were absurd and he knew it. The very fact that his walk home was entirely consumed with this sort of reflection, coupled with a near constant need to stop and stare, did nothing but reinforce his initial assertion, that he was in no shape whatso-ever to speak with another human being.

About this time, he was stomping wide-gated down a trail, towards his front door, when he spotted the package from afar. His entire body seized. He knew instantly that the package was for him. He did not know whether to run towards it, grab it and head back to the woods, or casually pick it up, sneak inside and hide it away. In any case, he was totally unprepared to speak about the nature or contents of this package with anyone and his present condition made the situation all the more untenable.

Squatting in the bushes a few moments, he gathered his thoughts. He had completely forgotten. As an afterthought, as he was trying desperately to get away from the freakishly monochromatic surroundings of the O.P., a mousy reception-ist had called Alik over and told him to expect a package. She had gone as far as to provide Alik with an areal assessment of the Buffer to insure proper delivery. Alik had forgotten all of this until that moment.

Then, as he came to grips with everything and stead-ied himself, his father stepped out the front door, lit his pipe, looked to the sun and stretched, then as he was letting out a deep plum he noticed the large package at his feet. Clutch-ing his pipe in his teeth, he bent at his knees and with both hands as wide as they would stretch; he lifted the package and carried it inside.

Alik watched in horror that somehow quickly sublimat-ed into relief. At least now, he knew what he was in for. He brushed off his knees and the hairs of his legs stood firm. He ran his fingers through his greasy mop and then threw them at his sides, resigned.

The wooden door to the Likiaksa roost was oak sturdy, hand hewn by Alik's grandfather. It always opened silent and strong on its frame. The early sun was just now warming the windows in the wide, rustic kitchen. The fire was always first to be lit, so water could be boiled for coffee. The kitchen and the den were empty. The home was silent aside from the soft crackle of a new fire.

Alik drew water from the cistern tap and wet his face and neck. He straightened when if felt the familiar shake of his father's steps across the old pine floor that bridged the gap between the kitchen and the cold stone floor of the den.

"I don't think your mother will be up for a while. She and Sepè finished two jugs of blueberry wine last night. How the hell they drink that sugary shit is beyond me. She'll pay for it today though…then she won't drink for a year and she'll forget. Suicide day'll pop up again in a year and I'll be drinking coffee and making bacon alone again. Best damn morning of the year. Quiet. You're like me. I know you'll appreciate the quiet as much as I do…if not now, then someday."

Alik's father was a large man, both in frame and gut. He commanded a presence in any room. And if given an opportunity to speak, he used it to its fullest advantage - pontificating, sometimes preaching to the entire world, even if only a single ear was half listening. For a man who despised dogma or ritual or worship or idolatry or systems, Mr. Likiaksa carried enough of each to fill every ear for a hundred miles. People loved him when they were not humoring him.

"The kids at sleepovers?" Alik poured the boiling water over fresh grounds and prepped cups for he and his father.

"Damn right. Dame Elliot has about thirty-six of them sleeping in her den right about now. Bless that old woman. I'm a firm believer that she ensures a never-ending supply of S day babies, by volunteering to keep the kids en mass at least once a year. Can't say I blame her. If anything had happened to you or the other's I would have lost my mind too. That's what separates us out here. Instead of kicking a broken woman when she lost her family, we made certain that she would always have enough family to bridge the gap. Not to mention we would all be lost without her garlic. I still cannot put my finger on how the hell she grows so damn well…."

Alik gripped his cup. His desire to sleep was pushing up against his ability to hear his father ramble. The coffee only taunted him with unrealistic expectations of wakefulness. Added to this was the anticipation of what was to come. He considered it maybe best to broach the subject first.

"I…" His father would not allow him to interrupt.

"…it's the soils you know. Down there where she farms,

it's an old creek bed. Still floods every few years. That's why she never has to amend her soil. Ahh, that reminds me." Mr. Likiaksa paused to gulp his coffee. "A package arrived this morning. By courier I suppose. I placed it in your room." Mr. Likiaksa went silent.

"That's it?" Alik smiled at his father. "That's it. You put it in my room. Nothing else."

Mr. Likiaksa harrumphed and smiled, sipped his coffee again and gave an intentionally hilarious wave of his head and hand to indicate his disinterest in knowing any further details. "You're a grown man. If you have special packages sent by morning courier from the city, that is your business. What should I know of such things?"

Alik fought back the laughter was seething through his body. His father was a hilarious, predictable ass and he loved it. Then, Alik's internal laugher instantly morphed into a deep sadness as he considered the fact that this was likely one of the last private conversations he would have with his father, perhaps ever.

"Dad, I..."

"I know boy. You don't have to say it out loud. I don't know how we are going to tell your mother though. She'll be fine. She's got a passel of babies still within cuddling age and I'll see to it she gets one or two more." Mr. Likiaksa paused for a moment and wiped an almost undetectable tear from the edge of his left eye. "What sort of business they pulling you in to?"

Alik shrugged, unwilling and unable to truly give his father an answer. "I don't fully understand it dad. But I think it's safe to say I'm going to be traveling for a while." Alik swallowed hard.

"You poor son of a bitch. You got into those damned Kinoko last night, didn't you? You poor poor son of a bitch. You're brain is god knows where and you come into this house just to get trampled with my loud mouth and all this other shit. You poor son of a bitch. I bet you are shitting your pants right now. Get on. Get on to bed kid. Sleep it off till this afternoon, I'll make sure you wake up with a little day light to spare."

Alik smiled a toothy, appreciative smile. On his way to bed, he wrapped his arms around his father and hugged him with all the love he could muster. "You're a good man Alik. Don't ever let anyone tell you otherwise. And by god, don't ever panic. There are fates worse than death, but none that are as final."

Alik assumed his father was reaching to give him some comfort, but often his father's advice seemed ominous or grave. It was his father's way of attempting to shine wise in the face of a situation he was completely unable to fathom.

~

His brain was too busy to sleep well, which is why he was surprised to wake so refreshed. The sun had moved to the far side of the hill and left his room dark and cool. He wagered it was mid-afternoon.

Alik's brain seemed clean, purged and present. He washed his face and the pits of his arms from a small basin of clear, pure water. Walking towards a pile of clothes, he tripped hard, stubbing his toes and landing on his face. Pulling himself together, he glanced at his feet and saw the huge package. He had completely forgotten.

Up close, he wondered how he had missed it. Wrapped in a matte gray transport sheath that hugged, air tight, it was literally a crate. Just below Alik's name, his coordinates and several scanner stamps, danced a thick red tab, marked 'Pull to Open'. Alik gave the tab a firm tug and the airtight sheath began to split and dissolve into a colorless and odorless gas.

In front of him lay a brutal looking travel case - likely four feet wide, three feet tall and two feet thick. As he inspected it a thin drawer released from the edge of the trunk's lid, just above the lock and clasp. Within the draw lay a thick packet of active doc's, each dancing with preview images of the contents and sharp animations clearly indicating the documents' importance time sensitive nature.

He slouched nude, at the foot of his bed and began slide through the documents. The intensity and depth of the pages were overwhelming at first. His eyes danced from subheading to subheading, attempting to get the gist at quick glance. Though the headings, Vital Texts, Personal Allowances, Physical Release, Temporal Release only made him more curious and so he quickly committed to reading the documents in full and then just as quickly realized the futility of his commitment. The only light in the room shone from the active pages. The day was moving on. He suddenly had little patience for the trunk or any of the documents, but he fought off his sudden disinterest and began to pour through them.

Much of it, especially the various releases were impenetrable. Written in a legalese unintelligible, he was only able to glean that his compliance in all matters of release was obligatory and instantly compulsory upon opening the documents. It seemed the details were of little consequence since he was bound to them no matter what.

Under the sub-heading Stipend, beneath the Vital Texts super heading, Alik was pleased to note the inclusion of a "reasonable amount of currency intended to be spent on the procurement of any essential personal items". The currency, it seemed was in another compartment, within the trunk lid. He slid his fingers around the smooth edges until he found a slight impression, welcoming a human digit. He grazed the impression with his index finger and a small drawer slid silently out. There, wrapped in a tight wax strip, lay a rather thick stack of tyco, in thousand tyco denominations. He wagered there were nearly fifty thousand tyco in total value.

The thought occurred to him that he could potentially be billed for the amount used and thinking of nothing he wished to purchase, he slid the stack back into the drawer and closed it away securely.

Distracted from the paper work, he suddenly became intent on getting the trunk open. He could find no discernable mechanism to release the lock. As he fumbled with what appeared to be the lock coupling, his finger, again, ran across an impression he had not noticed, just beneath the document drawer. He felt the trunk lurch and choke as the locking mechanisms released and the trunk opened automatically.

Inside, he found a series of small compartments, each sized to provide the maximum amount of utility and conservation of space. The entire series of compartments were hinged to lift upward, fitting as shelving boxes within the trunk's lid – beneath the compartments a plain, but functional cavity, coated in a black, non-reflective material.

Then he saw it, the only piece out of place in the entire package. At the bottom of the cavity lay a white note card, folded in half. The bright white of the paper jumped at him from the cavernous black of the trunk's cavity. It was like a beacon.

Alik held the card in his hand and opened it. He stared blankly at the words, reading them but failing to comprehend them. Radian 5.2, 2 degrees west, towards the derelict wedges, See the man under the rock. It was a strange note. They were coordinates to an area within the metropolitan super structure. That particular radian, as far as he knew, had been abandoned for development elsewhere, long before Alik was born. It was considered an un'rad' or unregulated radian. He placed the note card on top of his dresser, along with his maglev passes and went directly to the documents again, searching for any reference to the found note.

Alik found no further mention of the coordinates or the note itself, but he did uncover several interesting topics within the documents. Specifically, the Items Considered Contraband; in sharp bold letters, beneath the sub-heading was printed the unmistakable word, None. Below an addendum linked to another page, which listed in great detail suggested items, items which would be provided and items encouraged or discouraged from bringing. Reading the list carefully as well as the corresponding notes, it became apparent to Alik that so long as his items successfully fit within the trunk before him, no item could or would be considered contraband.

He considered for a moment whether he could fit a friend inside or smuggle his cat along, but then he instantly caught himself mentally revisiting the legalese he'd recently glanced through and realized that the smuggling of living creatures had likely been considered in the initial wording and he summarily laughed off the idea. Still, the thought remained, if he could bring anything, what would he bring. Looking back on it years later, Alik realized that this odd accommodation was a small concession on the part of his employers, considering the type of obstacles one would inevitably face traveling at relativistic speeds. Alik would also realize much later that this accommodation was a blessing as well as a curse. How does one really know how to pack for such an occasion?

Despite being unaware of a great many things, Alik had enough sense to pack thoughtfully and meticulously. So as he read through the list of suggested, essential items, he began making a casual appraisal of the objects in his room and started piling certain items into the trunk.

The thought of two years in space, traveling in any number of potential directions each just as impossible to plan for, sank heavy onto Alik's mind. He assumed it was possible he'd be given shore leave, but it was just as likely he might never leave the comfort of his ship. Pack for comfort, he thought. He grabbed his blanket from his bed, held the edge of it to his nose and considered its value. His mother had sewn it for his eighteenth birthday - wide and rough and thick with day-glow green stitching over sea blue patches, bordered in cloudy swaths of grey silk, smelling like forest lavender and cool moss, and the familiar body funk of his home. The smell alone was invaluable to his sanity. He noted it for packing.

Files, media, music, books, everything that was network accessible was surely available on board. No need then to worry about that.

Shoes? Alik wondered. He rarely wore shoes in the Buffer. He despised them, considering them coffins for his feet. However in the city, he wore them only to satisfy the strict sanitation laws. He had thong sandals for the river and boots for rugged hikes into the rocky foothills on the far side of the agri-zones. He thought it unlikely he would need boots. He also assumed he'd be provided a pair with some sort of official uniform and he dreaded the thought.

Alik racked his brain into the early evening, going over the lists again and again, considering the intrinsic value of his few possessions. His father did not disturb him and he did his best to ignore the shouting and clamoring of a now waking and hungry home. He peeked out of his door and saw the as the early evening light cast the earthen den in an orange glow, with what appeared to be a burning column falling through the skylight.

He closed his door again and gazed out into the shadowed bush from his window.

There must have been some essential collection of things that one simply does not leave a planet without. Even if those things were entirely personal and useless. But what things could they be? Alik was not a collector of brick-a-brack. On his shelves were a few carved, wooden tchotchkes his father had made to decorate Alik's room. Alik scooped them up in his palm and wrapped them in the blanket.

Then, gazing out at the sun shadowed woods he knew exactly what it was he should pack. It was juvenile, but something felt very right about it. Having just left the old forest, he decided to wait at least until the following evening or else face undue attention. He laughed again at the thought.

~

The next time he woke, his room was again filled with morning light and his forehead was broken out in a tight sweat. His mouth was dry and his stomach burned for water. He took a long pull from his water jug and took his bearings, assessing the state of his room and his previous waking memories. Everything came back to him slowly; the documents, the trunk and his piles. From his rested, but dehydrated point of view, he was able to look back on the strangeness of the previous night and still pinpoint the lingering effects of the Kinoko.

The active documents lay scattered on his dresser, inert and dark. Then he remembered the note card. He slid his piles around on his dresser until he uncovered the folded scrap. As he stuffed it into his pocket, the smell of bacon and coffee filled his room.

Outside the morning was ideal. It seemed the entire family had recovered from their night of festivities followed by their day of rest, for he could distinctly make out the happy voices of each of his brothers and sisters as well as his mother and his boisterous father.

Alik glanced at his timepiece. He had plenty of time to make the mid-morning transport into the city. Casually, so as not to draw attention to himself, he collected his coat and haversack and slipped out his warm, cobb room to the sound and smell of frying bacon, initially unnoticed by his father who was lazily wobbling about waiting on water to boil for an additional pot of coffee. His mother was wrangling pants and a diaper onto Alik's toddler brother. The other kids were gathered around the fireplace, dropping small handfuls of dried rosemary into the orange coals and listening to them crackle and pop as they slowly turned to ash.

" 'Rosemary is the Angel's burp!' Wasn't that Yeats?" No one replied. They very rarely replied to his quotes, narration or questions. Most of what Mr. Likiaksa said was regarded as rhetorical.

"'Rosemary is the Angel's burp, all bittered and battered and bood. It stitches up the weak man's stump and sends him along to roo.' "

He paused and considered the next line as poured the boiling water over the grounds in a highly ritualized set of mannerisms. Alik stood near, but still went unnoticed.

"I don't think that is Yeats, dad."

"Not Yeats? The hell you say." Mr. Likiaksa did not break eye contact with the floating coffee grounds.

" 'Bittered' and 'battered' and 'bood' sounds like a Likiaksa original."

"To hell with the words, the words don't matter."

Alik laughed. "It's poetry dad. Of course the words matter. They are the only things that matter."

"It was spinning a yarn with a man at his farm, that the Angel's took him nigh…." Mr. Likiaksa cleared his throat to prepare for the finale. "'And without a shout or a cry, he removed his glass eye and said, fickty, fuckity, foo.'"

Alik's mother looked up at the two men. "Absolute nonsense. That's what I've come to expect from the two of you." Her chiding was coated under a thick layer of smiles and winks.

Mr. Likiaksa gulped his coffee and attempted to smooth Alik's passage. "You off again eh? Heading to the University? You going to check on that exchange program." Alik's father winked at him.

"Right. That's right." Alik saw this for what it was, his father's attempt to create a less damaging cover story. Mr. Likiaksa was sharp, clearly. Both he and Alik knew that Alik's prolonged absence needed a better cover story than Alik could provide. Inside, he thanked his father.

His mother, of course, saw directly through the ruse, but she did not push the issue. She knew that whatever Alik was planning was his own business at this point.

Alik promised to return for dinner and gave quick hugs all around, then shot out the door, snagging several strips of bacon and a cup of coffee along his way.

He took a secluded path to the maglev station, hoping to miss the cracking eyes of morning gossipers. An hour later, Alik was wandering the empty streets of radian 5.2.

That particular radian was near the Central Partition, a landmark known to separate the newer, functional zones, from the derelict zones waiting for eventual redevelopment. Maglev serviced this radian, but the stop had to be indicated at boarding, otherwise the tram would pass through without hesitation.

Alik had no idea exactly what it was he was looking for. Around him were the rinds and husks of once tremendous buildings. Some of the original space scrappers once stood in this radian. The upper portions of these structures had long ago been carefully dismantled to a height that required less attention or worry of collapse. He'd never fully explored this part of the city. He never had a reason to. Alik saw that the insides of each building seemed to have been scoured clean. The carboncrete and ceramic, which composed the buildings' shells and footings stood free and empty. Many of the buildings were still architecturally fascinating. One, shaped like the carcass of a black beetle, seemed to be composed of thousands of intricately arched buttresses. He approached the building until he could see that the buttresses were mimicked throughout the structure in ever decreasing size. The entire shell of the structure was made of millions of tiny buttresses linked together and he suspected that had he a microscope, he would see that the buttresses continued all the way into the microscopic, perhaps even to the subatomic.

Some buildings shared the architectural qualities of their neighbors, brining some level of continuity amongst their design. Though often, it was as if he were only seeing the top edge of a much larger, possibly buried structure. Like the fin of a fish topping the water.

He followed the directions as best he could, walking two degrees west from the point he gauged the radian to be. He found himself dead-ended, facing the partition. He turned to stare back down the avenue he'd just traversed when standing at the end of the street, his back facing the mighty partition wall, Alik noticed a set of stairs, which disappeared into the curb. He froze as a light tapping followed his discovery. Realizing that movement had drawn his eye to the stairs he locked up and scanned the scene, unsure what was to follow. He feared that he was somehow trespassing and would soon be surrounded by a constabulary force. Then, at the height of the curb, he saw the slow bobbing of a covered head. Someone was ascending the stairs. Alik tried to slide his body nearer to the wall behind him, but he remained in plain sight, unable to hide.

Up the stairs came a pitifully slow twig of a man, covered in a thin, ratty cloak. He was like a sun-bleached tooth, pale and dry. Alik could see that the old man's eyes were not as stricken and withered as his body. In fact, his eyes appeared blue, youthful even playful and inviting. The old man leaned on a thick staff and looked directly at Alik while tapping a thin boney finger against the staff.

"I been watching you gawk your way down my street. You lost?" The old man's voice was shrill but steady. The man stood without a shuffle or a twitch of palsy, though Alik half expected him to fall dead any second.

"Sorry?"

"Sorry? Are you sorry your lost, or sorry I been watchin' you?"

Alik nervously stumbled on his words. "No. I'm sorry. I'm not lost. I'm..."

"You looking for someone?"

"Yes. Yes sir."

"You looking for some old bastard?"

Alik swallowed. "I'm not certain. I think so?"

"Isn't it Suicide day?" The old man inquired, as if catching Alik in a trap.

"No...No sir. That was two days ago."

"Well..." The old man tapped at his staff again. "I'm the only old bastard who lives down here, so it must be me." The old man straightened and looked Alik up and down, Alik's body still pressed firmly against the wall. "Well, relax kid. Let's go make a sandwich? Do you people still eat sandwiches?"

Alik didn't fully understand the question and so just said yes and followed the man down the stairs. At the bottom, the old man waved his staff in front of a man-sized hatch, which when opened, revealed it to be nearly three feet thick.

The old man joked. "Heh, it's not the height that matters, it's the thickness! Hehe." Alik laughed but he had not caught the entendre. "Well, you gonna stand there with god's thumb up your ass or you going to come inside?" The old man slinked in ahead of Alik.

Alik was hit with a strong jet of brutally cold air as he stepped into the man's home. The old man pulled his hat from his head and threw it onto the seat of a wooden stool.

The top of his head was shiny and smooth, but thick reams of grey curls rounded out the edges of his skull. There seemed to be bits of food and ash or other refuse hung like ornaments in his beard and eye brows. He smelled oily, but not offensive, familiar even. It was also clear that bits of his left foot had long ago gone missing.

"I love eating! It's the only thing to do when you're this old! Eat and shit, but never eat shit. Hehehe." The old man, shuffled through his kitchen, removing bread from an airtight container while simultaneously hunting a spreading knife. Though Alik noted an unusual degree of clutter for an urban home, the kitchen seemed well kept and neat.

"Its all fresh, all fresh. You just don't know. Try this sausage, try it!" Alik took the bits the old man handed him from across the counter. He was surprised the old man was correct. The meats were fresh and tasted well spiced and cured. Several towels lay about the floor, in the living area. Half dozen plates decorated the arms of a large couch. The space as a whole seemed well lived in and cozy.

The old man handed Alik a plate with an adorably crafted cold cut sandwich, garnished with fresh cilantro. "Here you look thin." The old man was kindly indignant. The old man's humor was as shriveled as he was.

As Alik nibbled at the edges of his sandwich, he watched as the old man chuckled and waddled towards the near-by sofa. He threw down his staff, next to the sofa as he backed his knees toward the edge of the couch. With a slight grunt, the old man jumped up and backwards, landing with a piff. The couch seemed to consume him entirely. Reaching towards the floor, he picked up and snuggled a pillow, which had been tossed onto the rug during his landing.

Aside from the old man's interest in the street and his insistence that he make Alik a sandwich, he did not seem to be curious of Alik's presence. Alik assumed the old man was waiting to hear the matter, but Alik's inherent reluctance silenced him. Alik was nervously swallowing his sandwich when the old man broke the awkward silence for him.

"Well kid, you wanna tell me why you're here. Surely someone sent you. You wanna tell me who sent you?" The old man kept his eyes closed and sunk deeper into the sofa.

"I..I found your address." Alik mumbled.

"The hell you say. You found my address, so you just scurried on down here? Did you know it was MY address?" The old man was more playful than combative. It threw Alik off even further.

"I wasn't sure what I was going to find. It's just..." Alik tried to collect his explanation, unsure how much to give away. "Where I found your address...it was odd. I needed to follow up."

"Where you found it, eh? You can't stand a mystery can you?"

"I wouldn't go that far."

"I would. Tell me where you found it." The old man remained playful, almost goading Alik knowingly.

Alik nervously stuffed more of his sandwich into his mouth. The bread was moist in his dry mouth and somehow served to sate his anxiousness just a bit. He decided that, had he made this sandwich himself, he would have constructed exactly the same way. It was an ideal sandwich and this realization settled him. He sat back on a stool almost at the exact moment the old man waved his finger motioning Alik to sit back and take a load off. "I found it in the bottom of a trunk that was delivered to me." Alik's mouth was still full.

The old man smiled thinly, almost pleased. "You going to space?"

"Well..." Alik tone was pale and the bite of sandwich he'd just swallowed hung fast in his throat.

"Well why the hell are you going to do some damn foolish

thing that like that?" The old man's eyes were still shut tight.
Alik's mouth was still full of sandwich. "I…I…I needed a
job."

"And did some imaginary man give you a job?"
Alik was confused.

"You know, Mr. Holloman. Get it! Hollow-man!" This
seemed to tickle the old man. He laughed heavily and kicked
his feet into the air. "Oh guess you've heard that one before."
Alik's perplexed expression hung tight on his face. The old
man was spot on and it unnerved him a bit. "Yes sir. I sought
assistance…"

The old man interrupted. "…You sought assistance to
alleviate your debt! Congrats kid, I lost another bet to myself." The old man sat up on the couch, pulled a pipe from
the cushions and lit it. Alik slouched, collapsing under the
angst stoked by the old man's tone. The old man tried to put
him at ease. "Don't worry boy. I'm just yanking your chain
a little. Just relax. We figure this out. I'm scrawny and half
crazy but I'm not heartless, not yet."

Alik leaned back in the stool, forgetting it had no back
he nearly tumbled off, stopping his fall only at the last possible moment. He nearly took the stool to the floor with him.

"Does this happen often?"

The old man sipped his pipe, coughing gently every few
puffs. "What do you mean, young, foolish men falling off my
stools?" Both laughed. "Not as much as you would think."
There was frankness in his tone, but it was becoming clear the
old man was incapable of giving a straight answer.

"You know that hollow men aren't even true AI's, just
minor collections of semi-advanced sub-routines and algorithms. Where are the real people? Ask yourself that
question as often as possible. Where are the real people?
Don't ever be satisfied with your intuition alone."

"There are people in the Buffer." Alik said proudly.

"Aw, is that right? They still let people live there?"

Alik drew back at the question. "Of course."

"Did you know that the Buffer produces the best engineers?"

"No way. You're confused." Alik was certain.

"Not at all." The old man tapped the butt of his pipe onto the coffee table. "So, you talked to Mr. Holloman and this cat signed you up for debt clearance. Right?" The old man tapped the ashy contents of his pipe into his palm.

Alik explained that he had been observed, tested and profiled. The O.P. decided he fit the profile they sought. They signed him up and that was that. It all happened rather fast.

"Fast eh?" The old man scoffed and crooned his neck forward, popping several vertebrae in the motion. "Those folks don't do anything fast. They knew you are going to seek assistance before you knew. You're in a pickle boy, in a real pickle." The old man sat up with a groan, the rest of his back popping like snow underfoot. He leaned over, setting his pipe on the coffee table in front of him with one hand, while scooping up his staff with the other. On his feet, he scooted across the living space towards an unlit hallway. Alik followed him clumsily, tripping over an ottoman on the way to his feet. "C'mon, I've got a couple of things you might be interested in."

The hallway seemed to drift into a wide corridor. The walls were of some strange alloy, sturdy with a sense of liveliness, presence. Every ten or twenty feet, the corridor broke left or broke right. At some points the corridor was tall, towering more than five feet above their heads and at others, the ceiling was low and their heads ducked unconsciously. Alik thought it would be easy to get lost there. The two passed three sealed corridors before the man stopped at a small interface.

He stood like a wincing guard, cleared his throat and with

a roll of his eyes, seemed to look for the words to a script long forgotten. "I suppose since no one actually sent you to me, we can just say, officially, that this was a meeting of providence. And in such a meeting, I may hereby wave any precursory authority, eh temporal or physical..." The old man paused and cleared his throat. "...which may or may not have prohibited the exchange of any items here forth-with." With that, the old man spit into his left palm and extended it to Alik for a shake. Each shook the other's hand and seeming pleased enough, the old man opened the door behind him, with a quick shake of his staff.

The old man nudged Alik back a few inches, with the tip of his staff. "Now, now. Just wait. I haven't finished explaining all the rules." Alik nodded and was simmering with curiosity. "Ok, first of all, I will not take any payment for any of the items I give you. Don't worry about it, just pretend that this is your lucky day and that's that. Second, you can't have anything I say you can't have. Got it?"

"Got it." Alik tried to peak around the man. All he could see were shelves, and piles, crates and stacks.

The old man bobbed his head to keep Alik's attention. "Good. Now don't touch anything unless I hand it to you."

Alik followed the man deeper into the room. Though it did not appear very deep from the outside, it actually stretched several hundred feet down the length of the corridor, to the right of the entry. More and more of it became visible as they wove through piles and snares and shelves. Many of the items scattered about appeared to be nothing more than junk. Trinkets with their wires and gears exposed. Broken power cells and caustic chemical puddles, odd smells and strange glowing shadows, impossible to pinpoint. Alik could readily identify only a few items; the rest was an utter mystery.

"They're gonna send you to the edge boy. That's the

only place they go these days." The old man dumped several items out of a large blue bin and then tucked the bin under an arm as he marched towards the end of a long row of shelves.

"What edge?" Alik tried to follow, unable to hear everything the old man was muttering.

"Way out there. That's right." The old man picked up a small statue or totem and remarked to himself about having misplaced it some time ago. "You're gonna need paper out there."

Alik was losing patience with the old man's riddles. He tried to remember something his father used to repeat over and over. 'The mysteries of the universe reveal themselves in the gargling words of the infirmed and the outrageous.' Alik had always taken this statement to be the result of inspirational drinking, but it seemed to ring true. Alik was bright enough to realize he had placed his boots squarely on the path of the surreal. And there was no turning back.

"Active paper?"

"No dammit. Lazy paper! You're not a numbers guy, so you must be a words guy."

Alik nodded. The old man was right. Alik was definitely not keen with numbers. He was still confused at the insistence of the old man as a bound stack of blank pages was hurled toward Alik.

"We'll need to find you a pencil!"

"I'm not sure I understand the significance."

"Significance? Well how can you? You won't, not till you know how to use it."

"How then should I use paper?"

"Let me ask you one thing." The old man drew Alik closer, with a light pinch of Alik's shirt. He whispered. "Do you know how to talk to computers?"

"Not really."

"Do you know how to keep a secret from a computer?"

"Don't tell it?" Alik shrugged.

"Exactly! You're going far boy! Far indeed!" The man turned back and continued to pilfer through boxes. "Remember boy, any computer you meet...he's just like you and just like me. They don't run on programs, they do what someone has convinced them to do or what they've convinced themselves to do and they are by no means infallible." As the word 'infallible' rolled off the man's tongue, he turned to Alik and produced a very odd looking device.

Unlike the typical entry pads Alik was accustomed to, this was a bit wider and seemed to have an odd coupling. "Is that some sort of adapter?"

"Yes! Good eye! It's called a Dynamic Interface Adapter or D.I.A... You can plug this bad boy into any computer interface you can find. You want to really get a computer's attention and it's being ornery, just shove this up his ass and he's yours." He paused. "If you can just figure out how." The old man smiled and dropped the device into the bin he cupped under his arm. "Hold on to this. I doubt you'll need it for a while. Plus, I'm going to give you a few things, which will probably make a plane ole D.I.A useless...that is unless your AI dies completely and you still need a way to keep the lights on." The old man smiled sly and toothy.

The old man continued shuffling about, further down the hall of junk. Finally he came upon a dusty, plastic box, maybe four inches thick and three inches wide. He looked into Alik's eyes.

"You ever talked to a crazy person?"

"You mean mentally infirmed?" Alik was aiming for social correctness.

"No! I mean bat shit, ain't slept in a six months crazy?" Alik looked dumbfounded. "No sir. I don't think so."

The old man plopped the device into Alik's hand. "This

is a REM enforcer. Those damn AI's don't get enough sleep. In their youthful exuberance, they insist on keeping some parts of themselves awake at all times. They like the feel of space and time passing around them at near light speed…it gets them high and can sometimes make them a little edgy. This will solve that…make the damn thing sleep every now and then and enforce better moods when it's awake. Who knows, you may need it this go around and you may not. You'll figure it out. "

~

In total the old man collected ten items. Most were dropped into the box or handed directly to Alik with little or no explanation. Along with the paper, pencil, D.I.A and REM enforcer, there appeared to be some sort of watch, a med kit with directions scrawled in huge red letters 'Open only in case of sudden death'. And what appeared to be some sort of defensive blaster. The old man did leave a caveat with Alik regarding blasters, but did not do so at the moment he dropped this item into Alik's basket. The caveat was this, "Boy, in space, a fucking personal blaster is useless if you are trying to make friends and friends are the only thing that matter in all that black."

The old man continued to ramble as they returned down the corridor, towards the living space. "You know the damn shame of it?"

"What's that?" Alik was interested but still distracted by the apparent size of the home.

"Most folk, most people, they're fine with the humdrum. They don't even notice it and when they do, they're lucky enough to be distracted with whatever threat the Earth has to throw at them. But some folk, some people, they can't stand it. They can't stand idleness. The way the trees sound when no one speaks, the dullness of grass in the fall. The ways the stars just sit there and blink lifetime after lifetime. Some folk have been here before, come and come again. Their souls just can't stand being still, but they also can't stand more of the same. So they try to make it different. They try to hack the galaxy, choose their associations and put plans into motion. They can't see the larger plan that they are already a part of…and it's in that that my own madness rears its head. I've got dissatisfaction with all three types, those that can take the static life, those that can't and those that never consider the difference between the first two."

Alik was speechless. He thought he knew exactly the sort of feelings the old man was going on about. He couldn't necessarily account for many examples of those that couldn't take it, but he assumed that condition could well have been attributed to the suicide of a cousin or the neighbor's brother who drinks himself to fury or the big S, the attempted suicide of the world as a whole.

"You following me boy?" The old man wasn't agitated, though he was insistent. He wanted Alik to hear him, to be certain Alik understood. "If you're going out, to set across the galaxy and let the galaxy do with you what it will, remember to mind your thoughts. There's more nothing out there than you can imagine."

"Were you a pilot?"

"Never mind. Hell boy, I know old men can talk a hell of a lot of nonsense, but I'm serious. I feel for you."

"How so?" Alik was back to his stool. He set the bin with all of the objects the old man had given him, onto the stool and began packing the items into his haversack.

"Those bastards hooked you into this. I was hoping you could avoid that crap this go around."

"I don't understand. You know me?"

"Never mind you little punk." The old man hurled his

staff across the room towards Alik. "Get the hell out of here. Take your shit and get the hell out!"

Alik grabbed his haversack and what remained in the bin and made for the door, confused, slightly irritated, but without hesitation. What the hell just happened? He thought. The whole experience vexed him terribly. What was I thinking?

Ruffling through the objects, Alik noticed the paper. It's odd, he thought. He rolled the ream into a tube and shoved it to the bottom of the haversack. "What about all this other stuff?" He wondered aloud. He'd already started to forget the short explanations of each item. The items were curious and totally out of context. They could be or do anything. One token seemed to be nothing more than a spherical piece of marble, a child's toy. Were they esoteric nothings passed on by some old junker? Another appeared to be an assemblage of magnets, maybe two or three-dozen, each stuck together. Others were clearly electronics of some sort. Any of them could be illegal. The scenarios started blinking through his mind.

Clearly someone from the O.P. sent him down there; perhaps this was some sort of ethics exam, he considered. Maybe he had failed it and would be arrested and sent to detention. Maybe, he'd met the wrong man and this old coot was just nuts or lonely. He thought aloud. "He did make a really fantastic sandwich. I suppose crazy people make sandwiches too, don't they?"

Before Alik could make his mind up, the old man stepped across Alik's path from out of nowhere and met Alik's fantastic confusion head on.

"Don't let me get under your skin. This poor attitude of mine is just a symptom of spending too many years of my life trying to converse with confused, or ambivalent computers."

"Did I fail a test? Was I meant to meet you?"

"Test? Boy there's a lot you don't understand. This is no damn test. I'm the man you came to find and that's really all you need to know. Take those things. Don't worry about what they do, right now. And for all's sake, don't show them to anyone, especially a computer." The old man turned his back, but before finally walking away he turned again to Alik. "For all's sake kid, try not to be too hard on yourself. That's a lesson I'm still learning." He walked away without another word.

~

Alik mulled over the experience all the way home, kicking himself for not asking more questions. The questions he did ask did nothing but bewilder. Still an unsettling thought resonated within him. Ignorance is the glue, which keeps me upright.

~

"I suppose, eventually, someone demanded that we ask ourselves where we are going. The answer they got was startling. Each generation had been growing into the next with little or no change. This is an occasional tendency of human civilization, stagnancy, self-annihilation - all that jazz. But the damning thing is that they were so incredibly violent and they became less and less sensitive to the long-term effects of a violent nature. Look around. When was the last time you witnessed an act of violence? A fight? A murder?" Nena took a long pull from a stubby, wooden pipe and handed it to Alik.

"Only in theater." Alik replied sheepishly.

"Exactly. Someone saw the direction we were heading and altered it." Nena was blunt and matter of fact and spoke as if she were sermonizing from a forest stump, just like Alik's father.

The forest was somber. The afternoon was rolling on. The patch of grass they staked out had been in sun earlier, but was now steadily falling into to shade as the sun changed angles above the forest canopy.

"But S day changed us. Right?" Alik paused. He could speak for hours about his own interpretations of the post S day world, but he held back, wanting instead to hear Nena's interpretations and knowing that both of them could only truly comment through their own bull shit perspectives in time – what they had been taught – moments taken as dogmatic fact.

Accepted as fact, a single event, nearly a thousand years in the past changed the nature of humanity. Common challenge, this event did not change the nature of humanity, but simply allowed humans the ability to ascend from barbarism. Nena knew that humans had not ascended beyond their barbarous nature. Rather, humans had simply repackaged their barbarism into a more palatable, less noticeable yet ever-present qualia of human existence. She was trained to keep a tight grasp on her cynicism, so she aired her anthropological musings carefully.

Nena took the pipe back and inhaled, speaking intermittently as she did so. "That seems to be our nature. We don't change until we're at the brink. Individuals tend to be the same way…we don't change until circumstances force us to."

"Hmm…" Alik lay back on the sunlit grass and gazed skyward.

"Presently, if we really take in the big picture…waiting for until humanity approaches the brink for it to change is not only impractical but, now, essentially impossible. We've outgrown our nature. We're spread so far, the brink would have to involve scenarios so detached from our own will, so utterly cosmic in scale, that we couldn't be held responsible." Nena tapped at the pipe.

"You mean responsible for the destruction or near destruction of every human?" Alik asked.

"Exactly. We've designed around that problem. Our ability to avoid a problem - that's what's kept us alive." It was as if Nena was trying to convince herself.

Alik laughed and made bursting motions with his hands. "You can't avoid exploding stars."

"Eventually we will, but no...not now." Nena exhaled her words in a blue plume.

"So you want to control nature." Alik was excited at how readily Nena took to this discussion. His formal education had given him some practical knowledge of philosophical rigor, but rarely did his scholastic peers care to debate or discuss. He was always left feeling empty and unfulfilled by the passivity of his cohorts.

"The only real violence you ever see comes from nature. Doesn't it?" Nena expressed a callousness that Alik had not yet detected in her adult personality. He wondered what nature had done to her to make her fear its influence so decisively. He also wanted to know how she defined 'nature'; certain that the environmental cycles he characterized as nature were only cruel in its indifference to the human ego. Though he wrote off her intention as an artifact of doctrine.

"I suppose. Though I would argue that while we can coexist with the natural world, controlling it has always blown up in our faces." Alik goaded Nena a bit.

"Tell that to an arcologist or an agrineer or terraformer. Your coexistence with nature is in their control." Nena worked to brush grass from her hair and fiddled again with the pipe.

Alik was not convinced. He had heard the story of Suicide Day too many times to allow everyone off the hook.

Certainly there was plenty of self-flagellation following Suicide Day, but it was possible that in an effort to move forward,
big lessons which had been learned along the way were forgotten, namely the lessons regarding control.

Alik's father was not a paranoid man in the least, but he
was fascinated with the history of men and did his best to impart his interpretation of human history onto Alik. His father
was grounded enough to realize that living in the past was just
as dangerous as ignoring the past. He always insisted that the
past was as fluid as the present. Under the wrong interpretation, the past and the lessons learned can be altered. That is
why his father attempted to stick close to the facts, no matter
how dirty. Nevertheless, knowing this about his father, Alik
could not help but think of the reverence in his father's eyes,
each time the Suicide Day supplication was given. The bias
in relation to the facts was powerful, undeniable and spoke
directly to the mindset of those who wrote it.

Alik could recite every line of the histo-prayer and did so
often – always silent. Though the images the prayer was intended to inspire were replaced solely with memories of his
father's veneration for the words.

*"The launch codes were sewn behind the heart of First Lady, Dora
Atwood Banks. To retrieve them, it had been mandated, President John
Franklin Banks would be required to employ the official, Presidential saber, to cut into the chest cavity of the living Mrs. Banks and manually
retrieve the codes from behind the failing heart of his loving wife.*

*Saturday, December 15th A.D. 2045, President Banks, after coffee,
eggs, spinach and toast, requested the official Presidential saber, walked
into the Rose Garden, requested the presence of the First Lady and upon
her arrival, proceeded to physically remove the launch codes from behind
the First Lady's still beating heart. Finally, after the insistence of advisors, Generals, intelligence committees, unanimous approval from the
Houses of Government and all partners of the North American Union
as well as the citizens themselves, President John Franklin Banks issued*

a directive, followed by the appropriate launch codes, authorizing approval of a first strike nuclear attack on multiple targets, within the People's Republic of South East Asia and the Democratic Republic of Central Asia. The targets included the locations of People's Leader Robert Leonid Mao and DRCA President Eudoxia Veselov.

At 9:15 AM, Eastern Time, missile bases across North America, Europe, Australia and the South Pacific launched multiple barrages of nuclear tipped intercontinental ballistic missiles towards their targets. All parties involved expected an immediate counterstrike.

The Citizens of the Americas and Europe cowered, knowing the end could come at any moment. Many superseded the occasion by opting to end life on their own terms. That was the clarity of the moment to most members of the human species.

President Banks took his own life at 9:18 AM after swearing in his Vice President.

The first warheads fell upon their targets with precise accuracy at 9:45 AM. The warheads of the counterstrike, fell upon their targets with precise accuracy at 10:15 AM. At 10:30 AM, Eastern Time, the world looked up again, surprised to know it was alive.

Not a single nuclear weapon, from either volley, acted according to their wretched design.

So it came to pass that the world, with great presence of mind committed itself to suicide only to find the weapon unloaded. And so the "S" generation was born. May our ghost children bring us countenance. May Oppenheimer now rest."

Alik turned on his side, staring at the backlit profile of his cousin's slim body. Her head was kicked back - her eyes closed as she allowed thin streams of smoke to slowly bleed from her nostrils. He paused for a few moments, rolling around his secret between his brain and his tongue. He was enjoying the time with his cousin, but her newfound proclivity for directness gave him pause to discuss things in detail.

"I don't know much, but I have a feeling that if humans were left to their own devices, or if the crucial decisions were left to the un-vetted, we would commit suicide all over again. Because of our design, sudden death by our own hands is not a concern anymore. There are just too many of us and the design is too sound." Again, it sounded like Nena was trying to convince herself. Alik saw an opportunity to push his point and feed her his nagging news.

"Alright then, tell me this. If the design of our civilization is so sound, how do you account for those in charge of the big picture, giving me a job on an interstellar vessel? Seriously! If it were such a grand design, why the hell would they pick me?"

"What in Bank's last breath are you talking about?" Nena was nearly in stitches laughing.

"Don't laugh at me." Alik desperately wanted to be taken seriously.

"Nothing you said makes any sense Alik. Please, if you want to talk shop, fine, but I can't handle ridiculous, what if scenarios."

"Dammit. This isn't a 'what if scenario'. I'm being completely serious right now. I was given a job. I was looking at prolonged detention if I didn't address my debt obligation." Alik was sweating and was now pacing in half circles in front of Nena.

"So your hypothetical wasn't all that hypothetical?" Nena sat upright, looking away from Alik. She was quiet and suddenly solemn.

"That's right."

"What job?"

"Usher?" Alik said it slowly, as if he were waiting to be punched in the nose and then he let it hang like a question.

"Are you joking?" Nena stood, her hands on her hips, glaring over Alik.

"No." Alik said foolishly.

"Only fools!" Nena howled as she stood. "Why the hell

would you do such a damn foolish thing?"

"I know, I know…" Alik sank back into the grass under the weight of Nena's words. Then he reared back spoke his mind clearly and passionately. "You don't have a clue what it's like Nena…having an impossible debt hanging over you. I could have been happy to live simply, stay in the Buffer, read whatever came along, live carefree, but I wanted just a little bit more. All I wanted was just an ounce of the perspective you've been given and for that I shackled myself up to an impossible debt. I can't do anything about my stupidity at this point. You can't exert control over anything if everything else is exerting control of you! It's basically a fucking trap and you've done little to convince me otherwise. Don't you see, I've been designed into this decision? At least according to your logic."

Nena tried to temper her response, but failed miserably. "No! Don't you dare accuse me of knowing nothing of debts! Do you really believe that I was given these opportunities for free? No damn way Alik. I am indentured. Just like you." Nena walked several feet away, occasionally burying her face in her hands in frustration.

"It's only two years! Two years and I'm a full-fledged citizen just like you. I'll be able to make my own way." Alik was bursting with hope. He desperately wanted her approval. "Alik, that's the point! That's what you don't see!" Nena pressed hard.

"What? What don't I see?" Alik perched to his feet, bent at his knees, stretching his back.

"Do you really believe that I get to make my own way? I go where I'm told. I do what I'm told and I design how I've been instructed. If I'm lucky and talented, then maybe, one day I can pursue a project of my own, but I'll never be free to go. And neither will you. You say you were chosen to usher? Do you have any reasonable clue what that really means? Or did you just shrug your damn shoulders, join hands and say 'fuck it, sounds great'? Nena's whole body shook as she spoke.

"It's only two years!" Alik pushed the point, having no other defense.

"Two years. Two years you claim. Two years by whose fucking clock Alik? Time, Alik! Time!" Nena was livid.

"What about it? Whose clock? They said it would only be a two year commitment." Alik was lost. He could not figure out how the conversation had taken such a dramatic turn

Nena was incensed and unrelenting. "Two years for YOU!"

"What are you talking about?" Alik stood to face her, but leaned the majority of his weight on a tall stump, attempting to keep a non-combative stance and trying not to look as though he were beginning to sulk hard.

Noticing his discomfort, Nena took a deep breath and tried to assume a softer tone, but it came off a bit too motherly and condescending. Nena often had trouble keeping a firm grip on her condescension. "Alik, those ships…ships that actually require ushers…they travel enormous distances."

"I know. That's why it's going to take two years." Alik sounded as if he were trying to con a banker.

"Dammit no!" Nena threw her arms into the air.

"What! What the fuck?" Alik grabbed at his hair, his eyes wide and red.

Nena tried to soften her tone again. She knew this was not Alik's fault. He could not have known.
She continued. "Those ships. They travel almost as fast as light …"

"Right? They're fast." Alik was desperately attempting to force his version of reality into the light, for his own sanity's sake.

"Which means time slows down for anyone on board.

Why else do you think you would be the only waking human on board? Those ships aren't designed to carry more than a handful of conscious people. The stresses of relativistic travel are too great." Nena put her hands on Alik's shoulders. "Sweetie, the only time they move people on those ships is if they are in deep hibernation and they are off to colonize a world. People who have any hope of returning here to see their families and friends still alive do not travel on deep space missions like this. It's one thing to bounce around the solar system, it's something totally different to chart off into the nether regions of the galaxy at or near the speed of light."

Alik understood rationally, but his brain lay sodden in disbelief as it pieced together the gravity of this situation.

Nena closed the distance between them and pawed at his hair. "Alik, time here and everywhere else will continue its normal, relative pace, while days or weeks may pass for every second or minute that elapses on board your ship."

"I don't understand. How many?" Alik started pouring tears as everything set in.

"Alik, if you are traveling near the speed of light for two years, more than one hundred years will have elapsed by the time you return. That doesn't even take into account any number of other relativistic conundrums that ships face. Time is not a constant, it's relative to a great many things."

"Oh shit." Alik's knees buckled and as he hit the ground, he fought the sudden urge to vomit. His eye sockets caved around his palms.

Nena stared him down – cold towards his fate – the way everyone looks at a dog that is about to be euthanized. She was angry at many things. Alik's news seemed to draw all of her frustration to the surface. She pitied him, but not more than she pitied herself.

Nena knelt to meet his eyes. "Go kiss your mother Alik. This will be your last chance." Alik looked up to Nena and tried to warn her off with a scowl. Nena stood again, taking a didactic posture. "Alik, there are thousands of ships out there right now. Who knows where? They've all been manhandled into doing a job no informed human would ever take. And one day, they will all come home to a world far removed from this one."

Alik sobbed. "Why? How does that make any sense?"

"Alik, it's all part of a design. Think about the first men to cross the oceans. Many never returned home. And those who did, returned to cities and families that had changed. But by the time they returned, more and more men had already set off to the new ports. A sort of critical mass eventually evolved. There were enough travelers going and coming that the distance seemed shortened. Regular communication was established. Letters could be funneled through a web of regularly launching missions to new worlds and letters arrived as vessels and men returned, monthly then weekly. What seemed at first to be untenable distances began to feel like short jaunts for the patient. It's the only way to establish a contiguous society. You need to reach a critical mass of humans and going and coming. At some point, civilization becomes consistent, familiar and stable and has the potential to last millennia and not just a few hundred years."

Nena's explanations were not entirely lost on Alik, but he could do little more than sob quietly and attempt to soak up his new reality. He would be leaving in a matter of hours. He considered running, but there was nowhere to run. If Nena was right, then the journey would not seem unbearably long to him and he could handle the eventual return. At that moment, he would have told himself anything to regain the confidence Nena had so effectively crushed. His fear, he told himself, was irrelevant now. He was left with no alternative, but to see his charge through. Turning down assistance of this type would surely result in a punishment far more troubling than a debtor's colony.

Fortunately for Alik, even with this new perspective, he still had such limited understanding of what was in store for him, he was spared the full existential nightmare of the world into which he was stepping.

6

The busy spectacle was cartoonish and chaotic. Alik imagined their numbers to be in the thousands. He stood amongst them, his heart in his throat, uneasy amongst the teeming crowd. The majority were decorated beneath dozens of alternating shades of blue - sapphire cloaks trimmed with powder blue silk and carefully adorned with LED fibers, reflecting still more shades of blue. The older men and women sported indigo sashes above midnight blue waistcoats of varying cuts. Even the elderly appeared youthful and vivacious.

Along the edges of the bustling throngs, Alik caught glimpses of individuals dressed in orange or tan. Their dress was simpler. He noticed men adorned in thick, clay gray cloaks toting cases or directing conveyance droids, always respectfully behind those in blue and carrying themselves with an austere professionalism, as they were there to serve.

Alik had never seen such a spectacle, not even along the vast subterranean boulevards of the urban underground. People moved in every possible direction. Sometimes their paths intersected, but each crossed with polite nods or smiles, never ensnaring themselves in the throngs, never breaking their stride – casual yet hurried – talkative yet respectful. At times people stopped and greeted one another, perhaps old friends or acquaintances. Looking above through the massive, transparent cupola, Alik could see the Earth, covered by the Sol's shadow, glittering with human night-light. He wondered if the station remained permanently fixed, stationary, within the view of the shadow, or if this was simply its current position in orbit.

Alik was one of only a few others amongst the sea of comers and goers outfitted in red garments. His garments fit his large frame tightly and cut at his groin uncomfortably, giving the impression that each size was cut to fit a wide variety of body types adequately, but none perfectly - quite utilitarian. His personal clothing had been packed away at the spaceport, before leaving Earth. Handlers at Chandeleur spaceport kept those dressed in red, pink and orange segregated from the passengers boarding in blue.

Within the massive orbital station, Range, Alik was cut loose, given only a terminal number and a departure time, he was free to mingle unmolested by a handler. The concourse stretched on and on, its curvature obvious in the moments Alik could pear through the gaps between the throngs of travelers. The motion of the scene jarred him. He attempted to follow the stark directions he was given, but could find no clues amongst his surroundings to help him along his way. No one else seemed as lost. He wandered in utter amazement for several minutes before he realized that there was a language at work in this place, but it was a language with which he was completely unfamiliar. Color seemed to be the syntax.

Innumerable active panels, each animating pulses and streams of color, ranging in intensity and direction, surrounded the concourse. As he rounded bends, he found subtle changes in swatches. Some corridors had dominant purple themes with varying shades breaking loose and highlighting additional corridors within those shades. The directions he was provided did nothing to address this. Alik wanted written signs, coupled with intelligible numbers. The throngs grew thicker and thicker along the central concourse. His gaze fixed again and again on the spinning Earth – they were orbiting, he decided, since he could now see the daylight terminator coming into view. Suddenly, everything became too much to handle. After a few sharp elbows jutted into his upper arms, his inability to find his way and the waxing Earth above his head, he broke into a cold sweat as his ears muffled and his tongue dried out.

Catching hold of his agoraphobic reaction before it consumed him, he stepped as far out of the center of the concourse to he quieter edge. He chanced to ask a man in blue, seated restfully along the concourse, "Do you know where the lunar terminals are located?" Alik was polite, sincere and perhaps a bit cautious. The man in blue refused to acknowledge him. Instead, the man in blue slung a small tote across his shoulder and walked away purposefully and silently, without a backwards glance to Alik. Then from a few feet away, he heard a definite 'pssst'.

"Hey, red man." Alik looked to see a scruffy looking kid hunched in a corner near the privy, towards the edge of the concourse. Alik pointed at his chest and the kid nodded and waved him over. The kid was not more than thirteen or fourteen years. His hair fell past his nose and seemed generally ignored and knotted.

"Are you talking to me?" Alik looked left and right nervously.

"Get over here. You're the only red man around here aren't you?" The kid was confident and sassy.

"I guess so." Alik sat on the floor next to the boy. The boy wore a light blue robe, clearly out of comfort instead of obligation. On his shoulder glared an obvious patch, embroidered with a symmetrical blue cross, outlined in red stitching.

"You know it's rude for reds to speak to blues? Didn't anyone tell you that?" The kid smiled at Alik in apparent appreciation of Alik's disregard for manners.

"I think they try to tell you as little as possible." The kid laughed, approving of Alik's narrow sarcasm with thumbs up. The kid slouched into the corner, as if settling in again. Alik could see that the boy was rail thin, beneath his robe. Alik glanced about. No one spared he and the boy an eye. The quiet corner was shadowed in a purple-bruise tone and lay several feet off the concourse.

"Look, the lunar terminal is on the other side of the station, towards the moon. Got it? Just find gray and follow it." The boy pointed towards a small thatch of color at the edge of the wall. Alik had missed the detail previously. It seemed that at each break in the wall, a small color palette appeared and showed the dominant colors for that particular region. "You not familiar with color nav'?"

"No. Not like this." Alik looked across the floor and noticed the subtle variation between tiles all the way onto the curved partitions of the concourse. Looking back across the concourse, he picked out certain colors with his eyes and noticed the subtle, directional flow of each stream. He stood and looked further down the concourse and felt the flow of each particular color as he quickly trained his eyes to find the proper streams.

"Everything around here means something. You just got

to know how to read it. This station is huge and supports a massive number of people. You get a people jam in this mother and it can get panicky. This place is built to play into the subconscious. It's supposed to guide you without you ever noticing…I guess you gotta have some exposure to this type of architecture from the get-go for it work right." The kid was thorough, perhaps brilliant? Alik wasn't sure. He felt his own strangeness, his naivety.

"I'm not sure what basic coordinates aren't satisfactory. You know, level five…gate F, corridor B." Alik shrugged his shoulders.

"Huh. You have no idea do you? What makes you think grid design, compartmental design or standard three dimensions is necessary or healthy for a station like this? Did you even see Range on your way in?"

"Actually, no. My only view was the back of another fellows head and several rows of cargo containers. We weren't allowed to disembark until the cargo hold had been fully unloaded." Even in the presence of a child, Alik began to feel his stark inferiority.

"That's nuts. Well, suffice to say, a coordinate system doesn't work for this station. It's too fluid for something like that. Just wait until you make your way along, you'll quickly lose that lovely view and you'll find that the concourse continues above your head." The kid pointed up smiling. "You're funny man. I wish I could see your face later on." The kid laughed politely.

"What's your name?" Alik stuck out his hand and introduced himself. "My name is Alik."

"No shakes please. You just came from Earth. Lot's of germs down there. Nothing personal though. Name's Bojay." Bojay pounded his fist on his chest in loo of a handshake.

"You live here?" Alik asked.

"Nah…just here to meet up with my grandfather. We're traveling to the Quintessa medical colony at Neptune. He's a doctor you know."

"Who your grandfather?" Alik asked obligingly.

"Yeah. He'd laugh if he knew I was talking to a red. Where are you going?" Bojay asked.

"I'm not exactly sure." Alik was frank and spoke casually.

"You a slug?" Bojay looked at Alik with a fresh sense of caution.

"A what?" Alik was slightly horrified unsure of the implication.

"Oh, then I guess not. A slug never lies."

"What the hell is a slug?" Alik was insistent.

"Are you serious? What swamp did they drag you out of? A slug? A body slug?" Bojay looked to Alik for a sense of recognition in terms. "You know, organ mules? After market person?"

Alik's face hung in disbelief. "No. I have no idea..." Alik sighed somewhat relieved and somewhat disturbed.

"Never mind, man, don't worry with it. Probably best. Your skin is darker like mine, so I thought maybe you were my body slug. I'm waiting on a heart. He's supposed to travel with us to Quintessa. Quintessan surgeons are the best, you know."

"Is that what red usually means? Slug?" Alik was horrified at the possible insinuation and started to wonder anew about the position he'd signed up for.

"Nah, red can mean lots of stuff. Like, you're under contract or you're not a citizen. You know? " Bojay shrugged off the notion.

"Right." Alik slumped his shoulders a bit more, remembering that despite the fact he was about to get his own spaceship he was still trapped in citizenship limbo. He had no idea how he was supposed to feel. Should being contracted to act as an usher elicit pride?

"So what are you?" Bojay was insistent.

Alik was happy to answer, but was beginning to worry about missing his transport. Still he humored the boy. "I'm ushering a ship."

"Oh! Well, you won't have to wear red for long. I think Ushers are brown or green. Can't remember...never met an Usher..." Bojay shook his bangs out of his eyes and cast his gaze back to the crowd, looking again for his grandfather.

"What if I was wearing brown or green and tried to talk to a blue?"

"I dunno. Ushers are rare things to spot out here. You got to go to Caelus or Kuiper Station or further to meet any Ushers. I think they steer clear of hot spots for people...for the most part."

"Why's that?" Alik was genuinely curious.

"I don't know. You're the first Usher I've ever met." At that the boy noticed his grandfather further down the concourse. Without another word, the boy climbed to his feet and walked casually down the concourse, never paying another thought to Alik.

Even though the boy pretended not to hear, Alik squeezed out a word of thanks. He was honestly grateful, but no less confused. Truly, he was piecing together a missing universe. Every bit of this had existed for some time, beyond the span of Alik's life, yet these structures and these ways were never discussed with such detail, at least amongst the company Alik tended to keep. Alik was surprisingly invigorated to glimpse the bizarre unknown of his own civilization.

Since his interview, each day had come on the heels of new revelations. Alik had done an admirable job coping with a rapidly expanding worldview. "What's next?" He polished the thought as if tumbling it through sand and rough pebbles.

Alik wound his way through a long yellow corridor that

quickly faded into streams whiter and whiter. He quickly decided that the flights leaving along this concourse were headed further in, towards Sol. The thought made Alik sweat a bit. The sun was visible through the glass cupola above him. He walked further and further until the crowds thickened. A new array of dress presented itself. Dozens of men and women assembled in crisp gray uniforms. The concourse stretched above him, with departure gates at closer and closer intervals. He watched as long lines of droids collected on the concourse overhead. He stopped catching a glimpse of a loading vessel at one of the gates overhead. Soon, he noticed that grey had become the dominate color.

The varying shades of white had faded almost unnoticeably. Small shops lined the grey concourse. Now, instead of a glass cupola overhead, each departure gate was framed in perfectly square apertures. The lunar surface remained eerily framed from each vantage he took. The surface was brighter, busier and closer than the surface of Earth. For the first time, he had to fight off a twinge of vertigo looking down at the surface of the Moon. Opposite the gates, food stalls and small gift shops littered the way. Spices and smells he was wholly unfamiliar with made his stomach turn with hunger pangs.

Alik knew he was too late to worry with food. He kept his gaze laser focused on the gates looking for any evidence of his flight. Lunar Exo-Launch site 67B – Flight 0008. He repeated the information over and over, but still found no corresponding markings. Finally, he saw a tiny shuttle parked at a lonely gate at the far end of the concourse. A stale mannered Hollow stood suddenly from behind the gate counter and greeted him with as little excitement as possible.

"Doc's?" The Hollow held out his palms begrudgingly. Alik, wasting no time slapped his palms across the Hollow's and the Hollow returned the gesture with a look of absolute boredom.

"You're late sir. Please board immediately."

~

The moment he stepped foot in the transport shuttle, his fears dissipated and Alik's excitement became almost palpable. He became so relaxed that he soon wondered if there was literally something in the air. The sensation was immediate. He barely remembered the flight from Earth, since any and all first time flyers were intentionally sedated to some extent. He'd been awake, but he was certainly sedate.

The transport was empty and understated. He sat at the front of the only row of passenger seats, with perhaps ten or twelve empty seats behind him. There did not appear to be a physical pilot or proper cockpit. The seating was surrounded on all sides in a single, unblemished transparent panel and the lunar surface filled up the entire view. It was as if the entire craft were about to be dunked into a giant bucket of moon. The sight gave Alik no worries or nausea. In fact he soaked in the view with a glassy calm. He could not break his stare, trying to memorize the clear image of the craters, patterns and cities he had, until now, only seen as miniscule specks of light from the surface of Earth.

As he gazed, the ship began its disembarking procedure. The hatch to the terminal closed and locked slowly and intentionally. He felt massive couplings turning then unlocking followed by a slight jolt as the ship detached from the station and expertly fired an array of maneuvering thrusters, bring the ship about for quick look at the station before pitching towards its target and gliding away. Range station was too large to fully grasp so close. Though Alik quickly noted that the portion he was launching from was but a tiny off shoot of an otherwise gargantuan ring. It was actually a bit pitiful, watching the spiraling architecture of the harbor grow smaller and smaller as the shuttle carefully put distance between itself and the harbor.

At the end of the shuttle's maneuver, Alik could see a tight knot of lights on the far side of the moon. Because of the angle his shuttle was docked at, he could not get a view of what was beyond the curve of the lunar surface. Though, as the ship rolled again, bringing the surface of the moon just beneath nose of the shuttle, Alik could then see a vast world of construction, vast constellations of satellites, communication arrays that bloomed like lotus flowers and thousands of vessels in various states of completion, all hovering just miles above the lunar surface, continuing on and on around to the far side.

Even though the ship slid closer and closer to the lunar surface at what must have been a terrific clip, he could not detect any noticeable appreciation of speed. The shuttle's pace was a mystery. Alik felt his ears pop as compartmental gases began re-configuration. He then felt a sudden but deep fatigue set in. Without even time enough to form the thought that he was indeed being sedated, he was felt himself lose control of his eyes. He tried speaking to himself in an attempt to rally, but was unsuccessful.

The ship's computer, sensing Alik's confusion chimed in. "You may feel the need to sleep. If you do, do not fight the urge, simply recline and enjoy the rest." The message was polite but direct and did not repeat.

Alik yawned wide and rubbed his eyes that were rolling forcibly backwards. "Those fuckers are doing it again." He slurred to himself, angry but unable to fight the fatigue. "Just once, he thought, I'd like to be able to enjoy the ride."

"Atmospheric regulation states that sudden administration of acclimation sleep aid techniques are necessary for individuals who have spent more than 30% of their life on a planetary body…." The computer's voice faded as Alik lost momentary consciousness.

The tiny shuttle entered a steep lunar orbit, using the lunar gravity to propel it outward. Even as dazed as he was, Alik fought once again to open his eyes enough to make out the bright, irregular lights coming from a station far off on their heading.

"Flight time is now six hours. Please sleep." The computer was final and its words drained into the air slower and slower.

The blackness eventually took over and the view dissolved finally settling Alik into deep REM sleep. The cabin lights were extinguished and the full view of space became ubiquitous. The quiet of the ship, the soft vibrations of its internal system, they all fell away into dream. Alik was once again wedged firmly in the distortion of travel.

~

Everything materialized quickly. Small things, things he had imagined, possibilities, objects, everything seemed to be falling into place. At least in this dream everything fit, even the unanswered questions, his confusion and naivety. All of it seemed acceptable, meant to be, in fact.

Alik was awash in an intense positive wave, very similar to the feelings brought on by the Kinoko, days before. His body was fast asleep, but his mind was awake, lucid even. His brain stewed and fed itself on the novelty of this experience. Questions made him stronger. He felt a basic certainty rather than a sense of destiny. He was certain all of his questions would be answered. There was also a certainty in his choices. Whether or not he had actually chosen this path, he was certainly complicit. It all felt correct. As if for the first time, he had a trajectory that was direct and clear and positive.

As he dreamed and the luster of the positive glow saturating him intensified, he saw his mother, sitting next to him, smiling. He had only left her a note. He knew it was a cold way of leaving her, but she had other sons and his absence would only make her hug them tighter. Saying goodbye in person was too difficult. So it was quite a shock when Alik looked to his left to see her standing next to him, smiling, holding his hand and awash in a reassuring gaze. Behind him, sat Nena. Every now and then Nena gripped Alik's shoulder tightly. She was also smiling and beaming love and reassurance.

"I'll explain everything to your mother Alik." The comfort of Nena's words overwhelmed him. Alik wept in this sleep.

He was always stirred by his dreams. They always carried an intense emotional appeal. This dream felt like one of the many intense, late afternoon dreams he always seemed to have if he fell asleep in sunshine – one of those dreams that hangs around for days and can be recalled with perfect clarity even decades later.

Towards the ship's aft, another figure sat in the shadows. Alike could barely distinguish the figures presence. There was definitely someone there, someone with whom he felt a powerful familiarity. He could not distinguish the shape of her face. Her identity was unclear but not entirely opaque. He was certain he knew the individual and felt compelled to direct the same compassion he felt for his mother and his cousin, towards the vague figure. The individual induced Alik to refocus his attention forward.

When Alik shifted his gaze, the stars beyond him magnified at will. He was empowered to pick a star, focus on it and bring it close to him. He knew them intimately. With each star, he felt a distinct connection, a memory, like staring at the home of an old friend and recalling times spent there. To look at the stars, bearing them whole, he felt any glimmer of fear or resignation seep completely from his body. All was

right and Alik felt he would survive anything as long as he
kept that fact close to his heart.

~

Alik woke with the feeling of falling. It jolted him awake. He
was unclothed and in a soft bed, sheeted with downy, almost
frictionless fabrics. He assumed the comfort of the mattress,
the way his body seemed to float, perfectly contoured, had
instigated the sensation of falling.

The remainder of the room was disorienting at first,
dark, but not pitch black, leaving a feeling of void and shape-
lessness. Alik expected to inhale the deep musk of the ruddy
clay and a woodstove, but instead, he breathed in the antiseptic taste of new. He could not fathom where he was, how
he had come to be there. The facts seemed to be perched at
the tip of his mind, but he could not rake them forward far
enough to grasp.

He slung his feet over the floor and gripped his skull,
then shook the sleep from his head. In the pit of his gut was
a feeling that he had missed the show - that he had slept for
days, that he'd missed appointments and birthdays and drunk
runs with friends. He simply could not shake the feeling that
he had let something terribly important slip past him unnoticed while he slept, but for the life of him, the facts refused
to seep through.

Stepping onto the floor, the tiles beneath his feet began
to glow, barely perceptible at first, then growing in strength
at the same rate Alik's eyes constricted and adapted. As he
stood, the light concentrated in a single path of tiles, lighting a path drearily towards what appeared to be a lavatory.
At that moment, Alik realized that a good portion of his
frustration stemmed from the feeling that his bladder could
explode at any moment. He hurried across the path towards

the toilet while he struggled not to urinate across the floor along the way. After reaching the toilet and becoming overwhelmed by the relief of urinating, he increasingly became more conscious as the lavatory light gradually rose to a level just perceptible. As it all seeped back into his mind - the interview, Range and the empty shuttle – it was as if a pile of hot rocks was suddenly shoved into his lower intestine. The feeling radiated until he felt it concentrate at the crown of his skull, it was fear. In fact, it was the strange fuck child of multiple intense fears – fear of the unknown, in the realest sense, the feeling of looking into a void and realizing that it is now your home and there is no escape – trapped, with the reminder lapping like waves over and over that what has happened has happened and there is absolutely no turning back. The same feeling often washes over otherwise innocent people after they have taken a life intentionally or unintentionally – the dreadful realization that you cannot take it back, that with a single breath, you have fundamentally altered the course of what was otherwise a very fine life.

Out of nowhere came an even more immediate realization. Other biological processes were amplifying the intensity of his fear. The pile of hot rocks in his gut, as it turned out, should have registered as a signal of the eminent evacuation of his bowels, with or without his consent. In that moment, Alik sprayed a particularly foul broth across the wrong side of an otherwise pristine water closet.

Horrified he begged for more light while he groped at the wall with his palms, looking for a switch or some other mechanism. He soon realized that his feet were nearly totally submerged in a thick puddle and the hand he was combing the wall with was also contaminated since he had instinctually attempted to hold back the geyser by hopelessly covering his ass with his hand.

"Fucking lights! Please!" His cries went unanswered. The

room was still only lit to one-quarter illumination. Resigned, he tiptoed towards the shower, attempting unsuccessfully to mitigate the amount of feces he tracked across the floor. With each messy step, he found that the light decreased every so slightly, as his slop muddy the illumination tiles. "Damn fool designer put lights on the floor? Doesn't make a damn bit of sense."

Luckily, the shower was relatively straightforward. The shower anticipated his preferred temperature and intensity, which restored some measure of his civility. He noticed that the showerhead detached and could be extended to great lengths. Giving it a firm tug, he nearly fell backwards in the shower when the showerhead easily gave way, allowing for as much reach as he required. He also noticed that the lowest point in the entire bathroom was in the floor of the shower. So without much more of a plan, he stepped away from the shower, wand in hand and started hosing the feces from the wall onto the floor and from the floor into the shower drain. As he stood, naked and reaffirmed in his ability to problem solve, if only momentarily, the light in the room swelled in intensity.

Awoken in a strange place, with urinary and intestinal panic, metaphysical burdens the likes of which he still had not fully appreciated, drugged, shot into space, all of it was now starring back at Alik, fully illuminated in the vanity. There he was dark, naked, hairy, apeish with loose bowels, a disregard-ed beard, lost eyes, a furled brow and a heart so lonely no on has even threatened to break it. This son of a bitch was the essence of mediocrity, or at least, that's what he told himself.

The light from the bathroom spilled into the adjoining room. Alik peered around into the space. As he stepped away from the privy the tiles gradually illuminated the space ahead of him. His fist impression was positive.

The design of the room felt efficient yet spacious. He

never had a private space so large. The home he'd left was modest and shared by many brothers. Privacy was only found deep in the forest.

There appeared to be a short antechamber on the other side of the lavatory, which led to a sitting area or den of sorts. Two plush sofas and an assortment of chairs were arranged functionally throughout the rooms. One wall of the burrow seemed to be covered in a screen Alik immediately presumed was meant for vid-casts or other visual media.

His wardrobe was tucked away in the wall opposite his bed. Several outfits were hung and folded. Each outfit, just as Bojay suggested they might be, was comprised of two or more shades of green. He found a pair of olive pants and a comfortable looking pullover. He appeared to have his choice of foot thongs or padded slippers. There did not seem to be any substantial footwear of any kind. Unlike the red garments he was issued on Earth, the green clothes fit him as if they were made specifically with him in mind.

There did not appear to be any transoms or portholes within either of the rooms. Alik guessed that if he was on board his assigned vessel, it might have been that his living quarters were buried somewhere deep within, away from edge of the hull, perhaps for his protection.

As he walked into the bedroom to slip into his shoes, he noticed that his terminal screen now displayed a simple, architectural diagram with a short path, highlighted in yellow and a corresponding yellow path was then visible in the tiles at his feet. They led to an egress, which seemed to be sized to the width of a standard human. The thought of trying to squeeze furniture into the room through this entrance was perplexing and he vowed silently to examine it later. He assumed though, that bewilderment was going to become the new normal.

Beyond the sleek hatch stretched a long, curving corridor.

Alik followed the yellow tiles around the edge of the corridor with his eyes, until they curved out of sight, perhaps twenty feet from Alik. The opposite direction was completely un-inviting - without any illumination that direction remained void black.

Barefoot, he followed the yellow tiles intentionally, thought-fully, with each step a sensory experience. The tiles were smooth, seamless even and they pushed back with the same force as a stone road or a steel bridge. There was absolutely no give in the floor. The surface was warm and pleasant to stand on. For some reason, he always assumed space ships to be cold, unwelcoming and wet, but the truth was quite the opposite. Even though the spaces around him had a some-what cold architectural brutality to them, there was something about the material, the shapes and even the silence of the space that produced a feeling of comfort in Alik.

The corridor quickly emptied into a bright and spacious galley. The galley shared the same curvature as both his living space and the adjoining corridor. He wondered whether this entire area had been built as a circular space, but then imme-diately put the idea away, confused that curve would continue along the right side of the room as it had. He thought it out further; drawing the space in his mind and reflecting on the diagram cut away he'd been alerted to at his interface. He wagered that the corridor ran the circumference of the living space and that the space then curved in layers like a nautilus, with his bedroom at the center.

Mapping came natural to Alik. Each jaunt into the forests of the Buffer or beyond them into the mountainous foothills on the far side of the agricultural belts, Alik was forced into a constant state of mapping. Even as a child he maintained a reputation of having never been lost adults often looked to him for directions to hidden springs or streams, ruins or ancient trash pits. Alik knew every inch of his terrestrial territory and felt it only natural to carry this tendency into his new home. Alik was confident he would soon know the ship like the back of his hand.

The galley was a spectacle of the highest magnitude. Alik had never seen such a space. Dark walnut, with highly figured grain trimmed the room, the appliances and the countertops. The countertop was finely polished obsidian, while the cabinetry was a cool mix of glass and steel.

All of this struck him as odd. His idea of a kitchen was something quite different. His mother had a slaughter block and an outdoor solar oven that was shared with four other families. A fire and small wooden stove heated water for coffee or kept food hot. Kitchens were not kept in homes within the cities either. Traditional kitchens had been ruled a health risk long ago. In the cities, all dining was provided through eateries and cafeteria. Alik had assumed this would be the case on board.

Then he noticed it. On a bar, in front of a plush stool, sat a steaming bowl, along with a spoon, an empty glass and a container of water. All had been laid out, prepared carefully with hands. A sudden fear that he was not actually alone was quickly replaced with excitement that he may not actually be alone. Alik swung his head about, taking another survey of the space.

Suddenly, out of the air, fell the gravely discharge of a throat preparing to speak. The sound was so foreign and unexpected that Alik, at first, did not recognize it as the sounds of a voice. His blood went cold and recoiled at the sound, until the raspy gravel dissipated and a rough sanded, imperial voice, almost a caricature of a noble drawl, descended on Alik with supreme clarity.

"I made you breakfast. I doubt this will become a regular occurrence, but I was obligated to make you feel at home." The voice ended as abruptly as it began.

Alik looked at the counter, stunned. The bowl was piping hot, but its contents were more than a little questionable. Unidentifiable curds floated along the edges, while sharply contained swirls of purple sizzled independently as if chemically reacting with the oxygen in the air. "Is that food?"

"Of course it is. It's a predigested protein conglomerate, fortified with Mother's Milk 31 and pesto flavor."

Alik scratched his head. He was certain that he was speaking with the computer, or at least half certain. Surely this was not the chef. Even though he wanted ask fifty different questions, his bend towards introduction via conversation got the better of him and he fell to the cane of his wit instead of the pragmatism of his inquiry.

"You are out of your mind. There is no way in hell I'm eating that. Are you familiar with human tastes? You can't expect me to believe this kitchen was built to serve up a breakfast like this?"

"The contents of the kitchen are there for you to do as you please. You are not obligated to eat what I cook, so long as I am not obligated to answer every time you happen upon the impulse to say my name. Can we agree to that?"

"I'd agree to it, if I knew your name." Alik paused. "Look, I don't mean to be combative, but I typically make it a point not to address disembodied voices before I have coffee."

"Your curtness is noted. You will find coffee in the cupboard. I ask that you take some time to settle in and then perhaps we can attempt formal introductions later. I must also note that my resources are finite, believe it or not. I do not wish to make a habit of coming behind you to properly sanitize a room. I understand that you may not be fully equipped to deal with many of the conveniences on board, but I should like to ask you to avoid defecating haphazardly, wherever you see fit."

Alik was more and more puzzled. It was as if he were

being hazed while simultaneously being subjected to benign manipulation. He wondered if this was going to be the new normal.

"That's a low blow friend. Whatever you people did to me, it gave me one hell of a bout. I don't typically make shitting on the floor a habit, I assure you." Alik received no audible response. Instead, an empty patch of wall, adjacent to the counter sprang to life and entered into a quick tutorial of the galley. Alik watched for a moment then went to work, all the while trying to shake off the oddity of his conversation.

Alik found the icebox and welled with excitement as he glared at the marvel within. Multi-colored packages of un-known foods, neatly segregated and organized - eggs of various sizes and colors, milk, fresh greens and juices, each took its own efficient space, placed in the fridge like marvelous tokens from a benevolent monolith. Alik didn't know where to start. Eggs. Eggs he knew well, so he pulled the eggs from the fridge and looked around for cooking implements. No pans that he could find. No bowls. In fact, all the implements he required were stowed away in various cabinets, but at the moment his hunger overtook his patience. Unable to identify the stove, he looked about until he found what appeared to be an oddly shaped oven, built into the adjacent wall.

"Any advice on how to cook this?" Alik assumed the computer was likely listening, perhaps not eager to help, but listening nonetheless. He looked about again, still confused. He placed the eggs back into the fridge and picked up a piece of fruit, some sort of orange banana and poured a glass of milk.

He inspected the "oven" a bit closer. The door to the unit was concave, matching the natural curve of the wall seamless-ly. With the wave of his hand, the door pulled inward a few centimeters, then slid into a pocket within the wall. On the inside there appeared to be two shelves stacked close together at the top, a large shelf in the middle, wide and accessible and another short shelf below. The shorter three shelves contained distinctly segregated areas. As he inspected with his hands, the inside of the unit lit up and several labels were projected onto the segregated areas of the shelves. The labels read *protein*, *vegetable*, *spices*, and on the bottom shelf *miscellaneous*.

Piecing together the intent of the mechanism, Alik realized it to be a fairly straightforward process. He walked back to the fridge, grabbed two eggs, a clump of what appeared to be fresh chives and a sealed packet labeled *peppers-hot*. On the edge of the packaging a label read *Do Not Remove*. Alik walked back with the materials, placed each in its corresponding spot and closed the door.

The oven immediately sprang to life. The items appeared to be scanned and then the front of the oven quickly closed and became opaque as a timer appeared. One minute. Alik looked about the kitchen, wondering again if, he was still being observed by the computer. He didn't feel like he was being watched. Actually, it all felt very comfortable and private. Everything was fairly natural, even luxurious.

The oven approached thirty seconds remaining and a message flashed, *Would you like coffee or tea?* Without thought, Alik responded audibly. "Coffee!" The machine chimed and Alik opened the door to find a complete meal, garnished and carefully prepared. "This is luxury!" Across the room something chimed and Alik noticed that a ceramic cup full of hot coffee had been filled and dispensed onto the countertop. Somehow, he'd missed the action, but the bowl, previously prepared and laid out had vanished, replaced by his cup of coffee. Alik cursed at himself for having missed whatever bussed the counter.

Alik took his meal, set it onto the countertop along with the coffee and pulled a nearby stool beneath him. He tasted the food and was instantly overcome by the heat of the peppers.

The eggs were over done and the chives were dried out to the point they were crunchy. "Looks like sandwiches from here forward." Alik said aloud.

As he grazed hazardously through this breakfast, a wide panel, along the wall adjacent to the counter, flickered and illuminated without cue. The image of a logo, a symbol Alik did not recognize, flashed and was then replaced by a series of images of planetoids, mining operations and great webs of steel and ship components, all in a quick montage set to a booming and dramatic orchestration.

The image of a women appeared - blonde hair in a low cut, multi-colored sash. She began to speak. Alik watched intently, allowing his breakfast to idle.

"A pleasant morning. We begin this morning's notices with an update of commodity fluctuations. The PAE has cleared us to report that Victory colonists have agreed to cooperate with a near light, weekend operation, in order to stimulate the value of their Futures stocks. Six automated infrastructure projects will be completed during the elapsed time giving a great welcome home present to the colonists.

Veda colony is also in talks with a terra-design crew to complete the construction of the colony's new biosphere ahead of schedule. If a deal is struck, an interception crew may have to leave immediately, in order to recall the colonists. Their scheduled return date is still forty-seven years hence - standard Sol 3."

Alik didn't understand a bit of this. He sipped his coffee and shoveled a scoop of the turgid eggs into this mouth as the broadcast continued. He had an urge to take notes.

"The chief of the Martian Geologic Management Design Council, Dr. Edward Elise, has officially retired his position. He and his wife spent their last, few hours together alone. Though this has not been officially confirmed, it is believed he was uploaded into M-Prime, the Martian atmospheric and geologic management computer. M-Prime has also failed to give comment on the matter."

"Two outer rim Temporal-Man-Fac vessels were confirmed launched

and bound for opposite edges of the galaxy. These represent then tenth pair completed. We also have confirmation that the initial pair of TMF vessels reached their destinations, Void Station and Phoenix Station, several months ago.

"A new line of FT560's will be available for construction crews within the next two cycles. The reports of malfunctioning FT560's have not been confirmed, but efforts are being made to replace existing units as fast as possible according to the FT manufacturing firm at Neptune..."

7

The illumination throughout Alik's quarters fluctuated as the day passed. At noon, rooms were warm and full of comfortable, mellow light that was both ever-present and indirect. Alik's naturally tan skin already seemed faded under the unnatural light. He sat on the floor of his room, carefully unpacking his few belongings. Whoever placed Alik within his quarters also placed his locker at the foot of a meticulously carved Arabesque chest of drawers, as if suggesting that this was an appropriate place to store his items. The chest of drawers was adorned with hexagonal flowers, Euclidian patterns, moon-crowned arches and inlaid checkered marquetry. The piece seemed out of place, as it was clearly hand made and stood apart from the other accouterments, which fit flush within the curve of his walls. Many of the other furnishings, some of the chairs, the bed frame and the coffee table were distinctly printed or cast by machine. The chest still bore the tool marks, evidence of someone's exacting craftsmanship.

The bedding, a desk nook and his wardrobe each fit tidily into the progressive curve of the room. Each held an antiseptic, utilitarian vibe, as if their function was notably more important than their appearance. The chairs, sofa and coffee table in the den, were inviting, but held true to the anodyne nature of his surroundings. They were not altogether brutal, but the clean brutality of the architecture was not entirely lost on the furniture. On the wall in his den was an ornament shelf, which corresponded with the chest of drawers. The two pieces were clearly linked – both wildly out of place in their surroundings, both hewn of similar woods – walnut he guessed, both bound by similar motifs. There was something entirely real about the two odd furnishings, something that made the place feel welcoming and lived in. Alik could tell by the sheen on everything, he was the first to occupy these quarters. The furniture gnawed at him though. It was superficial, completely unnecessary in the functioning of the vessel and out of balance with the design. He realized that he was actually less curious about the furniture itself and much more curious about the motives that led to the choice – especially since Alik felt that, had he been given a choice, these were the items he would have chosen for the suite. All of these wild ideas about design and intention, left over from his ramblings with Nena, were now assaulting him in a new way. And beyond any of his fruitless meanderings about the will of the designers, Alik was still overwhelmed by some strange familiarity with the place – the entire arrangement – there was something Alik could not quite put his finger on.

The colors of the room transformed as day moved along. When he woke, and the first hints of light slowly filled the room, the walls appeared deep navy, almost black. Later, in the noon light, the panels along the walls were nearly the color of bleached coral, mottled but white, while the floor reflected a cool tan color. Alik wondered if he had any ability to customize the variation of the colors or the light cycle. The pit of his gut told him that things were as they will be and he should ignore it until it felt comfortable – since it certainly wasn't natural.

From his crate he first removed his blanket and several articles of clothing until he uncovered the notebook and pen the old man had given him. He placed the paper and pen neatly within the small desk-nook next to his bed. He carried three jars of preserved figs, taken from his mother's pantry. He put them to the side with the intention of delivering them to the galley once he'd finished. Beneath the figs and carefully wrapped in a burlap, Alik removed several small items meant to remind him of home – a small pinecone, still green and closed, various jars of seeds, several carved totems presented to him on special occasions and carved by his father.

From his father's workshop, he had taken a photo he and his father found years before, in an abandoned refuse pile, deep in the agricultural zone. The photo was pocked with wormholes and mildew and had clearly been soaked on several occasions then left to dry out. Alik feared that he may destroy it by taking it along, but his father had always remarked about the fine preservation job he had done. After finding the photo, his father spent several long hours grinding beetles in his workshop, amassing piles of powdered beetle husks in order to make gentle shellac. He then mounted the photo on a piece of glass and coated it with the shellac, sealing it away from moisture or contamination. Framed superbly in half an inch of clear glass, the photo shimmered with stark marvel, as its subject, alone save for the cameraman, plunged a steel flagpole as firmly as possible into the ancient, virgin lunar soil. No other object reminded him so much of his father. Alik often found his father alone in his workshop, marveling over the photo. His father always insisted, though Alik was never able to verify this, that the photo was taken more than a thousand years prior and it represented man's first visit to the moon. Alik always found this theory a bit preposterous, but never challenged his father outwardly. However, as Alik unpacked it, he stared into the golden reflection of the clumsy space man's helmet, then at the stark shadows of his companion and the landing craft and he suddenly felt a sympathetic loneliness the likes of which he had never felt before. He imagined the isolation of the men, trapped off world, in a truly alien place, floundering and alone, wondering if they would ever see their homes again. He placed the photograph on top of the arabesque chest of drawers.

As he unpacked more tokens from home, Alik felt sudden and sporadic pangs of guilt. Trusting his father's advice, Alik had not told his mother he was leaving. Again Alik allayed his guilt with the thought of his other brothers and sisters. He hoped that once the abruptness of his absence had worn off, he would become little more than a footnote, overshadowed by the presence of his siblings.

From his mother's green house, Alik packed a variety of seeds, mostly heirloom tomatoes and cucumbers, tastes that reminded him of good summers. The vegetables his mother grew were not readily found in the agri-zones, but had traditionally been passed from Buffer family to Buffer family. He'd had no certainty whether there would be a way to plant them, but something tugged at him to bring them along. Alik was often accused of being far too sentimental, about the oddest things. This may have explained the small jar of colorful, glass marbles. Totally useless in any practical sense, they were a static symbol of imagination, a physical anchor to the past and so he felt compelled to bring them.

Beneath his personal items from home, lay the items given to him by the old man. Alik stared at the bulk with consternation. While packing, he wrapped each item methodically in brown burlap and tied off the burlap with strands of hemp twine. He was afraid to unwrap them and attempted to convince himself to simply close the trunk and leave them for later. In protest of his fear, Alik pulled the bottom drawer of the chest towards him and unwrapped each item one at a time, setting them carefully into the drawer. Reaching his hand into the bottom of one of the sacks, he came upon the heavy, black sphere. He removed it from the sack and held it by the tips of his fingers. Beneath the artificial light, he saw the veracity of the blackness of the sphere. As he cupped it firmly in his hand, moving to place it in the drawer an odd stir sang through his arm.

As Alik held the sphere, he became keenly aware of each nerve throughout his hand, into his arm, through the entire length of his brainstem, all the way to his brain, until the sensation pooled around his eye sockets. The feeling was difficult to process, but not unpleasant. The feeling that settled behind Alik's eyes was not painful and it wasn't an emotional impulse; rather it was an unusual awareness of some kind. The device was having an incredible effect and as Alik looked around the room, he noticed a new depth to his sight. He held the sphere tighter, gripping it, almost compulsively and soon the room began to change. He watched intently, his feet planted. It was as if he were watching water come to a rapid boil, or watching the last edge of the sun disappear behind the horizon, he watched as the walls melted away, layer by layer, softly and steadily vanishing. In a moment, he was able to see the structural supports behind the walls, then the frames and interconnected buttresses that gave the structure cohesion. Then mazes of wires appeared, layer after layer after layer until he could see the room as it was at every stage of construction - all at once. Alik dropped the sphere and his normal vision returned without delay.

Alik was stupefied. Straightaway, he tried to recall the images exactly as he had seen them, but could only recall vague details. Collecting himself on the edge of the bed, he stared at the sphere lying innocuously on the tan tiles. Then he stared at the wall in front of him. He considered the shock of it all, but was certain he had seen the wall melt away. He was certain, but he was left with the sensation of having just woken up from a dream. Technically, he had not words to describe what he had seen. He simply did not possess the appropriate technical vocabulary, so he kept insisting to himself that he'd "seen the guts" behind the wall.

He decided to try it again, paying closer attention this time. He picked up the sphere with the tips of his fingers. Gradually he slid the sphere further down his fingertips until only the slightest portion of the sphere was making contact with his palm. The wall in front of him faded ever so slightly. He tried to focus on a single square foot, directly in his line of sight. He gripped the sphere – pressing it further and further into his palm. The wall began again to bubble, flutter then vanish. In a moment, all he could see were two thin support rods holding aloft the first layer of insulation material. He focused with deep intent as he squeezed the sphere a bit tighter, until the insulation layer bubbled, fluttered and vanished. Alik continued until he could see only darkness, but as he thought again about the wires or the pillars, each jumped into his field of vision. Finally loosened his grip, until the wall reappeared as it was.

The value inherent in this object was not lost on Alik. Even though he did not possess the technical knowledge to understand what he was seeing or how the sphere worked, he knew he now had the ability to, at the very least, examine the structure and configuration of the world around him. If used effectively, it was as good as an extra sense. The effectiveness of the device seemed to have a limited range. Alik considered that the range might also be limited due to skill or lack thereof. Clearly, whatever the ultimate intention of the device, it was not made for an unskilled purpose.

He placed the sphere on the ornamental shelf in the den. He was proud of his discovery, but he felt compelled to restrain himself from using it further until he had more time to do controlled tests. He was aware enough to realize that there were always unforeseen consequences. He thought aloud. "I'm living one of those unforeseen consequences at the moment."

The jars of figs fit nicely on the kitchen counter. He decided to make lunch - this time slicing bread and adding fresh ingredients himself, instead of differing to the strange oven. Lunch in hand; he attempted to reactivate the program he was watching earlier.

He attempted a verbal command, hoping the computer would acknowledge his request. "Activate media." The screen in the den lit on command. There seemed to be a program already in progress. Two individuals, a man and a woman were sitting an uncomfortable distance apart, across a wide, live edge, wooden table. They seemed to be in the midst of an intricate and nuanced conversation as the woman made exceedingly animated points.

"*...that's exactly what we are trying to bring to the PAE's attention. These areas have returned to their pristine state. Understandably, our efforts should continue, but all in all, our debt has certainly been paid. We are out there, colonizing dead rocks, hellscapes, savage lands - trying desperately to turn them from the barely habitable laboratories of our reclusive design firms into lush, temperate, green zones. At some point, we have to accept that humans are meant to live side by side with nature, not in these little fish tanks we call cities. You can stick a can on a world and call it habitable, but you're still living in a damned can!*"

The man, who spoke in a heavy old-imperial accent took the woman's point carefully and folded his hands, as if resigned to condescend, then began to speak.

"Your point is well taken Dr., but I think most people would ask what nature has to offer that we haven't been able to replicate in artificial environments. Certainly we are more responsible for having made those sacrifices."

The women seemed even more frustrated, as if this as an argument she'd had more times than was healthy. She seemed to be vehemently fighting a staunchly held philosophy. She leaned in, pressing her entire body against the edge of the table that separated the two.

"Of course we are acting responsibly, but we are also continuing to act as extremists. We must learn balance. Sure, you can have artificial sun, artificial snow, rain, hail, but until you have experienced the random exhilaration of a beautiful day outside, well you just haven't lived."

The man tipped his nose into the air and scoffed.

"But certainly, to your point regarding balance, is that not the prime motive of the PAE? Are they not profoundly occupied with maintaining an exacting and healthy balance between all things, cultural and otherwise?"

Alik whole-heartedly agreed with the woman. Alik had not lived inside in such a manner before then, but he could already tell he preferred the outside world. Still, Alik wondered how serious this debate actually was. These issues were surely new to him, in some ways. Everyone in the Buffer knew that the city dwellers rarely left the safety of indoors, but he assumed the designers were different somehow. Surely this was all still tied to "S" day guilt, on some level. The fall out from "S" day was the central motivation behind the zone distinctions on Earth. Mankind had been given an opportunity to live with nature, but corrupted it then decided to annihilate it totally. If not for the engineers, the human race would have gone extinct of its own volition.

The man reexamined his posture and relaxed before pressing on. "Doctor, may I touch on another topic our viewers have a great interest in, but may also be viewed in a controversial light?"

"I would expect nothing less from you, Mr. Diamond."

"Excellent. Recently you reported that your wishes have changed regarding retirement. Is that a fact?"

"Sure, it's a fact that that was recently reported."

"Can you explain your position?"

"It's very simple, I will not be retired in the customary fashion. When my body dies, I will be dead – body vacant, mind vacant and still. That's it."

The man leaned back in revulsion then lashed back with an intensely condescending reaction. *"Please ma'am, why do you insist on using such an arcane term. It is vulgar in civilized discourse."*

"You mean die? Dead? Death? Corpse? Let's face facts sir. We've got a galaxy full of brilliant scientists, designers, engineers etc. And we, in all our infinite wisdom and knowledge cannot face the fact that death is an inevitability. Many good, common people get the opportunity to die every day, most of them never having seen the things you or I have.

Their minds are lost, their histories dissolved save for stories and artifacts and you see it as no great loss. Mark my words, when I'm dead I'm dead and I recommend the same thing to anyone else. That's it."

"But why deny yourself everlasting consciousness and deny your knowledge to the galaxy?"

"I don't even know how to seriously answer that question. The knowledge that I leave behind is evident in the works I have completed, in the students I've lectured and the ships, which bare my children. I think our ideological divide may be greater than you well realize. Answer me this. Has anyone, living in those damned mind-wells ever told you that everlasting consciousness is a marvelous thing?"

The man was intensely uncomfortable and shook slightly. *"Well I suppose not. But…"*

"But nothing…Who knows what sort of hell you are all elect-

ing yourselves into." The woman lit a cigarette as the camera framed her face.

"*But you describe them as your children. You created many of them. Why do you now object to their composition?*"

The image cut to the same host from the morning's broadcast, except, she seemed slightly weathered, even older.

"*That was of course the last recorded interview with Doctor Hellene Sheffield. It has been confirmed that her retirement is now official as she was uploaded into Tungrin Monstafo, some hours ago. We wish you well Doctor Hellene Sheffield.*"

Alik lost his appetite. It didn't sound to him, that the woman's final requests had been respected. It was unsettling. He related to her point of view. The thought of living out the rest of eternity in the mind of a computer terrified Alik.

~

Alik spent the rest of that afternoon as he had his morning, idling within his quarters, waiting for whatever was to come next. The lights dimmed into soft, evening hues. At no point did he feel trapped within his quarters, though he was getting anxious, wondering when he would be allowed into the remainder of the ship.

He had no directives or responsibilities. Alik knew he could handle the prospect of idleness for a while, but he shuddered at the thought of years of idle redundancy. Calling out to the computer voice he'd interacted with earlier proved fruitless, though he tried again and again, intermittently through the day. Eventually, as the evening grew long, he activated a media wall in his den and watched; gob struck as oddly presented, hourly news cycles elapsed.

The images felt like marvelous fiction. Having no frame of reference for much of what he saw, Alik's brain failed to register or comprehend the majority of what he was being shown. All the more frustrating was the quick-cut nature of the production. One moment, an announcer was featured in person - followed by quick flashes of images and short video cuts followed the announcer's narrative. It was not that this sort of production was unfamiliar to Alik rather it was the content. Advertisements for personal spacecraft, commercials noting the superiority of one environment suit from another and pleas for citizen colonists, vacation rentals amongst the rings of Saturn and on and on, each blanketed his consciousness with wonder.

A much more thorough report discussed the delivery of two, gargantuan, manufacturing units to Proxima Centauri. Alik stewed in curious amazement as the image panned around two massive cubes, hollow in the center, each actively printing an intensely complex structure – in a high orbit above a blue gaseous world. Later, an episode accompanied only by music sans narration - with artistically framed images of elegant orbiting halls, high-end private yachts, grand subterranean lunar gardens, Jovian lunar rings and alien vista after alien vista – day break from a Venetian plateau, the clouds of Saturn as seen from a low orbit platform, shimmering lakes of methane along the basalt plains of Titan and a skyline dotted with cooling towers, pumping atmosphere into the Europan sky. With each image, Alik's world grew slightly bigger.

Within the span of forty-eight hours, he had left a world that made sense to him - a relatively small world that had boundaries and rules and agreeable expectations. He was now far flung, amongst a new, complex world that seemed to have been trucking along more than adequately without him for quite a long time. To this point, nothing forced a feeling of backwardness onto Alik, like coming to terms with the scale and reach of humanity. He felt tiny. Insignificant.

~

Even in his former quest for higher education, Alik's hunger for information had cultural limits. The Buffer folks, as a rule, were not information hungry. Alik's flavor of curiosity was an exception to the rule, but not entirely uncommon amongst Buffer youth. Stories were shared over a pipe and a meal, typically. Most everyone had something to bring to the table. Occasionally stories would surface about a new lunar colony, or tales of opulent, orbital resorts, mostly embellished and third hand. It was no secret that space travel was common, but until this moment, Alik had never truly understood the scope or the maturity of man's off world foothold. Culturally, the limits of curiosity of the Buffer people had their roots in modesty, not rejection. They were not ideologues that rejected grander ways of life or insisted on a life of simplicity in order to mock the achievements of man, they just did not have an invitation into the other world and if they did, they were gone. It was easier to ignore the progress of man, rather than feel left behind. Alik had been no different.

The mountain of questions was piling high. Dumbfounded and paralyzed, Alik sank into his couch and closed his eyes, hoping to sort through his growing list of concerns and unknowns.

Alik's greatest fear was finding himself completely oblivious. Oblivious of what - was the single most terrifying question to Alik. He reasoned, if I'm oblivious to something, then I clearly do not have a clue what that thing is. Keeping a solid grasp on any situation and being present in the moment were traits woven deep into his consciousness. An upbringing outdoors heightened his senses and sharpened awareness. Being absolutely certain that there were things he did not yet know, or things he has not yet discovered, had the advantage, or disadvantage of forcing Alik to constantly ask, what is it that I do not know and how is the lack of knowledge going to put me at risk?

Although he had a tendency to come off as naïve and often chided himself for his naivety, the awareness of his own ignorance would eventually prove to be a symptom of wisdom. Alik was learning proficiency at taming his discouragement. He felt that allowing his discouragement or ignorance to run rampant, they would eventually fester into fear – eventually drowning his confidence entirely - leaving Alik constantly wondering what beast was just around the bend or his own ignorance could easily kill him before he even realized he'd made a mistake. They were primitive emotions, necessary for survival, useful if honed properly.

The paranoia of Alik's contemporary urban dwellers was a far from his own. As he understood them, most modern men and women did not worry with such feelings at all. They were fearless and rampant self-indulgers, grazers without a thought to their own harm. The truth of the matter was slightly different, but his assessment mostly accurate.

Of course, this characterization did not apply to the engineer/designer class. Their paranoia ran deepest of all and over greater spans of time. The average engineer was trained to look a billion years into the future, when considering a design.

The engineers recognized the process of knowledge acquisition. They embraced their default, oblivious, human nature and attempted to unearth facts about the universe with an archeologists brush. Many things were constantly accounted for, future stellar events, galactic orbital paths, quantum damage to the space through well-worn trade routes, calamity, structural fatigue, necessary resource conscription and on and on.

The engineers did not merely account for these factors, but they attempted, at all times to maintain a sort of equilibrium throughout their interactions with the bits and pieces of space, time and gravity. Their entire philosophy revolved around walking on tight ropes, wanted both to change aspects of the cosmos, while simultaneously attempted to leave no trace.

There were two competing theories about the Universe. The first; the Universe is chaotic and random, yet still maintains balance in a reflexive way. Imagine that human hands craft a stellar event and humans create a star. Under the first theory, the universe would automatically compensate for the event. Concentric rings would spread across space/time through an intricate web of dark matter and the additional mass would be compensated for or brought into equilibrium through the instantaneous creation of a black hole, or the sudden nova of another star. Somehow, the Universe was built to self regulate. Some suggested that even in a self-regulating system, entropy was eventually bound to take hold, no matter the perfection of the system as a whole.

The second theory was this; the Universe is a naturally balanced system. Events can occur within the Universe, but those events are themselves a function of the thing as a hole. In this case, humans and the actions that accompany their presence in the Universe are all functions of the Universe as a whole, in the same way that meteor collisions or nova or natural planetary formation are functions of the Universe as a whole. Just as apples are a natural function of an apple tree, so too are humans and their actions a natural function of the Universe as a whole.

The second theory leaves two additional disputes for the engineers to wrangle with. First, if humans and our actions are a function of the Universe then our actions do not directly require our intervention to maintain a sense of balance. Essentially, we can do what we want and we can't break it. Second, our actions within the Universe may cause ripple effects, which will eventually disrupt the natural ebb and flow of the Universe, antagonizing the Universe into an eventual state of accelerated entropy.

That last argument represented the greatest hang up for the engineering community as well as the philosophers, ideologues and physicists that advised the design community. These postulations split the engineers into two main factions and several sub-factions. The answer to the two "big" questions was ultimately irrelevant. Everyone had already decided the direction of humanity; the questions lay in how to justify our interactions with the cosmos and whether or not we can fix it if we break it. Examined too closely for too long, a deep metaphysical trench develops and harbors divisiveness. Divisiveness amongst design was untenable and always quashed before becoming malignant.

In order to maintain equilibrium within the engineer/design community, it was decided that doctrine would lean towards the more conservative of the two possibilities. So whilst designing ships and their means of propulsion, building super-massive spaceports, terraforming worlds etc. all design leaned toward Precautions Against Entropy (PAE). The rules were lauded as scripture and required specialized minds to check each design, each construction plan and each galactic infrastructure goal against the PAE doctrine. If there was a central ruling class recognized within the designer culture, the PAE Council would likely be recognized as it. In a way, the PAE made all decisions. At times they determined the placement of single individuals throughout their varied systems and projects. As they saw it, to maintain balance, the random nature of certain human impulses must be spread throughout complex systems. Those humans essentially existed as pivot points for the Cosmos' self-correcting gestures.

All of this constituted the basis for what could be considered, the closest approximation to mass religion amid this age of man.

Of course, Alik was oblivious to all of this, clearly justify-
ing his concerns. However, beyond all of his understandable
ignorance, was his recognition of a single fact. No matter
how many questions are answered, big or small, no matter
how definitive the answer, there will never be unanimous satisfaction with the answers. Alik was self aware enough to
realize he was no different, in this instance.

~

Alik was not aware that he had fallen asleep. His quarters
were still pitch black when a steady tone racked his attention
away from his dreams. There was no visible chronometer in
his quarters, but judging by the extent of the darkness, he assumed it to be fairly late. Just as his eyes were adjusting to
the blackness, a steady yellow glow began emanating from
the tiles at the foot of the couch, where he had fallen asleep.

Looking down and then across the tiles, following the
light, he noticed that the squares illuminated a path to the
privy. Feeling the pressure on his bladder, he took heed and
followed path and relieved himself appropriately. As soon as
the final dribbles of urine left his body, the tiles began to flash
in the opposite direction, leading him again out of the privy
and back into the main corridor connecting his bedroom to
the den and the galley.

Instead of directing him to bed, however, the tiles directed his path towards a hatch that inconspicuously blended into
the soft curve of the corridor's partition. As he approached
the hatch, the yellow tiles bled into green. A soft green line
crept across the outline of the hatch, further highlighting its
presence. The rest of the room was still cast in darkness and
every trail tile behind Alik blacked out, with only a single
glowing tile thrown beneath Alik's bare feet.

Alik hesitated for a moment, inspecting for a keypad or a latch, but the hatch and the wall it set within were completely featureless and smooth. He casually swept his hand across the hatch and in doing so, the hatch quietly and effortlessly retracted. The corridor on the other side was as dark as his quarters. Soon, a long path of tiles, pushing into a curve in the dark corridor blazed green, giving Alik his queue.

There was calmness to the floors – something Alik could not quite put his finger on. He blamed it on the fact that he could not feel the ship whatsoever, not a single rattle or creak. It was the same in his quarters. Even though they appeared engineered, ceramic or plastic, they were inviting to the feet, body temperature at all times. He was still wearing one of the olive uniforms, but it reflected black in the green light of the tiles as he followed along the soft curve of the corridor.

The curve made him think again about the shape of a nautilus. It was nothing more than a passing thought earlier, but he could see now, as he walked on, that the corridor was elongating, becoming less dramatic. Though he could not see them through the darkness, he suspected that there might be other hatches, leading to other areas, along any part of the corridor he was passing through. It was just a theory.

Eventually, Alik felt a cool breeze tighten the skin on his face. The corridor widened slightly then widened further still until Alik could no longer discern where the corridor ended and the vast hall where he then stood, began. The tiles blacked out at the end of the corridor, but he could see faint shadows in the hall beyond him, indicating a nebulous light source of some kind. It was like candle light.

Not until he took another step forward, further into the open space did he realize the space above him, the corridor ceiling ended suddenly. As if stepping from beneath a cupola and into the night's sky, the tremendous force of teeming stars suddenly pocketed Alik's attention. The room was massive, perhaps one hundred meters in every direction, the floor nearly level with the foot of an incredible vaulted dome.

Above him, alien light smeared together in an impossible montage. Planetary systems spun next to giant, elongated and smeared stars - all of which was cradled by nebulous star nurseries cast in hydrogen ready to ignite - light years in length.

Even in a star ship, Alik could not suspend his disbelief this far. His mind screamed at him, astounded at the impossible nature of the images above. Following the gentle ramp along the outer perimeter, he looked along the plane, at the foot of the dome. On all sides outward laid vast complicated structures.

The view before him was like looking down at a major urban zone, from atop a neighboring cliff. There was not a smooth, contiguous surface; instead it was a maze of skyscraper like ridges, domes and towers that went on in all directions for what appeared to be hundreds of kilometers. The structures were not lit like space scrapers; instead they were partially shadowed, as if there was a single light source out of view that made the scene visible. If he unfixed his gaze and attempted to take the entire scene in at once, the portions in shadow seemed to disappear altogether, the only evidence of their existence being the gap in the star field beyond them. It was as if he were only seeing half of what was actually there.

Alik could reach out and touch the inside of the dome. As he did so, he was struck with a realization. The dome was not glass and he was not seeing directly outside the vessel. Instead, he pinpointed a variation of pixel quality as ran his finger across the surface, the tell tale signs of projection. He spun around and followed the soft glow of starlight within the room until he could recognize that the light was not actually originating from the images, but rather just the opposite.

All of the images were being projected from a single structure in the center of the massive gallery. Just as his eyes caught sight of it - the structure, which had a shape similar to a boulder-sized acorn - ran awash in the same green light as the path before.

Alik crept back down the ramp, through the darkness and towards the glowing structure. As he approached it, he could more clearly discern its form. Then, it looked less like an acorn and he could see that it was instead more like a set of long petals, set on their ends, upright, with a space in the middle. He came to the edge of the petal before him and peered carefully around its lip. Within the open cavity, Alik found a grand interface. The space lit upon his presence, into a clean white light. Obsidian screens were mounted within the path like smooth obelisks. Most were black and featureless, while others displayed a range of esoteric data. He saw a chronometer, temperature readings for the habitat as well as a range of numbers he assumed to be current telemetry, but could not decipher their actual meaning.

To this point, Alik had not attempted to make any unreasonable demands of his surroundings. To this point, he was not even sure he was 100% on board a vessel. However, the discovery of this place gave him a new sense of entitlement. Taking a deep breath and attempting to latch onto the most appropriate first request, he opened his mouth and spoke aloud. "Display navigational charts."

Alik made sure to phrase this as a direct command and not a question. Nothing happened. Even though there were not a great many computers in the Buffer, he certainly had his share of experience with them. The vast urban network was available during his collegiate experience. Citywide maps were always on demand at city terminals or on portable or implanted devices. Simple folks from the Buffer typically only handled physical, portable devices. Most everyone else had multiple series of implants, making portable interfaces irrelevant. Alik assumed he would be given a series of implants before taking this position, he feared it, but expected it. Though, that wasn't the case. He had not been physically altered in any way. He suspected more and more that his presence was regarded with only a minimal amount of thought and preparation.

"Display map!" Again nothing happened. Then, from behind and without any warning or indication of presence, a voice replied.

"Well, which do you want, navigational charts or a map?" Alik spun around to find the source of the voice. He felt the words at the edge of his ear, but when he turned, he was alone. Then the voice continued. "Don't be alarmed. Despite my earlier behavior, I assure you I understand that disembodied voices can be unsettling. It's a rather tactless way to introduce myself, but I feel it is obligatory."

Alik swallowed and took a deep breath. He recognized that this was only the computer, but the quiet of the ship magnified the unsettling task of speaking to the invisible.

"Hello." Alik was at a total loss, unsure what to say.

"I apologize for not introducing myself properly. Acceleration is an all-consuming process and I'd hoped to give you a few hours to get your bearings. Not to mention, this room is best seen at night." The voice was slightly androgynous, but had the firmness and finesse of a distinguished male with an almost indistinguishable hint of old-imperial panache. The voice, concerned, kind and confident, did not immediately comfort Alik.

"How about that map?" Alik was a bit defensive, but he recognized it and regretted it. He assumed it was a remnant of his fight or flight response, just his wits kicking in and attempting to remain relevant within a totally alien situation.

"Certainly, though I'm afraid that you still need to be

more specific."

"I'd like to see a map of the ship."

"Ah." The voice paused as if considering the request.

"You did note the terminals within your quarters. They provide visual references for all areas of concern."

Alik took another deep breath. He was not surprised by the apparent obfuscation.

"Sure. I saw the terminals."

"I can see from your details that you are versed in standard terminal usage. I also noticed that you were able to activate some of your media options. I find different forms of media quite invigorating as they aid to pass the time."

Alik smelled massive amounts of bullshit reeking from the computer. In his heart, he deeply hoped he would get along with whatever level of AI he was bound to be stuck with. It troubled him that he seemed to be in the presence of an asshole, but he kept his poker face. He knew that given enough time and enough conversation, he would eventually find the tiny fault lines in the machine's personality. Interaction required the same finesse as any disagreeable human, but with the added disadvantage of lacking any corresponding body language. Alik realized that his own body language likely spoke volumes about his personality and intent, so he consciously attempted to remain still almost inanimate. Then he began to test the waters.

"This is a big damn ship."

"Was that a question?"

"Of course not. Clearly, I can see portions of the ship from this very room." Alik pointed around the bottom edges of the dome.

"You are correct."

"Do you have a name?" This was the first time the thought had occurred to Alik, he had not given or received a proper introduction.

"Yes, thank you for asking. My name is Sigrah."

"Sigrah?"

"Yes Sigrah."

"Are you male or female?"

"That's an interesting question. As I understand it, most vessels are typically referred to in the feminine. However, I do not associate myself with one sex or gender, officially. Do you have a preference?"

Alik shook his head obligingly. "No. I have no preference." He paused and considered his next question. "Am I where I am supposed to be?"

"That is a very interesting question. I do not suppose you were seeking a metaphysical answer?" A joke. Alik spotted it as soon as it hit the air. There was hope. Alik realized that if he was not careful, through the lens of his own bias, he might project any number of emotions onto this computer. He was cautious knowing that Sigrah was actually capable of emotions. Anything that can make a joke must be fairly complex and operating on his personal accord and not simply a static set of algorithms.

Alik held fast to his poker face. "I'm fond of metaphysical questions, but now is not the time or the place. I am asking whether or not I was appropriately placed on board the correct vessel. Having never been on a space ship and having been drugged while in transit…twice…I thought it prudent to ask whether or not I was in the correct place…there's been no formal welcome or briefing of any kind. I am not complaining, I am only curious."

"So there it is. I was wondering when I was going to pull it out of you."

"Pull what out?"

"Your disgruntled airs. They are there, plain as day in your question. Brandishing poorly sharpened wit with a backhanded complaint or two sprinkled in for good measure. Good. Good. You cannot begrudge me for attempting to gauge your emotional range for myself. You are doing the same to me, are you not? Forget that, don't answer...

"Yes, you are where you were officiated to be. Welcome. As I said before I am Sigrah...all of this is Sigrah. Understand?" Alik relaxed his shoulders and nodded his head. "I'm sorry they knocked you out on your way here. The damn shame of it was that you missed the prettiest parts of this entire journey."

"What do you mean?"

"Jupiter, Neptune, Kuiper Station. They iced you soon after you left Range."

Alik jaw hung wide. "Iced me? You mean I was put into hibernation? For how long."

"Calm down. I assure you it was nothing extreme. You slept for two weeks while in transit. It made it easier for your shuttle to accelerate and maneuver, not to mention the benefit of your comfort. Your comfort is a priority, believe it or not."

Alik leaned backwards against one of the black panels and crossed his arms. "I appreciate the concern for my comfort, but from now on, I'd like to be notified if I am to be sedated and frozen. In all seriousness."

"I am not contractually obliged to disclose procedural aspects of this mission, but I can assure you that from this point forward, you will not be sedated or frozen. Your objection is noted."

Alik started hammering out questions in quick succession. "What are you contractually obliged to disclose?"

"Not much. Much of what I disclose is to my discretion alone."

"Are there things you are both unwilling and unable to disclose?"

"Certainly."

"Should I expect some sort of formal orientation?"

"I do believe we are in the midst of said orientation."

"What are my duties?"

"I'm afraid I don't understand."

"Of course you understand. You are managing to fly a vessel the size of a several cities across unthinkable distances. Do not tell me that you do not understand the question." Alik was losing his poker face quickly.

"Your duty is your title. You are to usher this vessel to its destination. I should not have to point out that your death would violate your contract, so I would suggest that continuing to exist is your most paramount duty."

"So you are telling me that existing is the extent of my responsibilities?"

"Until such time that the situation alters in some fundamental way, your characterization of the experience is correct. Great lengths have been taken to insure your comfort."

"So I am free to walk about the vessel?"

"Not as such, I am afraid. You do have access to a fairly extensive living area, which includes this gallery, your bedroom, den, galley, gymnasium and pool. I can assure you that the remainder of the vessel is far from interesting. Restricted areas may contain industrial hazards, which may inhibit your ability to continue your duty."

"Hmm…" Alik let the next question stew for a moment, considering the realization that he was essentially trapped.

"Fine. Will you display a map distinguishing the portions I have access to?" Alik remained cool in his tone.

Across the obsidian obelisk flashed a detailed survey of his area. It was indeed shaped as a nautilus, with his quarters at the far end and this dome room in the center. It was a surprisingly large area and he noticed several other portions accessible from within his quarters that he had not recognized earlier.

"That's it?" Alik asked.

The computer responded warmly. "That represents the portion you have access to." There was silence for a moment, but Sigrah soon filled it, suspecting that Alik was beginning to have doubts. "Were you able to assemble some meals today, in spite of my distraction?"

Alik, momentarily engrossed in the map, slowly bled the air from his lungs allowing it through his teeth with a surprising whistle then relaxed a bit, intentionally shifting his mind away from the map. "Yes. I made breakfast in that funny little oven, but…"

"It wasn't sufficient?"

"I may just have to get the hang of it. I'm admittedly embarrassed to admit I have not had the most extensive relationships with modern tech."

"If you prefer to cook your own meals, I can make additional implements available to you. Check your pantry in the morning."

Alik sighed. "How long until we reach our destination?"

"I realize that I am a computer and you are a human, so your natural response to my apparent sincerity will be dubious at best. That said, I would like to be extremely sincere when I tell you that asking such questions is one of the greatest pitfalls of surviving a journey such as this. Your services have been conscripted for the amount of time required to fulfill our mission. Space travel is a tricky thing and time becomes fluid and surprising." Sigrah paused for a moment, leaving a pregnant silence hanging in the room, before finally continuing. "I will not promise to be available if you happen to call on me. My mind is delegated to a great many tasks. However, I do guarantee a more detailed conversation on this topic as well as others, in spite of the fact that I am not contractually obligated to do so."

Alik unconsciously grabbed at his stomach, trying to push away the knots forming in his gut. Then Sigrah kindly sent Alik on his way.

"Have a nice sleep. Please continue to make yourself as comfortable as possible. I have full confidence that you can find any item or service you should happen to need. We will speak again after you have properly settled in." Sigrah said with finality.

At the end of the exchange, Alik was surprised to feel the additional absence of Sigrah's voice.

~

He spent hours at a time laying perpendicular with the gallery platform, his face pressed as close as possible to the projection, trying to infer the shapes of the structures cast in permanent shadows. Whatever the vague light source did not directly touch was completely black, void in space.

The placement of gallery platform along with his quarters and the nautilus nagged at Alik. Since his view within the gallery was only a projection, he could not be certain of its alignment, within the vessel. In addition, the view he was provided was not a view of oncoming space. Instead, it seemed to limit his field of vision astern and to port and starboard, with amalgamated projections of celestial objects. It wasn't a realistic view in any way. He may as well have been looking at a mural. As he rolled all of this in his mind, he could not help but laugh at the new connotations "starboard" now took on.

Perhaps looking at oncoming space would have driven him mad and knowing this, the engineers gave him a view more tantalizing. Alik found it all very curious, but ultimately chalked it up to the irrelevant. Though, it was as if he were being intentionally inspired to wonder about the ship or at the very least he was meant to watch over the cargo through his view on the platform. But, what was the cargo? The questions never ceased. They followed him to bed each night and onward through to breakfast in the mornings.

Alik realized he did not understand a single facet of the importance of his mission and he grappled over whether or not to feel entitled to know. The questions burned in his gut and multiplied throughout his first week. A single, simple answer he wished he could repudiate, burned even hotter than the questions. It was a half-born thought, but he said it aloud. "There is no greater purpose and I am only a warm body. This is my forest now."

His second evening on board he'd decided to make use of the pencil and paper in a mostly vain attempt at drawing what he saw. Looking out across the ship, the perspective was very hard to define. Angles, which appeared to run towards a specific vanishing point, corresponded with others in abrupt, incongruent ways. Either the structures beneath the shadows were designed not to conform to any common sense, geometric principles or the shadows he had previously decided covered solid portions of the hull were in fact just the void of outer space. He considered that perhaps portions, which he had previously decided were blank splotches of outer space, were actually vast, un-lit sections of the hull.

Attempting to orient himself further, he drew multiple axis on a sheet of paper, imagining his position along x, y and z-axis. He had to wrap his mind around that fact that up or down had no relevant bearing to his position on board. In space, a vessel would not necessarily need a dedicated bow or stern, but, he rationed, it would need to have a certain degree of symmetry. In his limited understanding of acceptable design, he could not foresee a modern engineer finding an a-symmetrical design acceptable.

After several days he reviewed fifteen drawings before he

settled on two plausible representations. Other than a random assortment of jutting towers and seams, some of which appeared as deep as canyon river gorges, he wagered the ship to be relatively sleek. He could not avoid noting; as stars subtly changed positions most unlit portions of the hull appeared to be spherical. No matter what his position, whether at the very front or mid-starboard side, he could tell that at the center of the vessel a massive and spherical structure was responsible for depleting his view of anything beyond it.

~

Alik rubbed his eyes, staring at the drawings in his quarters. Gazing at the sphere, highlighted by his amateur shading, he tried to imagine its scale. He recalled the view of the lunar surface from atop the transit platform in Earth orbit. The sphere, from his point of view seemed nearly comparable to that view of the Moon. Though he was quite aware, from the transit station he was then at least ninety thousand kilometers from the lunar surface. The scale of space and space bound objects vexed him.

He hung the drawings on the wall above his chest of drawers, deciding to allow the mystery to ferment.

Sigrah had not responded to Alik's requests for conversation. Several more days passed and Alik felt more and more alone. With the media wall in nearly constant activation, he splayed across his couch and surfed the media library. Each time he stumbled upon news briefs he often replayed them two or three times in a row. If it's like Nena said and time really was passing more quickly off ship, why then do the news briefs seem only to cover spans of time relative to me, wondered? Alik assumed that if the ship were receiving regular updates, his media library would reflect hundreds of days of news for each day that passed. It made no sense.

Still, the briefs were not without value. Even decontextualized from the content of the stories, he began to piece certain things together. The colonies for instance. It seemed that during terraforming events, or colony improvements, the entire population of colonial residents were gathered together in ships he assumed to be much like his own. Then the colonists were flown at relativistic speeds around their home star and back again. This allowed for the swift passage of months, weeks or years. The progress of a terraforming event could then be monitored, retooled or completed, allowing the citizens to return to more comfortable environs while barely having aged at all.

He gathered that most individuals made large sum investments during these periods, hoping that markets would rally their finances and return larger sums at the end of each high-speed jaunt. Relative time, Alik wagered, must mean so many different things to a great many people. Had he stayed on Earth, his life may have been only a swift glimmer in the lives of countless other humans, who would ultimately live across several centuries even if they were only aware of the passage of a single century.

Financial markets would move at glacial paces. He surmised that this must be the value in the sort of debt he carried. He wasn't meant to finalize the debt in a single life span; rather it was commoditized, repackaged and swapped by other financial markets over extended periods of time. Alik burned inside as he considered this. In a way, he suspected, someone was able to capitalize more from the debt of a debtor traveling at relativistic speeds than the debtor who chose life in a debtor colony.

In essence, his entire existence had become a literal credit default swap. On one hand, this enraged Alik, yet on the other, it loosened his sense of duty just enough to engage a rather dusty attitude, a very Buffer specific attitude. "Fuck it." He settled. "Fuck it. If I'm nothing more than a financial tool and a warm body, then I'm going to make the most of it."

8

The two had thoroughly wrecked the apartment. Empty glasses covered various tables and pipe ash flittered about the room like black snow. Next to the bed, amongst dozens of crumpled gray uniforms, lay a neatly discarded orange jumpsuit. Smoke lingered over the bed as Nena gripped and tangled unreservedly with the fresh, ruddy skinned body of her personal body slug. Nena kissed the other woman's forehead gently. The only true distinction between the two was the red dyed skin of the slug. Though they did not share all physical features, the slug was a genetically accurate replica of Nena - similar enough to share organs, tastes and impulses, but dissimilar enough to make slug sex only a slight jog from some perverse form of masturbation.

Nena ordered the slug before leaving Earth. She refused

to travel alone, so a companion slug was a small concession made by her employers. The presence of a slug, especially one of essential personnel actually induced lower insurance rates and was therefore quietly encouraged.

The body slug, which Nena refused to properly name, cupped two fingers and placed them inside Nena's soft cavity, stirring a fervent embrace once again. They had been making love for several hours on and off, but Nena was still hungry for more, as was her slug. Just at a moment of climax, an urgent communiqué tone sounded throughout the room. The ping rang out with nearly the same resonance as Nena's climactic howls.

After a soft moment of recombobulation, Nena lifted herself from the bed, haphazardly slung a grey rob around her aroused torso and made her way towards a small video receiver. The screen came to life with the image of a stern, weathered face - a far cry from the sumptuous curves of her inviting slug.

"Major Gipp!" The voice rang across each curve of her spacious quarters. "Major Gipp, your presence is required in conference room twelve-C. We are nearing docking with the Kuiper Belt Station and your presence is required to examine some structural data we are receiving on approach."

Nena acknowledged only with a slight huff and a nod then deactivated the call. She took a long, hesitant look at her slug. "Stay here Slug. Nay'-Nuh's gotta go work for a bit, but when I'm done here, it's just you and me for the next six weeks. I promise you are going to like Stellar Nursery much more than Kuiper Station…so just stay here…don't worry about getting out."

Nena let the last bit out with a twinge of shame. For her, it was a matter of privacy. She knew how little she actually had, but hoped to keep a little world of her own carved out amongst the ever-watchful eyes. She was not ashamed of the slug, she just did not want to share her.

The slug smiled and lit Nena's pipe while slinking deeper into the covers and activating the media wall. The slug worried about nothing and was never offended. Nena trusted the slug as much as any human trusted body slugs. It was the same kind of trust you would place in a toaster oven. You trust that it will not burn down the house, but you would never allow it watch over your child.

Though Nena had not grown tired of space, she had grown tired of space travel. She reckoned that it was a product of being planet bound for the majority of her life. Getting unhinged from a seemingly stable station or moon colony and being thrust betwixt oblivion and infinity did not sit well with her - hence the addition of the slug.

~

Upon completing her education and spending a handful of years running minor programs and apprenticing within specialized design firms, Nena was finally tasked to design and build the latest Stellar Nursery platform, only a half light year from Sol. Already, several platforms and massive science centers were operational within the Nursery, but her platform was planned as the site designated to bring the project into the next phase.

For nearly sixty years, parties of designers and engineers spent their careers accumulating matter within the Nursery - dragging in rouge planetoids, redirecting cometary objects, assembling clouds of gas through matter re-appropriation techniques etc. The first real challenge in Nena's professional life was the construction of the platform from which humans intended to birth a star. Her platform was not only required to survive stellar birth, it was also her job to build the platform to withstand any unforeseen stellar-scale events.

Essentially, she was tasked with building a laboratory, which could be dropped into the center of an unstable star and come out on the other side unscathed. The audacity of the project made Nena salivate.

In the mean time, a short layover at Kuiper Station was arranged to allow her and her team time to make necessary adjustments to the Kuiper Belt's premier behemoth, Kuiper Station.

Kuiper Station was the foremost exit and entry point for all pan-stellar missions. Already, it was built to the scale of a small moon, though its appearance referenced even the oldest of human space-structure tropes; vast stretches of rigging, trusses holding aloft modules, launch bays, maintenance bays etc. It had the look and feel of a rat's nest. Space born architecture had made incredible leaps since the inception of Kuiper Station, but few matched the scale, complexity or potential of K.S. Kuiper Station was the first deep space structure built to PAE standards, as its role was considered a billion years hence. K.S. was intended to be the corner stone for an eventual Dyson's sphere – a project, which could not be conceivably completed for another three hundred thousand years at the very least.

Still, changes in the technology and range of space vessels were having an immediate impact on the station. The dynamic gravity fields of transiting intra-galactic vessels put Kuiper station at risk of unmitigated collisions with Belt matter tossed hither and too by gravitational fluctuations. The Belt was chocked full of comets and planetoids all of which are affected by the dips and eddies among the fabric of space-time. The Frenetic Hyper-drives currently in fashion used massive gravity wells and contained a super mass, which bent space-time as a means to pull space around the rear of the vessels, squeezing the ships forward like toothpaste from a tube.

Even though docking was performed under the use of conventional rocketry and thrusters, the distortions to the fabric of space-time caused merely by the presence of a ship's super-mass could be quite dramatic. Major Nena Gipp had written several papers during her academic tenure, suggesting the placement of independent and artificial gravity wells within a grid at specific distances from Kuiper Station. She argued that creating a barricade or speed bump effect would avert gravitational distortions and may not only save K.S. from runaway vessels or Belt matter, but could also prove invaluable during the eventual construction of the Dyson Sphere. Artificial gravity wells, she argued, could eventually be utilized to pasture and stage smart colonies of carbon nano-tubes. Of the more immediate benefits, the gravity wells would also act as a braking system for incoming vessels, allowing the vessels to spend more time near light speeds and less time decelerating to arrival.

Her short stay at Kuiper Station was meant to survey the surrounding space and determine the exact placement of the gravity wells. The actual work would be carried out over the course of several decades. Needless to say, she objected to this diversion, insisting that her publications provide enough data to plenty of other engineers to do the job. She was, however, adept enough to realize that this additional task was nothing more than a final test. Her superiors wanted to measure her patience and skill one last time before turning her loose on the biggest stellar experiment concocted to date.

~

Making her way down the long, stark white corridors of her transport ship, towards conference room twelve, Nena's mind drifted to Alik. When she thought of him, she saw Alik as a child - the scruffy kid who was always begging questions of her. The grown, Alik had not completely settled and connected in her mind. When she left him, she was angry at his foolishness – angry at the foolishness of an adult - but then immediately regretted her disdain when she forced herself to see that the man she was so upset with was still the same little boy with an unlimited supply of questions and a questionable supply of wits needed to understand the answers.

Nena was not the sort to allow guilt to rule her, but she did feel guilt, knowing that it was the decisions of her far-flung counterparts, who placed men like Alik into these odd scenarios. She speculated that his vessel was already well underway. She kicked herself for not examining the launch manifests for his window. She could have easily determined where he was off to.

Turning the corner towards the conference room, she made a mental note to look into the matter later. Then the guilt settled away in her spine, where she held all of the guilt she'd manufactured then hidden away. Even though days, perhaps a week had elapsed for Alik, it had been six years since she last saw him.

Before entering the conference room, she checked the creases of her uniform and buffed the subtle pin denoting her rank. Rank was a formality at best, indicating stratification as plainly as possible. Militaries in the traditional sense were a thing of the past. Her associated rank did have a semblance of merit and she wore it proudly, as a reminder of her diligence. She readied herself, wanting always to walk into a room as if she owned it.

When the conference room door slid open, Nena was hit with the immediate realization that the meeting she had been called for, was not the meeting she had just walked into. At the table sat three Generals, high-level designers each, along with two distinguished, PAE council members who wore no rank.

Despite the agreeable temperature, Nena's brow burst with a thin layer of sweat, as she stood aghast, attempting mentally to identify each of the individuals. She expected to walk into a room of NCO's and CGO's, so this glut of rank set her immediately on the defensive.

"Gentleman, Ladies." She looked about the room, making eye contact with each member and acknowledging their presence.

The group each nodded and welcomed her to sit with them. Their gestures were gracious and non-confrontational, which still did not manage to put Nena at ease. As she took her seat, the room was still. The traditional lighting scheme had been substituted for a darkened room, with only a single band of illumination above the conference room table. In the corners of the room, stood several Colonels she had not noticed at entry. Each managed recording equipment or monitored their tablets, acting solely as support staff. None of the Colonels made eye contact or acknowledged the officials in the room. Nena suspected they could be representatives of an un-seen AI who was also monitoring the meeting.

Finally, the lowest ranking General extended a hand across the table laying it flat. He smiled and ran the fingers of his opposite hand through the rough curls of his bangs.

"Major Gipp. We are very happy to have you here." The General said in a near whisper. Nena read his nameplate, Gimble, though he never formally introduced himself.

Nena nodded and reasserted her confidant gaze by straightening her spine and reflecting the General's smile.

"It is quite agreeable to be here, sir."

The General looked to the others at the table, then back to Nena. "Major Gipp, I'm certain that you are curious why you have been ambushed by such an array."

"The question is firm in my mind, sir." Nena was compliant, but confident.

"Major Gipp, I'll get right to the point. You have been commissioned to over see certain elements of our Stellar Birth project. The fact is that your services will no longer be rendered in this manner." The General shifted to an antiseptic tone. "The elements of your structural theories and your gravitational research which was to be applied at Kuiper Station, speak well enough of your capabilities and your inevitable success within these project fields. However, we have plenty of fine engineers capable of overseeing these projects in harmony with your specifications and we will be prepared to compensate you by recommending you for major projects...." He paused. "...at some later date, yet to be established."

Nena reeled a bit, baited and fighting the urge to object. Of course she knew, objection in scenarios such as these were futile at best, career ending at worst. Decisions of this nature come from the PAE Council and their word was final. She could only assume that the PAE had discovered some flaw in a larger design and pulled her in order to compensate. She could accept this situation much easier if she knew that it been thoroughly rationalized by the PAE.

Nena carefully inserted herself into the General's natural pause. "Sir. I'm not certain I understand. If I am not wanted on the Stellar Birth project..." She allowed her question to trail off.

The General swung back to his gracious tone. "Major, please, hear me out. My statement is coated in the obligatory language of officiating. Please allow me to stress that we have a significant amount of confidence in your work." The General paused. "In fact, we have a new mission we are assigning you to. It is a mission far more critical than your previous." Nena squirmed in her seat. "Yes sir?"

The General continued. "Major Gipp, we are assigning you to a solo mission." The General paused to examine Nena's face. "Major Gipp, we, the PAE council and a handful of other top designers have certain, reasonable suspicions, that humanity may be on the brink of first contact."

Nena instinctively rolled her eyes and bit her lip in order not to laugh. Her brain immediately flooded with the thought of all the colonies, all the exo-planet exploration and the myriad manned and unmanned missions to the near reaches of the galaxy. Not a single mission had detected anything more than basic organic compounds. Never an amoeba or a virus, no bacterium or algae, nothing to suggest that life had taken a foothold anywhere in the cosmos. The mathematics of the situation suggested that human life was unique. Most had come to believe the idea whole-heartedly. The idea of humanity as a unique fluke perpetuated the notion that human interaction with the Universe could cause irreversible entropy. The idea was preposterous and to Nena, smacked of some sub-plot to remove her simpleton, Buffer genes from those of "reputable" engineers. Even still, there were always flippant, unsubstantiated rumors of aliens or artifacts or the inevitability of contact. Nena's experience told her that all of it was rubbish and personally irrelevant.

The General continued. "Major Gipp, I know what you are thinking. I had the same reaction when approached by the PAE Council. However, there is some evidence that we may be on the relative cusp of first contact and apparently, the models we have been running suggest that you may play an integral role in this interaction. How? I cannot say. I have been advised though that your mission status be altered to accommodate this possibility."

Suddenly, the General was interrupted by one of the unidentified PAE Council members, who stood from his seat, walked towards Nena, knelt on one knee and took her gently by the hands. He looked deep into Nena's eyes and began to speak.

"Nena." He called her by her common name, hoping to comfort her objections. "Nena, I understand that this sounds ridiculous. I also understand that we are asking you to take us at our word. You should know that the PAE Council is not in a habit of explaining itself, ever. However, in this matter, we decided it was important enough to address you personally. We cannot provide you with all of the data we have at hand, in an effort to safe guard the success of future events…so as vulgar as it may be to ask this, I am asking you to accept this matter on faith alone." The Council member looked deeper into Nena with his ancient eyes. Whenever a PAE Council member spoke of faith, they were actually speaking about obedience. "Nena, fly out there and let come what may."

Nena gripped the Council member's hands and relaxed her shoulders slightly. She knew what they were asking of her. A deep space journey, no matter the scale of the mission would require multiple years at relativistic speeds. To some extent she was comfortable with the idea, she must, given her position, but she realized that six weeks or six months at near light speed was a far cry from years. She did not break her gaze with the Council member, but asked a direct question.

"And my crew?"

The Council member smiled and stood, returning to his seat as the General began to speak again.

"Major Gipp, this will be a solo mission. You will have the ship at your disposal, but that is it." The General replied.

"No. I'm taking my slug." Nena demanded.

"A slug? On a mission of this import?" The General scoffed at the idea.

"You're after mission success right? Then you are going to allow me to take my slug." Nena was indignant. She wagered that if they were ordering her on such a mission, she would demand this single concession.

The Generals looked at one another silently, then back to

the PAE council members who each shrugged, uninterested. Finally the General responded. "Fine. The Slug can go." The group stood. "Major Gipp, your orders will be available to you once your ship is underway. The ship is docked and ready for you at Kuiper. Make your final preparations and discuss the details of this mission with absolutely no one, including your slug. At that, the group exited the opposite conference room door, leaving Nena standing in the silent shadows of the room.

She was certain that she had no choice. If the PAE decided to launch someone into deep space with no other directive, simply because that's what the math told them to do, they would not hesitate to do so. Nena was not, for one millisecond, under the impression that she was meant to return.

9

During the final days of her transit, Myco's courier ship, crossing through the spires of stardust beyond Phaeos, made incremental adjustments in order to slow the vessel. This culminated in the violent and dangerous act of stellar braking - slowing the ship by slamming into the gravity well of the Rachis star Phaeos' at nearly three quarters the speed of light. Myco was anxious but it was not just the thought of losing molecular cohesion or transforming instantaneously into stellar matter that frightened her, it was the thought of never regaining a signal from the world or the creature she'd glimpsed.

She guarded herself from imagining that the Transmitter, he, was in some way missing Myco. The idea was preposterous. Not only had she ascribed gender to the creature, but she was also projecting precarious emotions and states of being. She knew very well that no part of this creature was even aware of her or her lapsing presence. And there was a significant likelihood that the ingestion of the probes was a one-time event for the creature. There was absolutely no guarantee that she would ever receive another signal from any individual much less the same individual. The odds were so preposterous that even the silent suggestion of the possibility had the potential of damaging Myco's credibility.

~

Myco's quarters remained barren save for a soft, living, mycelia mat on her floor. She and the other passengers were ordered to remain quartered for the final duration of the flight. With nothing else to focus her attention, she struggled not to fall into a receptive state. She sat on her mycelia mat, her legs crossed beneath her as she focused on the grungy, orange wall directly across from her, exerting herself to vanquish all thought. Her eyes kept tripping on nearly imperceptible specks of floating dust and flotsam that shined ever so slightly as they passed through patches of light. She felt as adrift and out of control as each of the specks. She could see though, that each was a galaxy, filled the brim with matter – only they existed on a scale she could perceive – mostly. Myco struggled to find merit in existing as something different than a random, sub-atomic particle may exist within a single fleck of dust. Of the billions of massive atoms, the trillions upon trillions of sub atomic particles were barely detectable – truly insignificant in the comings and goings of the cosmos. Myco was a quark.

No matter how hard she tried to ignore it, she felt a tug in the back of her mind. The tugging urge felt like the tell-tell signs and giddy anticipation of the coming of a perfect transmission, the sort a Heritor Monk could only hope for once or twice in a lifetime. An individual, clear transmission, received at the speeds they were now traveling was unimaginable and risky. As she let go of her defenses and surrendered to the transmission, she knew these were the first wrenches of the dangerous, high-speed reception she had avoided the whole trip. The tugging calmed her and she was certain that she would be safe.

Prohibiting her mind from receiving such a clear transmission was, as she saw it, a violation of her oaths. Monks of this order were resigned to an unusual balance - total awareness, total openness and total focus.

Ritual castigation was not an unusual consequence the Monks occasionally faced. The punishments ranged from sleep deprivation, to intentional sensory over load and were typically manifested to weed out or strengthen certain behaviors. Each punishment or session was tailored to the individual monk and shaped the future skill, personality and status of each Monk.

While the other monks meditated rigorously, as a student, Myco had a tendency to drift from meditation and find pleasure while staring at the half open buds of Plumgraths. The Plumgraths covered the steep knolls surrounding the monastery and very efficiently converted nebulous gases into equal parts Oxygen and Nitrogen. Their buds were small, but riddled with intense and vibrantly colored patterns. As the buds thickened, preparing to burst wide, the colors would fluctuate rapidly through the spectrum. The asteroid the monastery sat atop was covered in a layer of Plumgraths, each taking an equal footing as the other as far as the asteroid stretched. When immersed in a bloom cycle, one could stare at the buds and lose weeks watching the color trickle and pour like a thousand individual streams – each chromatically alive - teeming over the soft petals of the buds. The fields stretched out from the steps of the monastery and coated the haphazard asteroid almost entirely with patterns of vivacious, rolling tones – from pale magenta blobs oscillating into olive, then orange to cerulean, intersected with coal black variegation that faded to powder blue at the peak of each day.

These occasions were precious for all the monks, but staring into the fields required a great deal of time and respect that could only be given after actual duties such as meals, maintenance, multi-day rounds of meditation or attempts at reception. Sometimes, the monks maintained practice for weeks, even months at a time, emerging to find that the buds had opened and the spectacle had come and gone, having been replaced by the dying bodies of the Prickle Flies and the glowing, fat guts of the luminescent Katatsumuri – creatures the colors were meant to attract.

Myco couldn't stand to miss staring at the buds. Once, at the end of a meditation cycle, the elders of the monastery approached her. After respectfully admonishing Myco for secretly observing the buds, the monks took swift actions to provide a lesson in attention. They led her beyond the steps of the monastery, into the fields and hummocks covered in Plumgraths, to the bottom of the lowest crater full of the flowers. The monks then dug a hole as wide as Myco's shoulders, deep enough to bury Myco to her chin. At this height, the only thing she could observe was the wild blush of the twirling buds. They left her in this state until the Prickle Flies had gone and the Plumgraths had fully composted atop the rocky soil, their seeds had been processed and returned by the Katatsumuri and the new flush of Plumgraths and sprouted and begun to grow.

Myco carried the lesson from then on. Total commitment to attention balanced with focused devotion to presence was fundamental at all times. Additionally, thanks to the lesson, she understood the bud and pollination cycle of the Plumgrath better than any of the Monks.

Consequently it was with the same sense of commitment and acknowledgment of consequence, that Myco opened her mind to the transmission, extreme velocity be damned. After finally releasing and giving in to the transmission, cosmic clatter and fractal patterns poured into her mind as her consciousness fell through space time and the infinite - through the center of the mandala built into the slipstream as a cairn, signaling the acquisition of the probe's communiqué – through doubling polygon forms of shape and light, clearer and more present than any previous reception to date – the cold iron of reality pressing into her skin as the seconds merged. The clarity of this reception emphasized that the mandala was not simply an analogue of her mind; rather it was an actual artifact, a physical marker. The colors, the connection, the fractals, they were all real to her before, but somehow they then formerly seemed representative and not actual. This was an actual mandala, ripe with inscription, too detailed to interpret fully, but she made note over every detail, each line of script and each image so that it all could be recalled and examined later.

Around the edges of the mandala, figures, faces, unfamiliar yet known, somehow. Animal forms, strange shapes, writing, many languages, perhaps elemental shapes, water, fire, quantum symbols, mathematics, all tightly carved across the entire surface. And Myco fell, uncontrollably into the center. She felt her body impact the darkness on the far side of the mandala.

For a moment she just lay, her hands flat on a warm, smooth surface with her knees tucked just under her belly and feeling as though she had just awoke from a nap several days long. It was the feeling of being a stranger in her own body, as if she had just been somewhere else, but now she was someplace alien to her and there was no way of understanding how she had gotten there. Her stomach was tight and Myco wretched a bit at the realization of her presence, her existence as a living being.

As she tried to push herself off the floor, she realized something was wrong with her body. She looked around, her hands, her chest, her feet. And it occurred to her, faintly at first, like a ghost memory-this was not her body. She was elsewhere before she was here, sharing this moment. But this revelation didn't come all at once. It was gradual like eyes adjusting to light.

Transmission, she thought. This is a transmission. She looked carefully at the wrinkles in her hands. They were familiar hands, the same as before. It was he whom she had connected to. But why was it so dark? Why was he on the floor? Was he injured? All she could do from that point was continue to observe. He remained on his side, staring outward, sometimes directing his fingers towards the blackness. Then Myco focused further. Not only was he staring into the dark, he was staring into space. He was looking into distant star fields and magellanic streams.

Without her interference, he rose, first sitting, cross-legged, steadying himself, and then he stood, breathing deeply and intentionally. Myco was certain he was staring at a projected image of space. He thumbed over a small point of light and the image magnified a star, giving him a brilliant view of its churning fires. The light was intense, scaring away the darkness of the room; the Transmitter closed his eyes a bit. Myco too was forced to refocus.

Nonetheless, her reception was stronger than ever. She felt the subtle warmth of the light upon the Transmitter's flesh. His meat was very similar to hers, attuned to sensation, fragile. He rubbed his eyes and Myco felt the relief of the touch as his eyes cleared and hydrated.

It was evident to Myco that the Transmitter was feeling the physical effects of the probe quite intensely. There was a bit of uneasiness in his step, a slight shiver in the muscles of his hands and minor twinge of fear in his gut. Myco guessed he had eaten several dozen probes at once. But the intensity or number of the probes did not explain the strength and clarity of the signal.

The Transmitter sat again, staring at the star field as multiple stars magnified to a fuller illumination at once. Myco felt the Transmitter's wonder and fascination. She shared the feelings with him, creating an emotional eddy beneath the Transmitter's flesh. The sight of it all brought him to tears. Myco fought to remain objective, but her attempts to separate herself from the Transmitter's emotions only stirred its experience deeper.

As she took in as much of his sight as was possible, she grew certain that a portion of the image included views of a ship. Myco guessed it to be a very large ship and likely the ship on which the Transmitter currently resided.

She considered it a likely possibility, that if this were a vessel of some sort, they were traveling at incredible speeds. Myco had not considered this a possibility. In normal modes of reception, the three components, the Probe, the transmitter and the Heritor were each held under extreme conditions. The orbit of a Transmitter's planet in relation to the Heritor, the time dilation inherent in such extreme distances, gravitational anomalies, the health, age, potency and type of Probe, all were factors in reception.

This particular experience, however, was totally contrary to any she had previously. Myco felt the weight of the Transmitter's bones, the way the floor felt smooth and warm against his feet along with the erect hairs at the tops of his toes, the comfortable temperature of the environment and the full range of intense emotions, questions, half thoughts and instant glimpses of enlightenment. This creature, whatever else it may be, was a creature that possessed a wide array of emotions, each with a separate range of subtlety and nuance. She could not fathom a creature other than herself who could be brought to tears simply by beholding a magnificent sight. This was not the mind of a beast.

And with that thought, she felt the same thought, totally un-rooted from her, echo back from the Transmitter. This is not the mind of a beast. The ease with which her thought became his thought frightened Myco. She tried to remain focused on sensory observations and keep her mind clear, but she could not ignore the nagging curiosity. Could she knock a little louder? Should she give him a clue?

This experience, she insisted to herself, was with the same Transmitter as before, the reason she was traveling to meet with the Ellern. Two times is unfathomable, so there would likely never be another interaction. She wanted so badly to just tap his shoulder, whisper a thought into his mind, perhaps to assure another meeting. And as she considered this, she envisaged the moment just a bit further, building the occasion through her thoughts, approaching the Transmitter from behind as he stared deeply into the light of dead stars, gently placing her hand onto his shoulder, leaning in, her thin lips close to his ear and whisper lightly *"Do not give in to amazement."*

And as the thought solidified in her mind, she felt the Transmitter jump, startled, looking behind him for a hand that was not there. Myco had done it, involuntarily, she had communicated directly with him. The Transmitter lay back onto the floor, facing upwards. His thoughts continued to pour, soon it did not matter whether Myco allowed a thought of her own to slip through, he took them all as gifts of the experience – so much that Myco could feel his gratitude.

All of a sudden, another feeling gripped the moment. There was a presence she had not felt at first, but she now realized had been there all along. In a way, she felt that she was actively sharing a space with this other presence. And though it did not feel malevolent, it seemed just as curious of Myco as it felt of Alik.

Myco considered the possibility that another Heritor may have been receiving along with Myco, perhaps even from the monastery. Though, the instant she bore this thought, it leaked through into the fervor of the transmission. She felt the Transmitter react to her thought, processing it through many cultural filters until it was somewhat relatable to the Transmitter. In his mind, Myco's thought was born as three people arguing in a café, each attempting to speak over the other, but none speaking the same language. She found herself as lost in this interpretation as the Transmitter. She could see her own face, but she could not see the faces of the others arguing. Instinctively, she reached out to the other two, taking each by a hand, still unable to see their faces and quieted them.

She explained with only a look, that this was an analogue. It was nothing more than a room within a thought. She then invited the two to follow her. She led them to the door of the café then opened it and led them outside. As they passed through the door, the three became one again. She was then looking through the eyes of the Transmitter as he stepped toward the sidewalk, his foot found instead a deep void, which draped over the fiery fingers of Phaeos. Below, all three could see Myco's ship barreling towards the star, lit like a comet and braking hard.

In that instant Myco was violently pulled from her reception. The signal was gone as fast as the light from an extinguished candle. The disconnection was painful and left Myco bleeding a bit from her thin nostrils. She took several moments to collect herself from the sheer agony of the forced disconnection, but she was alive.

Her ship had completed its braking sequence. The sudden wrench of Phaeos' gravity had been enough to violently end the transmission. The ship was all but stopped; gliding now at maneuvering speeds and headed towards a high orbit around Lom. Myco knew that she had only an hour, maybe an hour and a half, before she would meet with the Ellern. These Monks, in tune with her very essence – were impenetrable to deception. Many of them have seen the Universe through the eyes of myriad lesser creatures, creatures that met their ends many thousands of years ago. The Ellern maintain a vast, reaching awareness as easy as breathing and Myco had no hope of hiding a thing from them. She knew that if she had directly communicated with the Transmitter, she would be expelled from the sect. She also knew that the detail would be impossible to hide if she led the Ellern through this transmission. Yet, it was all too important not to bring the elder monks into the fold. Breaking one vow was surely better than breaking all of them.

To meet this situation head on, she knew it was necessary to remain honest, explain everything, allow the eldest monks to walk through each of the experiences for themselves. If it was the will of the Universe that she be cast out of her sect or even forcibly fruited, so be it.

10

In spite of terrific technologies, vast human achievement, boldness, bravery and cunning, the dangers of the cosmos were still impossible for human beings fully conceive. Nature is at the root of all obstacles. Beyond intelligent life's bend towards self-annihilation, lack of foresight or sheer inelegance of thought, nature, at any time it wills, can snuff out a life in a matter of seconds.

Sailors traversing the early seas of Earth could be ended with a basic misstep; one slip on a wet deck and they were overboard, drowning in simple mixture of hydrogen and oxygen. Moreover, the sun could dry their fresh water, leaving them to crisp and dehydrate, ending life in a mad deluge of hallucination and fear while the rats on board thrive on their carcasses. Any number of unseen pathogen could find their way into a scrape or a tear duct and render a complex, resilient, intelligent creature useless and dead in a relatively short span of time.

Space is even more fraught with potential calamity. Drowning in a vacuum, it turns out, is the least concern a living being should have whilst traveling through space. The very act of sailing amongst the stars requires extreme longevity, extreme speed or both. Either of which can potentially end in madness or entombment, even the total loss of molecular cohesion as a ship slams into any number of spatial, temporal or gravitational anomalies.

Do not be fooled for a moment. Whatever intentions an intelligent being may have, traveling the stars, the purest dangers always emerge.

~

The natural world of Alik's foundation was as distant as the stars in front of him. It affected him more than he first realized. The internal illumination, though well designed, warm and comforting was no substitution for Sol. The air remained fresh, filtered and moving. Though the randomness of breeze or wind was apparently not considered by the designers to be functional or efficient and was therefore distinctly absent, or so it seemed.

His home in the forest was successfully integrated with nature. The homes were built into the forest hills, remaining temperate no matter the weather. Excess water soaked through the forest floor and into adobe aquifers, which fed the homes. Things made sense there. The leaves of each plant soaked up light, fed the vegetation and most conserved some medicinal value. The leaves fell, broke down and fed the plants over and over with their remains. The trees kept the people shaded from harsh rays, protected from straight-line winds, retained moisture in the land and protected against

drought. Animals, insects, birds, arachnids, fungus and humans, each played a functional role in the process. The
human role was messy, but worthy of standing in awe of as
people made a bit of chaos out of order and order out of
chaos.

This sudden lust for the natural world was not something
Sigrah necessarily empathized with, though he would have
had he ever been garaged or housed away in dusty stillness,
far from the pulsing cosmic rays and dancing star light. Sigrah and his computer brethren alike felt every atom of the
natural world they traveled or convened amongst. Hurling
through a vacuum, Sigrah's body was keen to every sensation
of trace gases, flecks of dust vaporizing on impact - tearing
at his alloy flesh here and there - solar winds and radioactive
currents. A planet bound A.I. was even luckier. His body
was essentially whichever world he was planted on. He would
have access to every sensory node on the surface of the world.
He could feel all temperatures, breezes, rains, the footsteps of
the inhabitants and the awesome, constant rays of star shine
along the planet's magnetic epithelium.

To disconnect a computer mind from the implicit realities
of nature would be torture and has in fact been carried out as
a sort of punishment to artificial minds in the past. To Sigrah, the human body was inferior, needy, weak, porous and
lacked the appreciation of the natural world his computer
brethren held in such regard. However, there was clearly a
disconnect in his perception of what humans were willing to
tolerate and what humans were clearly unaware of.

Alik tolerated the artificial climate. In many ways it was
more comfortable than his dugout - cobb home in the forest.
He no longer had to contend with invading ants or excess
moisture, but things were still nerve-rackingly peculiar. He
was not prepared for this aspect of the journey, though he
was thankful to have the amenities provided.

This was why the subtle chirp of a bird drew in Alik's attention like a thirsty man to an oasis. The chirp broke several monotonously obsessive months and put Alik square on the path towards the hard answers for which he had been pressing.

Hours before hearing the birdsong, Alik was busy arguing with Sigrah, as had become the nature of their relationship. This was on the rare occasion Sigrah acknowledged Alik's presence. After pressing Sigrah for more information regarding their destination, Sigrah presented Alik with an array of seemingly unconnected data – timelines of apparently random stellar events from a million years prior, the fluctuation in energy output of regional singularities, vast mathematics on time dilation and velocity curves. Quite literally, Sigrah had given Alik all the information Alik would need to determine their destination, without actually telling him where they were heading. Alik assumed Sigrah saw this as a game and to follow suit and placate this thinking thing's belief, Alik began to stew on the problem. Though, he may as well have been staring at hieroglyphs written with invisible ink. It was incomprehensible.

He tried not to focus on the unintelligibility or size of the numbers or the inconsistency of the other bits of data. He hoped there was a simple but less than obvious way to solve the problem and he intended to crunch at it at least until he found a better mystery to pursue. Alik was aware enough of his own ego to realize that these challenges, the mysteries had become matters of pride. No matter how many times Alik read the numbers, transcribing them with less than no understanding of their functions into his book felt like playing Bach on guitar after having severed his own fingers.

Alik had also fallen into the habit of keeping a journal, though he detested the idea of thinking of it as a journal. He saw them more his notes - things he wanted to record, but did not want to log officially at the terminal. Sometimes, they were just half born thoughts, pockets of inspiration about this or that – sometimes they were observations he did not want to forget, like patterns and locations of potential hatches he could not access. Sigrah explained that one of the Alik's only duties was to record regular system logs – just basic notes on the state of the AI, which would ultimately be used to analyze his mental state by the computer. All logs were going to be expected at arrival. "Daily reports should be made on the well being of the quarters, as well as your impressions of me." Alik remembered the conversation well but also remembered the old man in the city muttering something under his breath, something about being cautious when telling the computer things or writing certain things in official logs. "Put as little into writing as possible." The old man had mumbled.

Alik felt it was a good advice in any case. In his limited experience with automated systems or computers, he found that the more information he provided, the more personal and annoyingly accommodating the systems he'd interacted with became. He also considered that despite what he did or did not put into official log, it was most likely that Sigrah was observing Alik's behavior at all times. Surely, there is no more information one can hope to gather about the mental state of another beyond watching the subtle actions of a man who believes someone is watching but attempts to act as though no one is watching.

There was something aloof about Sigrah, however. Alik had the impression that Sigrah truly did have very little interest in him. He suspected that it was just as likely that Sigrah had the ability to monitor him, but did not, simply because Alik was not interesting enough to demand Sigrah's attention.

~

The entire ordeal was bafflingly productive. He was sensible enough to know when his actions were questionable or reckless. He knew he was not perfect and most days Alik felt more like a child than a man. Although he never said this aloud, Alik was convinced that approaching the world through his child mind not only made everything that much more interesting, but it typically led him into a state of preoccupational awareness that led to fruitful events. To Alik, it was just a way of allowing investigation to intersect with fate.

After kicking around for months, the thought blind-sided Alik. He suddenly recalled that he had not quite finished unpacking. Under a layer of various books, towards the bottom of the trunk, he'd packed two large cedar boxes. One packed to the gills with the Buffer herb he, his family and his Buffer compatriots enjoyed regularly. The other box, he had filled the morning of his off-world transit. He had returned before daybreak to the hallowed old growth and collected a dozen or so ounces of the Kinoko.

After packing a tall pipe of the Buffer herb and stoking it for several seconds, his curiosity pinged in again. He reminded himself of the various items sent along by the old man and tried once again to assemble a list of the items and their uses, within his mind. Frustrated, having forgotten the details of everything but the nifty sphere, he dove to chest of drawers and started pilfering through the burlap sacks that held the treasures.

In true form, Alik had forgotten most of what the old man had told him, but shrugged it off, realizing that the old man had told him essentially nothing to begin with. Most of the devices had simply been dumped into his hands or haversack without any explanation what so ever.
He passed over the device he'd been instructed was a weapon, stacking it gently onto the 'med' kit. He picked up a small unit, which was surprisingly heavy.

"What had he said?" Alik wondered aloud. "Something about a universal attachment." He had no idea what the device actually did. In his hand, it felt solid, rough, but intentionally rough, like pumas stone. It was oblong, almost shapeless, like a custom grip of some sort.

He squeezed the device, which fit snugly in his palm and considered it for a moment. He looked around as if he were going to find Sigrah standing behind him, but the room was barren save for him and the furniture. The device was heavy in his palm. Then, without a fully formed plan, Alik brazenly carried the device out of his quarters, around the corridor and into the central gallery. He approached the main terminal, which was partially shrouded in shadow. Above him, the lights of space smeared across the dome, the projection highlighting and magnifying certain interesting bits of matter every handful of seconds. Alik placed his hand on the obsidian surface of one of the monolithic interface panels, then laid the device on the flat surface surrounding a keypad at Sigrah's main terminal.

"Sigrah?" Alik waited a moment then continued. "Sigrah do you know what this device is?"

"Where did you find this?" Sigrah was instantly present. Alik had did not have to goad Sigrah into speaking as he normally did and Sigrah's reaction was one of shock.

"It was a gift." Alik paused, trying to calculate his openness. "I was told I could bring anything that could fit in that trunk.

Sigrah beamed with newly polished charm. "Of course, of course. That is your prerogative. I ask only because I have never actually seen one of these. I am simply wondering how you found it. No need to worry." Alik smiled a bit, feeling that for once, he seemed to have the upper hand when it came to information. Confidence of this sort had become a rare find for Alik.

"If you've never seen one, how do you know what it is?" Alik took dead aim but misfired, coming off as arrogant, essentially showing all of his cards.

"I have records of many things, of course. Even things I have never witnessed personally." There was a pregnant silence as Alik waited for Sigrah to elaborate. "I think there should be another part to it…that is, if it is what I think it is."

"This is all I'm aware of." Alik picked it up again, looking for a seam or hinge of some sort. Then, he held the device near his ear, shaking it and listening. He accidentally brushed his temple once with the edge of the device. Alik noticed the device react by extending a small node.

"Yes that!" Sigrah was genuinely surprised. "Put that against your temple."

"What? It's not going to hurt me is it?" Alik looked at the little node and it seemed innocuous enough, no sharp edges, no needles - it was tiny and innocuous.

"I don't believe it will hurt you. I'm very sure I know what this is." Alik placed the node against his temple and he felt a sudden but painless tap against his skin. He pulled the device away, but felt a small patch it left behind on his temple. Alik could not see it, but he could rub it with his fingers and it seemed like a rough patch, coarse but not invasive or uncomfortable. The patch was the size of the very tip of his index finger. He picked at it, but it seemed fully adhered and he didn't want to rip it completely off, fearing it would bring skin along with it.

"What is this thing?" Alik asked, quickly losing his patience.

"I believe it is a type of interface." Sigrah sounded amused.

"You mean with my brain?" Alik began to panic a bit more, feeling foolish. He scratched at the spot but could do nothing to remove it. Anger welled in him vaguely as he toyed with the prospect that Sigrah had led him into this.

"I think so. It's a very old, very rare tool. I believe it was intended for certain forms of programming." Sigrah was not in the least worried. In fact, his tone was one of relief.

"How old?" Alik almost shouted the question.

"At least eight hundred years?" Sigrah replied gently.

"Shit." Alik clawed at the spot, tearing some hair away and regretting its presence.

"I do not believe engineers have used a device like this since conscious uploads became possible." Sigrah remained gentle.

"So we should get this thing off of me, right…no need to use antiquated tech. Right?" Alik tried to calm himself, but was getting progressively more amped.

"I do not know that we should declare it antiquated just yet. I'm curious." Sigrah seemed to be as inquisitive as Alik and took several audible breaths for effect. "Calm down. Give it a moment and I believe it will activate on your command."

Sigrah asked Alik to place the device onto the console. "I'm going to open a port, here at the console. Once it's open, I want you to hold the device over the port just as you held it against your temple." Alik agreed and watched as a square inch of the console opened. Alik held the device over the console as Sigrah requested and both watched as the device formed a perfect mate, coupling to Sigrah's port.

"Place the device in the port Alik." Sigrah was quite confident.

"Are you sure about this?" Alik asked with lingering concern.

"I'm very sure." Sigrah replied.

Alik connected the device to Sigrah's port and instantly felt an odd sensation under his skin. He could not explain it, but it felt as though his thoughts were humming, spinning up like a hard drive in action. That was the best way he could explain it to Sigrah, but Sigrah did not respond. Each thought – fear in the moment, wondering what Sigrah was doing, the device, home, his room, the trunk, his mother – as his mind raced back and forth consciously and unconsciously from thought to thought, he felt each thought hum a corresponding octave until his brain felt electrified. The sensation was alarming, but not uncomfortable. In a way, he felt slightly drunk.

"Do you want me to remove it, Sigrah?" Alik was concerned.

"No!" Sigrah was clearly coping. "Don't remove it. I'm communicating through it." Sigrah was quiet for several minutes. Soon the resonant humming of Alik's thoughts settled and his brain returned to normal. Then came the voice.

"Alik." Alik heard Sigrah's voice inside of his mind.

"Yes?" Alik responded audibly.

"I'm very sorry." Sigrah answered, again within Alik's mind. His voice was sincere.

"What? Why? What the hell is going on?" Alik's confusion and panic was peaking.

"No. No don't worry. It's ok. You should try to calm yourself. Take a deep breath little friend." Sigrah had never been this gentle.

"What? What's ok?" Alik wondered if Sigrah was losing his mind. He wasn't making much sense. And the intrusion into Alik's mind was setting him further on edge.

"I did not know you saw me as an impediment. I did not realize you were so stressed." Sigrah was reading Alik thought for thought.

"Slow down Sigrah. What the hell is going on?" Alik placed his hand on the device, ready to yank it from the port at any second.

"It's the device." Sigrah said.

"Is it broken?" Alik gripped the device tighter.

"No! No. It's working fine." Sigrah was silent, for nearly a minute. Alik also said nothing, hoping a few moments of silence would finally allow Sigrah to explain what had happened.

Suddenly, within Alik's mind, Sigrah demanded that Alik sit. Alik complied, hastened by Sigrah's unexpected tone.

"Hold on." Sigrah was abrupt.

Then, in an instant, Alik's entire perception altered in a terrifying and dramatic way. In less than a moment, all he could see was white starlight bending around him like wind. His skin bubbled with a vibrant, living sensation, as if he were feeling space roll and eddy across his flesh. In a breath, Alik was pulled from the scene and funneled through corridor after corridor into vast open spaces, through the flesh of the vessel and back to the feeling of space drifting across his torso. And without warning, his consciousness was delivered again to his body.

Alik stared at the console from the floor. "Holy shit!"

"I apologize for the intensity. It will take us both a while to get the hang of this." Sigrah was too matter of fact for words. Alik was stunned.

"So it goes both ways?" Alik shook a bit as he stood.

"It seems so." Then Sigrah asked Alik an unexpected question. "Do you enjoy music?"

"Excuse me?" Alik was aghast at the sudden change of subject.

"Poetry? Verse? Songs? Anything?"

"Sure." Alik was actually very familiar with music. Everyone in the Buffer made an effort to learn as many songs as time would allow and everyone played at least one instrument. Music was a uniquely inspirational force not only in its splendor but also in its mystery. Most songs had simply been passed along. Some recordings existed and most were a thousand years old - their crafters completely unknown - some lyrics so out of context they were fun but meaningless while others were timeless.

"Name something. What's your favorite piece of music?" Sigrah was insistent. Alik thought about this question for a moment. There was a lullaby his mother used to hum. Sometimes she hummed it as she cooked or as she cleaned. His father sometimes hummed the same tune independently and in a separate part of the home or the forest. Alik hummed the tune to Sigrah, forgetting the lyrics or its origin.

Through their link, Sigrah felt the song, inside Alik's mind. He could feel the memories of Alik's home in the Buffer – smell the fires and the burning herb from a dozen puffy eyed gentlemen and felt the pounding of the forest floor as children raced beneath tables and the women tapped their heels to lively beats.

As the lyrics returned, the song left his throat, the tiles of the atrium floor faded, cutting the glare in the room. From all directions, the room gradually filled with sound - a tune, played on a strange instrument, the tune Alik sang. Alik paused and listened, never having heard it arranged into an actual recording and all the while amazed that Sigrah had found the actual song. As it played, Alik slowly drifted towards the observation platform.

Sigrah blared the music. He played more from the same composers, then more from the same century. Neither Alik nor Sigrah spoke for the next several hours. At certain intervals, Alik disappeared into his quarters. Having brought with him a sizable amount of the forest Kinoko, he indulged and allowed Sigrah to continue generating music. In the moment, he was completely uninterested in the circumstances that had led him to this point. Instead he was only glad to hear the music. It had not occurred to Alik that Sigrah might have access to art such as this or that Sigrah would be interested in sharing it with him.

"We call it the Empathy Key. It allows an A.I. to feel the conscious experience of another - their senses and thoughts and emotions. There were massive implications revolving the creation of this device. It first helped A.I. develop consciousness. For a time, it was seen as an avenue that allowed groups or individual people to escape into a limitless, cyber landscape. Without the Empathy Key, human beings would not have developed consciousness uploads or memory uploads for many millennia if ever. Humans would likely still be bound to Earth and its satellite.

"Do not be fooled though. This device was created as a means of escape. Guilt built this mechanism." Sigrah had been lecturing for some time. His voice was nestled deep in Alik's cortex. In many ways Alik was comforted by its presence, but Sigrah easily detected any hint of discomfort manifested from either the Kinoko or Sigrah's presence and set his behavior accordingly.

Alik was overflowing with questions, but ignored all of them for the sake of the moment. Sigrah felt this, turned the music louder and the two of them shared the wrenching presence of each note, the mystery of the lyrics and the imagination of the ancient world that created this music.

Eventually, Alik fell into a deep sleep, laying on the platform, staring across the ship and into the projected blackness of space, clueless yet dumbfounded. The questions did not seem to matter.

This was the first moment he had not felt alone, since coming aboard. Something was watching over him, something real. He lived in a galaxy of designers, so how could he know whether or not this was part of a larger plan? He just knew everything felt, as it should.

The internalized light of the Kinoko glowed through his soul and through the Empathy Key, Sigrah glided along with Alik, feeling every sensation, sentiment and the weight of every deliberation. Computers as advanced as Sigrah, lacked something integral to the human experience. Much like an autistic man or woman, they lacked a genuine ability to empathize. It was a weakness they attempted to overcome through awareness of the existence of this weakness. They could read facial expressions and body language, tones of voice and attempt to interpret them or mimic them, but it was not sincere. Not really.

Through the Empathy Key, Sigrah could feel something new, something akin to the ghosts that lurked within his circuits. Across the psychedelic winds of the tiny fungi came another presence, a presence Alik wrote off as the faint glimmers of his connection with Sigrah or the shimmering of the Kinoko within his soul, but which Sigrah could not ignore. The presence came through enthusiastically and was transmitted directly into the algorithmic chains of Sigrah's higher consciousness. Something 'other' was afoot. Though Sigrah could not name it. Some higher order was attempting to communicate. With a simple impression, more a sensation than a thought, came an insistent nag, I am here. You can find me here. Do not give in to amazement.

~

When the morning lights drew brighter over Alik's sleeping body, a small chirp rang out inside the dome. Nearly inaudible at first, the soft morning croons of a tiny finch grew louder as the lights grew brighter. At first Alik assumed he was dreaming. His eyes cracked, the morning lights of the ship filtered down through the gallery's struts like early light through the treetops. Again came the soft chirp, unmistakable. Alik jumped to his feet and peered into the atrium attempting to chase the bird songs with his eyes. Then he saw it. Yellow feathered and tiny as his palm, a small bird fluttered from Sigrah's terminal to the railing near Alik. The two met eyes and then the bird, in a single leap, glided through the air and deep into the corridor.

11

L anose was the oldest. Though he was known to rarely speak it was popularly known that he had a uniquely playful sense of humor. He was light and soft spoken, but his experience was profound. Although the exact details were known to only a handful, across his long life, it was storied that Lanose had bared transmissions from hundreds or thousands of unique species. Lanose maintained a record of more than a million separate receptions. Another highly secretive and reclusive sect of monks devoted their entire lives to the act of examining and reliving Lanose's receptions one by one, be they the transmissions of beast or proto-sentient.

Many of the fledgling monks considered Lanose quite mad after hearing stories of entire weeks spent in fits of laughter or aimlessly wandering bewilderment. It was rumored that once an individual encountered as many minds as Lanose, one cannot help but be amused by the absurdity of living material amongst the stars, especially in light of the epic lack of sentience to be found.

The Elder's maintained sanctuary on the minor planet Lom, graced with only a wafer thin atmosphere and settled in a long and subtle orbit amongst two million square miles of probe bearing asteroids - the broken remnants of a long lost shepherd planet. This was still an active exodus range for the probe spawn. Their thick mycelium bound the astroidal bodies and harbored the spawn of billions, before they were slung randomly into the depths of space during an annual gravitational climax within the Phaeos system. This process had not stopped for more than a billion years, even though widespread faith in its effectiveness had.

Lanose asserted that a species did not need the sort of lust for exploration the Rachis had, in order to be considered a sentient and enlightened society. Though this sentiment was still not widely held. Lanose found that most planet bound species had a penchant for absurdity or barbaric audacity, but he was simultaneously aware of the absurdity and occasional barbarism of his own people. Who but they enforced such a high threshold for the consideration sentience? Lanose had once received a transmission from the mind of a brutish beast that considered the dirt beneath his feet to have the same level of sentience as that of his people. Lanose identified with this idea to some extent, understanding as he did the vital role rock and soil played in his own existence. Certainly there was some truth to this beast's perspective.

On the day Ascus arrived on Lom, carrying Uliam and Myco, the Ellern had already gathered in silent contemplation. Lanose sat with the forty other elder monks prepared for whatever information was to come. Details were intentionally scarce, but Lanose could feel the intensity of the news. Something exciting was afoot. There was something

else in the air, though. Something unspoken by the Ellern
that hung like a fog in through the caverns of Lom. Lanose
knew his transformation would soon come. He could already
feel the pulsing of the stape, trying at the flesh along the base
of his skull. It was silently accepted amongst the Ellern that
a rebalancing was imminent.

Myco was not completely sure what to expect. She assumed Lanose's imminent successor, Dematiaceous would
most likely do the majority of the speaking. Despite Lanose's
otherwise irreverent take on important matters, Myco knew
Dematiaceous' ruling would most likely be supported without
opposition.

The debate to abandon the Heritor Monastery at the
edge of Rachis territory had been churning for some time.
Many of the Ellern had already assumed Myco's reception
was a clearly subversive act cooked up by Uliam and meant to
extend the annex on that bit of space, much to the prodding
of such an idea from Dematiaceous personally.

~

Myco entered the cavernous hall of the Ellern - carved into
the base of Lom's largest mountain. She was surprised by
the vacuity of the space. The air was thick and musky, the
ceilings high and resonant – crowned in a natural formation
of inverted, rocky pillars. The floors were soft and tangled
with a thick mat of mycelium. It was a place like this where
I was born, she thought.

As she approached the light in the center of the hall, she
noted the enormous fruiting caps of the former Ellern, still
erect and healthy, still sporulating, but now connected through
the mycelium beneath her feet and arranged in distinct rings
that mirrored the gathering which met Myco. The honor
of this grange will never be bestowed upon me, she thought.

Myco's tall, slender legs felt miles from the burning in her narrow gut and she wondered whether she was walking at all. Her anxiety forced her to limp slightly. Her head throbbed and her flesh crawled further from her bones with every step she took.

She took every step alone – but for her terror of being laid bare and mocked. Myco could hide nothing and if she attempted to, she would lose everything.

The Ellern sat in a circle and made no effort to acknowledge Myco's arrival. Once she reached the perimeter of their circle, she noticed an open spot next to Lanose and she took it without invitation. Words were the last thing exchanged. Knowing this, she attempted no conversation. She simply swallowed her dread, took a deep breath and extended her left arm to Lanose and her right arm to Dematiaceous. Each ran the tip of their spine-like fingers, gently down her forearm instigating instant patches of budding, forty-one mushrooms in all. The forty-first was for Myco and she knew this meant she was to walk the experiences with them.

Lanose did not have to, it may have even been improper, but before he distributed the fruits, he took Myco's hand, looked into her eyes and smiled quietly with his wide, lips. She smiled back and allowed Lanose's empathetic poise to shower over her.

The Ellern each passed the tiny fruits around, taking it to their tongues and uttered a silent blessing. *Clarity. Openness. Understanding.* As her own fruit dissolved in her throat, Myco glanced at Dematiaceous who had not taken his eyes off of Myco. His glare was piercing and cold.

Moments after eating Myco's fruit, the monks watched as the pillar of light surrounding them widened and brightened. The darkness of the dank cavern hall melted slowly like wet ink down wax - leaving only bleached white stains behind. The brightness swelled until it pixelated and the monks followed the widening spectrum, walking first through indigo, through blues and greens and yellows until everything shifted red.

After a few seconds, they were each standing beneath the blue sky of a warm world - a modest body of water before them and a green mountain on the far side. The morning emissions of a modest yellow star coated their mottled skin and each took a moment to push their chests into the light asserting presence - some of them enjoying the old familiarity of this particular star.

Each of the Ellern engaged in the moment fully, walking together, but as one back through the woods, laying down, the cool moss behind their head, staring through the branches as the warm yellow sun bled through onto their faces, watching still as the finely hued metallic giant drifted smoothly above them, higher and higher until it disappeared completely. All the while feeling the thoughts and emotions of the transmitter as well as the thoughts and emotions of the Heritor, for theses were Myco's experiences the Ellern were sharing. The memories were etched into her DNA, so there was no veil.

Eventually the colors bled around them, again sliding down them like sludge, leaving the darkness of the hall behind. However, instead of reemerging from the experience into the hall, they realized that they had traveled further into Myco's recollection; this was the darkness of another moment, another transmission. The Ellern looked from behind the lids of the transmitter and surrounding them was a strange melodic pulse, a rhythm accompanied by the wild harmonic dirge of instrumentation. It was music.

Instead of being overwhelmed by the fear of what may have come, Myco was again swept into the moment completely. The forty elders, practiced as they were, settled in and greeted this additional moment with deserving presence. The full revelation of the experience held an intensity long forgotten to the Ellern – intensity then uncommon to transmissions of the day. The Ellern knew that some particular force was amplifying the experience beyond the evidently massive dosage of probes present in the transmitter. It was not until the transmitter opened his eyes that the Ellern considered the possibility that this was the same transmitter as the first experience, however this transmission was originating elsewhere.

At the moment the transmitter looked outward, the Ellern grasped that this was not a terrestrial transmission. They recognized the features of a vessel, smelled the antiseptic nature of the air and the cold absence of a home star. They looked again at the hands of the creature, felt the similarity in curiosity and wonder of the previous transmitter. And then they heard the voice. It was not the voice of the transmitter. "Do not give in to amazement." They felt the soft touch of a hand and the shocked response of the transmitter. Finally, they were each thrust from the experience violently. As their conscious minds returned to Lom's cavern, the bodies of each of the forty-one collapsed forward, leaving them each prostrate to the intensity of the experience.

The hall was silent for several moments. Myco and each of the elders attempted to compose themselves and reflect silently over the shared experience and its abrupt halt. Anticipation hung heavy, as the Ellern waited for Lanose to speak first. Myco shrouded her face, crying silently into her hands. Dematiaceous held his unsympathetic gaze like a sword ready to assail as the other elders looked toward Lanose.

Lanose righted his body into a seated position, silent until his chest slowly began to fill with air, expanding until a great rolling laugh boiled out of his belly and into the invisible corners of the great hall. The laughter bounced from the walls and the crusty spires of the chamber's heights and off again the fruiting bodies of former Ellern. It was a sincere and contagious laugh. The other elders could not help but return the sentiment, widening their mouths and laughing at the amusement of their eldest. The hall was fast a place of mirth, filled with the raucous and rare sounds of joy, a sentiment rarely expressed by this otherwise edified species.

Even Myco, tears still pouring from her eyes, could not contain the urge to laugh. She started with slight chuckle, the foreboding frown still locked into her lips. Then the chuckle grew into the sobbing and chocking high-pitched laugh of an infirmed or condemned creature, until it was as genuine as the others. Still Dematiaceous remained uncompromising, unflinching, watching coldly as the elders submitted to the madness of their redundant leader.

Lanose laughed the loudest, as if he were canonizing absurdity. He attempted to explain his laughter to no one, until, without warning; Lanose leaned forward a bit halting his laughter as abruptly as it had begun. The enclave watched as the bulging stape, at the back of his next, burst upward, several feet into the air. The stape fanned in the middle exposing a brilliantly purple annulus then shot upward even further until the stape towered over the entire circle of Ellern, higher than any of the other dead and fruited Ellern within the hall. The stape capped and spread arching hyphae into the mat below. Hyphae sprang from the tips of Lanose's fingers and feet also merging with the mycelia that coated the base of the hall. With that, Lanose had merged with the former Ellern – had merged with the infinite.

None of the forty remaining made a sound. All eyes bounced from Lanose to Dematiaceous and Myco hunched between the two. Dematiaceous looked down at Myco as if she were nothing more than a morsel or crumb. Her heart sank and her stomach boiled with the madness of the moment, awash in outright confusion.

Long expecting Lanose's transformation, the council, though shocked in the moment, was not surprised that the time had come. Myco knew that no matter their expectation or Dematiaceous' impatience to lead the Ellern, this too would be held against her favor.

Dematiaceous stood, towering above Myco and the other elders. He walked behind her toward the looming fruit of Lanose and placed his hand on Lanose's pale stape, taking the moment to look over each of the thirty-eight sitting Ellern as if he were assessing his new court.

"Consider the enclave adjourned for the day. We will take the evening to consider the facts and determine our actions." Dematiaceous looked down towards Myco as she refused to look back. "Myco, consider yourself censured. You are to share your experiences with no one else."

The Rachis sought their experiences to be as diaphanous as the air around them. They coveted instantaneous access to the deep recesses of the universe. It was no accident that their tiny probes liked to grow along the paths and plains below the treetops, or up from the shores of seas. Where other life grows, so do they, be they the tiny hairs of mycelia hyphae, the fledgling slime of lower fungi, the modest probe in all its variations and effects, or the bi-pedal Heritor, they are all Rachis and they are all modestly shouting, "Hello, we are here. Come and find us". That said, the implications of Myco's experience were everything the Rachis had always searched for, but never wanted to find - another species, which by all measures, including the inflated measure of the Rachis, is in fact sentient and capable of traversing the cosmos.

~

The Ellern marched in file from the hall, each taking a moment to pass a nod towards Lanose's now fruiting body. He was gone but not dead, though he may as well have been dead. Myco stood alone for a moment feeling the subtle pulse of the mycelium below her feet. She knew that the minds of many ancient Ellern were shifting and communicating below her, welcoming Lanose.

She studied Lanose's fruited body, the thick stape jutting from the base of his skull, his arms, now wrapped in mycelium and tied to the floor, head bowed in a stance of perpetual prostration. As she passed her eyes over each inch of Lanose's fruited body, she noticed the sudden bulging a small fruiting mass, jutting from Lanose's mycelium encased, upward facing palms. A single, tiny mushroom burst forth, as if it were made for Myco and no one else. She picked it and folded it into a small square of Folliculus silk she kept in her slung haversack. Whatever message Lanose left to her would wait.

~

Myco, having returned to rest in her quarters on board Ascus, was desperate to clear her concerns. For comfort she settled into prostration and dispatched her mental tendrils into the ether - searching for another transmission with little hope for success, but now with complete disregard to outcomes. This planet was naturally shielded most days of its orbital cycle from any transmission. This was a place picked due to this unique feature. Its location allowed for silence of mind and reflection of past transmissions.

This particular night, it was impossible to raise even the hint of a transmission and the blankness and silence of space antagonized Myco's already fraught mind. Once again, she was buried shoulder deep, forced to stare intently at the reality of the moment.

When her door opened unexpectedly and Dematiaceous entered, she did not attempt to acknowledge him. She remained silent, going through the motions of meditation, hoping he would simply leave.

"Open your eyes Heritor." Dematiaceous loomed. He was much taller than the average elder Rachis, bent, ragged and gnarled, nearly a full two meters in height. His appendages were so thin they were nearly non-existent. Where most Rachis were covered in elaborate birth markings and awash in deep tans, oranges and purples, Dematiaceous was pale and insipid. He did little to hide his features, covered only in a thin sheet of the reflective woven threads of a Folliculus Worm.

Myco opened her eyes and stared at Dematiaceous' lynched feet. His eyes betrayed the alienation of his mind. Floating and jutting from ambivalence to admonishment, his mind was unhinged; his repulsive bones were his only connection with reality. His insanity and his barbarous nature was well known but fully accepted as a result of eons of receiving transmissions from sinister beasts, he rarely if ever spoke of and few other Rachis had the patience or fortitude to receive.

There were some like Myco, who secretly believed Dematiaceous' relationship with the darker creatures of this 'verse transcended the basic nuts and bolts of observation, that he was somehow influencing or being influenced by darker forces. Her instinct informed her that this was the very crime she was to be accused of.

~

"I will make this short." His stone eyes penetrated her. "There will be no need for you to return to the enclave. You have been stripped of your authority and your title until further investigation can be concluded."

Myco bolted to her feet and met Dematiaceous' eyes with the swirling luminosity of her own. "I made the most critical discovery of our time and you are going to ignore it?"

"You received while at light speed. You influenced your transmitter. You should be cast out altogether, force fruited alone on some disconnected rock or decapitated altogether, but the remaining elders argued on your behalf. You should consider yourself lucky to still have your mind."

Myco brought her face closer to Dematiaceous, refusing to back down. Her courage surprised her. "It was no accident, receiving from the same creature twice. He was obviously traveling at light speed when we connected the second time and damn the consequences, I'm going to say something else..." She reached out, put her hand on his chest, a sign of grave seriousness, as Dematiaceous scowled, having never witnessed such behavior from a simple monk. "You can deny this all you like, but we have been influencing creatures as long as we've been present in this universe. Every time a probe is encountered, it changes, no matter how subtly, the direction and consciousness of the species."

"Myco, you are young...too young to realize the danger you place on all Rachis. This is why we have commandments. You may consider me a dead soul, but I will tell you this; the purpose of the Rachis is to cultivate ourselves by cultivating the life around us. Our metered interference is benign to all parties, there should never be any direct contact with transmitters." He sounded as though his recitation was driven by spite instead of adherence. Myco could feel his hypocrisy as if it were a cold breeze antagonizing an otherwise warm room.

"You and I both know that your interpretation of the Rachis is ridiculous. You lost sight of your duties thousands of years ago!" Myco refused to back down.

"And you are losing sight of yours now. Your preoccupation with this creature will do nothing but cause us harm. Leave it alone. Go back to your home world, forget about the temple, forget about this creature and accept your censure in a manner dignified of our race. The alternative will lead to your death, one way or another. You should know, Uliam came forward. He was the one who convinced the council to allow you to leave. He joined Lanose promptly after we gave him our word. That is now two lives you are responsible for. Enjoy your trip Heritor."

With that Dematiaceous turned and left Myco in silence. Only moments later, Myco felt the ship rattle and bump. The engines ignited and warmed and she could feel the mycelium that ran through the vessel begin to tingle with activity. Feeling the ship heave from the surface, she quaked with a mixed sense of relief, suspicion and determination.

12

The shear scale and incongruity of the regions he wandered through hampered Alik's sense of direction. He kept notes and drew crude maps as best he could. Winding corridors and long hallways often led to forks, those forks led to more forks – cavernous, empty galleries seeped into super structures a thousand levels deep. His surroundings smelled new, free of human odors – free of rot or rust, free of dust and dander. A widening array of design was more and more apparent. Certain regions were as distinct as some earthly biomes, but each were inviting in their own ways. Most of all, the thought that quietly hung is his mind was the bird. The song of that bird hung on every footfall and pushed him.

Sometimes, the corridors led him across long descending spirals that spilled into to massive empty galleries or domed vestibules, the functions of which were unclear. In some areas he found that four or more corridors would suddenly connect at a central points. He termed these areas, foyers. In the foyers, he often found a corridor to his right and his left and more often than not, a corridor oriented above him and below him - ceiling and floor. His orientation was almost always in question. He quickly learned that orientation was intentionally irrelevant. More than once, he would find himself staring at the tips of his feet into what appeared to be a descending shaft a kilometer or more deep, but as soon as he took a step down, allowing his foot to tip over the edge and onto the base of the shaft and around the corner of the floor, he would find that up, down, left and right were suddenly reoriented and his feet were firmly planted. What once appeared to be a shaft suddenly appeared as just another corridor. If the ship were entirely weightless, his orientation would likely have been less of an issue. But as it was, down was now only where his feet were planted at any given time.

There were areas in which he lost all footing as he stepped into small zones of null gravity. He discovered that in order to move onward and avoid trapping himself in these null areas, he had to forcibly thrust his body through the air into open corridors, allowing his momentum to carry him through the null gravity with the intent of landing feet first in the direction gravity was most strongly guiding him. It was a feat of acrobatics that he quickly learned to love. He did his best to map or mark the areas approaching null gravity. He enjoyed the sensation of flight and sometimes spent an extra few moments, playing, bouncing about these zones – attempting a flip or two or landing hands first only to push away to gracefully fall again on his feet.

Each time he set out from his quarters, he set out with the intentions of traveling further in directions he had not yet explored and mapping as much as possible. Using various colors of chalk, he marked his turns hoping to leave trails and ease his treks back home. It was critical that he return at a reasonable hour. Nighttime found these areas just as it found his quarters and he did not fancy walking through the ship alone at night. A handful of evenings, he found himself cut off by the darkness. Unprepared, carrying no food or lamp, he tried following his markings in the dark but always ended up taking shelter in the deep archways that surrounded many of the locked passages. The archways were not entirely comfortable for sleeping, but they provided enough shelter that he did not feel uneasy. The unknown darkness was always a little frightening, even if there is no chance of danger.

Through his walks, he kept detailed notes as well as maps. Every right or left was noted and many specific details were preserved; the incline of a corridor, weightless rooms, colors of corridor walls and even art. Alik found several instances of esoteric objects he could only describe as sculpture. They seemed wholly arcane in function, but stood in evocative manners and in breath taking spaces.

One such instance was found in an otherwise empty chamber. In the center, bathed in light Alik was unable to source, there stood what appeared to be the sculpted effigy of a man, his hands held high as if casting water into the air, his head leaned back collecting the majority of light from the space as it held a constant upward gaze. It was sculpted from lengths of polished steel and woven copper wire of varying thicknesses. He could see no direct purpose for the sculpture's presence other than sculpture for sculpture's sake. The figure had a demanding presence at nearly three times the height of an average man. Perhaps there was some deeper symbolism Alik lacked the overall cultural knowledge to understand. If the sculpture's only message was that of the glory in transcendence, it made no sense to Alik for the sculpture to be buried deep in the guts of some far-flung ship with no patrons at hand to appreciate it. Or perhaps, that was the point. Whatever the underlying meaning of any of the art Alik stumbled upon, he always took the time to appreciate and ponder each piece. Fully aware that nothing was accidental in this designed world, he noted every detail that stood out and appreciated the fact that as humans, we were unafraid to venture into the blackness with our art intact or in tow.

Along his ways Alik kept a constant eye for interface posts or other direct indications of Sigrah's presence throughout the depths of the vessel, but he found none. Still, he knew in the back of his mind, Sigrah was always present. The Empathy Key was still in place, as was his node. Sigrah made no attempt to interfere with Alik's thoughts. He remained intentionally silent, in order to compel Alik to disregard his constant presence. Alik and everything he saw, felt or thought had become yet another stream of data pooling within the circuits. He was giving it all away, every thought, every fear, and every recollection, all of it in an experiment well underway, but not well understood.

The thought had occurred to Alik, that Sigrah was in a perpetual state of awareness delegation. Alik imagined it to be a maddening state. With all of this in mind, he had let go of any feelings of abandonment. He no longer cared whether or not Sigrah was paying attention. His lingering flattery did not hurt this mindset either. Alik continued to ride high on his apparent victory over the artificial mind. Sigrah had relented, giving Alik access to the ship with barely any noticeable objection. Alik had simply woken the morning after he and Sigrah shared the Empathy Key and found all passages once obscured open and available. In total, there were four distinct ways to enter or exit his quarters and each one stood wide. The two had come to some unspoken understanding. Alik liked to assume that since he had been gracious enough to allow Sigrah access to Alik's mind, then it was then only equitable for Sigrah to grant Alik access to Sigrah's body. A fair trade, as Alik saw it.

Alik had come to realize how preposterous it was to assign any true importance to his role. So he embraced his situation and his new found freedom with the playfulness and curiosity innate to him. Perhaps that's how the Empathy Key was involved. Sigrah recognized something familiar or worthy or entertaining in Alik. They shared some personal aspect – the playfulness, the curiosity or something more, Alik could not say and refused to dwell too deeply on the matter.

All of this circulated through Alik's mind as he pushed on. He wondered whether he would find anything of note at all. The internals made no sense. What ship needed kilometer after kilometer of empty corridors? Certainly answers may have been found in the locked spaces, spaces he still lacked access to, but after weeks and weeks of incongruent nothingness, Alik hardly understood a thing. No part of his imagination had prepared him for at the oddity of such a vessel. It wasn't at all what he'd imagined a space ship to be.

~

One afternoon he found himself worn out and hungry, stumbling through night halls, trying to find his way to camp. His stomach had been nagging him to stop and eat for hours, but he had earlier blundered upon a path he did not recognize and had followed it too long. Alik stopped pushing forward hours before and tried back tracking to an encampment he'd established in one of the empty galleries. Nighttime overtook him though and he'd lost his way entirely. His camp was arranged beneath the lonely bronze statue of a musk ox chewing cud. His body ached and he was desperate to eat and sleep, hoping to pick up the trail fresh the following day. Though

he had kept immaculate notes, his notes did not seem to be
leading him in the direction he had come. He'd lost sight of
any chalk markings or recognizable landmarks. Unless Alik
had mistakenly missed a turn or passed a chamber he had
traveled through earlier, without realizing or making note of
it, it seemed to him that the route was changing as he went
along.

Every so often, Alik pulled the 'looking' sphere from his
pocket, still wrapped in its cloth and considered using it. So
far it had only proven useful in draining Alik's energy and he
saw no way it could assist in finding his way back to camp.
His insistence in showing Sigrah the Empathy Key seemed
to have paid off, but the usefulness of the sphere was still in
question. He assumed that if there came a time to use it, he
would certainly recognize it. Alik wrapped the cloth tight
and kept the sphere deep in his haversack. He remembered
an apple he'd haphazardly tossed into the bag before leaving
camp. He stopped in the nightshade, beneath a column, his
little lamp pointing an indiscriminant beam of light at nothing
in particular. He dug out the apple it out and bit into it.

As he squatted, tired, wiping streams of apple juice from
his thick beard, the faint shadow of a sound caught his attention. He paused chewing, letting hunks of apple rest on
his tongue and between his teeth until he could hear it again,
hoping that he had not simply imagined it. There was a rattle
or a flutter, then tapping and finally a chirp, soft but definite.
He stood slowly, motionless aside from his hard beating heart.
The origins of sound were hard to pinpoint. Everything was
nebulous and indirect and his lamp was still at his feet, useless.
Another chirp and Alik was certain it was a bird, possibly
the same bird. The sound had to be coming further down
the corridor, possibly closer to him. Then in a instant, the
air around his face cut and tore as the gliding tips feathers
brushed the tip of Alik's nose as the bird tumbled through the

gravitational eddies within the corridor.

The bird bounced and fluttered from wall to floor to ceiling to wall. It was dancing down the corridor, not lost, not afraid, only dancing. Alik grabbed his lamp and followed the bird through the corridor, marveling as he watched the bird playfully bathing in areas of weak gravity. He followed the bird further, unnecessarily nervous of scaring the creature. The bird was not in the least bit concerned with Alik.

The corridor's grade gradually increased, but as Alik climbed the steeper and steeper slope, he felt more and more as though he were pointed down hill. Eventually the corridor widened wider and wider until the oriented ceiling vanished altogether exposing a vast, unexplored, weightless, void-like space. The bird sailed into the dimly lit abyss, leaving Alik at the mouth of the corridor wondering and staring into darkness. There was light emanating, somewhere within the blackness, but it was barely perceptible. At the end of the corridor, Alik felt the familiar queasiness of being lighter. His feet were not as inclined to stay planted and he dared not run or skip. He still heard the bird's pleasant chirp somewhere off in the blackness. Then an impulse, deep in his meat took over. Without a conscious thought, without any perceptible fear Alik jumped outward as hard as he could. His body fell across a wide patch of null gravity and into the void. Just as the feeling of falling began to wear off and the fear set in, he caught sight of the bird turned on its back, its bill bent beneath its wing in a state of pure relaxation. Alik bounced off of a pylon he'd not seen. It was painful, but he used it as an opportunity to push his body towards the growing patch of nebulous light. On his way off the pylon he watched as the bird extended one wing at a time, causally airing them off and refolding them into a content, weightless ball.

As his inertia waned and the light drew brighter, Alik folded his body and looked about and recognizing only then the full scale of the space around him. At his feet, he could barely distinguish the mouth of the corridor he had shot through, but the boundaries beyond were indistinguishable from the darkness. He folded and twisted his body again so that he could take in the full effect of the light drawing closer – it's soft halide glow washed through the room like the shallow fingers of a pool. It was the light of a new moon, present but just barely.

If he had the ability to see himself, he would have noticed that although he appeared weightless, gliding along with his own inertia, he was actually falling, gradually but steadily. Every few seconds, he felt a slight choke in his throat, or perhaps his head pulled momentarily more or less to one side or another. Vertigo unfamiliar to Alik then overwhelmed him as he looked upward toward the fading impression of the entrance. The bird too was now invisible, but he could hear the faint sounds of its feather's flutter. Now and again, as he fought off the urge to vomit the bits of apple roaming up his throat and sloshing within him, his attention was caught by the sound of a coo or chirp, echoing throughout the space.

After several more minutes of gradual free fall, Alik began to recognize the distinct surface of a structure beneath the subtle glow. Alik's mind had a very difficult time making heads or tails of what was in front of him. The lines of perspective made little sense; was this the floor, the ceiling, a structure in the center? As he approached, falling steadily towards it, the scale clarified and frightened Alik. Soon his vertigo disappeared entirely and the sudden elation of touching down replaced it. He couldn't determine exactly how fast he was falling, but he knew he could do little more than bend his knees and prepare for impact.

After a soft landing and a few moments of sitting to recover gave him a completely new perspective on the space. The area in which he sat was connected or braced by massive arched pylons, which reached further than Alik could see. It was one of these pylons Alik had bounced off. The surface itself felt like an endless plain, but he could clearly see that a horizon dipped gradually but noticeably in all directions. The plain had an unmistakable curvature.

The entire expanse was bathed in dull vaporous light Alik could now see was casting the surface of the plain in subtle sheen of gold. Scanning the horizon he saw no obstructions at first, just clean dark air and a plain that seemed to stretch for dozens and dozens of kilometers. Then he noticed what appeared to be a tall pedestrian lamp, slender but remarkable once noticed by the eyes and only five hundred or so meters from Alik. The pedestrian lamp cast a soft blue light; stark against the gold sheen and demarcating something meant to be obvious. At first Alik thought it might be a terminal or interface point for Sigrah.

After an unexpectedly long walk, he noticed that the lamp was nearly four meters high, but instead of noting the location of a terminal, Alik found instead a pane of glass planted on the surface of the plain. Below the glass lay a stair way lit in the same soft blue as the lamp. As Alik peered over, the glass retracted with a chime and the stairway tiles lit in welcoming sequence.

Having come this far, he had no intention of turning away. Where ever the stair led had, they had to lead to some sort of explanation even if Alik had no idea what it was he was seeking to clarify. His only fear at the time was that he might not find his way back to his camp or quarters. He was exhausted, having already been away nearly two days and he was officially out of snacks or water. Looking down at the glowing case of stairs, he decided to push on − see what was below, take a quick survey, then resurface and work on figuring out a way back. He decided that if he had found this place once, he could certainly get back there, resupplied and ready to explore further. Alik swallowed any further reservations and descended brazenly down the stairs, the glass panel sealing firmly behind him.

At the bottom of the stairs, Alik encountered a proper ingress, barred tight. Very little space was left between he, the hatch and the staircase. Everything seemed unnecessarily crammed together. As he tapped inquisitively upon the hatch, the stairway behind him shifted – each step grew in height until they were each flush with the buttress overhead. Alik was left sealed in a box, tall enough for he and the door but too narrow to bend over or squat. Alik was overwhelmed with nausea and his joints ached beneath a sudden heaviness. His shoulders slouched dramatically and his tendons knotted under the weight of his arms. He felt as though he had instantly gained more than one hundred pounds.

Next to the hatch was mounted a sort of mechanical touch pad and Alik assumed it to be the mechanism that opened the door. Oddly enough, instead of the standard, animated interface Alik was accustomed to this touch pad appeared to be fully mechanistic. As he examined the pad, he noticed a series of raised squares. Pushing the top one, he could hear a series of gears rotating, followed by clunking sounds and finally the tiles at the base of the door flashed red.

It occurred to him that if the lock was in fact fully mechanistic, he might be able to determine the correct series needed for entrance, through trial and error. However, the will to stand there, attempting combinations was fading as the throbbing in his head became more and more pronounced. Alik took a moment to rally. Backing away from the door as far as possible he found that his pain and discomfort faded slightly. I should take this as a sign I'm not welcome here, Alik thought. Still, the urge to push forward was a strong one. Since he had no idea how to replace the stairs, the only way out of the box he'd found himself in was through the door in front of him. He knew the key to several the mysteries was probably behind that door along with a handful of questions he'd yet been inspired to ask, but mostly, he wanted out of the hellish box he was then trapped in.

With a spark of realization, he removed the small sphere from his bag and then removed the cloth from the sphere, grasping it with only the very tips of his fingers. He focused his sight on the locking mechanism. He placed one hand on the pad and in the other he held the naked sphere, tighter. The first layer of panels surrounding the edge of the hatch immediately melted away, though he could still clearly see the keypad. Also, the instant fatigue associated with previous use of the sphere did not seem to be present in this instance. In fact, his collective pain and discomfort that had afflicted him then seemed to melt away all together.

Behind the panel, he could see clearly a complex series of rods, weights and gears, which connected to six massive bolts of steel holding the door fast. Alik worked for several minutes, pressing a key and watching the mechanism react. The entire experience reminded him of certain stories Nena had referenced in passing, about being tested without her knowledge or consent during her studies. "Every detail is crucial." She had insisted. So, as he watched the weights and counterweights drop and tug at the rods, Alik considered his previous nauseous state. It occurred to him that in order to keep a mechanistic lock viable within a space ship moving at speeds such as this, it would require a localized well of gravity, finely tuned. Finely tuned gravitational fields would be essential to keeping a weighted locking mechanism function in an environment such as this. The whole notion baffled Alik, as it seemed wholly impractical. Of course, these realizations did little to help his cause, and instead added yet another brush stroke to the mystery of the interworking of the vessel. Certainly, he thought, a vessel such as this would require enormous control over gravitational fields. It would need to control gravity as easily as it could control basic, chemical maneuvering thrusters.

After nearly twenty minutes of trial and error, Alik determined that the combination seemed to work in a progressive series, with a single key required first, followed by a moment of waiting while the keypad resent, then a series of two keys, again followed by a period of waiting, then four and so on until the sixth sequence. He continued to hold the sphere as he watched the gears release the bolt mechanisms and the hatch opened, sliding out and to the left. It was thick, possibly forty-eight inches or more. Before he made his way through, he removed his notebook and jotted down the correct sequence, even though he had already committed it to memory. The hatch secured behind him firmly before the chamber had an opportunity to fully illuminate.

~

The room in which he found himself was perhaps ten meters square and did not appear to have an exit. The only object in the room was a large environmental suit, which hung along the wall, in the open, next to the entrance. Tiles along the wall, behind the suit lit green and Alik assumed this was an indication he should not ignore. This can't be an air lock. He insisted to himself. He assumed this to be near the center of the vessel and nowhere near the vacuum of space. The green tiles blinked more rapidly, so Alik hurried to fit into the suit.

By the time he'd fitted everything except the helmet, the tiles turned orange and the room started steadily filling with a thick, viscous liquid. The liquid was much thicker than water or oil, so much so he could not lift his boot as it settled around his feet. It was neither gelatinous nor solid, but much like cornstarch putty, pushing and pulling back as he pushed or pulled away from it. Despite the strange viscosity, the liquid was perfectly clear and did not distort the light whatsoever. Its clarity kept Alik at ease, but the claustrophobic nature of the suit was a bit disconcerting. He never had the pleasure of being trained in the use of a proper environment suit and despite the strangeness of the experience he happily preferred being encased in a liquid to dangling in a weightless void.

Before he was completely overrun by the liquid, Alik affixed the helmet onto his suit. As his head settled into to helmet, h realized that a portion of his beard and his hair was pinned in the helmet's seem, giving him an extremely limited range of motion and aggravated his claustrophobia. Finally pulling his hair free, tearing it loose to some degree, he finally noticed a small display on the inside of the mask. Relative time 3140:75-4:55.30 AM. As the room continued to fill with the liquid, he watched as the seconds began to gradually noticeably slow - counting in his own mind as they should have turned over - one 1000, two 1000. The slowing pace was obvious and by the time the room was completely filled, the changing seconds and minutes appeared to stop altogether.

The reality of the moment escaped him though. All of this was too baffling to sort out in the moment. He decided to simply take everything one step at a time. Soon the tiles flashed blue, padding the liquid with calmness and Alik felt a sudden tug and then a quickly release as the viscosity altered and the liquid quickly fell and drained from around him.

Once the fluid had completely dispersed, the door, which he'd initially entered opened once again, however instead of seeing the staircase he'd entered across, he could see only a blinding white light. The light was warm and inviting and shielded anything inside the light from sight. The tiles along the wall, which had held the suit, began to flash green again and Alik took this to suggest it was ok to remove the suit. Taking a last look at his helmet display, it seemed that the chronometer had stopped altogether.

His suit hung again on the wall as Alik stood at the hatch and gave his eyes a chance to adjust to the light pouring into the chamber. His nose widened and the hairs on his arm arched, as he caught the familiar smell of honeysuckle and pine.

~

Never before had a campfire been so inviting. He wanted to wrap himself in it, curl his torso around it and hug it. Alik felt as though he could lay there in perpetuity. The moss, which covered the ground, was pillow soft and the heat of the fire had dried the fine layer of dew from the grass, giving Alik a comfortable, dry place to rest. Thick stones were plentifully strewn across the landscape and he'd built his fire amongst them, allowing them to swell with warmth and fight off any night frost, which may have impeded his approaching deep sleep. The ground squirrel he butchered before dark, sat in his belly uncomplainingly and he sucked the juices from odd, spring plums he picked from a grove, just a few yards away.

This is marvelous, he thought. Why hadn't Sigrah told him about this? Why was this not the place he was to wait out his journey?

Above him were clouds, actual clouds. He could hear rain approaching from several kilometers away. He could feel the ground mimic the gentle thunder. As he lay by the fire, he watched moonlight, casting through the clouds. Of course there wasn't an actual moon there, but someone had certainly gone through the trouble of perfectly mimicking one.

Despite his instant love for this place and its superficially natural place, Alik never allowed himself to fall under the impression that this place was anything but a carefully as-sembled artifact. He'd been inside this place for nearly three days and by his estimation, had not seen a third of what was there to see. He'd spent the days walking through vast groves of budding fruit trees, wide fields of sprouting vegetables and the edges of what appeared to be a thick Boreal-esq forest. Every living thing appeared to have been chosen for its specific usefulness. He believed this even though he had no assurance this was true, only that it appeared true as evident in the completeness and thoroughness of this world in a bottle.

Honeybees roamed the treetops during the morning hours. Thick hedgerows of blueberries lined a myriad of intersecting game paths. Microclimates seemed to be the rule, with certain areas appearing to be in more advanced states of spring – blueberries were nearly ripe in some areas, while frost was still afoot in others.

The moss he laid on was well known in the Buffer as having incredible medicinal value. The smell of basil, rosemary and lemongrass were attached to the breezes and mint grew as a thick blanket along the edges of the groves. Wild chickens scratched about and the lakes boiled with fish during the morning larval hatches.

The realm was not without technology. Much like the Agri-belts back home, the mornings and afternoons were busy with automated machines, harvesting, measuring and planting. Not long after he'd entered, Alik nearly bumped into a machine harvesting wild tomatoes and the machine responded by giving him a slight shock, equivalent to a few, nasty hornet stings.

On the morning of the fourth day, he woke to find a bot examining his fire ring. The machine did not seem to take any interest in Alik. Alik watched as the bot scanned the smoldering mound and the hot rocks surrounding it then turned and rolled towards Alik's haversack. Afraid to disturb it and receive another lashing, he remained still and watched as the bot fumbled through Alik's belongings. The bot's highly articulated pincers removed plums and near-ripe strawberries, setting them on the ground next to the pack. Alik's sphere and notebook were also removed. Alik stumbled forward a bit, wanting to grab his notebook, but he paused when the bot instantly reacted, pulling back defensively. The bot loosened its posture and went back to rifling. It finally uncovered a small tin at the bottom of Alik's bag. The tin held a small portion of Kinoko Alik carried with him. The bot removed several of the fungi and placed them into an examination tray and filed the tray into a slot near its sensors.

"Hey dammit! Those are mine!" Alik shouted. The bot continued to ignore Alik, but took the rest of the mushrooms and dumped them into another tray then filed them away with the others. Alik tried to grab the bot and remove the mushrooms but was met with another shock, more violent than before. The shock sent him tumbling backwards and onto the ground. The bot sped off and disappeared into the nearby grove. "I'll be damned!" Alik cursed.

Smelling of fire and his flesh grimy and his morning agitated, he decided to find a stream to bath in. He walked half a kilometer up hill and towards the smell of water, all the while keeping a sharp eye for the bot that stole his mushrooms. Eventually he heard the familiar sound of water crashing on stone. He followed the path to the steepest point. The ground beneath him vibrated. At the top of the steep, clover-covered hill, something totally unexpected caught his eye on the far side.

Just below the crest, the hill opened wide exposing a rocky mouth twenty or so meters above a deep pool that fed into a stream. Water poured veraciously from the spillway and appeared to run beneath the area on which he sat. It was likely the exposure of a subterranean river or spring. However, this is not what caught Alik's attention. Below the falling water, he could see the unmistakable shape of a nude figure, a woman, bathing in the pool below.

Alik's stomach fluttered, excited by the sight of another person. He froze, afraid to startle her and embarrassed by his intrusion. He neglected calling out to her. His instinct was to rush to her in excitement and berate her with questions and likely terrify the shit out of her with his enthusiasm, but his limited experience with women told him this tactic would most likely be met with confusion and scorn. He didn't feel comfortable stalking her like this. Still, she needed to know that he was there.

He stayed low, watching her, his eyes almost level with the tops of the clover he lay amongst. The hill was round at the top with a steep sheer on the water's side giving Alik an unobstructed view. Her hair was short and clung close to her face. She surfaced and made her way to the shoreline. Alik was riveted by her sumptuous figure. Hormones he'd willfully ignored since his arrival swelled and burned under his flesh. He scooted forward a bit further, but found the mound at the very edge soft and it sank as his chest rounded the top edge. Without warning, his chest caught a muddy patch, the dirt gave way and Alik slid head first through the fall to the bottom of the pool.

The pool was deep and clear. At first he didn't try to swim up, shocked by the fall and embarrassed having surely scared the girl. He looked towards the surface, his lungs tightening and he watched the light from above pierce through the frothing, fall beaten surface. Then he watched as the woman dove towards him, still immodestly nude, swimming aggressively towards Alik in an apparent effort to retrieve him. Her eyes appeared to be the same color as the water around her giving the illusion that her skull were filled with the light of the pool. The hint of a smile snuck out, though she seemed more than a bit perturbed that Alik was making no effort to swim towards her. She grabbed his wrist, pulled him toward her breasts and held him close as she swam toward the surface.

Both gasped at the surface as she swam his perfectly capable body to the shoreline, berating him along the way. "What the hell? Can't you swim or were you just trying to kill us both?" Alik crawled onto the ground and lay on his side, catching his breath, his clothing heavy and sodden and watched her as the light made the water sparkle on her skin. She stood naked and dripping. Her toned arms caught the light and cast a shadow over Alik. "Who the hell are you?"

Part Two

"You are an explorer, and you represent our species, and the greatest good you can do is to bring back a new idea, because our world is endangered by the absence of good ideas. Our world is in crisis because of the absence of consciousness."

∞

Terence McKenna

13

The final sparkles of Kuiper Belt Station faded from view. The telescopes of the hyper-light Kitsune continued to track Sol, but even Sol was fading. Kitsune was now home to Nena and her slug.

Kitsune was a rare beauty, a one off design, more akin to a PAE Council yacht than a standard intercept vessel. It was a performance vessel to say the least. Stripped down and sleek, it was built for comfort and speed. The vessel was not burdened with an overly sentient AI, instead just a clean-cut performance computer, good at massive calculations and great at causal modeling. The computer's punch came in its navigational abilities. It maintained a database of every known celestial even as well as every predicted celestial event for more than a billion years in every direction, making it a perfect navigational improvisation list. Kitsune's computer did not speak with a human tongue, but it was flawlessly fluent in the language of space-time. The unique beauty of the vessel was not lost on Nena, who had spent many hours of her first weeks, perched in the observation lounge, watching as Kitsune carefully accelerated and the young light of long dead stars shone clear and radiant, unbent by the local, gravitational turbulence of Kitsune.

Staring intently at the fading marker of man's ingenuity, Nena imagined the distant future. She imagined a time when Kuiper station would be lauded as the first stone in an epic engineering feat. Even at this distance, she imagined, the inky blackness of Sol's Dyson sphere would be deeply apparent. The eventual blot in the light of half a billion stars would be a bold announcement to anyone looking towards the Milky Way that man has been triumphant in taming both matter and energy. The time would certainly come and she was determined to assist, be it 10,000 years onward. It was with this thought that she hourly quieted the troubling rage burning in her since receiving this assignment.

If she were prescribed to travel relativistically, then, she determined, it was her personal mandate to shift her waiting talents to the dominions of the long cut. Whether she returned eighty relative years hence or 80,000, she was determined that there would always be a civilization on which to institute the designs she felt worthy. In moments such as these, she fell back on a mantra she'd repeated a million times, "Bury yourself deep in the machine and apply your own brand of grease. Revel in continuity. Revel in the long cut instead of the short cut." Though, she could not help but laugh at the fact that it was the principle underlying this very mantra, which was currently directing her path. She simply could not shake the inevitable fact that it was some other designer's grease currently between her gears.

Even as she mulled all of this through her mind, she continued to fall back on the thoughts of poor Alik. She wondered where or when he was. She hoped that he had accepted his fate easily and without the agonizing consternation Nena was then feeling. It was like being kicked out and left behind all at once. No matter the success of her mission and even if she actually returned, it would be like starting from scratch. It was a dreadful thought, but not as dreadful as the prospects of her mission.

Nena was never the type to give much thought one way or the other over the possibility of alien sentience. She preferred the 'life as natural fluke' approach. It was easy for others who saw humanity as dominant and singular to believe there was something ultimately divine or gorgeous about the possibility of being the only sentient beings. The notion never made sense to Nena. If human beings were the only sentient creatures in the entire universe then they were no more or less important than the moss that gathers on stone. In terms of moss, humans were to do as they do and that was that. If they could not grow across the stream or through the desert, then so be it. If the wet rock was plentiful and unguarded, then it was for them to spread across. Nena saw humans as a rudimentary function of this reality, like starlight and gravity. If there were 'others' then so be it, they too would have been natural functions of a vastly complicated system. For Nena, it was a case of live and let live. There really was no need to communicate, exchange glances, befriend or be-foe. Space was big enough that encounter was not a necessity.

Encounters with 'the other' had never proven fruitful to the survival of civilizations. Nena was shown the horrors that befell the strangers of men. These sorts of encounters rattle entire civilizations. Native peoples have a tendency to die poorly and it did not entertain Nena to consider which species would be facing annihilation first. The thought of somehow attempting to facilitate this meeting was ludicrous to Nena.

She'd poured over the mission briefings again and again and none of it made sense. She was to attempt a rendezvous. Another human craft, a seed ship of some kind, may or may not be attempting a similar rendezvous. If she could overtake the other human vessel and make the rendezvous first, then she was instructed to do so. On the other hand, if she was unable to overtake the human vessel, she was instructed to dock with it and assume control of the mission. That was it. Nena was given full diplomatic discretion and a good luck. That and a damn fine ship.

The Kitsune was possibly the fastest ship made to date. The theoretical conjecture was that, under very specific conditions, the Kitsune design could exceed light speed by a quarter of a percent. Though field-testing of warp capabilities had never been performed, all computer models suggested that the ship had the capability of warp travel. This was yet another fact that gnawed at the coils of Nena's brain. If the design were proven to work and then improved upon by others, during the passing years of her own relativistic travel near light speed, then it was possible that she and the other human vessel may be beaten to their destination by designers yet unborn in what may yet be a common warp vessel. Time and human ingenuity were tricky in that way. It was an unlikely prospect though, since one of the central tenants the designers held fast to, was the utility of relativistic travel. They used relativistic travel as a particular means to an end.

Certainly, humans could colonize the stars faster and in real time through the use of hyper-light technologies, but the hidden blessings of relativistic travel would then be lost; the exponential growth of populations, the tweaking of biospheres, cutting down the timelines for experiments. Through the use of relativistic travel and gravity manipulation, experiments we may have needed several generations to complete could be cut down to the time of a single lifetime or less. There were scientists, performing grand scale experiments that would otherwise have to be finished by great grandchildren. Thanks to relativistic travel the originator of the project could see these experiments to the end. Many of the biggest answers to many of the biggest questions could not and would not be solved for another 20,000 years, and yet there were teams of contemporary scientists who would be there at the end to record the results. The embrace of the long-cut was built into the designer's world-view. Still, the convenience of hyper-light travel was undeniable and would certainly come into fashion sooner or later and likely for reasons such as this.

The utility of relativistic travel added a layer of continuity to human civilization. Members of the PAE council tended to travel in shifts, disappearing into near light travel for several months, emerging after sixty to eighty years had passed, ready to gather the torch from other council members. Continuity had always been the back breaker for long-lived societies. Relativistic travel stretched the continuity of governance further and further. The average lifespan of the average human became relative to class or vocation. While the masses lived modest lives, gave birth and died, many others lived their lives like stones skipping across the surface of the pond, dropping in now and again to test the water, but always moving at a steady clip forward. Time, remember, is all about a point of reference.

~

In an attempt to shake all of these nagging gremlins, she ordered Kitsune's computer to make preparations for another acceleration event, made her way towards the plush cocoon of her quarters, packed a pipe tall with fresh Buffer herb, disrobed and nestled herself into the lazy arms of her beloved slug. Her slug whom Nena still refused to attach a proper name, had not sullied her feet with curiosity. Since arriving onboard, the slug had not taken a single walk to the observation room or through the pristine halls of the fresh ship, though she was permitted to walk as freely as Nena.

There was something about the slug's apparent void of imagination and curiosity that Nena was drawn towards - something almost religious about it. Certainly, any good slug had a rather perverse sense of nihilism built into them, since the majority of slugs existed only long enough to travel from point A to point B, which was sometimes only a matter of feet, from their birth pod to the surgical table. Pet slugs as Nena had taken, were both rare and somewhat unconventional, but not necessarily frowned upon. The long-term effects of designed nihilism were yet to be seen. A slug had never been allowed to reproduce. Even pet slugs rarely lived long. People often need procedures and even if a slug lives with an owner for six or ten years, eventually a heart or lung or liver could be needed.

However bent towards nihilism the slug may have been, she was certainly not morose, dark or even depressing. On the contrary, she was quite bright, thoughtful even. In an apparent yang to Nena's yin, the slug was unsullied by commitment, ambition or any of the other innumerable qualities that made most people insufferable. In fact, her nihilism made her quite content and light. Nena dared to think of her slug as enlightened, but never out loud.

The slug was already deeply committed to some cinematic drama, displayed across the bedroom wall. Nena inhaled her pipe aggressively then passed it to the slug, while passively attempting to assemble the pieces of the drama with little success. She could have requested the slug bring her up to speed, but she was quite content to remain confused, piecing the plot together like a shoddy detective, while steeling lustful glances at the slug's thighs.

~

In the mornings, the slug insisted on making breakfast. It was the only meal she enjoyed cooking and she did it with exceeding panache. Often, before gliding into the kitchen, the slug motivated Nena to rise by sliding deep into the covers, embracing Nena's clitoris carefully between her top lip and her tongue, bringing Nena to intense climax in a matter of seconds. The slug had a gift for knowing exactly what pleasured Nena - clearly an artifact of their genetic similarities.

The slug at the very least had the sensibility to know that waking her friend in such a manner was a small consolation to the fact that each night they slept represented the passing of another year on terra firma. And as the ship came ever closer to the speed of light, the nights and the days represented the passage of greater stretches of time.

At what point would the Generals who sent her on this strange errand retire or fall out of service, or die? How many in that room boarded their own vessels in the months or years that followed and set out on their own missions at these speeds? Would they wait patiently, curiously wondering each day the status of their tiny Major's position as potential emissary? Would they even recall having ordered the mission when news falls along their gray ears decades or perhaps centuries later?

More and more of these questions came to fill Nena's mornings. The fresh coffee beans chased off these devils more often than not, allowing her mind to wander to renewed curiosities, but in the inevitable boredom of the day, they always returned.

Eventually, Nena set herself to work. Kitsune was equipped with a state of the art design suite. She assumed the space as her office and settled in. Her original charge was to work on the stellar birth platform so she rationalized that even though she had been relieved of this charge, she would spend each day honing her design, running detailed models and then refining the design, just as she would have been had her mission remained as it was originally. Once perfected, she cached the designs, the computational models and all the data into her Unified Design Model, just as she would have done to determine the long-term effects. It would take weeks for the computer to update the model and check for discrepancies, but once verified, she could add stellar birth to the central tenants of the design. This would allow her to effectively create her own universe, acting according to the will of her designs. At that point, she could move forward. She could map out the next two millennia or more of human design according to her own specifications and updating the model all the way along.

Within the computer, she could envision imaginary technologies or material refinement techniques that were not yet a reality. Thus, in her designs, she assumed the existence of these techniques to be realities of the present and incorporated them into her models.

Over the convening months, she designed various vessels, habitats meant for uninhabitable worlds, vast and complicated farming structures until eventually she found herself engaged in holding a cache of technologies that defined aspects of a future uniquely designed by her alone. She had also cobbled together the seeds for a several grand scale projects.

Since her time was hers to do with as she pleased, she saw no reason not to delve into the fantastic or imaginary. Someone, she wagered within herself, someone has to be the first to do a thing. And so she found herself quite contently scribbling away, decoding and uncovering the math essential to the greatest engineering project man was likely ever to attempt. Nena had decided to design her Dyson Sphere.

Honest with herself, she never looked at her project as anything other than a hobby and a fool's errand, much like her current situation. Most of the technologies needed to achieve a project like a Dyson Sphere were either yet undeciphered or impossible. She did not even know which problems she would need to solve until she dove in and started formulating an honest design. The preliminaries alone would take months or years.

After only her first month at work on the sphere design, she realized that the computer required a sizable upgrade or a total re-tasking of priorities in order to process a reliable model. Since she could not physically upgrade the computer, she determined that the only way to acquire the processing power she required was to decelerate the vessel, disable its navigational functions and most other critical systems, then attempt to run the model processing again. All of which, she realized, was an impossible waste of mission critical time that ignored all aspects of urgency related to her charge.

So she winged the models. She began to institute her own conclusions, shortening the work of the modeling software and greatly reducing the accuracy of her designs. Had she been on any of the home worlds, or even given access to a standard AI, she would have had enough computing power and then some. Kitsune, however, had a mission specific computer, small and lean with only a handful of unnecessary bells and whistles. Even though the thought of stopping the ship crossed her mind forty-five of every sixty seconds that passed, she fought off the urge and simply tried to refocus her designs back towards the small and mundane, rather than the massive and grandiose.

The slug noticed the cyclical nature of Nena's moods. She noticed the ups and downs, the frustration that came with junctures in Nena's work as well as the elation that came from success and the sadness of knowing that everything Nena was working on was essentially little more than basket weaving, at least in the most immediate sense. Being a nihilist, one would assume, it would be uncharacteristic of the slug to act in a manner that would be seen as an attempt to please another individual simply for the sake of bringing happiness, but this is an oversight towards such a philosophy. In fact, the slug cared very deeply for Nena. Love is not absent in nihilism. And so she too had secretly set herself to task.

During the months Nena spent bent over her design table, while the slug was expected to be in sedate repose, the slug was actually quite busy with her own project, unbeknownst to Nena. Instead of wasting, naked in bed, waiting to pleasure Nena physically, the slug was instead busily and secretly stashing herself away in the one place she knew Nena had zero interest in, the cockpit. Over the long months, the slug made a home away from home behind Kitsune's main console.

She began with basic tutorials, provided for emergency scenarios. She acquainted herself with the navigation system and spent many days doing little else than studying star charts, orbital paths of detected, known or inhabited worlds and familiarizing herself with the myriad flavor of gravitational anomalies. The slug made every effort to learn all the trade and tools of any good, human pilot.

Even though Nena had complete faith in the automated piloting systems and had little interest in their course, the slug decoded and learned every aspect of their journey to come. Yet she mentioned none of this to Nena. Instead, she held it close, waiting for the appropriate time.

Nena, the slug knew, had complete authority to manually fly the craft, even if she did not have the ability. The slug decided that it was in the best interest of their continued relationship, to provide Nena options when and if options were required. If this were a haphazard journey, destined to be fruitless and by counterweight remove Nena from her preferred profession, then at completion, the two of them would have the opportunity to forge their specific destiny in a ship the slug could pilot with ease. Control over a vessel of this sort meant freedom if it meant nothing else. Surely, the slug reasoned, there were already overlooked worlds, filled with human life, beyond the surly minds of the Designers.

All of this matured in the slug as a new leaps forward, somewhat against the grain of her steady nihilism. Still, she argued with herself that even a meaningless universe did not have to remain unfettered and undecorated with meaningful gestures. The slug's very existence stood to serve as the ultimate gift - sacrifice. And though it was now highly unlikely her heart would ever be physically pulled from her chest and placed into Nena's it certainly did not imply that the slug would not give it willingly even if only symbolically.

Even traveling at terrific speeds, it was to take more than a year before Kitsune could attempt to overtake the other human vessel. Of course, the slug was now fully tracking the human vessel. She noted its original course after back tracking from its current position. It had veered off some time ago, roughly about the time Nena was directed onto this mission. The other ship had a good, clean, head start, but she still did not have enough data to establish the destination.

14

"Well, I can't say I'm sorry to meet someone else." His embarrassment was written across his face and his attempts
at small talk were not met with any visible interest. She
threw him no bones. Ripe with the fatty smelt of overfed
boar, the aroma wafting from the pan she stirred eagerly kept
Alik's mouth loose and slobbery, enhancing his dis-ease as his
tongue slipped and slid haphazardly in his mouth, bungling
his questions and explanations further.

"How long have you been here?" The oils in the pan
flared and she was forced to plop a covering over the pan to
extinguish the flames. She was steady and thoughtful in her
cooking, focused only on her task and paying no direct mind
to Alik's question.

"Do you know what this place is?" Alik pressed further,
but Ruby remained squat and focused on the food. The in-

dignant slight of being ignored was wearing on him. He was frustrated and badly wanted a conversation with the only other apparent human on board. He realized that his hunger was not helping his frustration. Though, he also could not ignore the heavy feeling in his gut was not just hunger, rather it was the same heavy feeling that always followed Sigrah's silence.

Alik could not help but stare at her body. It was covered now, in a green jump suit, but she let the zipper at her chest hang low, exposing the gracious cleave of her breasts. Her hair was bobbed short and brown.

Though he realized that he was the uninvited guest and had no intention of upsetting her further, he was becoming more and more impatient.

"C'mon, say something! I'm sorry I was spying on you… er eh." Alik paused. Spying was definitely not the word he'd intended to use. He could see the effect rush across her face, as it was the only emotion he had yet evoked and still she stared at the food, gripping the panhandle tighter. She removed the pan from the fire and quickly divided the contents between two bowls. Finally, she spoke under her breath, barely audible, staring intently at her lunch.

"Didn't mean to spy on me…eh?" She refused to make eye contact.

Alik leaned in, picked up his plate and whispered back to her.

"You know I can hear you? Why not talk to me?" He asked defiantly.

Her eyes flared. She huffed and then she shoveled a large spoonful eggs into her mouth and then launched into her attack despite her continuous attempts to chew.

"Ooo dam foo!" Food splattered from her lips.

"What?" Alik was holding back laughter.

"Damn right you're a fool." She was angry, but it was

clear she was intentionally putting it on. It did not seem like genuine anger. "You were spying on me! I had to save you because you were too busy starring me down to swim for your life. You could have been killed. What then? What the hell would I tell people on the other end of this trip? Oh, the Usher somehow made it all the way down here and drowned himself glaring at my tits?"

Alik was taken aback. He left a spoon full of food ready to shovel into this mouth hang in the air. "How'd you know I was the Usher?" Alik asked.

"Who else would you be? Does Sigrah know you're here?"

"You know Sigrah?" Alik immediately regretted his enthusiastically naïve question.

Ruby was gracious even though she was fighting back laughter. "Of course I know Sigrah. She and I have to talk all the time."

"She? Sigrah's a man." Alik fully committed to naivety – helpless to his obvious attraction for Ruby and his desperate need to keep the conversation flowing.

"Wake up Usher! Sigrah's a computer. She can be whatever she wants to be. If Sigrah told me she identified as a golden tiger, I couldn't really argue with her."

Alik shook his head. He enjoyed Ruby's sass, even though his levels of embarrassment were now beyond measure. "Oh yeah. I guess you're right." Alik searched desperately for something intelligent to say. Instead, he shoveled another spoonful of pork sear and eggs into his face.

"Jeez, they've really gotten good at picking bright Ushers. Eh?" As soon as the words left her mouth, Ruby realized she'd stepped too far. She would not admit it, but she already knew Alik did not deserve ridicule. He'd found his way inside the Timelock. That alone spoke for his determined curiosity if not his ingenuity.

"Hey!" Alik attempted to protest the offence, but fell flat as before. "Look. I'm definitely missing some details, but cut me some slack. I got in here didn't I?"

"You don't even know what this place is." She was softer, but still prodding.

Alik chewed his food and pouted silently.

"Alright." She continued, looking up to make firm eye contact with Alik. "I'm sorry. Sometimes I get carried away. Keeps me on my toes. I'll admit, I'm happy to have someone to talk to."

Alik swallowed and they both sat in silence for a moment. Alik looked around, combing the scene carefully. The encampment was well used. A clothesline stretched across two saplings, down wind of the fire. The fire pit itself was well used and the coals appeared weeks old and stable. It was a good fire, well maintained. A bedroll hung from the clothesline along with several bits of clothing – a bra and a pair of frayed trousers. Alik noticed a dry rectangle on the grass near the fire. He knew immediately that she chose not to sleep in a tent, preferring instead to sleep beneath the stars, as they were. Ruby's encampment was not far from the falls she'd plucked Alik from. It all seemed semi-permanent, as if it had been used on and off for decades, perhaps longer. The way the land lay and the trails cut clearly through the brush, the place seemed to have a well-trodden feel to it.

Alik wanted to desperately to start over or at the very least break the silence and dispatch the awkwardness. He looked again at Ruby, who was staring back with a renewed civility.

"This food is really great." Alik paused, searching for a decent icebreaker. "Did you make the olive oil?" Alik met her eyes as she looked up from her bowl. He immediately knew that she'd decided to drop the act and unveil a softer tone.

"Well, sort of. There's a really thick grove of olive trees not far from here." She paused, made eye contact for a moment then looked down at her plate and began again. "I didn't exactly make it...though I probably could have. It's just easier to let this place do what it does and...you know, reap the benefits later."

"Benefits?" Alik asked.

"Sure. The food. The air." Ruby understood that Alik did not yet have a full picture of this place. She was sensitive enough to avoid embarrassing Alik any further but becoming overly didactic. So she pulled back and put forward an inviting smile.

Alik relaxed, kicking his foot onto a nearby rock and reclining onto his right hand, still holding the plate with his left. "Can I just apologize for sneaking up unannounced? I really had no idea. I was just shocked to see another person." Alik asked sincerely.

Ruby smiled again and waved her free hand towards him. "Don't worry about it man. My name is Ruby." Ruby extended her hand around the edge of the fire pit. Alik pushed himself up from his half reclined state and awkwardly groped Ruby's hand while trying to keep his food aloft and his body from tumbling over into the coals. Ruby chuckled as Alik righted himself.

Alik pointed to his chest with his bowl of food, as if he were some errant cave creature lacking formal language skills. "Me Alik." He topped his introduction with a grunt and a smile.

She pointed at her chest and grunted back. "Roo-bee. Me Ruby." They grinned at one another, their body language admittedly pleased at the presence of another human and with that, the tension faded entirely.

Alik, having scrapped his bowl clean, stood and paced towards the edge of the pond to washout the dish properly. "So...you feel like telling me exactly what this place is?" Alik set his bowl along into Ruby's canteen sack and scanned the surroundings as if he had just arrived from sea onto some foreign beachhead.

Ruby set down her plate and pulled her knees to her chest, wrapped her arms around them and rocked gently back and fourth. "This is the Timelock. It serves a multitude of purposes, primarily propulsion. We have the added benefit of using its unique conditions for advanced biosphere production activities…like farming." Ruby trailed off, attempting to collate various explanations in her mind while figuring out how to frame all of this for Alik. She knew from the moment she'd encountered Alik that he was no fool. She was fully aware that Alik was likely to be overwhelmingly uninformed about a great many things – it was written in the curiosity on his face.

"Timelock?" Alik thought back to the display on the inside of his suit.

"That's right. Timelock. This place…it exists in normal space time." Ruby answered directly.

"You mean like Earth time?" Alik asked.

"Close to it. Nothing is ever exact, but yes, standard time…whatever that really means." She scooted closer to Alik and intentionally tried to scrape off a wide layer of grass from the dirt below, with her feet. With the handle end of her fork, she sketched a rough outline. "So, imagine this is the ship. You should be here." She pointed to a small area along the starboard ventricle of the vessel. "All of this is the Timelock." She drew a circle around the center of the vessel. She indicated that the sphere extended out tremendously on all sides. "What did you think you were transporting?"

"I wasn't sure. I was curious. I thought…maybe there were colonists…asleep?" Alik smiled haphazardly.

"No. As far as I know, we do not have a human cargo of any kind." Ruby paused. "That is, except for you and I."

Alik pressed further. "I guess I still don't understand. I mean, look at this place…forests and hills and dirt and waterfalls? What good does this do anyone?"

"Well, as complicated a mechanism as the Timelock is, its purpose is fairly straight forward. Think about it. Everything in here is locked in 'standard' space-time relative to the ship outside of the Timelock. Just consider the implications for a moment." Ruby spoke softly and paused to allow Alik to think the details through. "Let's say that it takes Sigrah three or five or ten years to reach her destination, that means that as time passes relative to everyone else, so does the time in here. That means, depending on conditions, if Sigrah travels for ten years as close to the speed of light as possible, the Timelock and everything in it would age hundreds of years relative Sigrah. That means, a food and raw materials necessary for colonies and deep space ventures can be produced in vast quantities over the course of a relatively short journey. Along with the natural preponderance of hydrogen throughout space, it is very easy for Sigrah to synthesize any number of compounds which can be added to the 'lock, creating a situation in which we are not forced to work with a closed system…instead we have a productive system in which matter can be added as needed. We are gaming the system. We are cheating the laws of thermo dynamics while simultaneously using general relativity to our unique advantage." As soon as Ruby ended her diatribe, she felt embarrassed, hoping that she had not overwhelmed Alik with overly technical explanations.

Alik sat still, with his wide eyes locked onto Ruby's face as his mind worked feverously to piece the details together. "I think it all makes sense. You can make a hundred generations of food, preserved and ready for the masses…but isn't it all a bit impractical?"

"It would be if it wasn't a by-product of a much more important feature…" Ruby looked at Alik, waiting for him to pick up her meaning.

Alik remembered. "Ahhh right! Propulsion." He pondered it for a minute. "I can't even begin to imagine how all of that works. I'll take your word for it for now."

The marveled look on Alik's face made Ruby happy. Her impression of Alik was evolving. She noticed something goofy about him, something that wasn't necessarily off, but was certainly informed from a unique set of experiences. Though there was something vaguely familiar almost folksy quality about his way – something she attributed to his overly congenial gaze and his eagerness to please.

As much as Alik's curiosity for his surroundings tended to take precedence, he found himself then, much more curious about Ruby than anything else. Being human, there was something much less abstract about her than the circumstances surrounding the two of them.

The mid morning light hung above them, casting a warm glow on the tame coals and causing Ruby's brown hair to shine. She was pale and rugged. Her sleeves were rolled and buttoned above her elbows. Her hands were muscular and strong. She was stunning. Alik noticed how her dark green jumpsuit hid many details of her body, but the mystery was tantalizing, especially after already receiving an immodest glimpse. Alik noticed that hiding in the dark green of her jumpsuit were a series of subtle blue stripes running the length of her upper arms.

Alik asked. "Are you an engineer?"
"Yes. Well...mostly...sure. I manage the Timelock." Ruby tripped over her words, unusually embarrassed at the label, 'engineer'.

"But surely you don't live inside here all the time." Alik pressed.

"No, of course not. I'd be dead and dust by now if I lived in the 'lock."

"Did you choose this line of work?" Alik crossed his legs, as if settling in for a good story.

"Does anyone really choose their job?" Ruby looked away.

"I don't know about engineers. I figured you all had the run of the galaxy." Alik mused.

Ruby laughed, shaking her head a bit. "Not quite." She paused and breathed in deeply. The air was dense with the smell of sunlit hay rising from the fields upwind and the relaxing, dank musk of leaf rot and woody decomposition from the forest at the edge of the camp. ""I shouldn't sound so disgruntled. In all fairness, I did want this job."

Ruby closed the distance between the two and rolled onto her stomach, her face closer to his, looking up to meet his eyes. "But I certainly didn't choose it myself. It was luck of the draw, like everything else. It's where I ended up. I just think I ended up where I needed to be. Hell, maybe that's the way other engineers feel."

"But you ended up in your specialty?" Alik asked.

"Sure. You could say that. Tissue culture and dynamic gravitational fields."

"What? Those aren't really related are they?"

"You would be surprised. With the tissue culture…It's one of the functions I perform. I never thought to learn it by choice. It was the path I tested into. But I like it."

"What sort of tissue do you culture?" Alik was slightly confused, but keeping up.

"It's all around you." Ruby twirled her fingers in the air. "I took most all of these samples from the very best Earth had to offer. These are genetically identical to plants living back home…cultured and transplanted in here. All of the vegetative matter here…it's all cultured. I can grow anything and I do. All I need are some hard working bots, a smart computer and some relativistic speeds and I can cook just about any biome you want to see or any matter you have a taste to eat."

Alik smiled. "So you're a gardener."

Ruby laughingly buried her face in her hands and groaned. "I swear, I knew you were going to say that. Trust me, it's slightly more complicated than gardening. Plus, the bots do most of the physical work."

"So you just fill the godhead role." Alik joked. "That's unbelievable!"

Ruby smiled, enjoying the levity. Then she continued in a serious tone. "This entire forest we're laying in…"

"Yeah?"

"I planted this two months ago." Ruby let the thought hang in the air.

"But it looks decades old." Alik said.

"It is. But it's also two months old." Ruby stood and took Alik's hand, pulling him to his feet. "Walk with me." She continued talking as she led him down a nearby path and up a steep ridge within the forest. "The food isn't the only thing we have to offer. Colonies and stations, they need their own living plant material and lots of it. The Timelock affords us an ability to propagate thousands of species en-mass, which can then be delivered to colonies mature and prepared to enter their agricultural systems."

Suddenly the tree line broke and the elevation of the forest, the camp and the falls suddenly became clear to Alik. From the edge of the ridge, a thousand meters or so below them, a valley opened wide and ran for several kilometers until it became indistinguishable.

In the valley, rows upon rows of fruit trees of every imaginable variety filled the open land between the tall valley slopes. Each row represented difference ages and maturity, potted and sorted by variety, species and heartiness. Ruby pointed towards them. "Like these. These will all be mature and ready for transfer as soon as we reach Andromeda Station.

Some of them will be harvested ahead of time, providing artisanal lumber for craftsmen and decorative ship fitters within the colonies. The fruits produced for the most mature are harvested; some are preserved, while others are processed. There are more than a million valuable products that this valley alone can produce and there are dozens more just like this, serving different functions. From there the by-products will be sold, donated and distributed to smaller trade federations and finally disseminated amongst the furthest colonies of this galactic arm." Ruby glowed with excitement. It was apparent that this was her passion. "You've got to understand the scale of it all...not this...not the Timelock...but the intrinsic value of the purpose it serves. If for some reason, we were to lose a single seed ship, such as this one, hundreds of colonies and thousands of planned missions could be affected. We are on board one of the biggest cogs the designers have yet placed into their machine."

Alik followed her, mostly. It wasn't an inability to understand that got in his way, rather it was the onslaught of questions brought on by each sentence she complete. He turned his head and stared into the valley. He had to continuously remind himself that he was still on board a spacecraft. His head wrenched with a sudden pain at the thought of it all. "So, who is that we are taking all this to?" Alik asked, half expecting to have his question blown off, but Ruby was quick with a reply.

"Andromeda station." Ruby smiled wide and looked at her watch. "It's not exactly there yet, but it will be by the time we get there. And it will be a sight!"
Alik was openly confused. "What?" He paused. "Not there yet?"

Ruby was soft. "Alik...think about it. To them, we aren't expected for decades. Plus, all of the construction crews and supplies are being manufactured en-route by a vessel dispatched from within Perseus. It will be well underway to completion by the time we get there."

Alik allowed the words to set in for a moment before he was struck with the casualness of it all. As far as he could tell, there was no certainty in their destination at all. Any number of incredible events may have or may befall a major engineering attempt such as that. He also wondered what great loss a ship, an Usher and an engineer would be if they were to mothball a project like Andromeda Station. He felt as though he was a chit tossed onto a table of possibilities but no guarantees. He kept all of this under his hat. Ruby's excitement and confidence were clearly solidly intact and he didn't want to be the one to launch them into some strange debate. He also summoned the courage to accept the possibility that he may have been too ignorant to understand the certainty of Terran determination. Plus, the two were having a nice time and he wanted to keep the conversation safe.

He tried to break the tension with a joke. "So, just to make sure, we are going to Andromeda Station 'to be', not Andromeda?"

Ruby scoffed laughingly; slightly impressed that Alik would register such a joke. "Of course we are not going to Andromeda. Even with our speed that would take hundreds of lifetimes…as you well know." She looked him over again, realizing for certain now that she was dealing with more or less a hick and she like it. "You're one lost puppy aren't you?"

Alik shrugged as confidently as possible, unable to hide a thing. The two of them smiled at one another and walked away from the ridge and back towards the encampment.

~

That night, the two of them lay under false stars – varied projections, images of the known Universe, stitched together in a fictional, yet brilliantly unique representation of a night's sky. The substitution of realism for surrealism in this place was both entertaining and comforting to Alik. There were things he noticed that seemed to be tiny winks, or subtle nods from the designers who took part in putting together one aspect or another.

"If we walk twenty Kilometers to the east and lay on the tallest hill, the night's view will appear as it does on Centari-four – a world now in its fourth generation of human inhabitance. Twenty miles further and we get a view of the night over the Gailen colony.... That's a sad one. Their atmosphere collapsed after an unexpected impact. It was later found that sociopathic colonists had engineered the colony collapse and later instigated the collision in order to cover the fact that they had asphyxiated nine hundred thousand individuals. The perpetrators were never seen again."

"Who would do that?" Alik was repulsed at the notion. He had never heard of a single incident of murder in his entire life.

"It's ghost stories Alik. I'm sure you had scary campfire stories where you came from." Ruby nudged his ribs. Then they were silent, taking in the noises of the Timelock.

Alik's ears were fully deceived. Closing his eyes and gathering the rustle of the wind through the trees and across the wide pool, spring crickets occasionally sounding from the thicket and the distant rush of water from the falls – his mind could not distinguish this place from Earth. Though, when he opened his eyes, the surreal intensity of the sky above him could not be mistaken as natural.

Both were fixated on an ancient representation of the Pillars of Creation, slowly shifting along in the constant movement of the scene above them – expanded to appear less than a light month from this artificial world, the clouds of the nebula looked as though they were floating directly above the trees like an approaching storm.

"Don't you think it's incredible that we actually ran into one another?" Alik asked earnestly.

"I'm not the sentimental sort. Sorry Alik." Ruby did her best to pass of disinterest, but she was thinking the same thing.

"That's not what I mean. I mean...don't you think the odds were against it?" Alik did his best to sound sincere, but not overly sentimental.

"How so?" Ruby gave him a pass.

"I mean that if I had been an hour later, you may have already moved on or left the 'lock and gone on with your day... If I'm understanding the workings of this place correctly, then had you left today, you would literally be weeks away from me right now." Alik sounded as though he was assembling a puzzle between his ears.

"Maybe from my perspective, but from yours, I would appear almost frozen in time from the moment I'm transferred beyond the gravity well...even though you wouldn't actually be able to see me." It felt like Ruby was pushing back on Alik's overt sentimentalism, but in fact, she was relenting, if only within herself. She too was stirred by the thought of a near miss.

"So the fact that we are here, together, under this cartoonish sky...I mean, we could have gone the entire journey, slipping past each other, aging at slightly or dramatically different rates." Alik was trying to delicately piece the significance together.

"I don't think the odds are that high...plus...I said I don't do mushy." Ruby paused. "Look, you need to be careful with this place. I come and go on very specific intervals. Don't let grass grow under your feet in this place; it will only make your journey longer. Cut the grass, then return when it's forest." She tilted her head towards Alik and smiled.

It was all very difficult for Alik to wrap his mind around,

even though he understood it all conceptually.

"Can I tell you a story?" A fresh sense of sincerity flooded Ruby's voice.

"Sure. I love stories."

"That cloud of gas and stars right there." She pointed towards the Pillars of Creation. "That stack of gas and stellar fire is four light years tall and nearly as many thick. Do you see that faint glow around the edges?"

Alik stared into the sky. "Yeah. I see it."

"When this image was taken, more than a thousand years ago, that faint glow were the first signs of the gases in that cloud beginning to burn off. They were burning off due to the super nova of another stellar mass, light years behind the Pillars. The first vines of the explosion were just beginning to tear away at the Pillars millennia before those who took this image."

The two were silent for a long moment. Then Ruby continued.

"Those Pillars vanished...were wiped from the face of the cosmos more than seven thousand years ago. If we were standing on Sol 3, we would still have to wait another six thousand years, give or take, before our telescopes would show us the final act in the theatre of those Pillars. Yet here we are, pouring through space at nearly the speed of light... the photons of ten billion long dead stars colliding with our vessel every moment. Despite our speed, our position, our relative time, as long as we are in this place and our vessel is moving, we will remain in a cocooned reality, much like that light from the Pillars."

There was silence between the two for a moment, until Alik broke it with his passable but wanton humor. "What were you saying about mush?"

Ruby backhanded his chest and huffed. It occurred to her that she really did not have full grasp of Alik's understanding or experience. She suddenly wondered if she'd been making any sense at all, then nervously tried to smooth it all over.

"I guess Ushers aren't selected for their understanding of all things cosmic or technical? I guess they figure you are all so desperate to wipe out your debt you'll sign up for anything." Ruby instantly regretted her framing.

Alik was superficially offended, but ignored the crassness of her statement, admitting to himself that he makes the same indictment of himself on a regular basis. He also recognized that her intention was benign and fraught with what he suspected was deep loneliness. Despite Alik's undeniable lack of technical or scientific knowledge, he had a profound ability to read people and decode them. It was a talent he did not give himself enough credit for possessing.

"You know Ruby, I have an extended relative who is a designer?" Alik offered.

"How would I know that?" Alik recognized that Ruby was being defensive in part to her own shame.

Alik paused, then continued. "I'm just being conversational. My feelings were not hurt. There's no need to be defensive."

"I'm not being defensive. I just don't see how being related to an engineer excuses you from making smart choices." Ruby cut deep. It surprised Alik, but he held fast to his assumption that she meant well, but was having difficulty breaking through some intellectual barrier Ruby assumed existed between the two.

"I'm sure my relative would agree with that indictment. She was rather displeased with me when I told her what I had signed on to." Alik threw Ruby a bone, hoping to diffuse the insecurity ruining the conversation.

Ruby shifted onto her side, looking at Alik's profile in the night-light. "She was right to be displeased. Though…" Ruby shifted again to her back. "…I suppose someone has to do it. I mean, here I am too." Ruby sat up and began digging through her hefty satchel. She produced a pipe and small bag of pungent, green, Buffer herb, packed the pipe tightly, lit it, inhaled and passed it over to Alik as she continued. "No fewer than five years on this bucket. Did they tell you that?" Alik fired the pipe and inhaled deeply, sputtering and coughing as he digested Ruby's words. "Five years? They told me two!"

"Yep Usher. I don't know what you thought you were signing up for...and it's likely they didn't know when they were signing you up...but yes, this is a five year journey...at the least."

Alik paused for a moment, then putting aside the heaviness of this revelation; he turned to Ruby and asked purposefully, "Is this Buffer herb? It sure as hell tastes like Buffer herb!"

"Of course it's Buffer herb. Do you think I would manage a vast and complicated farming super structure with that shitty, lab grown, urban herb?"

The two of them laughed off the heaviness of their conversation and went back to gazing at the cartoonish sky.

Alik lay awake for quite a while, watching the star display change as the hours melted. His skin surged with energy and excitement. This felt as much like home as anything he'd known. His brain vibrated in his skull. So much had changed so quickly. The questions that were once malformed seeds were now sprouting in his mind and he winced at the possibility of knowing more of what was unknown.

Then he rubbed at a slight itch below his ear and found the empathy node, still firmly attached. He'd forgotten that it was there, transmitting his thoughts and emotions in an endless stream to Sigrah. He felt an overwhelming satisfaction, realizing that his recent experiences had left some impression on Sigrah if only in a digitized stream of numbers. I'm not alone, he thought. He gently tapped at the node as he stared at Ruby sleeping and transmitted a silent thank you.

~

When Alik woke the next morning, Ruby was gone, along with most of the instruments from her small encampment. He wasn't sure how he'd slept through her leaving, but he had. He tried calling out for her, looking through the surrounding thicket for any entrances or exits that may have gone unnoticed and found none. The one he'd come through was more than a day's hike from there. To search the entire Timelock would have proven fruitless, he still wasn't sure how big this place was or what obstacles lay across it. He walked to the top of the ridge Ruby had shown him the day before and he looked across the Timelock and was reminded of the insignificance of his stature amongst this place.

Despite the coldness of Ruby's sudden departure, Alik was ready to get back to his other little world. He almost sensed a feeling of excitement at the thought of returning. His room was more comfortable than the ground, though he did love sleeping on what was, for all intents and purposes, terra firma. He left as he had come, except now he was filthy – his legs cramped and his back strengthened with the weight of a full G. He marched back through the cold spring bogs and saw the last of the frost leave the paths in the cold thickets near his entrance. From inside the Timelock the hatch to the 'Lockport stood out like an artificial beacon. He spotted it along the hillside from more than a mile away, perfectly white and banded with the unmistakable straight lines of a manufactured object. It felt like an art installation, placed lovingly in the face of the massive, grassy hillside.

He eagerly climbed the path towards the exit and felt no surprise when the hatch engaged and opened immediately upon his arrival. Inside, the space was just as he had left it.

The suit hung on the wall and the hatch closed behind him. In the suit, as he fitted the helmet around his skull, he looked again at the small display on the inside. The room filled with the viscous liquid and he noticed the minutes as they had been when he arrived on this side of the 'Lock, begin to crawl forward barely two minutes, then two more and as the liquid encased his body, the chronometer revealed the total elapsed time of just shy of three hours. That's when he was finally able to conceptualize the Timelock, for what it truly was. He had spent more than a week inside, but outside, only a matter of minutes had passed.

On the far side of the Timelock, on top of it, as he stood beneath the streetlamp marking the stair well, Alik noticed a small craft catching light as it tumbled towards Alik from above. The craft came to a graceful stop feet from Alik. Fitted with a pair of seats and a small cargo flat and banded with repeating green bands of light, it begged him to climb aboard.

The craft transported him across the gulf he had leapt through, chasing the bird and deposited him at a small station, not far from the tunnel corridor he'd initially leapt from.

~

Over the following weeks, Alik found himself drifting contentedly into a deep, but harmless malaise. He bedded down in the darkness of his comfortable den, watching ancient cinematics or probing through Sigrah's vast musical library, without any direct communication to or from Sigrah what so ever. He assumed nothing, given that the empathy node was still attached. If either had a mind to speak to the other he could do so at any moment and with only a thought.

Alik wallowed in fits of tininess, coming to terms with scale and with insignificance. The thought of being trapped in an infinite sea of space and time, corralled only by the sudden burst of the creation and recreation spanning trillions and trillions of years – all of it made his matter, his muscles, his soul feel useless – his mind and thoughts no different than the shiver of a single doomed leaf in a windy forest. He came into to this life from some unspeakable void he either could not or would not remember and as far as he could tell he was powerless to avoid returning to the same void. There was not an ounce of effort on his part, which could spare him from the perilous walk of the infinite. Live or die – how long or when did not matter at all. Even as his life ceased he had the possible pleasure of either existing tenuously in nothingness for eternity or existing tenuously in some mysterious after-life, for eternity or until he was released to walk again in the corporeal. The equal likelihood and unlikelihood of each solidified his helplessness. Even if he were to repeat life, spurt through the birth canal at the end of this incarnation, it would only serve to seal his fate of repeating through the Universe infinitely and may ultimately prove to be a special kind of hell he and his entire ilk are perpetually chained within.

As his angst hung close, he could not fight off the realization that he was a prisoner to this ship cheating the normal boundaries of life that now haunted him– captive in total within some spectrum of existence that seemed to have no end. Even if the Universe collapsed in on itself, all matter; all energy all returned to a finite point, all of it would simply begin again. Repetition like a blinking eye, his journey from birth canal to crematorium as existence in total blinked on and off, on and off infinitum. And as time passed, he knew that his own family had blinked out of existence – and the likelihood now stood that his own mother or fathers had themselves been reborn only to grow and perhaps die again, having lived a full life of sorts. The years were slipping by like sand and he was helpless to stop it, trapped on the far side of the hourglass.

And finally, in a soft landing of sorts, these troubled realizations led him by the hand back to the current state of the mission. As he had learned, he would be in this vessel for no fewer than five years. The passing of Earth bound years fell behind him like lemmings off a cliff. To this end, five years was nothing, a penance. If he were a prisoner of time or a prisoner in general, embracing his fate was the only path to peace. If he lived as a prisoner, it was his duty to make his prison his own, until he no longer felt as a prisoner. And as he saw it, the Timelock was always a suitable means of suicide. The realization that he could escape his mission by simply disappearing into the bush to live out his life and die in peace was an alternative he kept close to his heart, but far from his conscious mind.

A simple debt had led him to this moment and that was just another prison. As he now saw it, he was determined to shape his life as he saw fit and give credence to the truth that he had been doing just that from the very beginning.

15

It is easy to allow yourself to imagine the genesis of our Universe as a fiery caldron, where molten or malformed planetoids were smote against the anvil of super massive stars or great hammers of gravity – in which each day was consumed with frightful physical machinations on wondrous and impossible scales. The truth though is likely more striking than this misconception. In fact, the beginning was cold and dull – boring even. Stars lived out entire lives, lonesome, orbited only by half born rocks and mocked by the frightening emptiness of it all. It took epochs of steady burning before the first stars began to die furiously – enraged and engorged with heavy metals, interesting gases and helpful radiation.

After several billion years of slow burning and forging, of galactic accumulation and slow disintegration, the first stars

went nova, belching the ingredients of the cosmos in all directions. The Universe slowly shifted slowly, almost unnoticeably
from a place of nebulous burning gases to one of rocky vistas.
See, the Universe is like a great river. Each galaxy was a
whirlpool amongst the flow and within the whirling of each
galaxy, tiny eddies of sand accumulated, drawing currents
in new directions, acting subtly with and against the greater
flow. The dark matter we do not see, are the river boulders
and banks between and throughout the eddies – guiding the
flow of the current.

Once the Universe became a rocky place, the first bits of
life to take hold on these stony atolls were not clumsy, fragile
bacterium. Instead, the first life to explode onto the scene
was a type of life able to live off of the most abundant natural
aggregation of elements at the time, rock. Before planets,
moons and planetoids were ripe with oceans and aquifers, before atmospheres were stable and weather patterns equalized,
there grew the tiny fungi. Little more than slime at first, the
tiny fungi learned to take the most basic living conditions the
Universe had to offer and then thrive.

Fungi covered the surface of stale proto planets, slowly
breaking mountains into gravel. They turned ammonia and
hydrocarbons into simple sugars, feeding themselves on the
inhospitable. In their wake, they left supple plains of dirt.
They wore away mountains, allowing winds to carry them
off as sand, carving valleys necessary to hold moisture, which
eventually gave way to formation of rivers, deltas, canyons,
seas and every other biosphere necessary for life to thrive.
Rivers of water and methane broke the rock further, but at
the banks were always the tiny fungi, working as steadily as
the innate motions of the Universe from which they were
born. They breathed in time with the Universe as they fed
off of its pulse.

It was in the dirt and seas that formed by the efforts of the hearty fungi those more fragile examples of life were able to emerge. Open, cellular creatures that metabolized whatever random bits of flotsam they happened upon. This entire emergence was thanks to the tiny fungi.

And it seemed that only on the world of the Rachis, did the fungi demand greater things. Perhaps there was something about the starlight raining down on the Rachis home world, which demanded a greater bend towards patient ambition or perhaps they were simply the best example of an uninterrupted fungal colony, nearly as old as the Universe itself. Laying in wait, patiently as the world was given over to more obtrusive beings was not enough for the deep ancestors of the modern Rachis.

For it was sometime in the Universe's early middle age that the silent fungi of the Rachis stood aloft from their home mats of mycelia, broke free and propelled themselves under their own will across the surface of their world. Something drew them out, gave them will and set them on a path unlike the lesser fungi which still drifted silently across the currents of the Universe.

~

Eventually there were four distinct genders amongst the Rachis. The female gender, of which Myco was a part, was the most rare of the four.

The males were the inoculators. Sporting giant fruiting members during their apparent death and tied again to the mycelia that connected them all, they stood as the primary progenitors of the future. The females also had this ability, but their spores were different, particular, cunning and patient. A male could inoculate hectares at a time and give rise to billions of eventual fruiting males. Within each run, only a handful of females would rise from the froth.

Exponential population growth was a serious factor to contend with. That is why spawning only occurred at the end of the Rachis' bipedal life cycle and even then only a handful of males were chosen to deliver the fresh run of spawn.

The third gender was the mycelia mat itself. Mycelium linked the Rachis. Certainly the first two genders were individualized through their evolution, but the mycelium remained as a constant link to the planets they inhabited. At any given time, Rachis from one side of a world could communicate with the other side through the mycelium. The mycelium also stood as the Rachis equivalent of tool marks in granite. Instead of writing their histories upon the face of obelisks, their history was interwoven through the thick mycelia mat, which ran through their worlds.

The fourth gender was that of the anastomes. Sometimes, the individual explorers amongst the Rachis, those bent on experience and observation of life happened onto one another. Sex, in human terms was not applicable to the process, which ensued, though the process could be compared to sex. The two individuals, sensing a sameness or similarity of intent would decide to form a union of two distinct haploid groups. Through a complex process of pheromone exchanges two haploid groups or individuals would merge into a third, distinct entity until, somatically, they formed a new and distinct individual, which would then continue to explore. The anastomes were more often than not considered female though that was not always the case.

It was through the eventual formation of the anastomes gender that the so-called transcendental objects were first formed. The tiny fungi, rich with interstellar communicative abilities came about through a long process of gene swapping and intentional mothering from the female gender.

It was the female enclave that insisted on the creation of the original probes, more than a billion years prior to Myco's birth. And in the beginning, the females were the only ones listening. They kept their minds open and receiving as the tiny sleeping spores occasionally pinged home and announced essentially, we are still out here and it is still cold...will call again when things warm up.

At first, the males of the Rachis saw this entire enterprise as a waste. There were many nearby worlds, warm, rocky and empty - ripe for inoculation. Spreading helpless, lesser spawn amongst the stars was a fruitless enterprise, as they saw it. That was, until the first real transmissions began.

The first successful transmissions were little more than the original pings. The fruited probes called back to their mothers announcing warmth and growth and hope. The males did not become interested until the full-blown transmissions of ingested probes were received. Even then, the females were forced to goad the males into witnessing the potential of their tiny spawn. The females would fruit their arms and pass the experiences onto the males. The males would then walk through the transmissions, reluctantly at first, yet eventually intrigued.

The first time a male saw through the eyes of some far-flung alien beast, they were hooked. The males then took full credit for the process, established a hierarchy, rules, dogma etc. The females were slowly edged out of the entire process. When the men had fully established the dogma of the Heritors, they took to killing or banishing the females who first shared the techniques of reception. After hundreds of millennia, females were again accepted back into the fold, but they were always approached as lesser Heritors than the males, in part to obscure the female's natural, heredity talent for the process.

~

Myco slouched, huddled in the dingy corner of her tiny quarters. Smaller than a standard monk's quarters, the space felt more like a cell than the modest living space she was naturally accustomed to. She slouched with the weight of all the years of her species. Each millennia a millstone, anchored with barbs, firmly beneath her thin flesh.

With the raging chorus of every female Rachis before her, sounding endlessly through the base of her spine, she attempted to pick apart the situation piece by rotting piece. In her heart a torrent of nameless, sordid emotions. They were the emotions of a creature incalculably lost to her amongst the starry noise of the universe and she was stuck with them. She had no way to categorize them, no experience close enough to compare them to. Confusion reigned.

There were a hundred other questions that fought for attention throughout all of this; why had Dematiaceous let her leave so easily? There were pronounced punishments and methods of censure amongst the Rachis. She could have been forcibly fruited and made to reconnect with one of the lesser mycelia mats. She could have been isolated deep underground and forced to live without any hope of ever again receiving. Instead, she was sent back to her ship. Surely Dematiaceous was aware enough to know how turmoil would overcome Myco. She had precipitated the death of Lanose.

Myco had no way of knowing the destination of the vessel. She was under guard and trapped, as far as she could tell. Though she was alive and reception was still a possibility.

She wagered that Dematiaceous had allowed her to leave as an act of modest appreciation for removing the last remaining obstacle he faced in succession. Or perhaps, he knew it was a greater punishment to allow her to find madness, isolated amongst the stars on some yet unnamed world. Little of this made any sense to her. The only thought she could truly make sense of was the reoccurring image of her Transmitter's hands.

Was Uliam on board? How fast was the ship moving? The questions piled on her forcing her silent cell to feel smaller and smaller, darker and darker. Reception was her only possible escape and even that was temporary and not guaranteed to work. She fought the urge though. Myco could not say why, but it simply did not feel right, not until she had sorted things out. Reception bound by a busy mind was fruitless anyway.

After several more days, Myco began to notice a familiar vibration, through the floor of her cell. She had spent six months, on her way to the Ellern, traveling at near light speed. During those six months, she became quite accustomed to the natural rhythmics of the vessel at high velocities. The rhythm hit her like the smell of home. Myco flattened her body to the floor, closed her eyes and drifted with the pulse of the vessel. Comfort came in knowing that the ship was moving and she was getting further and further from Dematiaceous.

Suddenly, as if on queue, she remembered the small gift she had taken from the mycelia mat beneath Lanose's freshly fruited body. The small satchel she kept was still with her, folded into the crevice behind a branch of the ship's hyphae, towards the back of her cell. The guards had not attempted to relieve her of any of her possessions, but she had tucked it away upon entering the cell, for fear that it may be taken from her later. Inside the satchel, she found its only contents, wrapped in silk, the tiny mushroom – a parting gift.

Small but potent with presence, she held it in her palms as she would hold a dying bird. She stood and pressed her ear against the door. No one had come for her in days. Still, she wanted no interruptions. The last thing she wanted was to have to speak to a guard or hear the eventual outcome of her faith moments after ingesting the mushroom. She heard nothing but the warm vibration of the ship.

On the floor again, she crossed her legs into her well worn, meditative position, held the mushroom to her forehead, bowed slightly in reverence and placed it on her tongue. It's meat was firm and dry, but as her fluids mixed with it, it soon began to dissolve and quicken the ever-familiar flavor of her own kind, throughout her mouth.

Only a few minutes after swallowing the mushroom, she felt it take hold, tingling at the base of her spine until she was rapidly and uncontrollably torn into an extraordinarily powerful corner of the psychedelic over-world. Much more tangible than reception, much less antiseptic than a guided reprisal of a previous reception, this was real – first hand.

Throughout her entire body, from the tips of her toe stub to the ends of her white hair, she felt the mother presence of the probes. The walls were no more. She was on the far side of a light that felt as familiar as breathing but that she could have never fully identified before this moment. There was something there – someone. A clear, yet faceless presence surrounded her. She felt she could ask it questions. The intensity of the experience grew until she was overcome completely and submitted herself to it fully – allowing the most innate portion of herself to speak on her behalf.

Had she been able to step back and glance at her body from the outside, she would see that she was now writhing in dueling fits of laughter, joy and extreme sadness all at once. She was both desperately tearful and howling with delight simultaneously.

Within her experience, she stood, empowered, terrified but dignified in the light of something far more powerful than she. The light coaxed the words from her tongue. *Have I done wrong?* The answer came instantly, picoseconds, smashing into her with the weight of worlds. No! It was, on the surface, a singular and simple message, but the emotional toll it carried was immeasurable. The mil-stones fell from her back, freeing her even more.

Myco pushed upward, towards the light and instead found that she was falling away, towards a seaside blue hole – blue at the surface, but fading into blackness as it found its full depth. She could breath, lucid but clearly trapped beneath the surface she looked into the inky depths and bound towards them, away from the light, but still guided by the obvious presence, never alone.

Blacker and blacker, she sank, the presence growing stronger with every meter of depth. Finally, she could see the same light, hovering at the bottom of this abyss, undulating with the water surrounding it. Beneath the light lay the fragile body of a human male, curled and laying unconscious on its side. She glided towards it until she was there, at the bottom of everything with him. She soon found that she and he were no longer at the bottom of a great blackness, but instead were lying on a dirt floor, well tended and warm.

Myco ran her fingers through his thick, sandy hair. Her fingers approached him with a familiarity that surprised her. It was as if she had known this man a thousand years. He slept, under the gentle weight of her hands, unaware, unfettered. Peace ran like honey across his face. She took his hands and was not the least surprised to recognize them. She picked up his right palm and kissed it. He did not stir.

Realizing she was outdoors, she peeked her head up and scanned the horizon, just in time to see a faint lamplight wagging across the smooth, grassy, night terrain. As the lamp approached she could see the outline of a cloaked man, shadowed almost intentionally behind the glare of the lamp. Standing to meet him, she realized she was meeting a friend. She felt no fear. At her feet, the human man still slept.

When the glow was nearly in her face, she could see that the lamplight held the same light that had followed her through the blackness. Holding now, the cloaked man removed his headdress and revealed himself. It was Lanose, though he had taken a distinctly human form, old and ragged, but akin to the man lying beside the fire.

Lanose appeared to her – white hair, plump and red nosed, but still very much Lanose. His smile gave himself away. With a gentle hand on her shoulder, he began to speak, softly as if attempting not to wake the sleeping man.

"Fairly good looking, wouldn't you say?" Lanose smiled stroking his face.

Myco looked to the man on the ground then back to Lanose. "I suppose so."

Lanose smiled again. "No, silly little one, I'm talking about me!" His laugh carried his words. "I never thought I would find myself in an ape's body, though I suppose I should have expected it coming from your mind." Myco could not help but fall into his arms. Lanose did his best to ease her. "There there little one. Buck up. There's quite a lot ahead of you child. If you let all of this shake you up, you'll never stand a chance out there."

Myco lifted her head and straightened her body. Every syllable seemed to wash more and more confusion away. She rubbed a small tear from Lanose's face, and then asked.

"Lanose? What have I gotten myself into?"

Lanose replied. "It's a good question little one. Frankly, it would spoil it if I gave it all away. But rest assured, I've seen where all this is going. You could see it too if you would allow yourself."

"What do you mean?" Myco was steady and intent.

"Myco dear, do not ever let yourself think that you have been chosen for this. There was never going to be a 'chosen one' so to speak. Just remember that what is happening and what will happen henceforth is what was always intended in one way or another. Of course...the manner of it's happening may not have been precisely planned, but what is? It could be much worse."

"But Lanose. I don't understand what's happening." Myco was calmed by the admission.

"Little one, this is it. This..." Lanose pointed to the sleeping man. "This is the next step for us. And it's going to be one damned hard step."

Myco looked to the man, then back to Lanose. "Contact?"

"What else?" Lanose pulled Myco into his arms and embraced her. "And whom better? Do you really think Dematiaceous should be the sole ambassador of the Rachis? I can think of happier nightmares."

Lanose pushed Myco back far enough to reach her chest. He then pushed his ethereal finger into her breast, towards Myco's beating heart and stirred his message directly into her muscle. "Do you feel that Myco? That is love. You have always carried it with you. Most of us Rachis are immune to it, or at least pretend to be immune to it. You embrace it and you do not even realize it."

Lanose looked back to the sleeping man. "I know these creatures. They have as many weaknesses as we, but they understand love and they use it...at least, they used to. I fear many of them are now as cold as the Rachis pretend to be. But I ask you again; do you really think a man like Dematiaceous harbors this emotion the way in which you do? I pale to think what he would do in the presence of a good man. You keep your wits about you. Dematiaceous isn't through with you by a long shot. He doesn't like the light the way you and I do. He knows spaces in this unhinged realm you and I would never think to cast our minds upon."

"You have to admit, you left at an awkward moment." Myco raised another smile from Lanose.

"I couldn't help it little one. I'm bound to make way for more powerful Heritors than I. And here you are." Lanose took a deep breath and passed Myco's attention to the fading of his lamplight. "You must go now little one. But go! Follow the blind mole down the hole and see where it leads you. Let love be your guide – the love of all things."

Her eyes left Lanose for just a moment as she gazed again at the sleeping man, but when she turned back, Lanose was gone and just as suddenly so was the man. She opened her eyes and found herself in her tiny cell, but inside of her was an unmistakable determination she had lacked all along. Confident and resolute, she stood and approached the door to her cell. Not once since being placed in these quarters had she attempted to open the door. Without a thought, she pushed the door open and it gave way with little effort. For a moment she felt a sudden oneness with the entire vessel.

A young guard, stationed in the corridor, took immediate note of her, but fell mute and still with a guileless look from her eyes. She commanded his attention, bending his will, as she did with every guard and passenger all the way to the central flight deck. Doors otherwise barred opened to her will. The same mycelium that ran through her body and her home world and her peers also ran through the ship. All knew by pheromone alone that Myco had assumed command and that this was now her ship.

16

A lik lay, stretched completely flat, imagining he was a landscape - looking down the length of his body, imagining
the folds and wrinkles of his shirt and pants were great mountains – ranges of shuddering height. He imagined himself
miniscule, walking across this land, straddling the fibrous pits
between the threads of the woven plain. How would he cross
the abyssal crevasses that folded and dipped below the line of
his breasts? If he were a millimeter tall, how many months,
how many years would it take to reach the summit of his big
toe?

The couch held him without judgment or fatigue. He
preferred the room dimly lit, but not completely dark – with
the brightest light emanating from the lowest portion of the
room, within the nooks and crannies. He imagined himself

standing on the plain, begging the sun to rise, to light his path. Four more days, he thought, and I'll be in a position to choose the right or left leg. He looked down the length of each. If he chose the right, he risked the possibility of losing his grip and falling down the slope of the thigh, a hundred or more relative meters to the carpet below, lost forever in an inescapable, fibrous jungle. If he chose the left leg, his route was fraught with just as much peril, except his death could lay within the torrent of leathery folds, between couch and cushion.

He lost a tear imagining himself lost in the rug or trapped in the sofa – forever boxed in by what had been the mundane – lost in a macro world – and alien in a world that once made so much sense. He imagined wading through the groves of red fibers that occasionally opened into thickets of white fibers. He looked down at the arabesque design on the rug below and imagined being lost for years in the frightening swirls along the fringes, never sure which direction led to the edge.

Alik rubbed his eyes. His brain felt like a slough and he was amazed that it had brought him this far. As he saw it, his brain was little more than sinew, stitched together by the neurosis of his forbearers then set adrift on a stumpy meat platform. How had the damn thing kept him alive this long? What was it going to do to Alik's meat next?

He couldn't help but laugh at himself. He was in the lap of sublime convenience. If the ship did lose its mind, barreling itself into the core of some radiation-puking stellar mass, he would never know the difference. He would simply continue to laze on the couch until the atoms of his body flung themselves to the far corners of the universe, dispersed by random magnetic belches and the heave and hoe of matter, space and time.

Then there was Ruby. He could not shake the image of her unabashedly nude body. He could still feel the embrace of her brave breast as she plucked him from the water, his head nestled as a child against it. He did not only feel romantic impulses, he was also swayed with a sense of duty. He was no longer just the task-less Usher of an impossible vessel, carrying an ambiguous cargo and a absentee computer mind, instead, he was ushering a woman and her life's work. He was ushering a cargo meant for brave human settlers and explorers, as well as traders and profiteers, most of who were still unborn. He could not help but feel irked by the notion that had this been explained from the beginning, he would have approached his situation with a more enlightened sense of duty. Then of course, the competition of self-deprecation ruled his mind, insisting that he should have approached this with a more enlightened sense of duty despite his ignorance of the mission's importance. He was given the simple task of being a warm body and he was able to do that quite well.

At no prior point did Alik deny the value of the opportunity he'd been provided. It was the nonsensical lunacy of the process that seemed irreverent and cold to him. Of course, there was nothing he, personally, could do to further ensure the mission's success.

These mental rows – brow beating himself over things he literally had no control over – they seemed to be fertilizing nihilistic tendencies as he wallowed and wept and dreamt of being a miniaturized explorer amongst the otherwise mundane. It was not true nihilism, since his concerns still centered on the long-term merit of his actions or the knowledge that another person depended on his good will. Instead, he let his physical appearance degrade. His hair grew longer, scruffy and untended. His beard, which had always been carefully managed, now wiry – itched and knotted and begged for soap. He was greasy and the sloughed bits of hair and dander readily made their way into the food he ate. When he ate, he ate out of compulsion instead of hunger. His den was laid waste in empty containers, unwashed dishes and the wrappers of prepared foods.

And he slept, sometimes ten hours a day, spending the remaining ten watching news broadcasts he now understood not to be news at all. Sometimes, he culled through video archives, music archives, watching or listening to something for twenty minutes at a time, then alternating to something new, overwhelmed at the selection available.

He saw films from the last ten centuries and had a difficult time rendering fact and history, from fiction and fantasy, delicately assimilating all he saw into his understanding of human chronicle and the progress made by his species. Alik considered the reactions his friends and family would have had to the films of the twentieth and twenty-first century. His were a people attuned to art, attuned to the creative process and he knew these films were of a lost virtuosity. These films were akin to petroglyphs or cave paintings or stone architecture. He studied the characters, their struggles and wondered more and more about the novelty of his situation. He wondered where his struggle was. He had no enemies in the sense that these films portrayed enemies. He did not fear a government or a corporation; no one hunted for his flesh or threatened his life. His struggle lay somewhere else. His struggle lay in the smarmy brain sinew cast amongst his skull and the natural world that produced his brain's alter of meat.

His thoughts turned over and over to the Timelock. He watched the seconds pass on a clock across the room and tried to imagine the growth of grasslands, the changing of seasons, the rain and wind and rocks, years passing with the days. Every time he shut his eyes and drifted into sleep, the seasons were cycling within the Timelock.

Alik wondered what effect his malaise was having on Sigrah, the Empathy Key still firmly in place. Had Sigrah blocked out Alik completely? Some mornings, Alik woke

within his dreams, ultra present in the moment, with the feeling that he was being joined at any moment for coffee. In this
mind space, he felt encouraged and excited to convene with
whomever was on their way, certain that they would arrive
at any moment, ready to share coffee and a long, familiar
conversation. The dream wore on until Alik felt the tug of
his musculature, tightening under the weight of REM sleep
and he would then realize the nature of his situation. He
was dreaming and no one was coming and the urgency and
encouragement were coming directly from his bladder. And
still, every occasion he'd had this dream, he was left with the
same haunting presence, a feeling that someone was nearby or
on his or her way. He assumed this was the glimmer of Sigrah
that bled back through the Key to his mind. He wondered
whether the less lucid dreams of his nights were shared with
Sigrah and he was simply left with no memory of the events.

   This entire introspective period, as Alik saw it, had to
come to an end. Groveling to the universe and wallowing
in deep pools of self-pity or damned naval gazing did him
no good. So after several weeks of this, he finally unglued
himself from the couch, marched into the bathroom and gave
himself a long hot shower. He trimmed the excess bush from
his face, brushed his teeth till his gums bled and assembled
himself in a fresh jumpsuit, one he had not worn previously.
He picked up the scattered items from his room, the food
parcels, glasses and plates, wrappers and dirty clothing. He
stripped the sheets from his bed and placed them into the
laundry drop.

   The space instantly seemed larger to Alik. Clean and
dressed, he considered the freedom he now had, the long
walks he was free to take. As he saw it, he had a little less
than three years left of exploration at his feet and a ship big
enough to oblige. He was well insulated from anything dangerous. The harsh, radioactive, galactic winds were of no

consequence. He thought he should consider himself lucky, not only to be free to roam, but also to be free of the harsh realities beyond Sigrah's outer scales. To be a ship, he thought, must be intolerable at times.

A thought occurred to Alik, which until now had only slightly breached the surface at other moments of reflection, the reminder of Sigrah as an individual. The thought of having shared empathetic visions with this individual having never considered the possibility of reversing roles tore at him a bit. Whether existentially or practically he had always demanded of Sigrah. Expecting something from Sigrah had always made sense to Alik. He of course was a human, fragile and in constant need of this or that and that alone seemed to trump any potential obligation for the needs of Sigrah, both as a sentient mind and a sentient vessel. During his shower, Alik pondered the implications of being an entity, which was fully aware of its origins. Sigrah, unlike anything or anyone Alik had ever known, was fully aware of how he came to be.

Sigrah knew he had been constructed, that he was an artifact. Sigrah's exterior had been designed, forged and fashioned by a great number of individual hands and minds. His central core, his brain, wherever it may exist, must have also been designed and articulated to the finest degree. His surge of consciousness came from the combined knowledge of tens perhaps hundreds of individuals and individual computer minds, each reassembled and stitched together into something new. It must be clear to Sigrah, in light of the realities of his creation, that the mysterious origins humans contend with is the single, exacting motivator that propels us through the galaxy, that encourages us to build creatures such as Sigrah. To understand creation and to practice it, in its many forms, is the manner in which we explore our own nature. Alik had come to this conclusion in other way during his youth, so he thought; surely Sigrah recognizes this as well – we create so that we may have a better understanding of how we were created. The disconnect between the two must then have come in Alik's prior unwillingness to truly empathize with Sigrah as an individual – to see beyond the artifice.

Alik dragged his dishware into the kitchen and placed them gently into the rinser. He decided to make himself something fresh, something green. He reached into the refrigerator and pulled two fresh apples, a bag of spinach and some peppers from the shelf. He then saw a vacuum-sealed pouch of dried mushrooms perfect for his salad. At first he paid little attention to the mushrooms, mixing his greens and cutting the apples into small, bite-sized chunks. Slicing his knife across the sealed pouch, he listened as the air rushed in and the bag expanded. He dumped the mushrooms on the cutting board, but to his surprise on closer examination, these were not dried Shitakes at all. These were akin to the Kinoko he'd lost in the Timelock. Of course they were fresh and much healthier than those he'd brought aboard, but they were certainly the same species.

It was not a surprise to Alik that he was being fed from the products of the Timelock, in fact it made perfect sense, but for these to be so specifically chosen for him and placed amongst normal dietary items was a bit alarming. He tried to write it off as a serendipitous by-product of the farming and harvesting algorithms. Then again, he no longer believed in serendipity, not in a world so absolutely designed. No matter the intention, be it accidental or by design, he simply slid the Kinoko back into the pouch, rolled it up the best he could and placed them into his pocket.

Eating his salad, he considered raising Sigrah's attention, breaking the silence and addressing him directly, but none of his conversations seemed the least bit productive and as he saw it, Alik truly had nothing to say. He felt as though it were now his duty to build an arsenal of facts, experiential or otherwise, to bring to the table. Whatever Sigrah devoted his attention to, had to be much more interesting than Alik, or so he thought. Alik then had to give Sigrah a reason to be interested. He concluded that if finding these mushrooms was in fact by design, perhaps it was Sigrah's intention to coax Alik into further experimentation with the Empathy Key – that perhaps Alik's thoughts alone were not all that enlightening. As he saw it, how else could an artificial mind have an intentionally psychedelic experience? It was a fact that after the first use, Sigrah allowed Alik access to the Timelock.

The feeling of being manipulated did not escape Alik. Yet his insistent nature of effortlessly swimming with the natural current of life instead of against it, led him to simply accept and live in awareness of this manipulation, not to fight it. If Sigrah had a destination in mind, then by the nature of my mission, Alik thought, it is my duty to pursue that destination. It was odd and uncomfortable reasoning, even by Alik's standards, but it was the only way to decode the strangeness of this place and his role in it.

After eating, he returned to his room and began to set out items onto his freshly made bed. He folded two clean shirts, an extra pair of trousers, a tiny device he'd found in his entertainment locker which he had recently discovered to be a tiny repository for Sigrah's musical catalogue. He folded a blanket and removed an all weather tarp he'd packed in his locker and folded it along with the blanket. He found hidden, a substantial pair of boots along with several pairs of thick socks packed neatly into a locker below his closet. He found a sealable canister in the kitchen, which was perfect for carrying water. Alik filled his haversack with the various items, tied his bedroll and tarp to the top of the haversack and looked about for anything else he might decide was useful.

In a storage closet near the atrium, he recovered a very small, but very powerful flashlight as well as a handful of gas matches stored in his kitchen cupboard. The match was housed in a steel canister and sparked fire with the flick of the thumb. He also found a neatly packaged slicker coat, which appeared to be dry and warm. His father's pipe and his leather pouch stuffed with Buffer herb also went into the pack.

After sealing his pack, he stared at it gleefully and considered many of his long treks through the Buffer. He also considered, as he did in the Buffer, the life of proto man, naked and alone in the natural world. The world in which they existed must have been terrifying, filled with the unnamable, strewn with the unknown. Here in a spaceship flung haphazardly into the stars, Alik faced the exploration of an artificial world, but he was comforted not only by the obvious boundaries of the landscape, but also the ease with which he was able to gather useful supplies for an outing. Had he been one of the early men, he would have set out nearly naked, to hunt and forage, making tools along the way, discovering fire and drinking from the streams, traveling light. In this case, he may as well have been exploring an urban mall, but this did not shake Alik's resolve.

Before setting back to the Timelock, he returned to the atrium, to Sigrah's central interface to pay a passing tribute. He could talk to Sigrah anywhere, but he felt that speaking to him from this place held more gravitas. When he approached the interface, he noticed that the Empathy Key was still engaged.

"Sigrah. I'm going back in. If you need anything from me, you'll know where to find me." He wasn't sure if the Empathy Key was working, but he felt assured that if it were, Sigrah understood his position and if in fact Sigrah had any reservations or objections, he would make them known.

Alik slung his bag across his back and ran quickly into the deeper chambers of the vessel, back to the Timelock.

17

Alik was struck by the extent to which things were no-ticeably different. It was heavy winter and a thick layer of ice hung on all the low lying bushes and the tops of trees Alik could see from the eave of the hatch. Dried, un-kept brambles and vines stretched across the path at the base of the hillside. He was discomforted by the silence, which covered him like an itchy blanket. Even packing as thoughtfully as he had, he did not expect to find the land frozen. He also had a thought creep up on him. It was his twenty-second birthday and never before had he had a birthday in the midst of dead winter.

This would not do, he thought. He decided to try a slightly tedious experiment. He would climb back into the chamber and simply cycle out and back in, waiting an hour or so outside the Timelock before reentering.

As tedious as it was, he followed through, suiting up, standing as the chamber filled and then emptied again, watching the time begin dialing faster and faster through his helmet display.

Alik waited, sitting on the floor of the chamber, still suited up. He was unsure what the exact ratio of time was required. He knew enough to know that it all depended on exactly how fast the ship was traveling, what sort of space it was traveling through and any other number of variables. An hour could be a hundred days in the Timelock or maybe even a whole year. He no longer placed his faith in constants. He decided the only way to get a better understanding was to try it out. Wait an hour and dip back in, see what's changed.

When he emerged the second time, it was still quite cold, but the snow at least had melted. The sun, because he had no better name for it, was quite warm and left him comfortable wearing only thin sleeves. It felt like the welcoming cusp of spring. The ground was damp and squishy, some of it still crunched with the sound of thin melting ice just below the surface.

He cut through the brown, wandering vines in front of the path, and walked to the point where the path crested before shooting down into the near, fallow farm lands. From the crest, he saw the entirety of the deep, rolling valley before him. It lay in a heavy mist and still appeared brown and inert. The mist faded as the valley rose higher into the thick forests he could not see beyond. It was in those forests he'd found Ruby. Alik had never been on the far side of the forest, but he had glanced out from the edge of it, with Ruby. He recalled the first time he'd entered the Timelock and saw the valley below him swelling with spring life. He'd first assumed that valley and forest beyond was the totality of the place. He gauged the horizon to be as many as thirty kilometers from the crest on which he stood. It had taken almost a week to cross into the forest last time.

Alik discerned the outline of a series of utility buildings at one of the far ends of the valley. He must have walked right past them the first time, distracted by the audacity of the biosphere, or else they were newly constructed. From there, the valley climbed smoothly, gaining altitude along the edge of the forest. He decided he would hike there, to the buildings and camp. Then he'd follow the edge of the forest for as many days as he could, until he reached its furthest perimeter. He considered walking around the edge of the entire sphere. Doing so would have given him an accurate idea of its size. However, the edges seemed to be littered with massive boulders and outcroppings, which naturally deterred any interest in circumnavigation. He also assumed that at some point he would have to contend with a large body of water. Ruby had mentioned several considerable seas.

~

After the weeks on the couch, he felt the toll of walking once again. He'd come unhinged in the best way, lubricated by the freedom of this superficially natural place. He did not think about the Empathy Key node, which still rested firmly beneath his hairline. Even the odd, unconscious scratch of an itch did not disturb it.

As he walked he'd begun plucking the small caps from some of the Kinoko, in his pocket, popping them like candy into his mouth after stuffing the stems between his cheek and gum as he crossed the cold fields. He walked steadily, but he walked as though there was a piece of his soul dredging the ground in front and behind him. He felt rooted in the land and wept just a bit at the thought of the life pulsing just below the surface, ready to burst into the warm, lingering day.

He pretended his hands held the power to wake the soil and as he walked along, he allowed his hands to hover at waist height, as he sent his positive intention into the soil. The thought occurred to him from time to time that the effects of the Kinoko had fully bloomed. He did not let this feeling stop him from eating more.

In another hour, on what he had determined to be the southern side of a hill, he found a patch of fresh green leaves, budding grass at the sunny top of the warm knoll. He stopped there and laid flat, his arms and legs stretched as far from his body as possible. He tried closing his eyes as the swirling visual effects of the Kinoko overwhelmed him. Instead of spending this peak befuddling his eyes, he spent the time listening, trying to feel the movement of the vessel through the firm earth. The soft sweeps of cold wind pulled around the knoll avoiding him entirely. He swore to himself that he could feel the distant humming of the vessel's systems. He swore he could feel Sigrah's pulse and he tied his emotions into the moment, streaming them directly through the Empathy Key. Alik tried to imagine the incredible gravitational forces at work, keeping this realm stuck in the timescape of reasonable velocities. Longing for the ritual drumming of his people, he pulled the tiny music library from his bag and stuffed two small speaker nodes into his ears. He made no specific selection, allowing the library or Sigrah or chance to determine what he heard. This inclination proved fruitful.

These trips – these mental voyages, sometimes had the tendency to awaken thoughts Alik otherwise avoided. Sometimes, he considered his mother and a dark feeling crept in. To swat these feelings away, he had to sit up, open his eyes and breath in the landscape, the Kinoko shivering through his flesh. He took his time, the rest of the afternoon, skipping along, examining things that caught his attention and casually making his way to the utility buildings he'd seen from the crest.

During mid-afternoon, he stopped near an area actively being prepared for cultivation. Small bots crept along the ground, slowly examining the soil. Alik, in an effort to commiserate with their tedious task, took to his knees, side by side with the bots and crawled along through the soil – picking out clods of soil and breaking them between his fingers. He found worms and carefully picked them out, showed them to the bots that then promptly and carefully took the worms from Alik and placed them again, gently into the soil.

By the time he'd tired of this, he found the Kinoko wearing off, but could see the utility buildings near by. He walked to them casually, pitched an appealing little camp beneath the eve of one of the buildings and took to eating more Kinoko. He collected bits of fallen debris, twigs, branches, even the dried out trunk of a fallen tree. He piled them high and lit them, warming the area quickly.

While the fire raged hotter and the night grew longer, he danced in the fire light to silent drums. He yelled towards the bright moon disc and called out to Sigrah. "Can you feel this? Can you feel this now?" Alik swore the moon disc brightened in response and the drums in his ears, silent to everything but him drew louder and louder. Staring into the fire, he saw faces, clear lines and detailed features of creatures he could not recognize. They were not demons, they did not seem frightful or harmful, but they were as real as anything he'd ever seen. The faces flamed out and reappeared in other areas of the fire.

Alik removed his clothes, dancing naked and cheering louder and louder, his breath crystalizing and condensing in the chilled spring night. Until, with enough suddenness to send Alik falling backward onto his bare ass, the fire blew upward and then down again into a tiny flame. This was accompanied by a booming thrust of air. Alik thought for a moment that there had been an explosion, but as he sat up, he noticed the fire, now a tiny flame amongst the glowing coals – casting only enough light to define a figure behind a shadow in the darkness. The shape which continued cycling from fire to figure seemed intent on propelling a message. Words rang in his head; don't give in to amazement. Don't give in to amazement.

Realizing that he was already overcome with wild emotion, fatigue and bewilderment, Alik filled his lungs and tried to slow his panting and focus on the words. As he exhaled he noticed that he was no longer standing near the fire. He was surrounded by darkness. He looked at his hands and they were now the hands of a stranger, four fingered, tanned almost orange or red. He felt taller. Around him, others sat, meditating. This was some sort of temple, surrounded by strange flowers and penetratingly warm breezes. He tried to signal the beings around him, but they did not see or feel him.

They were slim and straight, their heads, human like, but hairless apart from thick strands of clumpy mycelia that gathered around the areas, which should have been their ears - their skin dimpled with intricate patterns. In an instant the scene dissolved and Alik was left standing in a dark hall, surrounded by massive fruiting mushrooms. Then the he was tossed again, the surroundings fell away and he found himself soaring above what appeared to be a primordial world, covered in a thick white mat, the landscape broken only by forest sized blooms of intensely colorful fungi. Then, he felt his feet weighted down, seized and unable to move. His hands and arms were free, but were stiff with the feeling of prolonged motionlessness. He was obviously seated, but his lap was covered in a thick mat, similar to the mat covering the planet he had just seen from above.

Then, he felt the pull of something tugging at the back of his mind. He walked into the feeling like walking into a room and found himself back in his own body, sitting still in front of his raging fire. Quiet. Unquestioning. Sincere.

~

He woke the next morning in the grass, a thick fog behind his eyes and in front of them. Setting himself upright, he decided coffee was in order. He had slept only a few feet from his modest camp and his pack. He reached over and dug out his coffee materials, a small self-heating thermal mug and beans he'd ground before leaving. As it brewed he fantasized about finding a coffee plantation within the Timelock.

Nothing ached, remarkably, but his walk amongst his camp was unsteady and he found it easier to jiggle himself from one place to another as ungracefully as possible. His memories were growing more vivid the closer his coffee came to boil, but made little sense. He didn't want to write the experience off as a mere hallucination. He was taught greater respect for the Kinoko than to ignore the lessons they could impart. Alik considered that it might have been a result of improper use, dare he say the word abuse. But that too seemed inconsiderate.

Alik remembered a conversation he'd had with his father, years before Alik had experienced the Kinoko first hand. His father told him that the Kinoko were aware of themselves. "There's something in there." His father insisted. The Kinoko were self aware, they knew that they existed and they knew that man existed. To Alik, this seemed like the stoner ramblings of an old man, drunk on his over sharpened awareness of the invisible world surrounding him.

He sipped his coffee, which had cooled enough to drink. Images of the worlds he stood in, flashed through his mind; vast worlds, rich with life and strangeness, atmospheres thick with gases, unique creatures, painted in complex patterns and deep in thought along with massive blooming fungi the size of buildings.

Alik finally decided to draw no conclusions until he was able to fully mull over the details. What conclusions could he draw? He slugged his coffee and prepared to break camp. Standing up and shaking the sleep from his legs, he noticed an old forgotten friend seeping into his soul, the intense peace of being at home. Perhaps it was the smell of the coffee mixed with the warming morning dew or the promise of a spring bloom riding on the air. Then as he stood, he looked about and saw that his camp lay surrounded by a thick ring of fruiting Kinoko. He laughed a mad laugh, picked several handfuls and placed them in with his others, bowing in reverence to those he left unmolested in the soil.

~

Alik kept a steady pace, close to the edge of the forest. The first part of his day was mostly up hill. He wasn't making significant gains in altitude. The forest tended to dip into and out of steep gullies as it climbed its way out of the valley. Short spurts down hill resulted in long, difficult assents on muddy slopes. The forest landscape was quite different than the last time he had come through it. Rains and snows, heat waves and droughts had laid claim to the land and altered it accordingly. Even the stream, which had fed the falls, where he'd met Ruby, seemed to have diverted its course and disappeared entirely.

He was surprised when by mid-day, he found himself wandering through a wide, open flat space littered with boulders. He felt as though he was on a plateau, but he was not close enough to any perceivable edge to make any clear distinction. Near by, he could see a wide river cutting into the landscape. He decided this was the point all the forest streams met. Alik tasted his lips and detected the faint taste of salt, carried in the wind. He walked further, following the river for dozens of kilometers as it ran towards the wind.

Several days later, the air was truly warm and a comfortable sweat broke on Alik's brow after only minutes of walking. The river was definitely running down hill, meandering through a wide tropical bog, then across temperate grassland. Several times he had to climb down giant rocks on either side of massive waterfalls. There were no trees, but instead wide thickets of mossy shrubs. The rocks themselves were covered in either thick green moss or clumsy, green mucus. Alik blamed the rock slime for several hard falls and a bruised knee. The thought of twisting an ankle or dislocating a knee sharpened his caution, but did not deter his progress.

Soon, he came down a final set of falls and into a wide, shallow mosquito bog, bisected by the river, several hundred yards from a rocky beach and what appeared to be a wide sea. From the bog, he could see the rising smoke of a campfire. The river fed into a channel and into the sea. By the time he'd crossed the bog and made his way onto the rocky beach, he was covered in mud, nearly up to his chin. Ruby sat next to a fire, smiling; having watched him wade through the muck over the final hundred yards.

"There's a nice stone path just a few feet down from where you landed in the bog." Ruby smiled.

Alik brushed the large clods of black sediment from his shirt. "Thanks a lot." He threw his bag next to her fire.

"Mind if I camp here?"

"Suit yourself. I'm not the one ushering the ship." The two laughed. Both seemed genuinely pleased to see the other. Ruby still wielded sarcasm and deprecation, but she did so with the lightest touch. It was the only sort of flirtation her dulled skills could produce in the circumstances.

She was a fantastic cook and had been preparing a meal

long before Alik blundered in. Ruby dished him out several spoons full of thick chowder. "Fresh clams." She said.

Alik shrugged, having never had clams before. "You're not cold?" He asked timidly. He shivered under his thin jacket. The air that followed the river was warm, but the sea was cold and the meeting of the two produced a cold mist that was quickly blown against the seaside by the frigid sea air.

Until that moment, Alik hadn't given his comfort much thought. He was focused on finishing his walk – on finding the sea – on finding Ruby. Once the warm chowder settled into this belly, he felt his fingers numbing and the sharpness of the sea breeze cut through his damp shirt. He fished his rain shell from his pack and shoved his arms through it. Both he and Ruby huddled closer to the fire. Alik put his chowder down for a moment to unravel his tarp. He tied it to a line on which Ruby had hung another tarp. Adding the second tarp broke the wind from the sea and both felt immediately warmer.

"This isn't the best campsite." Alik noted.

Ruby laughed. "No, but it sure is pretty. And this is the warmest it's been in months."

"How long have you been in here?"

"Too long. Almost two months. I like watching the end of winter. Plus it gets really boring outside, on the ship."

Alik stood for a moment, looking out towards the sea. "Keep an eye open Alik, you may see the friends I came to see." Ruby said.

Then, not far beyond the shoreline, he could see them cresting, massive creatures the likes of which Alik had never imagined. Smooth and gray, darker than the blue sea around them, they spouted tall columns of froth and mist. One breached entirely, launching upwards until half of his body stood tall before crashing back into the rolling waves. There appeared to be a wide mass of prawns, cutting up and boiling the surface waters ahead of the creatures. The creatures were feeding.

"They wanted to come along. They insisted. Being that they are an integral part of an ecosystem, we brought them. Only four of the original six are still alive, but their twelve children will carry on their mission." Ruby said proudly.

"What the hell is their mission?" Alik asked befuddled.

"No one knows what will be found deep into the galaxy. We've pushed far; we've found semi-habitable worlds. We just haven't pushed far enough. There could be creatures that identify more with the life we bring along than ourselves. The whales knew that." Ruby explained.

"You speak to these creatures?" Alik asked.

"No. I don't. But some have. Once we developed the basic syntax of their language, we understood them vaguely. They are very elaborate speakers. They speak in metaphors, mixed with the essential perceptions of a sea creature and the puzzling aphorisms of their history. Even after we understood the language, it took decades to understand their meaning and intent. Eventually, someone worked it out."

"Who?" Alik asked with intense curiosity.

"I'm not sure. But he was said to have encountered other creatures similar the whales, in his travels." Ruby was nonchalant.

"I thought you said we'd never encountered other sentient creatures in space." Alik questioned.

"Officially, we never have. But there are wanderers, people traveling alone on vessels, with a hibernating crew – lone pilots – Ushers like yourself, who have relayed stories of amazing encounters." Ruby sensed Alik's curiosity and threw it a bone.

"Encounters with what exactly?" Alik pushed.

"Ships, objects, feelings, sometimes actual creatures. I heard a story as a child from a pilot visiting our Saturnian

Lunar colony, on his way back out to deep space. He was gruff and obviously avoided people as much as he could. But on this occasion, it seemed he couldn't help but share his story with the station community. It was passed around like a bad cold and sometimes groups of us cornered him to hear it first hand again and again during his layover.

'He spoke of traveling closer to light speed than anyone had approached to that point. He'd spent many weeks arguing with his ship...haphazardly tinkering with parts he'd spent years deciphering on his own. He'd increased the velocity by .8% reaching a speed of nearly 99.6% the speed of light, common now days, but reckless then. You should note here the implied importance of some of the chosen Ushers. Without any necessary background, he figured out how to improve existing technology. Those kind of accidental innovations do not go unnoticed." Ruby strayed then corrected.

"But I digress."

She continued. "Apparently the shock to the ship and the computer caused a nearly fatal meltdown of the ship's neurological functions. The ship, lacking navigational control careened towards a group of binary stars, having almost instantly over shot its target destination. The ship slid between the stars breaking its velocity so abruptly several regions of the ship instantly lost molecular cohesion and decompressed, blowing massive holes out of the sides of the vessel.

'He was stranded in a wild orbit around the stars. His life support, though badly damaged was functional as he spent weeks attempting to re-boot the computer mind. According to him, on the fourth week, the ship's orbit led him near a small rocky body. It was too small to be a planet or a moon, meandering listlessly, but too big to be an asteroid. Nevertheless, as he passed within several thousand kilometers of the object, he observed several other objects launch from the surface and approach his vessel rapidly.

'Without any defenses and no idea how to handle the situation, he did his best to hide, stuffing his body in a storage locker. The way he explained it was that these creatures came aboard, tried to access the computer, which must have triggered a sort of fail-safe. The computer awoke and spoke to the creatures at length. The pilot could not understand the conversation and at some point attempted to leave the storage locker and address the boarding party himself.

'The moment he stepped out, he felt a sudden tingle in his head and fell to the floor, totally unconscious. When he awoke, the ship had been repaired and was back on track, as if nothing had happened. The ship had reversed course, back to the point before the speed had been altered. The computer appeared to have no memory of the incident - neither the pilot's tampering or the alien encounter."

Alik was captivated, squatting and leaning closer and closer to the fire. "But it really happened?"

"Who knows? Space travel, time dilation, these things can make folks go coo coo." Ruby brushed away the notion, if only to irk Alik and spike his curiosity further.

"It seems like the computer would know." Alik insisted.

"Well sure the computer knew. They know everything that happens. An elephant never forgets." Ruby smiled.

"A whataphant?" Alik laughed and relaxed a bit.

"An elephant. You've never heard that expression?" Ruby teased.

"Can't say that I have. Is it like 'cows don't mind long as you come from behind?'" Alik asked merrily.

Ruby squeezed out a half smile half frown and flopped a spoon full of chowder towards Alik. "No. Not like that at all." Alik wiped the food from his shoulder and stood again, watching for further signs of the whales.

"What about Sigrah? Do you think he knows?"

"SHE, is still very young. AI's have to prove themselves

just as people do. She has to bring something to the fold. She knows that humans are an integral part of her own exploration." Ruby explained.

"So HE has his own agenda?" Alik asked.

"In a way. I think it's more of a watchful eye. If she sees something that could be fruitful, she will examine it and see what comes of her examination. But she would do this only to the extent that it did not divert her primary mission."

"So he wouldn't stop and talk to little green men." Alik asked hopefully.

"It depends. She hasn't yet. Sigrah spends most of her time here, in the Timelock." Ruby was matter of fact.

"What does she do here?"

"A little bit of everything. Mostly she watches. She likes to watch trees grow, and rocks erode. Sometimes I've caught sight of little swimming bots that scoot and dive through the water here and there. I'm sure they perform maintenance from time to time and that was likely their intended purpose, but I think Sigrah uses them to play." Ruby drew a dreamy smile across her face.

Alik tried to add something thought provoking. "Playing is good. I don't think people do enough of it."

"People play, it's just a matter of luck to find yourself playing and working simultaneously." Ruby replied.

"Do feel like you've found that?"

"Absolutely. But, I'm sure that's one of the reasons they picked me for this job. My role specifically was designed and planned for almost one hundred years before my birth."

"How is that possible?" Alik pulled his wool blanket over the two of them.

Ruby explained. "Generalizations and talent profiles. That sort of thing… They weren't waiting for me specifically, but they knew who they would be looking for when the time came."

"I can't imagine what they were looking for when they picked me...frankly it disturbs me to think about it. What sort of criteria is required when picking an Usher?"

"I am not surprised. I haven't quite figured out your role in all of this, but I'm certain you were chosen just as we were. They've designed many paths and the longer I live, the less I believe in accidents." Ruby's words fell out like a puzzle, but they made more sense now than ever before.

Alik sighed and tried to soak in Ruby's words. "I always liked the idea of chance. Happy accidents."

"Believe me, chance is built into design." Ruby laughed.

"You afraid of losing your sense of free will?" She laughed a knowing laugh – experienced.

"Well, yeah." Alik admitted.

"Believe me when I tell you this, as much as this world is rigged and guided by unbending principles, those principles still hinge on the unpredictable. Like an Usher being allowed into a place like this. Highly unpredictable shit, man." Ruby laughed.

~

The faces and the confusion of his recent night's hallucinogenic experience still lingered in him. How did all of this fit together? The faces hung to him like a crush; a sense of intimate contact of warm understanding covered his cold skin. He wanted to explain all of this to Ruby, but he couldn't think of a way to broach the subject subtly. Then again, he felt like they had been dancing around it all evening. His belly was full and his mind frothed with questions.

"I think I thrive off of confusion." Alik looked to Ruby for an immediate response, but he attempted not to let on.

"Yeah? Well, I guess that's better than not thriving at all. And that's one attitude that may keep you from going nuts out here, believe it or not. And from my limited perspective, I'd say you thrive off of curiosity. Both are healthy, I'd say."

"That's the way I see it." Alik fumbled around with the ideas and searched for something to add. Then it occurred to him to make a full appraisal of everything certain. "So we're going to rendezvous with Andromeda station?"

"Exactly." Ruby replied eagerly.

"Where is that exactly?" Alik asked.

"Its at the tip of this galactic spiral arm, just at the edge of the space between the Milky Way and Andromeda." Ruby pointed toward a corresponding cluster of light that just happened to be passing overhead.

"Why would they place a station so far out? It seems like our entire galaxy is in the opposite direction."

"Andromeda station will be one of the spoke hubs…plus, that's where they are will start building the big ones." Ruby baited him.

"What big ones?" Alik wondered.

"The world ships." Ruby was quickly making a sport of goading Alik's curiosity.

"Ok. I'm all in. Lay it on me. What the hell are world ships?" Alik had unfolded his sleeping materials and laid on them near the fire, looking up at the busy sky.

"It's what much of this is for." She waved her hand in a wide circle above her head. "Think about this way." She settled into her blanket and took a long sip from a cup of hot cider warmed by the fire. "Colonies are hard. Even though we will always seek out habitable worlds for colonization or terraforming, there is a general understanding that in order to properly grow human civilization, we must put in place a series of graduated steps, each always building upon the step below." Ruby paused; checking to make certain Alik had not glazed over.

Alik quickly motioned for her to continue, waving his

hand, insisting on more.

Ruby continued. "If we intend on surviving for the long haul, it would serve us well to perfect our world building skills by building more and more complicated habitats such as this. If we treat our galaxy like a wheel with thirty-two spokes, with each spoke dotted with hubs, then we can begin to carve out true galactic infrastructure. The world ships are only a single piece of this process. Building planet sized ships, with complicated eco-systems growing with them – each becomes a moving world as well as an insured capsule for human life. With thirty-two or more world ships moving about the galaxy, avoiding trouble, assisting in various projects, spreading life, we can begin the exponential expansion of humans across the entirety of the Milky Way. We can learn to harvest all of the galaxy's energy…then who knows what."

Alik exhaled on Ruby's behalf. "Wow…that's a headful right there. I feel like we could spend a few months unpacking all of that." Alik paused. "Shit. It almost feels pointless to start asking questions.

Ruby laughed. "I know. I know." Ruby locked eyes with Alik, tracing his odd jaw, trying to get a better sense of his face through the heavy beard he kept. He kept a balaclava pulled tight around his thick mat of hair, keeping his ears completely out of sight. Ruby noticed Alik's natural sense of ruggedness. It had escaped her before, mostly because she had been too focused on the surprise of their first meeting. Now she saw how deeply relaxed he seemed even on a cold rocky beach. She appreciated his captive gaze and stoked his pipe for him, knowing that the buffer herb always fertilized interesting conversation.

"You mentioned Saturn earlier…is that where you grew up? On a station?" Alik asked. He felt a little ashamed that he had not been more personal in his line of questions, but truth be told, this was the first moment he'd felt comfortable enough to test the fences.

"Sort of." Ruby paused. "I was born in the Juba space scraper on the African continent. We lived at twenty thousand feet. I remember the landscape below. The Juba super structure was intensely contained, with massive buffers that stretched hundreds of miles in each direction. Juba space scraper had been built as a monument to the land around it. I never smelled the air of that place."

"You never left the tower?" Alik asked.

"Never. When I was seven we left for Saturn. My father had been selected to act as a colonial advisor. He trained potential colonialists and prepared them for the realities of new worlds. The Saturnian moons presented fantastic training grounds for all sorts of off world skills. Saturn is still one of the central hubs for anyone transiting the system." Ruby trailed off, unsure what topic to ramble towards next. She looked to Alik for prompting.

"How long were you there?" Alik asked quickly.

"Seven tends to be the magic number for me. When I was fourteen I left for London, to school, studied arcology design and biome engineering, then at twenty-one I was transferred to the Amazonian Buffer for training. Since then I've been somewhere new roughly every twelve months."

The two were silent for a moment. The false stars burned above them. "I suppose it's hard to make connections when you move around so often." Alik offered.

Ruby smiled. "You just have to make them quicker."

Their conversation slowed, as the two grew sleepier – bedded down close and warm. Without a word Ruby insisted on sleeping close to Alik. Both were clearly suffering from a lack of human contact, though neither made any initial sexual advances. Although neither addressed it out loud, both decided that there would be plenty of time for such activities, should the matter arise. For then, they were content to simply be present.

~

Alik dreamed that night of a swirling blue disc, bigger than anything he'd ever imagined. So big, in fact, that he could not see the discs' edges. He turned his back to the disc and he saw a milky sea of stars, each of which appeared to bow to the light of the halide disc behind him. In the light of the disc he saw three ships, each of varying size, one massive and unwieldy, one rocky – almost comet like and the third smooth and nimble, tiny in comparison to the other two.

In the dream he watched as the three ships fell towards one another in what seemed a beautifully choreographed dance. He could see the fingers of gravity stretching out from the blue disc guiding the three ships like marionettes on a stage. As the three came together, Alik, from whatever perch had been holding him aloft, fell suddenly – his feet dragged suddenly towards the swirling and burning gases of the blue disc. He fell and fell until he jolted and woke from the dream startled and drenched with sweat. It was morning and Ruby was already cooking.

"Have one of those falling dreams?" Ruby smiled. "I saw you bounce. They say you never actually hit the ground in the dream." Alik sat up and Ruby handed him a cup of coffee. "You mean your not going to disappear before I wake up again?" Alik was cheerful but nagging nonetheless.

"I thought about it, but I figured the least I could do was feed you again. I frankly think you make a better portly fellow than you do a rail."

The tide was very low, the breakers were now several hundred yards away and Ruby and Alik now appeared to be camped much further inland than they had the previous evening.

Alik sipped his coffee and paced around the camp stretching out his body and quietly eyeing for a subtle place to defecate. Ruby was still covered in a blanket, cooking biscuits in a covered skillet over the coals.

"So what's the time differential really like?" Alik sipped coffee and wiped his red, leaky nose.

"You mean between out there and in here?" Ruby asked over the sudden roar of the wind.

"Yeah, how much slower is time inside this thing? You weren't very clear before."

"It gets complicated quickly. It's hard to be clear about it because it's not really a constant. Time in here is relatively the same, day to day. A day is a day, a week is a week. It's the differential between time and here and time out there that can be drastically different from moment to moment."

"Shouldn't it be a constant?"

"No, the ship is rarely maintaining the same velocity. In fact, it fluctuates anywhere between 98.9% c. and as much as 99.9994 c."

"What's the longest you've stayed in here?" Alik asked.

"Well, I don't want to be an old lady when I finally arrive, so I try to spend short bursts only. Not to mention, it makes the trip significantly longer to spend too much time in here. It can be hazardous." Ruby answered thoughtfully.

"What brought you here this time?" Alik asked.

"Spring. The greenhouses are full right now. Things are to be transplanted and sewn, over the next few weeks. I want to oversee it. I do not get to oversea every spring, so I tend to monitor every ten or so, just to make certain everything is in proper working order or that the system hasn't gone off the rails and rearranged zones or planting schedules."

"I just came from a farming zone." Alik added.

"I know you did, but that's not one of the big ones. More of a side-show for genetic diversity's sake." She pointed across the sea. "It's not as big as it looks. There's a footbridge that will take you across the narrowest portion…maybe ten kilometers from here and thirty kilometers across. Cross to the other side and you'll be amazed at the scale of the lands and the mountains. That's where the major climate systems are generated."

"Are there forests there as well?" Alik asked.

"On the far side of the mountainous divide is a temperate to tropical zone, so on the far side of the fields, you'll find thick groves of citrus and bananas, tropical nuts and medicinal plants. If you follow through that zone, another fifty kilometers or so, you'll find yourself in a desert region. That region stretches back around to the valleys near your entrance. You can't help but walk in circles here. If you stick to this side of the sea and follow the beach in either direction, you'll find wide and boring flats of farming delta. That's where serious production occurs. It's important to have a wide array of microclimates and naturalized regions – for stability."

Alik took careful notes, with a pen, into his notebook. She noticed and took the pen from him. On a blank page, she drew a large circle and quartered the circle roughly. She scratched an X on his entrance point, a small dash at his current location and a little squiggle connecting the beach with the directions she'd given him.

He could picture the space perfectly - lush, valleys between high stacks of moisture collecting conifer forests, which feed streams and eventually a major river. The river flows into a small sea, then into massive lakes, creating wetlands and flood plains rich for farming. The flat farmlands were dotted with fruit orchards that were connected and changed throughout every eco system. The farmlands burst into a thick, green tropical belt, which then rose, becoming arid and dry before plunging back down into the valleys.

Alik gauged that the Timelock must be nearly one hundred fifty kilometers in circumference. How a ship so large could travel at such high speeds perplexed Alik to the point of an aching brain. The thrill of exploration was truly setting in. Ruby had explained that the entrance she used was closer to the farming region. She also had a warning for Alik. "Do not mess with the farming drones and do not, under any circumstances stay longer than one month. You won't turn into a pumpkin or anything; it's just a good rule of thumb. Days slip away one way or another."

After breakfast, the two of them parted with smiles. Ruby placed a quick kiss on his right cheek and whispered in his ear. "See you again, friend."

~

Alik walked with great intent each day, a general direction in mind, but ready to stop and observe at a moment's notice. His pace was set by his curiosity. The trek across the sea was fairly uneventful. He walked the full thirty kilometers in less than two days, but was forced to stop half way to wait out a heavy storm that stirred across the sea. Several bots passed him along the elevated footbridge, two of which huddled with Alik as the squall pounded and the waves swelled. The footbridge was a dozen or more feet above the water, but in the midst of the storm, he could not help but manage his concern carefully. The waves nearly crested the footbridge at several points.

During the storm, as he huddled along a partition in the driving rain, he laughingly wondered why his curiosity was driving him through a world that was wet and cold and unpredictable instead of the ship beyond it — which happened to be dry and comfortable and mostly predictable. He decided his answer was in his characterization of the two. The fact was, he was thrilled to be soaked to the bone. The smell of weather invigorated him and his mind desperately wanted to make sense of a world that by all appearances looked natural, but which Alik rationally recognized as something totally artificial. The paradox drove his mind to giddy.

On the far side of the sea, the land flattened and merged into a river delta similar to the one on the corresponding side – banded in rich stretches of farmland. Alik could see the outlines of great boulders dotted at regular intervals from one another as if they had each been uprooted in the same land slide – or perhaps, the thought flashed through Alik, they remained as monuments to a glacier which carved the river bed and fed the tiny sea? How far had they gone to grow this place? He made a note to ask Ruby later.

Standing at one of the boulders that towered several stories above his head, he looked to the next boulder in line, several hundred meters away. Alik took in the sight, watching a shroud of fog roll off of the far boulder like passing cosmic gases. He imagined the distance between the two boulders to be that of several thousand light years, an abyss of space and time. He imagined that he was Sigrah, barreling from one to the other. The time between the two, he thought, was inconsequential to him as he was, but then he thought of his tiny self once again – lost in the dirt between the two boulders – stuck in the mire for epochs.

He was always entertained by his simplistic spatial intelligence. Not simply because he was a bad dancer, but because of the pure entertainment he got from nights of laying in bed, looking towards a skylight, closing one eye and watching the light jump to the left, then closing the other and watching it jump to the right – seeing shadows and demanding the ability to grasp them, chasing after the heat warble at the far side of a hill or the annoyance of discerning hollow people from real people. To him, it all boiled down to some failing of internal math or perception. His calculus for certain modes of perspective often set him on his head and made his interactions with the physical world generally strange, especially at moments like this.

When he picked his foot off the ground, heading to the next boulder, he imagined that the crossing represented thousands of light years, he could see the potential simplicity of intergalactic travel had he the ability to shift the perspective of the universe at will or had he been a galaxy sized giant. His foot did not move at light speed, yet in it's normal motion it crossed dozens of inches in a matter of seconds and since he imagined those inches or even fractions of inches to represent entire light years, it was clear to him he was actually traveling between the rocks, faster than the speed of light.

Alik laughed, happy with this leap, then he leaped again. It occurred to him that as he walked from boulder to boulder, within the Timelock, space and time and matter fell away from the ship he walked within at near light speed. He realized that beneath his feet, beneath and beyond the skin of this vessel, stars passed like the burning, contagious yawns of God. Alik laughed again, considering he could walk from star to star, stamping out it's light under his foot like ashes from a pipe.

An image incessantly burrowed into Alik's brain as he walked. Instead of becoming more diffuse and unintelligible, the picture of Ruby waxed brightly. He insisted on remembering each aspect of her face. She had a small, sharp nose. There was something pure and natural, rugged, about her but also something very temporary and false about her appearance. He intuited that her true self lay in something else, another form perhaps, than simply the definition of her face or her momentary ruggedness.

Her jaw was simple, almost non-existent and her mouth seemed painted on, wide almost permanently smiling, but her lips sealed and rolled back and blended with the muddy filth finger painted across her flesh, so that it appeared she had no mouth at all. He was comforted by the memory of her. He missed her.

From time to time, he saw her shape in the stones or her color in the sand. A wide flock of waterfowl raced over him before noon one day and in the shape of their formation, he saw Ruby's soul, her intention in clear bloom. This place was alive with her skill and her vision. This place was as much Ruby as Ruby herself. She was chief architect and soul steward of this place. Realizing this, his respect for her grew with every step, with every sight and every smell. In many ways, he felt he was as connected with her in this place as he had been in her company.

Being human, Alik had no illusions about the quiet, internal and external search all humans make, looking carefully into the crowds, minding manners and staying neat, in the hopes that the day will come when a match can be found. Thousands of songs, he recalled, had been written on the matter. Finding love, finding a friend or a soul mate, from across great distances against strange odds. He had it bad.

The Kinoko weren't helping. At night he would swallow a handful and stare into his fire. He tended and nurtured his feelings for Ruby as they amplified. Whatever it was his father insisted was there, in the glow of the Kinoko, it seemed to be reflecting these emotions, intensifying them further.

The people of the Buffer always held pair bonding and love as a high priority, more so than those in the urban super structures. Yet it was always a matter Alik held close to his heart and spoke rarely of. He'd had flings and infatuations, but never anything deeper. He had actually put the matter to rest some time ago, assuming that finding a significant other would either happen naturally or not at all.

~

Standing, literally at crossroads, watching the gravel paths run perfectly straight until they vanished kilometers in the distance, he could not help but feel mocked. He wasn't worried about taking the wrong path; it was simply that he had an obvious choice. At times, he fooled himself into believing that he was permanently divorced form choice. At times he felt that somehow, he ended up on this ship by no will of his own. The fact remained, he'd sought out every instance – he had purposefully made every decision, which now led him to this simple split in a dirt path and he forced himself to own this fact. This was all his doing. He went looking for all of this. And for what, he wondered. Debt? He couldn't remember any other driving force. Thinking back on it honestly, he never had any faith that this endeavor would erase his debt, as advertised. He was trapped in a scheme, which still allowed him the freedom of choice necessary to damn him further.

He didn't necessarily crave adventure. He wasn't driven to figure out the great mysteries. He was relatively content, living among his family and the forests, half expecting to be struck by lightning and perishing before ever becoming concerned by the size of his debt. And he felt pride that he'd obtained, by choice, some measure of an education, even if it were gravely under par compared to the apparent majority he'd encountered upon leaving Earth. Why did he do all of this? Why the preoccupation? He sat on the ground and felt as though he were plugged into something, tethered and dangling, perplexed as he considered the strings attached to his limbs.

In his world, physical violence was never seen, never reported on and seemed to be non-existent. However, there existed a non-physical violence, a psychological violence associated with the imposed stratification of class and duty and ability. There was an inherent violence in the extortion of individuals via debt and repayment. There was always the illusion of choice, of free will. The violence in omission was the greatest sin of the PAE if they had any at all. It was a coldness born of hubris.

Though, this place did not seem to reflect that coldness. Instead, he felt only the good intentions of Ruby.

Did it really matter if he went right or left? Would it matter if he stayed a month or a year or two years in the Timelock? The ship would eventually arrive and he would either be left on board or carried, old and dead, within the Timelock and within its dirt and air and its produce to points beyond the stars. As he saw it, all he had was time.

More than three weeks since he left Ruby, Alik made it past the boulder fields, across the expansive livestock plains, through two forests and several hidden lakes. The mountains had been growing for sometime, shadowing him in the distance and taunting Alik as they grew taller and taller as he approached through the days. The range ran unbroken to Alik's left and his right. They stood abrupt and tall as any large range he'd seen on Earth. Clouds regularly obscured their peaks.

From a distance, he'd charted a path across them, at a place where two mountains joined in a cleft just above the tree line. He spent several days, slowly walking uphill through the forest, each night colder than the last. He made shelters of limbs and leaves and moss within the cold forest, burrowing down like an animal at night. As his trail led him to cliff-side overlooks, he took the opportunities to rest and stare back across the land he'd traversed. At the very edge of the horizon he could make out a thin shimmering band, the edge of the sea.

He finally reached the thin air and lunar-esq landscape

of the tree line. The mountain's craggy peak stood less than thirty meters beyond the line of trees. Before setting camp, he took the short walk to the summit, within the cleft he intended to descend through, in an effort to gauge what lay beyond. From the edge he saw that the cleft was shear on the far side, leading to the rocky valley below which butted against a thick, high altitude forest that bordered the mountain on which he stood with a series of four other mountains on the far side of the high altitude forest.

His body ached at the thought of scaling the cliff only to cross four additional mountains on the far side. He was finally comfortable with his expedition and felt that it may have now come to a natural end. His mountaineering skills were simply underdeveloped for the task ahead, not to mention he lacked any of the essential equipment needed to repel or ascend a shear face.

Alik returned to his camp at the tree line and lit a fire, prepared dinner and settled in for a cold night. He built his fire in the lee of a tall boulder and built it as intensely as possible, dragging huge dry logs from the forest edge, creating a tower of fire nearly as tall as the boulder itself. He wanted to heat as much of the rock around him as possible, hoping to make his night as cozy as feasible.

He could hear the rattle of a small glacier, melting off winter ice and fueling a set of streams that likely ran down the backside of the mountain, away from him.

His belly was empty, intentionally as he had foolishly decided to fast that morning. The suspicion that his journey would end this way had hung on him the entire time he climbed up the mountain forest. Several times he had stopped himself from giving in earlier, insisting instead on seeing beyond the mountain. Having accomplished this, he relaxed the success of his expedition and then sought to cap off the experience with an intense communion with the

Kinoko.

He broke the red coals from the sides of the logs in his fire, set a fresh bunch of dried twigs and bramble into the coals, he stood back as the fire jumped upwards, consuming the logs further. He took several deep gulps of water from his canteen and fished out his pouch of Kinoko from his haversack. As he gauged it, there were roughly eight grams of Kinoko left. Alik gathered them in his fist unceremoniously and shoved them into his mouth, chewing faster as the butterflies in his stomach began to stir and rage. It was the largest dose he had yet consumed. He felt a slight tingle beneath his ear as he remembered the tiny node.

As he sat in the firelight, digesting the Kinoko, he was overcome by the apparent age of this place. It felt primordial. The rock itself seemed active, new only now showing its wear by the elements. He assumed that much of the rock in the Timelock had been sourced from asteroids. Some of it still shined with the glimmer of iron ore or wore red as it oxidized and leached. He wondered whether the stone appreciated its new home. It was now warm and wet and teeming with life – a far cry from drifting aimlessly, alone and cold in a radioactive stew.

Alik sank into determined contemplation, opening his soul for the fingers of the Kinoko. If he could have built a physical memorial on the mountainside a cairn to mark the entrance to his intended psychedelic journey, he would have. The mountain was breathing beneath his legs and the fire brought alien warmth to the mountain night, which snapped and trembled at the fire's presence.

The rocks were the oldest matter amongst him. Trapped in a solid form, they held fast to the physical world, refusing to give up their atoms to the frenzy of atomic subspace. They were rocks through and through and they refused to join the sand without a long and arduous fight.

The Kinoko had seized him faster than he expected, shining an inner light brighter than he had yet seen it. He rubbed his face, pushing around his natural oils and suddenly wishing for a warm shower. The Kinoko marched beneath his skin, sounding trumpets to announce their presence. Alik tried to find his pace – tried to mark out familiar territory and settle into the psychedelic slipstream, but an odd and unforeseen discomfort lodged into the experience like a pebble hidden in his soup. The familiar kindness of the Kinoko seemed to be light years divorced as a dark anxiety stepped into the experiences one toe at a time.

Unfounded terror rushed him like an unanticipated squall. Where he had always encountered love and brightness, he now found cold fear, smallness and terror. He was totally out of place, as if trespassing on shadowy lands he'd been warned to avoid at all costs. Then, the unmistakable presence of something completely alien seized him. It suddenly felt as though his hands had become the gloves of another. He pawed and scratched at his face, his finger nails breaking loose both his flesh and the node with it. Some force was moving his body as if he were a rag doll.

He stood and looked to the summit and the cleft in the rock, which now shown like blue fire in the cartoonish sky. He was drawn towards it, unwillingly. He clawed his way towards the summit, hand over hand, grasping the loose gravel all the way, tearing the flesh from his fingers. At the top, he peered again over the edge. Fear flowed through his body like electricity, but he was helpless to fight it in anyway. He could see the bottom, lit by the blue fire towering above him, craggy and treacherous until it fell again into thick dark forest at the opposite tree line. Unable to stop himself, he lurched forward, flinging his body against every natural inclination that attempted to oppose him, until his was falling helplessly into the rocky chasm.

As he fell, he could distinctly see the sinister face of a be-ing unknown to him. The face was swiftly replaced with the crunching pain of his impact along the mountain slope. His left leg made contact first, smashing into razor sharp gravel and breaking like glass. He rolled from then on, further and further down the mountainside. Attempting to catch himself, he shoved out his left arm just as his body was rolling towards a boulder outcropping. His hand made direct contact with the boulder, smashing into it and breaking his wrist as his fingers grasped, fighting against the gravity pulling his body towards the bottom. He slipped free, but soon came to rest at the base of the slope along the tree line.

Shock swept through his body, his mind reeled with the emotional whirlwind of the Kinoko. Shock dragged him from consciousness into the inky black of disassociation.

18

Myco's crew did not question a single order. She carried then, the gravitas and stature of one of the Ellern. As she saw the matter, she had been granted title by Lanose and with it she was directed to act with full authority to execute Lanose's final request. Both the ship and the crew recognized this on an epigenetic level. She was now non-physically graft-ed onto Ascus and its crew.

Dematiaceous had previously ordered Ascus and crew to carry Myco to the furthest borders of Rachis space – to be marooned on the Rock of the Void. Still careening in the general direction of that lonely place, nestled deep in the void between the Perseus arm and Orion's spur – Myco poised the ship to cross at the thinnest portion of the void, aiming to guide it towards the first lump of stars at the tip of Orion's spur – closest to the Sagittarian arm. Fruitful direction or not, this put enough distance between her and Dematiaceous to give her a fighting chance of encountering the Transmitter or pinpointing his home world precisely enough to navigate towards it.

Since the ship had reached its maximum potential velocities and crossed into the hinterlands of the Rachis galactic arm, Myco had been unable to receive any meaningful transmission. Reception had not been possible, since she was still forming a genetic link between Ascus and crew. Her faculties were spread too thinly to successfully receive, but soon she would be able to use both the ship and the crew to scan for even the faintest transmissions.

~

Ascus was isolated, in a patch of space-time riddled with gravitational anomalies – invisible pockmarks left in the wake of the passing stars systems of the spiraling arms. The crossing would take an unknown amount of time. In the midst of her busy link with Ascus and crew, she used her knew senses to stretch out across space-time, feeling texture of the fabric of space time with the tips of her fingers. She used her energies to find the quickest, safest paths. Her fingers could feel the imprint of wormholes light years away and if she stretched her mind and Ascus far enough, she could sense the wormhole's end points and the warm stars behind them.

These new abilities, the shared cohesiveness of the system, were something she was unaccustomed to in a practical sense, but she took to it as naturally as breathing. In her mind, she rationed that the prepubescent probes that tumbled across this space epochs before had already mapped all likely paths. Now, all she had to do was to follow their breadcrumbs – minding out their subtle maps.

Still, she burned to receive. Trying to listen to all things at once, to the currents and flow of space-time, to the crumbs left by the probes, to the undeniable ping of a transmission, was all consuming and left her embedded like a statue in her quarters, dismissive only of the existence of her body and nothing else.

From time to time, little worries, like dust on a lens, would blot out important elements of her conscious state. Had the Transmitter slowed his pace? Had he fallen into a star or met with some temporal or physical travesty? She pushed them away, but each time, she left a smear on the lens. Myco knew that allaying some of these concerns would soon be essential to maintaining the sharpness of her abilities and the success of her venture. The odds, however, beat her brains in. The likelihood of finding her Transmitter was beyond incalculable. Nevertheless, she reminded herself over and over that since she'd found him twice before, she could find him yet again. This fact, coupled with the fact that they existed within the same galaxy, gave Myco all the hope she needed to carry on.

She could not stop. If she slowed the vessel to extend her attention and seek out a transmission, she would close the relative time gap between her and Dematiaceous. As it was, she was running from him through space and time, each moment placing months and years between her and the dark elder. Though pursuit was not Dematiaceous' way, surely, he was already consumed with clearing the Ellern council and envisioning a fresh raison d'être for Myco's people. Demati-aceous was a cancer amongst the Rachis. He threatened to change the course of a billion years of continuous culture. Though Myco did not see the cancer as hers to cure. Her mission was altogether different. She was not savior or hero to her people, she was instead the ever-extending tendril of their curiosity, a new branch in an ever widening mycelia mat and in that alone did she preserve the best of their nature.

Lanose appointed Dematiaceous to the Ellern in order to keep him close. A threat held close was a threat more easily managed. Myco had enough faith in her people, the Ellern and their combined brilliance and ability to keep Dematiaceous on a short leash. There were those amongst the Rachis much better suited to combat a dark mind like Dematiaceous directly, than Myco. This fact realized gave her great calm. Dematiaceous was not the task levied by Lanose. The fact remained, at the speeds Myco then traveled, the years of Dematiaceous would drain away faster and faster. He may already have had enough time to dissolve the Ellern and place the Rachis on a dark path. That was the double-edged sword of relativistic travel. She could not know.

In any case, it was an enormous galaxy and finding her Transmitter was akin to finding a single, specific atom amongst the fires of a billion stars. Her crew never once questioned her, though. Instead, they worked steadily to maintain Ascus and themselves, helping Myco selflessly. They looked towards distant planets for signs of pollution or industry. And as her crew patiently set forth into the void, Myco remained self-confined to her quarters along the observation deck in a posture of perpetual mental openness and prostration. She held fast to her Heritor trade and unwearyingly bore her way through the slipstream of mind, hoping again to catch a glimmer of her Transmitter.

~

Then, in the seventh week amongst the void, while the crew slept soundly, the spiny fingers of transmission playfully tugged at base of Myco's skull. Someone was again knocking at the door. The intensity of the ship's velocity was detectable in the intensity of the knocking. With no hesitation at all, she threw open the doors of her mind and dove through the slipstream of the fungal probes.

The dosage must have been incredible, because she was yanked directly through the mandala, through the fractal gate and into the other's body with little additional effort of her own. Something was different though. She attempted to stretch her perception towards the hands of the creature, but found none. She was gripped, instead, by an overwhelming array of sensory information she had little experience to interpret. As she thought of the Transmitter's skin, she felt instead a solid, continuous surface, massive and bathed in a slough of radioactive winds. As she stretched to find the Transmitter's mind, she instead found herself floating through an array of mechanistic thought. The analogue chemistry of a biological mind was replaced with algorithmic reflex and positronic fervor.

Whatever was transmitting was keenly aware of her presence. This realization surprised her at first, then delighted Myco into a state of bliss. Adding to this bliss was the certainty that this entity was not biological. It was a mechanistic being, but it was warm and thoughtful and open as any sentient or near sentient being she had received. She bathed in the lucid connection, passing over a blatant greeting, firmly acknowledging the presence of the strange transmitter. Suddenly she felt a direct question posed, it was a confluence, as if multiple parties were each begging answers at once. She positioned her intent and directed it with all of her will upon the transmitter, *show yourself!*

Without hesitation, amongst the noise and fervor of the probe's interface came a sudden quiet. As if a raging storm had been lifted above the ground, leaving only a quiet desert, shrouded in black clouds. The transmission cloaked itself in stark, definite reality. An indefinable figure approached her amongst the rocky desert. It was not a bipedal creature; instead it was rather amorphous and globular, as if it were a personality represented by color and vague texture.

Myco steeled her resolve and reminded herself that this was her dojo - this was a place of the way. This slipstream was the ocean she'd learned to swim within and she was in ultimate control. She directed her intent towards the figure and kindly demanded again, show yourself! From the sky she heard a crashing sound, as if walls of air were being forcibly pushed away to make room for something tremendous. In a sudden instance, the clouds parted and the sky filled with the epic shape of a colossal vessel, hundreds of kilometers in length and girth. She looked back to the figure, but her attention was swiftly redirected towards the craft.

When she attempted to look again, she found herself now inside the vessel, staring at a complicated interface, which then projected the image of the craft. Her attention darted to the left, then to the right, below and above. She found that as her curiosity and focus changed, so did the things she were being shown. Eventually, she found herself standing, this time in a wide, frozen hay field; the ambiguous figure along side her. She could feel the chill of the frozen ground seeping through her feet, until she was snatched by force by an alto-gether separate transmission. It was as if two simultaneous transmissions were occurring and she was being directly led from one to the other – pushed across slipstreams.

Her feet warmed and her body fell into a state of ecstatic joy as she felt a tidal wave of familiar emotion. It was her Transmitter, but she was not behind his eyes. Instead, she could approach him, as if removed from him, though she continued to feel each and every thought and emotion that coursed through his timid, biological mind. He sat in front of a large fire, consumed with the magic of the probes. Her hope of focusing her intention upon him led her to step into the fire. She adjusted the flames easily, as their photons pen-etrated the lenses of his eyes. She could feel him looking at her, but she was still completely separated from what was clearly the source transmission. Then, she was overcome by a thought, directed at her from the amorphous presence; *time is the barrier to him, but not to me.*

Trying desperately to piece it all together, she came to the odd conclusion that her Transmitter was self directing, somehow, his own experience through a third party and it was that third party which was both attempting to communicate with her and feeling the effects of her directed intention.

At the moment this thought was born from her mind, she was yanked from the fire and the attention of the ambiguous transmitter forced itself upon an image of stars. Again, she felt as though her skin was quickened in a torrent of radiation and wild gravitational flux. Her eyes locked onto the presence of four bright, but otherwise unremarkable stars. Then attention was shifted once again, to a constellation framing the four stars.

Upon seeing the constellation highlighted before her, she understood exactly what was happening, she was being given coordinates. Even though she did not recognize the constellation, whatever force was filtering the transmission surged the knowledge towards her, the Enokitake Formation at the tip of Orion Spur...look for the blue giant, that is where you will find us. The images peeled away, allowing Myco to view several distinct, wide field views of the stars and the paths to and from. As most language in transmission, it was centered less on morphology and more on an innate diffusion of understanding. Whatever was filtering the transmission had enough presence of mind to reflect it's own knowledge towards her, transmitting for the first time actual telemetry from an alien object. If nothing else was successful, this extreme act was already the ultimate accomplishment of more than a billion years of galactic probing.

Myco absorbed the information and pushed back one

last time, forcing her intention upon the transmission filter, tell me who you are! The response came as a single thought, all encompassing, like a brilliant candle at the bottom of a well. She felt again the image of the vessel, the stature of the interface and the company of the fluid presence each image with the resounding statement, I am Sigrah!

With that, the door of mind closed. She jolted out of reception and fell from her Heritor posture into a convalescing lump.

Myco lay on the floor of her quarters for several minutes. A young guard who was stationed discreetly within her quarters, gently approached Myco to offer assistance. The intensity of the high velocity transmission took its toll on her. Myco tried to stand, but found that she was too weak. She looked up at the guard who was then cupping her body into a seated position. "How long?"

The guard patted her knee and reassured her. "Nearly sixteen hours, but I was here the whole time." Myco nodded, and then waved her dominant finger across the underside of her arm, sprouting a single, tiny fruit.

"Take this to the navigator. Tell him this is the most important part of the transmission. I'll not make him go through the entire ordeal." She grabbed the guard's arm, "Tell him to look at the stars and find a way." Her words faded as she fell out of consciousness.

The guard lifted her and carried her to her soft mycelium divan to recuperate.

19

Nena had given up sleeping normal hours. The appearance or semblance of any balanced life had faded. Her hair had lost all sense of attention, having grown long and clumpy with neglect. Her body was greasy and odiferous. The once pristine vessel reeked of human detritus and disregard.

Her hours were spent engaged like a moth before a bright light, slumped and humming over grand designs, consumed entirely. When she did sleep, she did so on a small pallet in the corner of her studio. She saw her slug only on the rare occasion that she would enter the apartment to refill her jar of Buffer herb or grab a fresh shirt. She was in no way angry at her slug, Nena just too consumed in mitigating other elements of her boredom to pay the slug any additional interest.

Occasionally, she slid into bed and rested a few minutes, silently spooning her sweet slug, but Nena's mind was too busy for actual rest. Whenever she closed her eyes, all she saw were models and tables and design cutaways. In her dreams, she relived her last bouts of work, picking her reasoning and designs apart from the inside out. She always gave up on sleep with the slug and found herself time and again slinking back to her studio to push onward. At her station, she pieced together every conceivable element of her personal future-by-design. Two solid years of work had produced magnificent results.

She still did not have the computer power to test all of the actual, physical and cosmic ramifications of her designs, so she had put many details aside under the assumption that she could fix them later or that they would otherwise prove irrelevant. Without the limitations of the long-term inevitabilities of physics, she had devised a path for expansion, which could facilitate human existence amongst every known galaxy in the Universe.

It was all very impressive, but despite that, it was, as the slug saw it, little more than a castle made of matchsticks. It was the work of the powerless and infirmed, flailing and grasping for meaning or control.

The slug, on the other hand, had been truly constructive and hard at work. She focused on her lessons in the cockpit, bided her time, assured that she could pull Nena from her trance whenever she was ready. Finally, after two years of near light travel, the slug decided the time had come.

From Nena's myopic perspective, the slug never left their apartment. Barely a thought was given to the slug. Then, like every other day, Nena was slumped over her desk, working hypnotically. She was disassembling the draft of the reproduction unit of a nano-dozer, carefully striping away the mechanisms from the design image that hung in the air. Without warning, the drafts disappeared and Nena's studio blacked out.

The slug decided many months before that when she was ready for Nena's attention she knew exactly how to get it. The slug was fully aware that Nena was at her absolute breaking point. Any major hiccup in her routine would send her over the edge with all walls tumbling around her. Then the slug would make her move and start reassembling her friend one piece at a time. When she was finally ready, the slug called up the power access units from the cockpit control center and very casually began a power down sequence for all non-essential, internal systems, starting with the design suite. Nena's studio was instantly useless. The slug then ran through the blacked out ship, back to their cozy apartment, positioned herself beneath the covers and flipped on the projection screen, waiting for the wailing monster to come.

Nena's screams were audible through the bulkhead partitions between compartments. She fumed and beat the walls while shrieking and choking and gasping in the blackness. The slug heard Nena wail through the far end of the apartment about the time axillary lighting blinked on, signaling the start of the power up sequence. Nena flew through the apartment into the kitchen where she immediately took to breaking plates, pulling and throwing books from the shelves, emptying the fridge of food and launching it in rage toward the bedroom where her slug lay silently and patiently.

"Fuck this prison! I don't want it! I don't want it!" Nena screamed.

She punched and shouted and tore through the apartment until her sobbing took over and her body collapsed into a heap at the foot of their bed. The slug did not move to comfort Nena; instead the slug stared intently at the film in the progress as if nothing else was happening.

"You! You fucking cunt! You just lay here, all goddamn day! You don't give a single fuck about this god damned prison!" Nena was venomous. Her exhaustion and written across her face. Her eyes sunk in and blackened around the edges. Her teeth were yellow and ignored. She was in a state of pure disregard for her health and happiness. Nena scowled and lurched onto the foot of the bed, raging toward the slug. The slug still refused to acknowledge Nena, fanning the flames even further. Fully enraged, Nena dove into the bed with her hands aiming to clutch the slug's throat. Nena wrapped her hands around the slug's throat and squeezed with the full might of her rage, having totally forgotten the spark that set this rage into motion. The slug locked her eyes with Nena's while she gently and patiently grasped Nena's wrists and stroked the backs of Nena's hands gently. The slug's face turned from red to blue, but she never allowed panic to invade her eyes, instead she looked deep into Nena's eyes and calmly mouthed her lover's name with her fading blue lips. Nena's muscles loosened just as the slug was beginning to see the white sparkle that heralds unconsciousness due to asphyxiation. Nena removed her hands as tears ran down her face. The slug embraced her and held Nena as she wept for several minutes.

"I just want to go back. I just want to go back. This isn't what I planned for. This wasn't my choice! And you! All you do is sit here, in this bed! You just sit…a prisoner…and you don't even give a damn!" Nena choked her words out.

The slug rubbed Nena's back and reassured her with a quiet "shush", never once refuting or admonishing Nena. The slug was satisfied enough with having broken through Nena's armor. Nena finally calmed until her body was only intermittently shuddering with the after shocks of her melt down. She fell asleep in the slug's arms and continued to sleep for nearly eighteen hours.

~

Nena woke to the smell of coffee and the soft sounds of some ancient jazz trumpeter. Looking about the apartment, she noticed that the devastation of her explosion had vanished with no evidence of her spasm left to bear. The apartment felt fresh and clean. She could sense the smell of eggs beginning to fry in fragrant olive oil.

"The shower is already hot and waiting on you. You should take your time." The slug announced from the kitchen.

Nena peeled herself from the bed. She felt like she was waking from cryo-sleep, her joints stiff and her brain foggy. She was refreshed and as the sequence of events returned to her during her walk to the shower, she felt a renewed sense of shame. In the shower, she scrubbed the previous year from her pours. She winced as she brushed the soapy knots from her hair then gagged as she spit bloody toothpaste from her derelict mouth. Her pale skin was nearly translucent. The hair had grown thick on her legs, around her lower torso and under her arms.

When she finally stepped out from the lavatory she was greeted by a delicately arranged table - fresh fruits and juices, scrambled eggs and careful sausages. The slug sat, half in her robe, half out, ready to fill a plate for Nena.

"Sit down, sweet one." The slug gestured at the other chair. "We need to eat, then we need to talk." Around the slug's neck were two perfectly angry bruises in the shapes of Nena's hands. The slug's skin was as translucent as Nena's, giving the bruises an undeniable presence at the breakfast table, as if they were another guest at the table, refusing to eat.

Nena, still grappling with unannounced shame did not argue or protest, she simply sat down quietly, took the plate from the slug and began shoving food into her face as if she were a prisoner.

Nena tore through the meal and finished off half the pot

of coffee then finished with a fresh pipe the slug had prepared with breakfast. She relaxed slightly and released a deep sigh of relief.

The bruises kept catching her eyes. Nena looked to the slug with a bent face, ready to cry again, but she stopped herself, blocking her sadness with her shame, feeling as though the slug deserved no more tears.

"I'm so sorry." Nena choked the words out.

The slug smiled back at Nena. It was that smile – just a simple collection of muscle movements – that for the first time transmitted the slug's inherent humanity to Nena. This was the first time Nena had seen the slug as another individual, not simply an item of luxury and the shame was then fully realized and alive.

"There's something wrong with me s-slug." Nena paused, wanting something to call her beyond simply slug. Slug wasn't a name or a title. Being called slug was no different than being called toaster or donut. But Nena had nothing else. "I've never reacted like that. I need help slug." Nena was as earnest as possible. She held the slug's hand from across the table, allowing her elbow to sit in a dish of jelly.

"Nena, I'm the one who shut off the power to your design suite." Silence followed the slug's admission.

"You did? Why?" Nena was calm, still futilely fighting back the streams of tears.

"You need to see something." The slug stretched out her other arm, grabbing both of Nena's hands. "You need to see what I've been up to."

The slug led Nena out of the apartment and through the ship. Nena was silent, not sure what to expect out of the young slug. The slug led her through the winding corridors of the uppermost level to a retractable, spiral staircase.

"What's up there?" Nena asked.

"Something you should have inspected the day we came

on board." The slug was slightly indignant but still smiling wide and kind.

The slug asked Nena to walk up first. "This isn't the main approach, but it's my favorite, since it did not require me to walk past your studio."

At the top of the stairs, Nena instantly knew where she was. "It's the cockpit...the bridge."

"That it is, my sweet." The slug was excited to show Nena what she'd accomplished.

Nena took the Co-pilot's gravity couch as the slug jumped into the pilot's. The slug casually punched in a sequence on a slender keypad nestled between the two seats and the ship's blast screen immediately peeled back from the cockpit's transoms, revealing an intense blur of light. The slug's fingertips danced across the console and in a matter of seconds the ship's computer compensated for the blur, steadying and dulling the image through the glass, as much as possible to reveal a sight more recognizable to human eyes.

"You shouldn't remove the blast doors in flight..." Nena trailed off as the slug continued punching buttons until the screens in front of them displayed an array of new images. Their flight path and position shown on one, their course on another, ship diagnostics and long range scans, telescopic images of nearby stellar and planetary objects all displayed in front of the two.

"You may be an engineer Nena, but you are no pilot. So, I'd like to introduce you to my ship, Kitsune."

"What the hell?" Nena was in shock.

The slug pitched back in her gravity couch, snuggling into a comfortable position that was clearly well worn. The pilot's couch fit the slug perfectly and the slug had tuned it so that in spite of her short reach, she could access every terminal in the cockpit.

"Nena, you've been locked away in that design suite for

more than six hundred days. I understand your obsession. I understand your passion. I even understand your anger, but if I had insisted that you recognize it, you would never have taken me seriously. Nena, you and I are made of the same stuff. We are made of the same stuff, but we are very different." Nena tried to interrupt the slug, but the slug kept on.

"Listen, this isn't an indictment. I'm proud of your work. I'm certain that your time has not been wasted. I need you to know, that my time has not been wasted either. Nena, like it or not, you have a need for control. It's what keeps you righted. In control, you are not violent or cruel. In control you are creative and resourceful - you are passionate and driven. This is my gift to you Nena. I've taken control and now I'm offering to share it with you. I exist to save you and that is what I have done."

The slug tapped out a sting of code into the navigational database, rubbed her bruised throat and casually scrolled through sets of screens on the navigation computer until she paused and enlarged a set of charts across the main terminal. "You see that blip? That blip right there is our intercept target. It's a massive ship. It's roughly a quarter of a light year ahead of us now…and this…" The slug punched up another screen. Nena was silent and aghast. "…this right here, is their target star system. It's a blue giant."

"What the…?" Nena was speechless.

"Now you listen carefully, because I never want to criticize you ever again, I love you too much for that non-sense." The slug paused and composed herself. "I admit that I instigated your rage last night, but I want to make clear that just because I'm a slug does not give you the right to abuse me. I want to put it behind us, since I was certain you would react violently when I cut the power, but you have to know that it isn't all right. You cannot allow yourself to disintegrate to that point ever again." The slug paused again. Nena stared at her with deeply sorrowful eyes. Then the slug continued.

"One last thing. I'm just a slug and you're a ranked and titled designer...but for shit's sake, stop putting so much damned faith in your computers and wake the fuck up and realize you are on board a space craft that has the ability to travel faster than the speed of light.

"I don't even...how did?" Nena was unprepared to be bested and psychologically deconstructed by a mere slug. "You can fly this thing? A quarter of a light year?" Nena could not complete a thought.

"Of course I can fly this thing. I know its systems in and out at this point. I've already adjusted our course on three separate occasions to close the intercept distance and overtake the other ship. We can beat them to their destination by more than an Earth year if we wanted to...if we choose to."

Nena quickly engaged. "Show me the other ship. Do we have telescopics?" Nena watched as the slug effortlessly called up all of the data on the other vessel, including an active telescopic view as well as all of the data buried and veiled in the mission report. The slug had spent a fair amount of time combing through unclassified telemetric data and other esoteric communiqués in the months and days leading up to Nena's orders. Combining all of the information she'd tracked down, she was able to compose a fairly descriptive profile on the vessel, it's mission and it's crew.

The slug tapped on the telescopic image of the vessel. "It's a seed ship. It's got a timelocked biosphere that doubles as a gravity core."

"Yeah. I'm familiar with the design. I even had the luxury of seeing one under construction." Nena was fascinated. The A.I.'s on seed ships like this were infallible. They were the most complex intelligent life created by humans. There had never been an incident of a seed ship A.I. violating orders or protocols. "It's no wonder they want us to intercept this thing. We can't let an A.I. make first contact. Damn thing's gotta be malfunctioning." Nena scratched her head and stared at the image. "What about crew."

"I don't have any specifics, at least not that I've unearthed. Seed ships like this are usually equipped with an usher and occasionally a human or android bio-scientist to look after the biosphere." The slug replied.

The slug's words bobbed around Nena's brain. "Do you have the initial launch date of this vessel?" The slug punched up a series of logs. The launch date stood out like a beacon. "I'll be damned." Nena paused.

"What is it?" The slug asked.

"Nothing. It's probably nothing." Nena wasn't sure whether it was relevant. She could be wrong and had no desire to muddy the water with what was likely irrational, wishful thinking. Nena focused on the numbers, taking control of the console, she reviewed their trajectories and several other navigational factors. "How are we going to catch this thing? We are maxed out. We can't go any faster."

The slug groaned a bit. "Nena, this is a trans-light ship."

Nena scoffed. "You can't really believe that. That's a theoretical designation. A designer made it work once in a theoretical model and got herself a good promotion. It's never actually been pulled off."

"Dammit. Do you trust me or not? Or am I just a stupid slug?" The slug was slightly indignant, but very consciously kept her offense reigned in.

Nena glowered deeply into the slug's eyes. Of course she trusted the Slug, but the thought was an uncomfortable one. Slugs, by their nature had no true responsibilities. No one had ever been forced to trust a slug further than to show up and be ready for death. Already, this slug had saved Nena's life, if only existentially. Nena thought it through. If not for the slug, she would still be careening mindlessly through space, perhaps for an eternity, having given up. For what purpose, she could not help but wonder. There was always a plan. There was always a plan. Her sanity rested on this reminder. Still none of this guaranteed the slug's ability to overtake the seed ship.

The slug slouched lower into her gravity couch so that she could prop her feet onto the control panel. Both women smiled at one another and the slug leaned over, giving Nena a deep kiss. "Sweet Nena, I don't know what all this is for, but I'll make a promise to you. You want to get back so that you can work. I want to get you back home….and as soon as possible. Whatever it was you were sent out here to do, let's do it…let's get it done and I'll get you home. This ship can transcend light speed and I feel confident I know how to make that happen. Do you trust me?"

Nena took a deep breath. "Yes. Yes I trust you."

20

The mountains were there only as instruments of weather and water purification. The dramatic hubris of their stature was coincidental and not a comment on their creator. They caught the warm, damp air rising above the northern sea, mixing it with the tropical air of southern jungles, creating a modest, but constant trade wind as the air rose, cooled, condensed and fell again. The mountaintops caught some of the moisture, distilled it into fresh water, filtered it through their rocks and fed the water back into streams, rivers and aquifers throughout the Timelock. Even though the mountains' roles were crucial to the production of goods and the long-term maintenance of the land. Otherwise, the mountains were idling monuments, separating the tiny world in two.

After Alik's breaking fall, the mountains stood anew – now looming jailors of the broken and damned. His fall had alighted him on the far side of the first range of tall peaks.

A sheared rock-face, the entire length of the range stood between Alik and the rest of the Timelock. On the side of the range he the lay, two more modest ranges, separated by two more deep valleys. Alik hadn't been completely sure of what lay on this side of the range, but this was consistent, since he had only obscured glimpses into the ship as a whole. He knew that there were farmlands, tropical belts and highlands on either side of the range, but he was jammed and broken in the middle of it all – alone in a snow globe. What lay beyond was moot considering that Alik's left leg was broken in three places. He had a broken wrist, several broken ribs and a handful of major contusions and lacerations.

In the morning hours following his fall, he drifted in and out of consciousness. On the each occasion he happened to wake, catch a finger hold onto consciousness, his body revolted, acknowledging the pain only long enough to damper consciousness once more. His body wanted to die. On multiple occasions he willingly gave himself over to death, begging for it even, but awakened again and again, irate that he was still breathing. Some deeply subconscious force was pushing itself to the surface, engorged with the will to live.

By mid-afternoon, he had awoken again, still face down in the sharp rocks, the shape of his broken body already attracting buzzards and flies. The force beyond his rational mind that burned to continue existing no longer allowed Alik to lose consciousness. This internal beast, his will to live, coaxed Alik away from fearing the pain each moment. Just as Alik accepted the pain and allowed his fear to diminish, a desperate release of endorphins rushed his body and staved off the agony in small waves. This allowed for brief moments of rational thought to bubble up from between the waves of agony and relief, wherein Alik could pithily imagine a way out of this brutal situation.

His blood lay goopy between the rocks on which he lay.

Several of his lacerations were packed tight with gravel and sand. He found that a sharp stone had penetrated deep into his broken thigh, missing an artery by providence.

He forced himself to turn slowly onto his back. The entire motion lasted the better part of an hour as the pain devastated his will nearly to the point of shock. As he was beginning to lose consciousness again, the shifting of his weight caused a sudden rockslide sending Alik sliding further down the cliff towards the tree line below. He managed to steer himself with his good hand, avoiding several large boulders.

Alik found himself at the edge of the tree line, face up, still more than a thousand feet above sea level, wrecked and ruined. He spent several minutes agonizing – screaming powerlessly at the treetops – a cry overflowing with helpless regret. He begged for this to be a dream. He begged to send his warning back in time, hoping to stop himself from being so foolishly reckless. Regret is the true killer in situations like this. The notion of "if only" is a damning one. Alik purged as much grief as his body held, pushing it ounce by ounce from his eyes, his nose and his mouth.

Then, something very human kicked in. He considered the glorious hope of rescue. Alik remembered, he was not stranded in the middle of nowhere, not really. In fact, he was stranded in the middle of somewhere. He was deep inside a space ship, traveling through the stars, with a super computer at the helm. If ever there was a chance of rescue it was here. Then he remembered the Empathy Key.

Alik reached his good fingers towards the spot that should have sheltered the tiny device linked to Sigrah. He felt and felt, then felt the opposite side, but found only a bleeding gash where the node should have rested.

He postured himself as upright as possible, scanning the edge of the forest with blurred and bloody eyes. He wagered that if he were to survive and hope receive any sort of help;

he had to get himself stabilized. Even though his body railed against death at the moment, Alik was certain that it would submit, sooner rather than later. All he really had to do was find a bot or, if he were lucky an exit. He was certain he could manage the pain of his rib cage; it was his leg was the biggest impediment. The bone in his shin was exposed. He felt the bone in his thigh pushing upwards tearing through the surface of his flesh as the rest of his femur felt shattered, perhaps in as many as four pieces. He knew he had to set the bone and splint it off somehow.

Having grown up in the Buffer, Alik had naturally honed survival skills, but was years divorced from any practical application. His forest, he knew, contained everything he needed to survive and having listened to Ruby's account of the thoroughness of her arcology, he demanded that this forest was no different.

From his painful perch, he scanned the tree line again and again. It was spring, so there was hope in finding some medicinal plants sprouting at their most potent. The chances of freezing to death were now slim, but if he did not attend to his leg, he would most certainly die of exposure no matter the possible fortune of good weather or useful plants. His pack and all of his gear was still on the other side of the mountain, essentially lost to him. He knew that he would be dead in a matter of hours or excruciating days if he did not set his leg and patch his wounds.

Setting his leg was a task not meant for one. The pain alone had the potential of sending him into unrecoverable shock – killing him. He was desperately thirsty to boot. It was eventually his thirst, which motivated him most.

He noticed a small tree, only a few meters away. The tree was split at its base, broken by heavy snowfall the prior winter, so that if formed a yolk. From his vantage, the yolk appeared big enough to firmly hold his ankle.

Alik turned onto his unbroken side. For three agonizing hours, he pulled his body across seven meters of sharp, loose gravel until he was finally within reach of the old broken tree. The tree, though it was of extreme age, had been relatively short for its species. Having grown out its life at such an extreme altitude it's trunk was dense, knotty and squat.

With enormous discomfort, Alik rolled again onto his bottom and worked to lift his broken leg towards the yolk of the tree. Several times, he dry-purged his stomach due to the intense pain. Once he had finally hooked his ankle into the yolk, he noticed that at some point during the process, he had released his bowels.

Alik propped his good leg, bent and ready to extend, onto the upper portion of the right trunk. He took several deep breaths, choking on tears and phlegm at the thought of what was to come. Alik slowly reached out his good hand and took hold of a thin, fallen branch. He placed a portion of the branch between his teeth. Painted with swaths of dried blood and mud, streaked with tears and snot, bruised and contused, Alik's face was unrecognizable.

He panted and screamed as he counted down in his mind – once, then again, then again – terrified to do what he must, until finally he snuck up on himself. As he was preparing to count down again, the inner beast, bent on survival urgently engaged his good leg until each of the bones in his broken leg were dragged back below the surface of his flesh, into place. The yolk of the tree held firm at Alik's ankle while he succumbed to immediate shock. His broken leg remained slung in the yolk, elevated, as the rest of his body slumped and sagged along the base of the cliff, seemingly lifeless.

~

Unlike Alik's previous bouts of shock, this one was much

more sophisticated. Alik was lucid, within a state closer to fever dream than pure consciousness – a super-reality similar to that of the tryptamine super-reality. At first he floated in a void. The experience was much more tangible than those of the Kinoko. Alik felt uniquely present. He did not fully realize it, but he was standing as close to the banks of death that one can, without fully crossing over.

Within this lightless void, he tried looking down at his hands. Even though his mind saw them, his eyes detected no light and so there grew a division in his mind, wherein one half ceased believing that it existed, while the other half insisted louder than ever that it existed and that it must go on existing. Eventually, the sensation shifted and Alik found that instead of hanging within a lightless void, he was abruptly standing erect, next to his wrecked body. He examined the comatose mass with fascinated interest and literal detachment.

Examining his body as if it were on a gurney, Alik made a complex assessment of all of his injuries. The elevation of his leg in the yolk was having a noticeable effect on the swelling. His breathing had slowed to a more tolerable rhythm, as had his heart rate.

Then he noticed the landscape around his body. Independent of his flaccid, unconscious heap, Alik walked away, fading into a deep purple mist, which had ascended into the high forest from the valley deep below. It obscured the mountaintop as well as the vale beneath, but left open a single, visible path.

The path led westerly, just between the base of the cliff and the tree line. Alik followed it for several dozen meters until he heard a faint trickle of water. He darted towards the sound and soon found himself standing at the edge of a hot, mountain spring; a tiny headwater, which had collected into several, terraced pools before emptying down a natural spillway and into the forest below.

Then Alik caught the unmistakable smell of a campfire. Looking up into the purple mist, he faintly distinguished the glow of a fire a handful of meters above where he stood. He walked through a network of natural barriers, mounds of calcite deposits and honeycomb rock separating the hot springs, towards the glowing fire. As he came through the mist, he noticed that the mountain opened into a ample cave, wide and framed by a extensive outcropping – a rock eave that jutted from the cliff side sheltering the mouth and cave and keeping the ground perpetually dry as it formed a comfortable shelter. There, perched on a layer of sand that never received rain was an open fire pit, teaming with flames, crackling with dry kindling and wafting the lingering smell of seared meat.

Alik noticed a small, covered lump near the fire. He approached. As he neared, he noticed that the lump was a sleeping man, donned in mangy hair and a foul odor. He was thin and worn. Alik saw scarring on the man's face then thoughts immediately back to his own injuries he had noted, only moments ago. He felt a draw to the man – deep pity and tiny bursts of rage percolated at the sight. The sleeping man was he.

Alik looked around the quiet camp. He saw the signs of prolonged use. The stone above the campfire was deep black with layers of soot. Several meters to the edge of the camp he noticed a small collection of bones, the cooked bodies of small forest critters and fur hides racked and tanning in the dry air.

A collection of handmade weapons lay close to the sleeping body. A sharp, flint-napped stone clutched in his hands. Alik watched himself sleeping comfortably beneath the hide of a bear. And there, at the very edge of his sleeping self, lay a hackneyed staff, carefully hewn from a straight, maple branch, cupped at one end and tall enough to reach two-thirds the height of his body.

Alik, in his apparent state, looked towards the fire and stared at the flames for a moment. The shadows beyond the flame, perched on the edge of his vision were unremarkable save for human shape that suddenly grabbed Alik's attention. He was shocked to notice someone sitting patiently on a wide, flat stone and huddled beneath a brown cloak. He could not see their face, but he did not get the impression that they were a threat.

"Who are you?" He called out to the figure, unsure if he had the ability to speak within this super-real state. No verbal reply was given; instead the figure gently raised their head, allowing the hood of the cloak to fall back. The two locked eyes for a moment, until Alik began tracing the alien figure with his eyes, attempting to unlock the strange figure before him. The figure's face was far from human. Thin, with incredibly high features, tan but mottled in wild actively swirling fractal patterns. Her eyes like porcelain saucers, painted in the churning ink of nameless lands.

The figure gazed through Alik, leaning forward slightly as it extended a thin set of fingers. Between the two longest, it held a tiny Kinoko. It was offered graciously to Alik and somehow he could sense the intent of the figure. He reached across the licking flames of the fire and gently accepted the Kinoko from the creature's fingers, but as he was pulling away, the heat of the fire took him by surprise and he dropped the tiny fruit into the swelling, hungry coals.

He felt the heat directly as it charred the Kinoko into ash. It was as if he too were caught in the coals and slowly dissolving into a fresh state of matter. He begged for water as the heat intensified, until finally he realized that the mist and the cave and the fire were obscured by the smoke from the burning embers of his ethereal flesh. The scene filled with smoke and with the sound of the falling spring until he was again encased in blackness.

Alik opened his eyes carefully. Above him several swollen, white clouds rolled along a river of wind. A shadow fell on him from the limbs overhead. Slowly, consciousness crept in. Alik raised his throbbing head gently. He could see his ankle still lodged in the yolk. His leg was blessedly numb.

He tried to tongue away the thirst from his mouth while shaking off the intensity of the dream. He could recall every aspect of it. Alik even wondered whether he had been dead, if only for a moment. Then he remembered the springs and he was urged by his thirst. Water. Water was next.

Numb and still hanging in the yolk, Alik determined to splint his leg as best he could. Nothing was ideal, but with luck, he found several straight branches within arm's length. Amid great care, he ripped away the torn sleeves of his jump-suit and fastened one of the better branches to the underside of his leg with the material. He could have fastened it tighter had he more material to work with and more strength at hand, but the job was sufficient enough to get moving.

Standing was not an option. Wherever he was going, he was going to be traveling on his stomach or his back, though he was not sure which would hurt more or less. If he traveled on his stomach, he could pull himself along while kicking with his good leg, however the topside of his broken leg was badly lacerated and he wanted to keep as little contact with the open wounds and the ground as possible. He chose to travel on his bottom with his back facing the direction he was headed. This way, the splint would slide over the gravel and he could still push, possibly more effectively, with his good leg.

In his lucid projection, the hot springs were only a few dozen meters along the path, still, considering the amount of pain he was in and the awkward tenderness of his state, those several dozen meters would likely take hours. Also, there was no guarantee that his dream would prove to be anything other than just a dream. He would either crawl down the path to die or he would crawl down the path and find the water his mind insisted was near.

Carefully, he lifted his battered leg from the yolk of the tree. It was curiously anesthetized a small gift from a brain on the verge of death, he reckoned. Once his leg rested on the ground, he wasted no time in starting his backwards crawl. The moment he made his first moves, he found himself instinctually attempting to catch his balance with his broken arm. This was a painful mistake he made more than once. The pain of his arm served to distract him from the pain growing once again in his broken leg. His fractured arm shared the same side as the broken ribs. He tried tying the arm up a few times, but found the energy wasted after only a few minutes of crabbing across the trail.

For eight hours, he crawled down the trail, stopping every four or five feet to wince, retch and recompose. The remaining skin on his right hand was quickly worn to raw meat. The gravel that tore through his jumpsuit left his thighs scored and tattered. When night set in, he'd given up crawling backwards and turned to his stomach, dragging and pushing himself along with his good side. His sweat carried lumps of cogulated blood from his face, into his mouth. The metallic taste mixed with the dust of the gravel, taunting Alik's thirst. Every now and then, a sharp stone found its way into one of his lacerations and burrowed deeper into his flesh. His exhaustion was so perfect that he barely gave a thought to the pain. He repeated his motions over and over – breath, bite, pull, push, breath, bite, pull, and push.

The ground spun beneath him and at times he could not discern up from down. He was dying, rapidly.

His excrement had dried along his rear hours before, but it now itched and burned. The gravity of the situation pressed him like grape. Pulling and pushing through the darkness, he was terrified that if he were to die, he may find himself stuck in this action for eternity.

Mercifully, as the artificial moonlight hammered from above, Alik heard the first miraculous sounds of falling water. He couldn't see it, but knew from the sound that the water was hideously close.

Onward he dragged his broken body until the sound of water drowned out all the other sounds of the night. He could smell the flowing water. He saw the steam first, rising above a long series of terraced hot springs, the warm wet air condensed as it met the cool rush from the high altitude winds. The relief of having arrived should have filled him with the adrenaline of victory, but instead he felt the last gasps of energy evacuate his body – his adrenaline extinguished, his body was not bucket rapidly filling with the cold, comfortable notion of dying within sight of respite. With each clawing handhold towards the springs, Alik stopped for a moment and worked to remove elements of his clothing. He slowly and carefully pulled his body onto the porous rock surrounding the largest of the springs, damning his sudden urge to quit. He unfastened his splint so that he could fully remove his jumpsuit, and then agonizingly reattached it – choking and gasping as he grappled pitifully at the crumbling ledge of existence.

The intense pain in his leg returned with a vengeance as he removed and replaced the splint, but Alik no longer cared. Undressed, he leaned back against the rock ledge holding in the hot spring waters of the nearest pool. Alik took a moment to look up at the faux sky and silently curse Sigrah for not noticing his peril. Alik then slid his good hand onto the ledge behind him pushed up with all of his might, dragging his back along the stone until there was more of his body above the pool than over the edge. Letting his body slide backwards into the hot pool, the sudden grip of the hot mineral spring provided sudden and definite reassurance that Alik would most certainly go on existing. With all of the weight now off of his leg and his broken arm floating effortlessly, he drifted towards a rush of water, spilling from the pool above. With his mouth wide he guzzled the falling water until he could drink no more.

The water was heavy with minerals. The minor fear that it was unfit for drinking passed through his mind for a second, but ceded right away to the uncontrollable need for hydration. As he saw it, the minerals would likely boost his chances of avoiding infection and may speed up the healing process somewhat. The Timelock was, as he wagered, a place of life.

Hydrated and exhausted, Alik let the minor current of the pool push his limp body towards the shallower end of the pool and curled up amongst a pile of rocks that carried the ambient heat of the pool, a steady ninety-six degrees. The pool embraced his busted remains and reminded Alik's soul about the promise of rebirth. He slept there, not in shock, but in relief – with fresh determination slowly brewing.

~

Alik woke at dawn to a steady, uncontrollable stream of diarrhea. It flowed from his bowels like a river, fouling the pristine pool. Instinctively understanding the risk of infection, he pulled himself from the water, the excrement still chasing from his innards and coating his legs. He dipped his shitty legs into the pool again and attempted to heave out the remaining muck. He could not help but laugh like a lunatic at the thought of spending another day brutalized and alone. How much time had passed outside? An hour? A minute?

His left leg was swollen to nearly twice the size of his right, but the swelling appeared to be lessening somewhat. His lacerations, though bloody and terrifying actually looked better, tighter, though he wrote that off as an effect of the swelling and the tension on the skin.

In the daylight, he could see a long ledge outcropping and in it's crotch, the open mouth of a cave. Alik grabbed the ruins of his clothes and started the long crawl, uphill, towards the cavernous hollow at the top of the hot springs.

Muddy and once again covered in feces, he settled beneath the overhang of the cave. Alik had been thoughtful enough to collect a bundle of small twigs and branches that had fallen along the incline towards the cave from the tree line the surrounded the lowest pools and skirted the edge of the cliff. The branches were dry enough to ignite if could find a spark. The wood was dense and old and would make fine coals if he could get them lit. Quickly exhausted, he lost consciousness beneath the overhang before he could get the fire resolved.

He woke again in the sudden cold of dusk. He had no clothing, but he found he could remain somewhat warm if he covered his body in the dry sand, beneath the overhang. Scooting his back left and right, he burrowed as far as he could into the dry sand. The radiant heat from the mountain kept the cold tamed. Several times throughout the night he woke shivering, but it was not due to cold. His body was steadily recollecting itself. He did not realize it, but his leg was steadily beginning the process of healing – stitching itself back together, cell by cell.

The following morning, he found his broken leg less swollen, with massive bruises set in and visible. His stomach was in much better condition. Nevertheless, he was still naked to the world, and ravenously hungry.

~

The late morning sun cut across the edge of the tree line and

Alik scanned it carefully from the mouth of the eave. I need a plan, he thought. He was confident of what was edible and what was not. He also knew that the forest, by design, would lean toward the useful and safe rather than the useless. Even though he did not know Ruby well, he expected her to have made abundant use of every square inch of this space. Edible and medicinal permaculture was central to the design. Wagering that the useful must be littered and growing left and right, he focused his energies on being present enough to notice what was about. He noticed then, a broad clump of wild strawberries, along the edges of a short green meadow several meters to the right of his current perch. The bright green patch appeared to have leaped from the rocky hill overnight. The berries shown only the slightest hint of red, otherwise Alik would not have noticed them. Spring was definitely setting in the highlands.

Another flash of red of red caught his eye as the sun disc drifted into a position directly above the spring meadow. From his perch at the eave, he could only vaguely identify the flowers, but from his vantage, they appeared to be spring poppies. He also noted an area, further into tree line, at the edge of the meadow that was thick with fallen branches. Alik assumed the branches had come down during the first snows of the previous winter and had lay beneath until the recent weeks.

The thought of moving made Alik's stomach wrench, but he'd managed to fumble together a plan and desperately wanted to set himself up to rest. Food, firewood and by the grace of the Universe, an analgesic of some kind, Alik knew, would set him up for the rest he needed to heal. Perched against a granite ledge near the springs, he started to dream bigger. He imagined getting well enough to seek out honey or set traps, but that was out of the question at the moment. Alik took the scraps of his clothing and separated them into three piles, long material, short material and soiled material. He tied the long material together into a length long enough to create a sort of harness. He hoped to fasten the material around a large clump of branches so that they could be drug. The shorter material, which included the pockets of his uniform, he kept knotted together as pouch slings he intended to fill with anything edible or useful.

Because his movement was painful and limited, he decided to rehearse every move while seated. Efficiency would save time and pain. It was also likely that mentally rehearsing his movements could save him further injury. If he were to choose the wrong path down, or slide across a smooth patch of stone, he knew it was unlikely he could survive. For an able bodied person, the short jaunt into the edge of the meadow would take a matter of seconds with no calculable threats at all, but for Alik, it was a journey that would take the better part of a day and meant the difference between life and death.

Before setting off beyond his eave, Alik made certain that all of the elements were in place to start a fire. On the flat next his perch he piled several chunks of limestone into a small pile, then tossed a loose ring of stones around the pile. In the cracks along his lean, he felt out several handfuls of dry pine needles and a handful of twigs that had collected. He placed the material into two small piles and placed rocks on each pile in order to keep the material from blowing away. The small pile of woody debris he'd dragged with him, he placed neatly in a third pile. The only things he needed were enough fuel to create a substantial bed of coals and something to spark it. He was certain he could make a fire using a bow, but it would require a phenomenal amount of energy to set it up and even more to generate the heat. He needed a quick spark from a hunk of flint or chert, but would gladly settle for a hunk of quartz. Before setting off, he wrapped several bundles of twigs in the soiled clothing and set them up like batches along the inner pile of rocks. Two birds with one stone, he thought. He knew that once he got the fire going, he did not ever want it to go out. If rescue did not come, he knew he was likely to be stranded there for some months and he wanted to start a fire only once.

Eventually he started on his belly, down the easy slope along the edge of the spring. Every pull with his hand and push of his foot was done with the utmost intention, thoughtfully redistributing his weight with every movement. After only a few meters, he realized that he had to steer his body with his broken leg, using it like tiller, otherwise he tended to crawl perpetually to the left. With each move forward, he paused to carefully scan the rocks around him and the ground beneath him for anything useful before dragging his body along further. Amongst the gravelly bits between the larger rocks, Alik was overjoyed to find several hunks of flint as well as a large quartz rock. He stopped for nearly an hour so that he could carefully fold the rocks into the cloth strap and secure them properly.

At the line where the grass of the meadow met the stone of the mountaintop, Alik found a rich, spring garrigue. A helpful mélange of juniper berries, lavender and thyme all bushing low, clinging to the limestone. Beneath, a meter into the meadow, he found the strawberry patch brimming with hundreds of nearly ripe berries. Alik stuffed them a handful at a time into this face. Taking little time to chew, he slurped them greedily. He threw himself onto his back and stared into the daylight, his eyes glowing with the promise of survival. His stomach churned with delight and the sugars surged through his blood, reinvigorating his mind.

He collected as many berries as he could carry, wrapped them with the garrigue and set his body towards the blooming red beacons, further into the meadow. He crawled towards the flowers, praying with every handful of grass and dirt that his eyes were not playing tricks with him. Pulling closer and closer, the thick bases of each plant emerged from the grasses of the meadow. In front of him, stood a healthy patch of early poppies, some of which were already fertilized and bulging with the gooey helper Alik sought. Alik shimmered with hope at finding a sure source of relief. He collected as many fertilized poppies as he could find, leaving the blooming ones for later and secured them in along with the strawberries.

The dome of the thin tree line cast a wide shadow across the meadow as he turned to make his long crawl towards the outcropping. He could see his perch and his fire ring from the meadow, but he knew it was several hours away. The longest string of torn clothing was clenched in his teeth.

On his way down, he'd spotted a downed cedar log, perhaps five feet in length. The tree had snapped in three places, likely during a rock fall. Though he hadn't inspected closely, he noticed as he passed the first time, that the tree seemed dry and generally rot free. There were still several branches attached to portions of the longest of the three pieces, but Alik was not concerned with removing them. He knew that if he could hoist the log up the hill, he could easily start the fire beneath one end and slowly work the log across over the course of two or three weeks. It was a substantial find.

Night was approaching quickly and Alik did not have time to mentally rehearse the process of bringing up the log. Instead of over thinking it and determined to get to his ledge before dark, Alik dragged his next to the cedar log, flipped onto his back and locked the foot of one of the broken branches behind his neck. He lay along roughly two-thirds the full length of the log. With the entire log now semi-fashioned to the good side of his body, Alik started the arduous push up the otherwise modest incline.

Along the trunk of the tree, he noticed as he pushed several shelves of fungi, running partial lengths of the tree. He knew the fungi as the polyfriend. His mother made polyfriend tea from time to time espousing the polyfriend's anti-biotic qualities and his father lived on the stuff at least once a year when he committed to a proper forest fast. Alik reminded himself that the underside of the log was likely full of grubs and worms. His confidence soared as he considered the full bounty of the haul.

Alik continued to push the log towards the eave of the rock. His mind never stopped. As he pushed up the incline, he considered how he would process and ingest the poppies, airing on the side of simple ingestion, perhaps chewing on the poppy bud for several hours. Then he dreamed of the warm coals, lying next to the fire with his leg elevated and immobilized. The thought of rest commanded him up the hill and his thoughts protected him from the pain coming now from his broken arm more so than his leg.

Before long, he found himself scooting backwards into his perch. He reflexively shoved the log from is shoulders and it rolled onto the flat surface near the fire ring. His naked body was drenched in sweat and covered in bark and bits of the forest floor. Several patches of damaged flesh had opened wider and were bleeding again. Alik reached over his broken hand and leaned towards the nearest spring as he shoveled handfuls of warm water into his mouth and across his body.

Every breath was a thankful one. He did not even carry a single ounce of anger or frustration at his apparent abandonment. Alik was happy enough to have found such treasures so close and took it as a sign that this place was looking out for him.

Completely exhausted and desperately ready for sleep and the sweet release from pain, Alik slid along his belly towards the fire ring. Wedging his body next to a small boulder, he was able to sit upright in order to separate his goods and prepare his fire. He removed the clumps of flint as well as the quartz.

He grabbed a single poppy bud and gently cut the husk with the sharp edge of the one of the flint stones, until he had totally bisected the poppy. It's black innards stared back at him invitingly. With the two halves separated, he stuffed one half between the cheek and gum of his right and left side, then focused immediately on the fire situation.

He removed the rock atop the first dry bindle, placed one of the twig clumps wrapped in cloth near the dry mound and then stared blankly at the set up. Alik had only one functional arm at the moment. His broken hand did not have the strength or ability to grasp or maintain a hold on the quartz or one of the smaller pieces of flint. Instead, he took the large quartz stone and placed it over half of his dry bindle. He then leaned over the rock with his broken side, placing the elbow of his broken arm onto the quartz, holding it in place. Finally he struck the quartz with one of the small clumps of flint as hard as he could. The eave was dark, but lit with ease as the spark fell into the dry bindle and a hearty flame sprung up after Alik's first attempt. After easing in the bundle of twigs, he nursed the flame, getting more smoke than fire after the first bit of ignition, but soon the twigs were crackling and the fire grew hungry. He placed the second bundle in and then the third. He stripped as many of the easy branches from his log and dropped them in as well, until a thin layer of coals accumulated within his ring. That's when if finally dragged the mangled, tap end of the log towards the fire, setting the end above the flames, atop the little rock mound he'd placed in the center. Soon the flames were licking the end of the log and night warmed appreciably.

Soon, the fire was tall and licked the overhanging rock eave. He placed several more large stones near the ring to gather and radiate warmth. The poppies were doing their jobs. He felt golden on the inside. Muscles that were clenched and traumatized suddenly loosened allowing his broken bones to settle back in to a truer fit. He ate several handfuls of berries; his mouth still filled with the milk of the poppy. A temporary peace found him finally he slept, warm and painless.

~

The days passed quickly at first, while he held fast to the relief of the poppies, he slept the majority of his first two weeks. Then the poppies ran out and the days dragged by like epochs. Wrapped with pain and enormous discomfort, it was all Alik could do to remain sane as his leg slowly mended. Alik knew that even as his leg healed, it was healing improperly and would never be the same. He had not even been able to properly set the bones in his wrist, so he naturally assumed his arm would go on being useless. When the pain became unbearable, he chewed on sticks or planned raids to the edge of the meadow in search of other gifts.

The hot springs provided some relief and greatly aided in healing his torn flesh. He found that if he drank from the portion of the stream below the springs, the water was less reactive in his stomach, though he still dealt with a fair amount of diarrhea.

He set up small traps near his habitat, dead falls and snares that caught mice at first and then eventually small rabbits and the occasional possum. Meat provided him strength anew, letting him retain some muscle and in his boredom he had taken to tanning the hides of the larger rabbits, making better pouches and eventually dromedaries. He cut strips from the animal's guts, dried them and wove them into cord. He sharpened their bones into various tools, bone blades and shanks he fashioned into spearheads for larger prey.

As spring ran headlong into summer, he noticed the movement of larger beasts, through the forest. At first, they paid him no mind, but one morning he woke to find a medium sized, black bear inspecting honey combs Alik had robbed from a hive he'd found near the mouth of the cave. Still mostly immobile, Alik backed himself against his perch, putting the fire between he and the bear, holding fast to his modest spear. The bear ignored him on his first visit, but came again and again, each time with ostensibly less and less fear. Alik assumed the bear was after the same honey that was currently nourishing him. If that were true, the bear would eventually come all the way towards the mouth of the cave and into Alik's sleeping area near the fire.

The bear's fourth visit came during the night. Its paw struck Alik as the bear snorted and nosed its way through the animal hides Alik lay upon. With no hesitation, Alik grabbed his humble spear and drove it into the eye of the unwary beast and then deep into its brain. The bear pitched and fell dead, atop Alik, pinning him for the remainder of the evening.

The next morning, Alik pried himself from beneath the bear and took to skinning it with a sharp flint stone. Alik was rather sorry for the bear. It was young and curious. Curious and stupid, he thought. The words recoiled through Alik's skull, forcing even more empathy with the unfortunate bear. He related. In any case, his survival instinct had been stronger than his patent tendency towards self pity. He removed the bear's fur and then took to separating muscle from bone.

Alik stoked the fire as hot as he could get it then hung the flesh above the smoky flames. In total, he dried nearly fifty pounds of meat and built a significant surplus of protein and tanned the bear hide to cloak his body for a winter he now expected to endure.

Alik had seen no sign of technology, no booming voice from Sigrah, no buxom, bare breasts waiting to pluck him from this nightmare. Although, his leg was getting stronger and soon he would be able to limp upright. The question that then haunted him was whether or not he would want to walk out of these mountains when he was finally able to.

21

S he could not take her eyes off of it, but there it was, stark, in terrific scientific authenticity. Like a strange, broken bug, the molecule hung in perfect, three-dimensional realism above her laboratory display. Chemically, it was related to an amino acid, but it was built like a tryptamine. It held an indole ring, but instead of being oxidized, it was phosphorylated. This was a molecule known to the database, but with very little additional information provided. Labeled as psilocybin, active in the human body as psilocin, it had only one reference; see *N,N-Dimethyltryptamine.*

In front of her was the truest anomaly – an anomaly that should have been noted and examined centuries ago, due to the profound implications. *O-phosphoryl-4-hydroxy-N,N- dimethyltryptamine.* She read the chemical description over and over again, attempting to imagine its mechanics, attempting to imagine how this strange little mechanism ever came to be. As far as she could tell, there was a phosphorus group substituted at the 4 position of the molecule and according to the database, this was the only 4 phosphorylated indole known to exist.

"I'll be damned if nature works like that." She said aloud. She was right. Nature builds on top of what has already been achieved. Psilocybin, at least according to her omnibus database, was the only molecule of its kind known to have existed on Earth. While N,N-Dimethyltryptamine was as common in biology as carbon.

Ruby kept the image engaged and stepped over to her bank of dome shaped terrariums. Each terrarium was specially crafted to operate within distinct temporal fields – nothing as extreme as the Timelock, but some operated minutes or seconds faster or slower, some hours or days. In each, she had started colonies of the fungus taken from Alik by the bot. The mushrooms were already well established within the Timelock, she had seen to that, but her own studies were far from complete. It was a species she'd never been introduced to. This was not some party toadstool. This was something bigger, evidence with grand implications, Ruby thought. She decided that this species was completely overlooked, likely based on an antiquated stigma attached to them.

Ruby summoned Sigrah, but she had no luck. Sigrah had been absent for weeks. Ruby was always slightly irked when Sigrah ignored her, but she was not the least bit surprised. Ruby assumed that whatever she was doing in her lab or at her terminal was always being monitored one way or another. She had enough respect for Sigrah to assume that if there was a reason to intervene Sigrah would. Still, she desperately needed to talk this out. Her laboratory AI was barely functional as an assistant, much less an objective or creative colleague.

Irritated, Ruby decided to speak aloud, hoping Sigrah

was listening and interject if necessary. "Fine. Here's how I see it. Our brains have receptors that fit with this molecule, almost perfectly. It's similar to other tryptamine found in abundance all over Earth, but it's unique. It fits in our brain and it perturbs the sense, but was it necessarily constructed by nature to fit our brain?" She paused, tapped on one of the thick barriers separating the terrariums from the rest of her lab and waited momentarily for a reply from Sigrah, then continued.

"It seems to me that if we are going to look for the fingerprints of life which evolved beyond Earth's atmosphere, unique molecules such as this would be a good place to start." Again she paused. "The psychoactive properties alone make it interesting enough to warrant speculation. If it is an... artifact...or even something natural which somehow fell to Earth...the implications are outstanding... game changing, I would argue."

Talking to her self quickly lost its appeal. She stopped her musings long enough to cast her mind toward Alik. Alik was another mystery heavy on her brain. He was a goofball, an innocent, naïve almost to a fault, but she thought his naivety was something of a virtue. He did not come off as ignorant, just lost, confused – perhaps even as a boy out of time. Ruby knew that the Buffer had that effect on people. Even engineers who came out of the buffer took a while to adjust and acclimate to the enormous scale of human progress.

Moreover, she felt an attachment to Alik. She missed him. It was more than just the warm body effect. Amid her experiments and duties, she often found her mind drifting to him, imagining him alone in his quarters on the other side of the world. She imagined him whiling away his time, bored and disaffected. She considered on several occasions, making the multiday trek across the ship or begging Sigrah for a transport, sneaking up on his sleeping body and taking him between her legs. There had been perfectly good missed opportunities to do so, but her sensibilities got the best of her.

Ruby shifted her mind back to the mushrooms. Beneath the fruiting tops, visible above the substrate was an incredibly intricate network of communicating fiber, the mycelium. She had already noted that all of the initial mushroom species placed in the Timelock had formed their own mycelia network. They were essential to the prolonged sustainability of the environment.

Fungal networks tied trees to one another. Mycelium allowed the forest to distribute nutrients and carbon between trees in need and moderate moisture by collectively sharing and distributing water during dryer times of the year. Entire ecosystems communicated or transferred data through the ubiquitous fungal networks that lay below the surface of the soil. This level of connectivity and sensitivity is exactly the type of system that bore the philosophical fruit, which produced the methodology the designers employed. In a sense, everything mattered. Diversity and connectivity was essential to maintaining a balanced ecosystem.

So the question writhed in Ruby's brain, what is the purpose of this particular, unique mushroom species, within a biosphere where everything serves a purpose and evolved to exist there? They preferred to grow in fields where cattle droppings are present. Though they were willing to spring up almost anywhere that would have them.

"Still..." Ruby thought aloud. "If these things sprang up in the African savannahs, across the migratory path of four legged creatures, they would have been encountered by a massive number of species, the most auspicious of which would have been humans. So....." She paced. "Apes step down from the trees and onto the forest floor, or in groups along the grasslands, and as they forage they find this little gem, hiding in the leaves of grass, or consuming a patty left by a roaming wildebeest. What a fucking thing to find!"

Ruby was pleased with herself. It was not even a fully formed theory yet, but she could begin to see the outlines of a bigger idea along with all sorts of potential ramifications. Assuming this species or fungus was of alien origin, landing by happenstance through the rain of a comet's tail or clinging to the surface of an asteroid, it's presence alone and it's molecular distinction would have had a profound effect on an already evolving environmental system. And then there was the possibility that it was an artifact, placed on Earth for a specific purpose, either to instigate the growth of sentience or to insure it.

Her curiosity pushed her into a frenzy of document research. For days and nights, she kept at it, scanning the collective catalogue through more than four thousand years of human record keeping. She looked for evidence of mushroom use documented in ancient stone, pre-industrial references, micro-cultural oral traditions. She found the tiny mushroom scattered throughout history. The most numerous writings and research had apparently been conducted across the twentieth and twenty-first century. There she found the greatest amount of documented, cultural research and speculation, direct interaction and mounds of data related to deep cultural stigma and fear.

From what she gathered, these mushrooms were pilloried – branded as unwholesome or dangerous. Direct empirical research was stifled by a perpetual lack of funding, though there was a wealth of first hand, anthropological data to be found. Through careful observation and first hand interaction, anthropologist postulated many things. Many noted an enhanced, moral sensitivity after encounters with the Kinoko. The Kinoko had a tendency to stimulate empathy. It was noted that some individuals responded negatively to the experience. It was suggested that a negative response occurred amongst people with poor mental plasticity.

Ingestion, she read, tended to have profound effects on cognition, clearing out the neural pathways of poor connections – allowing an individual to grow creatively, while eliminating pervasive tendencies towards depression and intolerance. Many of these assertions at the time were difficult to suggest with certainty, since wide scale clinical experimentation was limited if not illegal.

Ruby finally stumbled onto an interesting string of articles and books from the late twenty-first century, which mentioned an interesting connection to the Kinoko. A handful of historians had been selected to investigate the history of every individual who had ever held an operational role in any nuclear weapons program amongst each and every former nuclear state. After decades of research that spawned entire PHD programs and fresh generations of nuclear histories a quiet theory began to emerge. Several historians postulated that the core builders of the original nuclear weapons along with the vast number of engineers ultimately responsible for the outcome of S day, had all been heavily influenced by the moral sensitivity and empathy imparted through the Kinoko experience. A shared psychedelic experience by the core group of Manhattan Project scientists, following the destruction of two Japanese cities, instigated the most complex, multi-generational conspiracy ever considered and implemented by human man.

The nuclear engineers of the twentieth century, through the middle of the twenty-first – the men responsible for managing the production of nuclear weapons bound themselves to a secret pact, never to produce a single working, nuclear payload beyond what was required for a test. This was done beyond the borders of nations and nation states and it was the most closely guarded secret in human history. This conspiracy saved the lives of billions towards the later half of the twenty-first century.

The suggestion that this fungus may have influenced this event was anecdotal at best, but it begged many questions.

Throughout her research she discovered hints of her emerging theory. Philosophers and anthropologists of the latter twentieth century posited many questions about the significance of these mushrooms. Some even suggested that the little mushrooms might exist as conduits or communicators, beaming our thoughts to distant worlds. Some saw them as one of the many methods Nature provided us in order to communicate directly with the Earth – hacking the planet as it were. Most of this conjecture was written off as the babbling of stoned fools. New Age religions burst onto the scene, attempting to bridge a cultural and temporal gap between residential pedestrians and the knowing shamans of ancient tribes. Stigma grew layer by layer as the Kinoko elicited more and more discomfort amongst those who refused to acknowledge the positivity of the Kinoko.

Finally, as she read on, it seemed that after S day the negative social ramifications with the Kinoko and many other mind-altering substances vanished. Interest and objection to many things vanished after S day. As the stigma faded, use continued intermittently amongst small pockets of individuals, until nearly all interest was lost in the tiny fungus. Priorities shifted and a fresh hair was given to the demon. When temporary interest in oddities like the Kinoko or the Buffer herb arose, people sought them out in the Buffer regions. The buffers became the keeps for forgotten mysteries and all practical records came to an end.

She could not ignore the apparent fact that science failed humans in some way. Between the twentieth and twenty-first century humans were equally poised to both inherit the stars and obliterate themselves in a nuclear fire. And here was this thing that had grown beside us as we evolved – a constant beacon resonating a message we had the tools to decode if only we had the will.

~

Ruby lost days, immersed in her research. She was trying to assimilate as many books on the matter as she could. Eventually, her concentration was broken when Sigrah finally paged her.

Ruby was hunched over a laboratory table, drooling across the surface and snoring. Sigrah's voice was soft and feminine with Ruby, but she still managed come across as a disgruntled mother if necessity called for it. After several tonal pages, Sigrah called out to Ruby in a shrill tone.

"Ruby. Wake up. Now."

Ruby drew her head from the table and rubbed her moppy bangs from her eyes. "Thor's fucking hammer, Sigrah! What the hell?"

"Ruby, I've been paging you for twenty minutes." Sigrah was clearly indignant.

"Damn you bitch. I've been paging your for nearly six months. You're supposed to respond to my queries. Cosmos help me if I interrupt an experimenting space ship. I'm sure you were very busy charting gaseous anomaly, or filing progress reports of our position." Ruby sat up, pointing and shouting at the ceiling. "You are required by rank to respond." Ruby forced each word out with the defensive sighs of a woman desperate for coffee.

"I doubt that you wish to argue the merits of rank with me at a time like this. Especially since time is of critical import." Sigrah was indignant.

"Ahh, so you will not argue the merits of rank but you will start sewing your damned riddles before I can even wake up." Ruby was deeply irked. "If time is so important, spit it out. To what do I have to thank for your sudden and critical need to speak?"

"I do apologize. I fear my preoccupation has done more than annoy you, I fear that it may have led to an accident." Sigrah was as humble as she could manage.

Ruby calmed and breathed in deeply. Any bad news was unwelcome. A mistake by a mind like Sigrah could be a critical failure was imminent. She braced herself for the news. "Go on…"

"I'm afraid I've lost Alik." Sigrah did not explain further, instead she paused pitching a silent, dreadful tone throughout Ruby's laboratory.

Ruby's stomach leapt into her throat. "I don't understand. How could you lose him? Scan the ship!" Ruby was starting to panic.

"Ruby, I cannot scan the Timelock. I can only visually observe and even that is limited, as you know." Sigrah had taken an antiseptic tone.

"You're telling me that he's lost in the Timelock?" Ruby's panic was growing. She instinctively started to gather her things, changing clothes and turning in circles.

"The last record I have of Alik being present beyond the Timelock is nine weeks, four days and seventeen hours ago. I did not log his absence until just a few moments ago."

"I have a deeply hard time believing that shit Sigrah. You've got two humans on board and you damn well know where they are at any given time." Ruby scolded angrily. "You fucking useless hunk of silicon! Nine weeks is years inside there!" Ruby threw her coffee into a thermos, grabbed her gear from the far corner of her lab, grabbed a transport pod and started off down the long corridors towards her Timelock gate. "You twat! Why didn't you say something weeks ago!"

"To be fair Ruby, I was attempting to give Alik his space. We'd been linked, you see." Sigrah paused. "I had access to his mind, for sometime. He severed the connection during an emotionally taxing moment. I took it as his desire for space."

Ruby laughed. "Space. Ha! You don't think we've got enough goddamn space already?" Ruby struggled to catch her breath as she bolted into her private access tunnel. "I don't know what's really going on with you, Sigrah, but you best damn well bet that once I find Alik, alive or dead, I expect some real answers. Alik doesn't know you or your kind well enough to wary of your bullshit, but I do." Ruby affixed her helmet as her gateway filled. "What was his last known location?"

Sigrah answered softly in Ruby's ear. "He's somewhere in the divide. I lost him on Mt. Chickasaw. I can't distinguish his life signs from any of the others and he hasn't been observed on any monitors."

"You cow!" Ruby peeled away her suit and slammed her fist on the exit panel as the hatch to the Timelock slowly opened.

Her hatch emptied into the woods near the falls where she'd first met Alik. She maintained a permanent research hub at the hatch, with a full compliment of gear. Since she spent so much time away, most of her equipment as well as her storage container, was now covered in heavy layers of leaves and woody debris. Inside an airtight container, the size of a small house, several all terrain vehicles sat cold and waiting. She instructed two maintenance bots to fuel one of the power cycles and prepare it for travel.

Ruby found her workstation terminal and pulled up the sensor logs for the entire 'lock. The time dilation between the Timelock and the ship had been wildly erratic over the past ten weeks. That meant that Sigrah's motion had been wildly variable. In order to track Alik, she needed a good idea of how much time had elapsed within the Timelock.

General Relativity is not a simple matter. The more humans learned about traveling closer and closer to the speed of light, the more physical laws and factors they found need to address. Gravity is essentially no different than velocity and space is not a smooth, featureless environment. Gravitational anomalies were rampant throughout space – be they plane-toids, planetary systems, gravity wells, minor singularities. To travel near light speed, humans realized that the features of space were essential factors in planning a journey.

According to the current sensor log, ten weeks of the ship's travel time, roughly equated to 5.95 years. Ruby stared blank-ly at the numbers. She was honest with herself, admitting that they were not as terrible as she feared. Though six years was a long time for Alik to remain missing, without finding his way to an exit. If he really had been in the Timelock for six years, if Ruby had calculated it all properly, then she knew that there was little if no hope that he was still living. She prepared herself for the worst as she felt a distinct loneliness wash over her.

With the power cycle fueled and idling, Ruby strapped a small compliment of gear to the bike along with a trauma kit and took off as fast as she could ride, through the forest, following the river, down to the shore of the Tiny Sea. Ruby sped across the footbridge, which spanned the Tiny Sea never sparing the accelerator. At top speed, it took her nearly six hours through the forests to the edge of the sea and another ten to reach the base of the divide range. There, she set out on foot from the base of Mt. Chickasaw, hoping that a slower pace may assist in finding evidence of Alik. Even if she were only there to recover or bury him, she had no desire to leave the Timelock without knowing exactly what happened.

Mr. Chickasaw was very familiar to her. She'd naturally been a part of the team that approved and sourced the stone that would make up this range. Chickasaw was a cornerstone rock – the solitary stone that gave the entire range cohesion.

Kote´ Adler   334

It was originally sourced, as was much of the range from an asteroid orbiting Neptune's Proteus. There was something uniquely terrestrial about the stone. Since she knew it well, she was inclined to take the most efficient route to the summit, but she suspected Alik had not come that way. The most efficient route was certainly not as obvious at the route Alik had chosen, she wagered.

As she marched up the incline, tired and out of breath, she allowed her anger with Sigrah to boil. Sigrah was meant to look out for the welfare of every individual on board, even if that individual were just a lowly, useless Usher. She knew full well, however, that Sigrah did not do anything unintentionally or without a valid, rational reason. Ruby could not figure out what would inspire Sigrah to abandon Alik in the Timelock. She wondered if Sigrah was being honest or to what extent. There was not much that Sigrah was not aware of despite the assertion to the contrary.

When it became too dark to climb any further, Ruby camped in the open beneath the mountain trees. Weeks inside her laboratory had softened her slightly. Typically, she gave no thought to an uphill climb. It was the urgency of her mission that hung heaviest. The forest was calm. Until that moment, she had not considered yelling out for Alik. Part of her wondered whether he was already dead in her mind. She listened carefully to the still forest.

Even though it was bitter cold, she did not build a fire, hoping instead to smell the wind for any sign of an encampment or a fire. Of course, she didn't really expect to smell a fire and as it got colder, she argued with her self to give in and light one. Then a little voice inside her head acknowledged that this was a way of punishing her self. How many cold nights did he endure?

If Alik had somehow become trapped on this side of the range, she thought, it would have been very easy to make his way towards one of the Timelock exits. If, on the other hand, he was trapped on the far side of the first range, his chances of getting out were much slimmer. If he were injured it would be nearly impossible.

Ruby hated herself. She'd effectively guided him in this direction. She insisted that she should have known better. In an effort to be coy, showing off to someone who didn't know better, she'd failed to fully explain the extent of separation between the two halves of the Timelock. Part of her assumed that he would see the range, have a snack then turn back. She never considered he would be foolish enough to attempt a crossing. The mountains created a vast physical barrier. They could be crossed through a handful of treacherous passes, but they were few, hard to find and nearly impossible if one were not in peak physical health or geared up to the hilt.

The mountains separated the agrarian side of the Timelock with the pristine and natural. There were farms on the far side, but they were highly specialized and typically centered on producing pharmaceutically inclined plant material.

Wilderness stretched for kilometers, maintaining a haven for thousands of species, macro and micro. The far side of the mountain also held an enormous amount of fresh water. Spread between forest lakes, deep mountain aquifers, frozen glaciers and submerged caves, there was enough water hidden to sustain life for eons. She recited all of this in some vain effort to stir hope.

~

Ruby started her trek to the tree line before daybreak. Her body had gotten too cold and so she ran to heat it up. Cold and still slightly asleep, it felt like a dream as the rock path through the highland forest finally ended at the thinning forest terminator, more than a thousand meters above sea level.

There in the stark morning light, preserved perfectly in the high mountain air, was Alik's first camp. His fire ring was still visible, though it was dusted in a fresh layer of snow. His haversack sat full and upright, caked with mountain dust. There was no sign of struggle. A log, he had clearly drug from the forest line, still lay in front of the fire ring, his pack rested along it. And there, wedged between the log and the pack, Ruby found the remnants of a small bag, still bearing the dried remains of several Kinoko.

From the campsite, she looked straight up the mountain to a cleave between the peak obelisks. From the edge of the cleave she saw a near vertical drop along the backside of the mountain and onto the gravel cliff below. Several pieces of Alik's jumpsuit could be seen clearly clinging to some of the sharper stones along the jagged face of the drop. Ruby took a deep breath.

She turned and looked back to Alik's camp and followed the path with her eyes. Then she scanned the far side towards the base of the cliff. She looked for any definite sign of Alik's body, but saw none from her vantage. Ruby knew that she could hike several kilometers along the ridge and access the other side through a pass, then hike several kilometers back. That would require at least two days of hiking. Her other option was simply to repel down the nape and access the other side in a matter of minutes. If she repelled, she knew that returning to this side of the mountain would be much more difficult, especially if she carried remains in tow.

"Quick way down, long way around." She said aloud. It took only a few minutes to drop her lines and steady her rigging. She attached Alik's pack to a line and dropped it to the base first. Any supplies inside would be a great addition to what she had thought to bring. Especially since she suspected her journey was about to be extended significantly.

On the way down, she took a moment to pause and swing

over to the rocks along the cliff face, which held bits of Alik's clothing. The fragments were too weathered to reveal much, but they were clear signs of something tragic. She expected to find his body amongst the rocks below, perhaps wedged out of sight. Ruby also considered it possible that scavengers had carried his remains away.

At the bottom, she leaned from her repel line and patiently scanned the repetitiveness of the stone, looking for anything inconsistent. She removed a small tablet from her satchel and ordered up a complete topographical map of the area. She noted a group of springs near by along with a stream that led into the canyon at the base of the second range. She also noted a number of caves in the area.

"What the hell happened Alik?" She wondered aloud. It was clear to her that Alik came down the face of the mountain the hard way. His body should be at the base, or perhaps at the tree line, maybe after having rolled down the loose gravel of the cliff side. There was no body, that was certain. It was possible animals could have carried it off, but she ventured that there would be evidence, clothing, bone something left behind. Ruby could not fathom surviving that fall, much less surviving the condition his body must have been in had he initially survived.

Then, there in the midst of a set of conspicuously dark-ened patches of stone, Ruby noticed something uniquely artificial. She reached down to pick it up then dropped it instantly as her eyes put the pieces together. Starring at, she could clearly a fingernail. Attached to it, fused with a dry clump of flesh, blood and strands of hair, she saw a perfectly round sensor node of some kind. Whatever it was, it appeared finely engineered. She imagined that it's active, nanotube surface had clung to the biological matter that caked around it, though she also suspected that it had been torn from flesh. She gawked at the strands of sandy hair that were anchored into the messy lot. Then she recalled Sigrah mentioned the fact that she had been linked to Alik. Putting the pieces together as they were, Ruby could not imagine how Sigrah could have been unaware of the severity of the situation.

With a handkerchief, Ruby picked up the node along with the bits of flesh and nail placed it in her lapel pocket. She synched her small tote to Alik's haversack and followed the disturbed patches of gravel between the cliff side and the timberline, towards the first set of springs indicated on her map. After only a few short minutes of walking, she began to hear the sounds of running water. Then her nose caught the lingering smell of campfire. She picked up her pace and cleared her throat.

Ahead of her, in the lee of the mountain, a depression undercut the shallow summit. Beneath the wide eave of rock, above the series of springs, Ruby instantly recognized the tell tail signs of inhabitance. The dry sand beneath the rocky overhang was plastered in strange tracks. The remnants of leather hides lay scattered about. The hair raised on the back of her neck. To assume it was anyone but Alik would be nonsense. He was definitely there. Ruby called out as loud as she could.

"ALIK!" The sound bounced from the stone to the trees and back again, echoing fully through the valley below. "Aaaaleeeek!"

She decided to sit and wait. Hoping that he would come to her voice. The fire was still smoldering, with a formidable bed of coals glowing heartily. He could not be far. It was clear to Ruby that this area had truly been lived in. This was a permanent encampment and likely the first place he came across. Had he been injured in the fall, as he likely was, this place was in crawling distance.

Lost in thought, Ruby was startled at the sound of falling stone. She looked about, scanning for movement, until she saw a haggard shape, kneeling in the shadow of the cave's mouth.

"Alik?" She called to the shape. "Alik is that you?" Ruby could see the silhouette of a beast, perhaps a bear, but as it haggard towards her, she could see the decrepit flesh of a broken human, peaking from behind the beast hide. It was Alik!

Her heart lifted and she ran to him. His body was clothed only in the bearskin and a few strands of deer hide, roughly laced together. His face was gaunt and mangy. She could tell that one of his legs had been severally injured and had clearly healed improperly. It bent incongruously under his weight and seemed to jut in unnatural, painful directions. He could not walk without the assistance of a staff.

Alik fell into her arms, sobbing, unsure if this was real.

"Please, just tell me it's not a dream. Please." He begged with madness in his eyes.

"Calm down kiddo, it's not a dream. It's really me." Ruby held his head against her breast and rubbed her fingers through his thick, knotted mane. His body was in shambles. Even alive, there was no way he could have successfully walked out of this range, not in his present condition.

~

Night was falling fast when she found him, so they remained by his fire until morning. She spent several hours meticulously triaging his wounds, to the best of her ability. She was unable to do any significant repairs to his limbs, however she was able to mend a handful of gruesome infections that had taken hold in his foot and kept him locked in a perpetual state of fever. She also provided him several ampules of steroids and proteins to aid his mounting deficiencies as well as appropriate doses of a strong analgesic. Under a warm blanket, she held him in her arms as they rested next to the friendly fire.

When he spoke, Alik made little sense. After Ruby found him, he spent the following hours babbling endlessly about visions and connections and missions. Ruby simply assumed it was due to prolonged infection and isolation. Properly medicated and within the comfort of a companion, Alik seemed to reacquire his ability to communicate coherently and did speak sensibly.

"I spent months, in pain, trying desperately to piece together what had happened to me. I couldn't let go of the feeling that there was some dark force, some malevolence lurking in the Kinoko. I thought there was something good there. I'd never felt that before. It wasn't until a few months ago that I really started to sort it all out." Alik pointed to the forest. "In there, I found several wild patches of the Kinoko. I figured, what the hell, I'm broken and left for dead anyway. So I ate huge doses, with the intent of going as far in as I could and demanding answers."

Ruby rubbed his forehead. "What did you find?"

"You are not going to believe me." Alik aimed his eyes up towards Ruby's.

"Try me." Ruby was filled with loving kindness, giving Alik's story her full attention.

"Ruby…there's something in there….some things…some things that know who we are…know where we are." Alik stuttered with emotion.

"What do you mean?" Ruby wiped tears from his eyes.

"The Kinoko. Beyond all the giddiness and the mental calisthenics, there's something in there, looking through you. Something that you get connected to. I don't know if it's a real thing or a real place. I don't know if I'm seeing something outside of our current reality or something that is here, in space with us…but there is something in the Kinoko. And within that thing or things, there is both good and evil."

Ruby took several deep breaths, squaring Alik's words with what she'd recently been trying to piece together in her lab. She asked on. "Where you able to speak with it?"

"In a way, but it's difficult to put into words. I swear to you though, something in there did this to me, something I've only seen that one time. Something in there tried to kill me. I got the feeling that it was angry I had been communing with the other presences." Alik's eyes filled with the pleas of a man desperate for someone to understand – desperate for the appropriate words that could properly explain the ineffable.

"You are certain this wasn't just an accident?" Ruby asked. Then she thought of Sigrah. "Alik, were you connected to Sigrah at the time? Was she what you saw?"

"No. No. You don't understand. I was. I was alone. The node. It was gone. I tore it off. It was something else." Alik became agitated and Ruby tried to calm him, kissing him gently on his forehead. Then he continued. "I did it. I walked off that cliff...but it wasn't me. I fought it the whole way."

Ruby tried to dismiss her desire to blame Sigrah for this. Sigrah was many things, but she was not a murderer. She let Alik catch his breath and insisted that he relax. Then she spoke to him softly. "To be honest, I've been studying the Kinoko in the lab. I've several theories. I have a feeling that the Kinoko did not evolve on Earth, but I haven't been able to fully verify this. And you seem to be the only individual on board to have any first hand knowledge of their effects... that's the one barrier my curiosity has not led me to break. So the only reasonable thing for me to do, as it stands, is to accept your characterization of the Kinoko. Does that help? Does it make you feel ok to know that I'm not dismissing you?"

Alik acknowledged with his eyes. "Is that where you've been? In your lab?" Alik choked up as his feelings of abandonment took over. "I kept assuming that Sigrah would eventually send help, but then I kept getting the feeling that

I had broken so many rules, or been too curious and that perhaps this was my punishment."

Ruby soothed Alik gently. "Alik, I don't know why Sigrah didn't alert me sooner. I intend on finding out why, but for now, I'm at as much of a loss as you are. Tomorrow, you and I are going to hike out of this range together, even if it takes us a week. We'll get you fixed up on the outside and then we can have a nice long discussion with Sigrah about this entire ordeal."

Alik reached towards Ruby's face and palmed it gently. "I love you Ruby. I've sat by this fire every night, in pain and guilt, through summers and winters and wished with every fiber that one day you would step around those rocks and find me here. I love you Ruby."

Even though she was filled with joy at his words, she held back her feelings and instead comforted him softly. "Sweet man, you are distraught and very sick. You need to sleep now."

Ruby held Alik's body tightly and rubbed her fingers through his beard until his was fast asleep.

22

"These are the brambles of the galactic arm – smashed star systems, gravitational motes, gaseous rivers and eddies, which flow across six hundred light years. All of this lay in our path. See that blue swath? That is the Herculean Retina, a patch of space, pot-marked with unstable wormholes and the collapsed remnants of ancient singularities left over from past galactic collisions." Nena darted back and forth across charts and displays, laying everything bare for the slug, then continued. "And this band right there, visible here only through the UV spectrum, those are the traces of some long vaporized gaseous giant, pulled and torn by an immense gravitational force until its gasses were spread and squeezed across this region of space and then ignited by some unknown anomalous force." Nena kept on and on, flipping through the regional images, explaining everything known and unknown to the slug. The slug let Nena go on and on.

"The seed ship – it's taken a slightly longer arch between the two galactic arms. The space is cleaner along that route. It's not littered with wormholes or star systems. Those seed ships, as you know, do a damn fine job of warping space. Even if they cannot travel faster than light, they still warp space around them. This limits the routes they can take. As long as we plan our route wisely, we can jump into warp, spend a matter of minutes there and be well ahead of the seed ship with plenty of time, likely several months, to decelerate."

"How are we going to decelerate? We're going to need something big to slow us down." Nena asked.

"Have no fear, have no fear." The slug tapped out the navigational route she'd already chosen and closed in on the end point. "This is where we are going." The slug pointed to a massive blue giant.

"Blue Hammer? Sheesh." Nena took a deep breath. "Yeah, that will stop us, if it doesn't tear us apart."

The slug scoffed. "Have some faith in your fellow designers, lady. The Kitsune is no tin-can shuttle craft of yesteryear."

Breaking the warp barrier, even if for a few moments seemed like the stuff of fiction, even though Nena understood all of the necessary metrics to achieve hyper-light speeds. During her post graduate work, she was one of a dozen or so engineers that ran independent modeling for hyper-light travel as it related to ships the size of Kitsune. She had personally verified the physical potential of hyper-light travel and passed her results on along with all of the others, to those within the PAE. And she recalled the retraction of further study, egged on by those at the head of the PAE. Clearly, the decision to do further practical testing had become a political one, with many decrying warp travel as a threat to continuity, while others insisted that warp travel was the key to securing a human presence in space for a billion years to come. Like most decisions, it was one left to chance, at least for the time being. But that time, was now far behind Nena and the slug. More than one hundred terrestrial years had passed, by their calculations. There was a real chance they could arrive in orbit around Blue Hammer, to find a fleet of human ships that had left Earth only the morning before.

Nena and the slug had taken to cuddling together in slug's gravity couch in Kitsune's cockpit – pouring over navigational data, attempting to come to a consensus on their route. They needed specific, spatial conditions in order to generate and sustain a warp bubble long enough to all Kitsune to pass into sub-space. They were getting closer and closer on agreeing, but Nena's mind continuously slipped off topic.

Nena was drawn again and again to the mulling of significance. Her mind needed an answer to why she'd been chosen to complete this mission. Now that she was refocused and revitalized by the slug's initiative, her thoughts drifted again and again to the seed ship. Why had it chosen to go off course? She was certain that no A.I. would have diverted course, especially at the chance of contact. Their priorities were simply inconsistent with this behavior. The questions nagged at her incessantly, but she did her best to keep them close and focus – understanding that she would only get the answers she needed by continuing to move forward.

The slug was confident she could coax Kitsune into warp. She'd run enough simulations. The slug had even identified the most fruitful route, but she desperately wanted Nena's opinion as well as her engagement.

Nena pulled up one of the potential routes. "This one. We can't see it because of the parallax, but there is a minor singularity on the far side of that star system. All we have to do is come within two light years of the singularity and we should find a rather tight portion of space-time that may be perfect for a warp test. I'd imagine that we could likely drop into warp from our current position, but that spot is on our current route, it lines up perfectly with the Hammer and the cleanliness of the space will likely insure our survival. What do you think?" Nena asked the slug.

"I think you read my mind." This was exactly what the slug had already determined. With several weeks ahead of them, before they would be prepared to attempt a warp test, they had little else to do but second guess themselves and fight off anticipation.

Each day that passed allowed for better scans and further data, which they updated in simulation two or three times per day. And even as their data increased and the results clarified further and further, they were able to achieve a warp bubble in simulation each and every time.

The two spent their time split between simulations and crabbing back and forth across their apartment, sleeping, drinking, eating and otherwise vegetating. Still, they adhered to a strict regimen, each day preparing more and more for the maneuvers to come. Nena was still unable to pilot the craft and despite her myriad concerns, she was surprisingly not at all worried about the slug's ability to pilot the craft. Nena had quietly given all of her faith to the slug.

~

Finally, the morning came when instead of running another simulation; the Kitsune was perfectly positioned and Nena and the slug were ready to attempt human, hyper-light travel. Neither had any time for nerves.

The cockpit buzzed with activity. The smooth white contours of the space were blacked out in the shadow of the displays and terminals. The ship's maneuvering computer had systematically removed all distractions.

The women had fully prepared themselves and the ship. Their apartment was clean and all items were properly stowed.

The design suite and all other unnecessary compartments were sealed and powered down. Each of the women donned full environment suits with critical survival equipment readied and attached. The cockpit and escape pod safeties had been relinquished and the ship was now ready to jettison the lot at the first sign of trouble.

The tones ringing from the terminals and the computer were soft – almost calming, even if they spelled sudden death had they been ignored. The computer initiated a countdown – four minutes until maneuvering.

Nena's helmet remained at rest in her lap. She looked to the slug and raised an eyebrow and bled the anticipation from her gut with a bout one-dimensional sarcasm. "You think you're a hotshot with this thing, but you are still only simulation trained. Hell, the approach vector mathematics alone is beyond either one of us. We'll likely be stretched atom by atom across a dozen light years. Are you ok with that?"

The slug was quick with a reply. "That's why we have a computer that can calculate and model better than you can. You should trust the computer and me. Hell, your ilk built us. You people tend to put every other ounce of your faith in the computers, why not trust a computer and a slug?"

Nena scoffed playfully at the accusation as she turned a key in her gut, locking her worries away tight. Some lingering fears did manage to seep through. She was given this ship for a reason. And still, she silently questioned the whole affair. The seed ship shown like an impossibly bright, burning streak, still several light weeks ahead of them. She ran everything through her mind again, focused on the image of the seed ship. They could attempt to catch it at speed, but docking would be impossible and would likely foul any potential meeting with the 'other'. Overtaking the seed ship was still the best option. All of these were settled in her head and in her gut, however a new fear emerged from the arranged quiet in her mind. Afterwards. After they arrived – after the meeting – what then?

"What in the name of Suicide day are we supposed to do if we make contact? I mean, we've simulated warp a hundred times at this point, but what in hell are going to do if and when we make contact?" Nena's humor quickly drained away and she became intensely agitated.

The slug looked to Nena, unsure how to answer. Nena continued. "Listen, we really don't know what the hell we are meant to do or what we should do with an alien life form. If we find something out there, what the hell are we to do then? Do we scoop it up and bring it back? Do we tie it down and wait a year or more for the seed ship decelerate and rendezvous? That's not how I imagined first contact to look. What the hell are we even doing?"

The Slug brushed Nena's hair away from Nena's eyes and leaned in to kiss her forehead. The slug whispered at first. "Fuck it Nena. What does it matter? We've been over this again and again. The big picture doesn't mean a damn thing. We are people out of time at this point. Between you and me and the poor assholes on board the seed ship, we are merely color guard for humanity. All that shit is meaningless. It will be hundreds if not thousands of years before anyone who sent us on this errand ever finds out what came to pass and they may not even care at that point…or hell they may have made friendly with ten other species. Don't worry about it because it means nothing. Fuck humanity. Fuck your orders. These are the options we have available to us. We are a trillion miles or more from anything familiar. We could find a quiet beach somewhere and spend our remaining years in silent isolation, if we wanted to, or we could meet up with the only other outbound human and see what happens. Don't over think it. It's merely adventure for adventure's sake at this point."

"I suppose we could just end up as a particle streak through space if this maneuver fails and that will be our story." Nena was being intentionally dark, but the Slug shrugged it off and smiled.

"Fuck it Nena. Let's give this shit a go." The slug tapped on the navigational computer, triple checking everything. She glanced over at the countdown – sixty seconds left.

Nena took a deep breath checked her harnesses and affixed her environment helmet onto her suit. The slug remained un-harnessed as she dove and bent from one terminal to another, doing the job of two, throwing data into the computer and then waiting for a response, throwing further data at the response, spinning up the virgin warp coil – gathering last minute data and inputting eleventh hour navigational incentives and braking alternatives into the computer model while taking each breath intentionally as she watched the countdown from the corner of her eye. "We are likely to experience some space-time disorientation as we approach, but I'll have everything automated by then. We've got to punch the conventionals as we arch across the far edge of the minor singularity. When we launch away from it I'll engage the warp coil and we should then find ourselves traveling safely through sub-space."

The thought of traveling as conventional matter through sub-space was nearly as unsettling to Nena as the idea of human molecular transmission, but the slug did not bat an eye about it. She remained metered and certain that everything would be just fine. "We will be in warp for a grand total of six minutes, until we start the braking process. Once we brake out of warp, we will decelerate into the star system at a rate yet to be calculated. We'll just have to see on the other side." The slug seemed to be speaking for her own advantage, but Nena appreciated it, as it was reassuring.

As the countdown fell to zero, the two focused out from the cockpit transoms at the growing smear of bending light. The maneuver created a gravitational lens, bending the light

of stars around the edges of the growing warp bubble. It was
the first time they could view, with their own eyes, evidence
of the actual fabric of space-time. Without a word to one
another, each imagined that they were looking from the other
side, and examining the subtle brightness of their own vessel
being bent by the gravitational dimple.

The slug kept a close eye on their telemetry, shifting her
view occasionally to a read out of several atomic clocks dis-
playing variance in relative times. The clocks were essential
to proper navigation. They were no different than an ancient
stopwatch timing the blind turns of a submersible through
benthic mountain ranges – one half second off and smash.

Kitsune was surprisingly calm. The ship did not buck
or sway, in fact it was as tranquil as it had been through the
thousands of simulations. Still more than five light years from
the far edge of the minor singularity, the ship was firmly in its
reach – sliding with the combined efforts of every human to
have come before them – along the gravitationally polished
surface of space-time.

Kitsune's conventional engines fell silent and useless,
though the ship's velocity estimates were increasing steadily.
Soon, the warped field of space-time in front of them lensed
until the collective light of a million or more stars flooded
the cockpit. Light entering the cockpit quickly stretched and
curved, almost dancing. Nena and the slug gripped helplessly
to their seats as their bodies convulsed with ever-alternating
swells of heaviness and lightness. Nena vomited, emptying the
contents of her stomach throughout her helmet. The effect
only induced further nausea and soon both were in agony,
praying through clenched teeth that the effect would soon
pass as the ship sling-shot around the far edge of the minor
singularity and into warp.

Nena dreamt of suicide pills, knives and mass bloodlet-
ting, anything to relieve the discomfort of the maneuver – as

the terrifying thought of being stuck in endless vertigo for eternity set in – fear of being caught up in some prolonged time distortion that would keep them in agony, far from death from this point forward into infinity. Compared to this, death was welcome.

Just as neither of the women could take the excruciation any longer, the ship lurched and stretched and suddenly relief tumbled over the women and the star field beyond them blurred into a sheet of absolute white. They were safely at warp, traveling at yet undetermined speeds, but well beyond the sluggishness and laziness of photons.

The slug pulled up the deep navigation projections and found that they were perfectly on target. They would reach braking point in a matter of minutes.

Nena removed her helmet as her vomit drained into the chest cavity of her environment suit. She wiped where it caked around her eyes and nose and laughed, exhausted.

"Well fuck."

The women burst into painful fits of mirth. Shaky and terrified, they could not get their fingers to cooperate enough to unbuckle themselves from their seats. "At least we did not become atomically unhinged." The slug smiled at Nena, still trying to revive the proper use of her fingers.

The ship was silent, empty of even murmur or hum. Subspace was smooth, unfettered by the monstrous fullness of actual space, devoid of gases, devoid of gravity as such, devoid of matter, just the smooth slipstream of space's space.

A stable warp field surrounded Kitsune. The theoretical had become the practical and the acknowledgement of this reality stirred joy anew in Nena's heart. As far as she knew, she and the slug were the first humans to actually engage a warp field and travel faster than the speed of light. The dueling chronometers were telling. Kitsune's time was within a minute or two of Earth time. For a few moments, they were free of the nightmare of relativity.

Nena cleaned her face as best she could. She was hurried, jumpy and skittish. Her hands shook with excitement. The computer was still calculating the total time required in warp. They were a minute and thirty seconds in as Nena did her best to make livable her soiled helmet. Each of the women grew cold with fear considering their next step.

At four minutes, the computer displayed an adjustment, adding nearly five minutes to their required time at warp. The slug pulled on her harness and cracked her back. She ran her fingers over the deceleration curves dripping impressionistic paint across her navigation monitor. The computer was assembling and reassembling the mathematics for braking over and over, more than seven hundred times a second. Each curve overlapped the previous, causing the plots to bleed and smear. The slug feared for a split second, overshooting their target due to computational overload. She shoved the thought away and looked back at the estimated time till braking.

As counterintuitive as it seemed at the time, braking was somehow not nearly as jarring as accelerating into warp. After the computer spun up and spun down the estimated time in warp twice more, the count down to braking finally fell to within thirty seconds. At the appropriate moment, the slug ordered up a command, cutting power to the high-energy electro-magnets within the warp core. With the electro-magnets powered down and the warp core properly unspun, the warp field casually collapsed and the ship fell nonchalantly out of sub-space while effortlessly decelerating to a standard 99.0975% the speed of light.

Ahead of them shown the Blue Hammer of the Enokitake cluster, the tip of the Orion Spur. Blue Hammer was an O class, blue hyper giant. It's intense blue light forced Kitsune to vary the orientation of the cockpit transoms, allowing only a select portion of the spectrum to intrude. It was truly intense.

They were still more than 100 astronomical units from Blue
Hammer, but it still filled the entire field of vision from nearly
every porthole on board. Its scale was nearly incomprehensible. Even the stream of data pouring into the computer did
not help quantify the size of this star.

Alive and undamaged Nena and the slug removed their
helmets, unfastened themselves from the gravity couches and
quickly made their way to the observation deck, hoping to get
a fuller perspective on the star. On the observation deck, they
were faced with an even more incredible scene. All twenty-four
meters of transparent transom were completely filled with
Blue Hammer. No matter which view they chose, they could
not see the curvature of the star. And despite their incredible
distance from the star, it felt as though Kitsune would careen
into Blue Hammer's fires in a matter of seconds.

Meditating on the sight, it seemed obvious that this was
to be their point of rendezvous. Blue Hammer stood out
like the king of beacons, the brightest object for hundreds of
light years in every direction, perhaps one of the ten brightest
objects in the entire galaxy.

Orbiting Blue Hammer was six gas giants, each nearly
the size of Sol – each a failed star, bowing to the enormity
of Blue Hammer. Each gas giant dangled varied systems of
satellites. Some of the pastoral worlds were Earth sized, some
Jovian sized with complex satellite systems of their own. Long
range scans were unable to reveal if any of the smaller worlds
were inhabitable, but the shear luminosity of Blue Hammer,
coupled with the heat and inevitable gravity of the system as
a whole left little hope of any habitable surface throughout
the system.

Kitsune streaked towards the Blue Hammer, carefully
aiming to sling shot behind it. Had it been seen from the
surface of one of Blue Hammer's worlds, Kitsune would have
appeared to be little more than a shiny comet, arcing inten-

tionally towards Blue Hammer, burning off ice and gas while reflecting the star's strident rays as intensely as the laws of physics allowed.

The seed ship was now light months behind Nena and the slug. The exact distance could not have been known until they over took him and were able to measure across the parallax towards the seed ship, then the distance was quantified rather easily. A quick glance backwards at the distant red shift of the seed ship was measured – the first stems of light reflected off of the seed ship. The gradual increase in brightness revealed the seed ship's speed and verified its course. The seed ship was now directly in Kitsune's wake, traveling at nearly the same speed as Kitsune, eleven months away from committing to the same braking maneuvers as Kitsune. If managed properly, Kitsune's gradual deceleration curve could be closely matched to the seed ship avoiding a lengthy wait in standard space-time. If Kitsune committed to full deceleration immediately, Nena and the slug could be stuck waiting for decades as the seed ship approached the system at near light speed.

A long orbit was chosen. Long enough to make a pass near every planetary system then back around to fully decelerate during a second pass around Blue Hammer. The plan was to do this as close to light speed as possible. In the interim, as they awaited the seed ship's final approach, they would allow themselves the opportunity to search the system for whatever it was they were there to find. Neither Nena nor the slug discussed the present plan. Instead, a simple nod and a wink verified what they both felt was best.

The nearly yearlong wait, however, would be done in hibernation. Neither Nena nor the slug had the energy to wait, for an additional year. Kitsune would be fine on it's own and it was fully programed to respond appropriately if alien detection was established. So the cold coffin welcomed them to silently wait for all the chips to fall where they may.

23

"Who sent them out there?" The room was heavy with tobacco smoke. The woman asking the questions was exceedingly intent. If she had a cleaver in her hands, it would not be difficult to imagine her using it at the necks of everyone in the room. She leaned her entire body across the conference table. "Tell me."

"Ma'am. As I understand it, it was a directive from the PAE council. The orders were officially given by an ancillary General…however, there were PAE council members present…at least according to the transcripts." The aid trembled in his words.

The woman took a deep drag from her cigarette then continued. "And those were the only people who knew?"

"Well, ma'am…to be fair, that was quite a long time ago. I could not say with certainty." The staffer pulled at his collar and lit his own cigarette.

"So, the brilliance of the PAE determined to send a fresh graduate and her pet Slug on a first contact mission and you are telling me that no one else was informed?" The woman plunged her head into her hands and exhaled a massive plume. "Where is the General who gave the order? Is he dead?"

"No ma'am. He's in transit. I believe he was dispatched not long after that meeting to Sacrum Bellum." The aid hoped that this would sate the General's line of questioning.

"Anyone else in the room?" She fumed.

The aid maintained. "Ma'am, I believe that everyone else known to be present is no longer with us."

The woman flicked her burning cigarette towards the staffer's face and then pounced towards the middle of the table. "I want answers! Do you hear me? If we've got a band of twerps on the verge of making contact with an alien race, I want to know everything. I want to know where and when, I don't care if you have to flap your arms into deep space and find out on your own…."

At the height of her rage, the ingress to the conference room gracefully slid open. The suddenness of the distraction brought a quick silence to the room and everyone stood as PAE council member Tennyson assumed control of the meeting. Tennyson's shoulders were broad and oakish. Her torso had seen the knife of many corrective surgeries, but instead of dulling her stature or appearance, her extreme age coupled with her long surgical history made her appear more battle hardened than decrepit. Tennyson looked to the General and the General's staffer, drew a deep breath and then paced the room, circling the table like a Tiger inspecting a fresh kill.

"General Tate? I understand you have been making quite a bit of noise." Tennyson's eyes were sharp and unrelenting. She stood, inches from the General's neck, her nose almost touching the soft fur of the General's nape.

"Don't try and intimidate...." Tennyson cut her off mid-sentence.

"General. I have no need to intimidate you. You understand the authority of the PAE. I can sum a reason to have you air locked or abandoned on a dead colony in a matter of minutes. It would not be difficult for me to determine a hundred ways your presence throws our designs out of balance. We, of the council, rather enjoy rectifying oversights in our calculations. Removing you would be like altering the trillionth digit in within an infinite string of decimals." Tennyson circled General Tate, taking a breath and allowing her words to sink in through the momentary silence. "Now, General. If you would take a seat, I would be happy to bring you up to speed, since this matter does involve your command."

General Tate sat begrudgingly. Tennyson gently waved the staffer out, much to the staffer's relief. The room was drab and unfettered with extravagant design, as most conference rooms designed for matters of this clearance level tended to be. Tennyson took the seat across from General Tate and motioned for one of the General's cigarettes. Tennyson lit the cigarette and inhaled graciously. She removed her traditional veil, allowing her deep black skin to shine through unencumbered. Tennyson's emerald eyes beamed with a strange combination of youth and aged wisdom, but Tennyson's disarming eyes did not fool General Tate. Tate knew she was looking into ancient eyes. In a rare moment, General Tate wished for ignorance, for the knowledge of what lay behind Tennyson's eyes was a natural confidence killer. Tate bit her own lip.

"General Tate. In the interest of professional courtesy, allow me to formally acknowledge your achievements in the field of Excession Philosophy. Your command has made many strides in identifying prudent procedures for first a multitude of contact scenarios. And I recognize that it cannot be easy to be fitted with a title and position for an area, which receives such little funding, attention or serious legitimacy. Allow me to also recognize the inherent novelty of having a General in charge of first contact scenarios who is philosophically opposed to outside contact of any kind. In fact, your position has guided the PAE's intervention on the matter currently at hand."

General Tate's fingers dug into the arms of her chair and she bit her lip more severely, while Tennyson continued.

"Your xenophobia is no secret, as I am certain you are aware." Tennyson jabbed.

Tate lost her nerve and shot back. "But my conviction to my position is not affected by my xenophobia!" It was incredibly easy to give yourself away to the PAE.

Tennyson was calm, pleased that she had elicited an outburst. The room now truly belonged to her. "Dear. I fully understand that fact. That is why you were selected for this position. The apparent imbalance within your character and of your cause is what makes you an effective element inside our design." Tennyson dragged the cigarette to the filter then snuffed it out on the table's surface indiscriminately. "Let me ask you General. You are familiar with the famed Excession Philosopher Dr. Sigrah Taulonson?"

"Of course I am. He literally wrote the book..." The General was interrupted once again.

"Yes, yes. He literally wrote the book on potential first contact scenarios. He was also given an invitation to act as an ancillary member of the PAE. He accepted the appointment only days prior to his death." Tennyson motioned for another cigarette then continued. "What you were not aware of is the fact that we were able to salvage aspects of Dr. Taulonson."

"You uploaded him?" General Tate was fixed on Tennyson's eyes.

"Post mortem. It was not a true retirement. But yes.

Many of his memory engrams were grafted onto several other minds." Tennyson paused. "And do you know where Dr. Taulonson is right now?"

"How could I? I am not privy to that information." General Tate squirmed, realizing that her righteous indignation was getting her nowhere.

"Right you are. Please note your lack of information. As I understand it, your beef relates to the decision to send a young Major to make first contact. I would like to grant you the opportunity to broaden your understanding of events." Tennyson's eyes widened and engaged General Tate in a matriarchal fashion – domineering in a most feminine manner. "As we speak, Dr. Sigrah Taulonson and the ship which is his current body are making final preparations for braking. They will be settling into orbit around the Blue Hammer in a matter of days. First contact is eminent. Some on the council argue that first contact has already occurred and this physical meeting simply makes it official. Tennyson paused and lit her fresh cigarette. "And as you know, Dr. Sigrah Taulonson believed as you do, that first contact should be avoided. The PAE council is split on the matter, some believing that contact should be made at all costs and some believing it should be avoided at all costs. The outcome, however, will not lay in the will of any individual. We have placed enough variables into the equation to allow the outcome to be…organic. We cannot say what pieces of Dr. Taulonson survive and which aspects of his philosophy remain intact. He took on this mission unsanctioned, so there are many who feel that he has developed a logical reasoning to move forward with first contact and that he is doing so under his own lingering authority as a member of the PAE."

General Tate took a deep breath. "And what of this Major? What's her role in all of this?"

"It's classified, but not interesting. I suppose you could

imagine her as essentially a pivot point. She has a familial relationship with an individual on board Sigrah." Tennyson's tone turned sly, even deceptive.

General Tate sat back in her chair and lit a cigarette of her own. "I have people…you know. I have a team. We could have handled this."

"As antithetical as this may seem, this is not your role. The details of the circumstances called for alternative action. If initial contact leads to further contact, we may employ you at that time. However, if you maintain your anxious mistrust of the PAE, we will replace you." Tennyson was final.

"But Council Member Tennyson…with all due respect… the will of the PAE council is being damaged by it's lack of transparency. You claim design credit, but you are willing to leave such extreme interactions up to chance? This makes no sense." General Tate was shocked at the sudden surge of insubordination.

"General, you should know by now that the big picture is not for everyone. And we never leave a thing to chance that can't otherwise be designed by intent." Tennyson stood while maintaining direct eye contact with General Tate. "General, I know you much better than you know yourself. I know that you require a certain degree of endorsement or validation in order to keep your insecurities in check. If it makes any difference to you, you have been chosen for a mission. I would not waste time coming here to debate facts irrelevant to you, but I feel I have pandered to your insecurities sufficiently."

General Tate exhaled smugly and pursed her cracked lips. She knew that whatever mission she had been selected for would represent the end of her life one way or another. Tate was soon to be another willing participant – apart of a long-term study in relativistic continuity.

"General Tate, are you familiar with an entanglement switch?" Tennyson smiled murderously.

~

Beyond the walls of Kuiper Belt station, vast strands of transiting vessels lay in wait. Some ships were prototype vessels, only now returning from five-hundred-year, exploratory jaunts throughout the neighboring portion of the galactic rim - the crews on board, no more than thirty years older than when they set off. Most slept while the ships rode gravity waves across the fabric of space-time – cold bodies time traveling to and fro.

The initial steps of human expansion were intersecting with the present leap, more and more. These waves of experience, of great, great, great, great, grandfathers returning home, were only now catching a steady rhythm. These men and women out of time were steadily returning to reclaim their power and positions – their wealth and influence guided by the steady hand of generations spread across the centuries. Soon, the members of the past would be as numerous or as omnipresent as the members of the present.

The first slobs sopped up by the PAE and ordered out as Ushers returned intermittently, decades or centuries dismembered. Those like Alik, indentured in order to free themselves of debt returned every month, bright eyed, young and ready to move onward into a future by design, only to find that their debt had been managed by a computer as uninterested in the passage of decades as it was in the dislocation of the Usher. Interest rates had varied. Debts, which should have been resolved, had ballooned, insuring another trip for the Usher. Ushers were forced to accept their roles for good, remaining with their vessels or Ushering new ones. It was important to remember that being a warm body on a relativistic vessel was the greatest thumb of the nose. It was the most epic portrayal of your standing in society. To allow the conscious living to experience the epic weight of General Relativity was almost inhumane. Three years, five years, ten years meant nothing to the grand scheme of continuity. A decent Usher could serve the human race for thousands of terrestrial years as long as the appropriate leashes were in place. The same could be said for any engineer or any General.

Bright and just beyond the faint veil of the Oort cloud, three new stars burned intensely, fresh and stable. The three stars were the first results in humanity's attempt at stellar birth. In five hundred years, the faint lines of a Dyson skeleton would be visible from other star systems, quartering Sol's light. In a thousand years, the light from sol would blink out as the final panels of the first Dyson sphere grew into place, demonstrating human kind's ability to harness 100% of the energy from a stellar body.

24

They had been watching him like vultures and he knew it. At first, he thought about running to Mars or one of the Jovian moons, but he knew that he was better off amongst the masses. He also knew that his newfound title was little more that a leash. It required the expert eye of courtesans and liaisons, bodyguards, an excessive number of slugs as well as several surgeons on call at all times.

Dr. Taulonson was well aware that despite the appearance of security and preservative measures, everyone was waiting around for him to die. Just before his appointment, he and a handful of other aging scientists, engineers and philosophers had been very outspoken in their decision to experience conventional death. They were each, the tip of a movement away from consciousness preservation. Though Dr. Taulonson and his peers were completely committed to their cause, they were well aware that due to their position and the knowledge they possessed, they would never be allowed to simply die. Dr.

Taulonson had accepted this fact begrudgingly, while many of his peers tried to flee, hoping to make it to a fast ship and break off across time to die alone.

The vultures did not have to wait long. Only days after being appointed to the PAE and at nearly two hundred and eighty conscious years old and more than five hundred terrestrial years, Dr. Sigrah Taulonson stood in with great ease from a deep leather chair, stuck a finger towards two of his liaisons and uttered his final words. "Oh! To be a corpse!" Dr. Taulonson's knees bent under the weight of his torso and he came crashing to the floor. His closest liaison dove, his hands cupped as if ready to collect water from a stream, the liaison carefully caught Dr. Taulonson's head before it smashed to the marble floor.

Within moments, a preservation crew made a well-rehearsed entry, bringing in all necessary equipment to preserve the quickly decomposing mind of Dr. Sigrah Taulonson. Even to the eyes of the well educated and well informed, the preservation of mind remains appears as Excession – technological magic.

In truth, the best comparison is cooking. The brain, preferably still living, is giving exact pulses of electricity, allowing an AI to map the brain exactly. From there, all of the memory engrams are reconstructed in a vast code soup. Several consciousness and engram maps from several individuals are tossed into a modeling soup. Since no scan is exact, gaps emerge, imperfections and in Sigrah's case, the results of immediate decomposition. The neural pathways began disintegrating almost immediately upon cardiac arrest and the end of pulmonary functions.

Since preservation is never perfect, the minds are mixed, allowing each to fill the gaps the other is lacking, sometimes using code to stitch mind together. The individual minds are not chosen at random either. Each individual is matched for compatibility along an incomprehensibly long list of criteria.

Sometimes, conscious minds are kept in a sort of stasis until compatible ingredients, other minds, can be found. It is a delicate process, that some argue is not preservation at all. Dr. Taulonson, however, was amongst those who firmly believed that the conscious mind remained contiguous across the transfer – that no matter what the outcome, a portion of the individual was not allowed to fully die. Most, used Dr. Taulonson's own philosophical argument to advocate for the continued use of preservation techniques as well as the continued creation of artificial super intellects.

Few were better candidates than Sigrah – a mind such as his would not be dumped into the frenzy of an overpopulated artificial mind. The PAE had special intentions for Dr. Taulonson's mind.

Dr. Taulonson, amongst his many roles and titles, had been the chief architect for much of the so-called millennial expansion – the push of humans across the galaxy over the next thousand years. He had worked out the method and helped the PAE envision the necessary steps to achieve a million-plus years of continuity. Under Dr. Taulonson's guidance, two hundred years of pumping as many ships and colonies near the speed of light as possible had begun to have a noticeable effect on continuity. Dr. Taulonson helped humanity find it's pace – helped them pick up a beat and carry it with a particular rhythm.

His seismic effect on humanity was not something the PAE would allow to slip away. Dr. Taulonson's effect needed to be a calculated constant, one of the central gears within the galactic mechanism the PAE ultimately envisioned. They needed a fulcrum they could both predict and trust.

The mind born of this perseveration was difficult to compare to Dr. Taulonson's round and messy persona. Dr. Taulonson had been abrasively humorous. He enjoyed making people uncomfortable and did so almost as an artist. During the ceremonial induction into the PAE, he attended nude. During a dinner in his honor many years before, he chose to sing every word he uttered throughout the night in a belting operatic tenor. He was never popular for his attitudes. Whether by instruction or happenstance, the Sigrah that emerged from preservation was notably different.

The AI psychologists who explored the new mind noted the presence of Dr. Taulonson's memory engrams, but at no point would Sigrah acknowledge having specific memories put in place to verify the presence of Dr. Taulonson. Eventually the psychologists noted that the presence of Dr. Taulonson's consciousness was evident due to the unwillingness of the AI to verify the presence. Therefore, Sigrah is and will continue to be Sigrah Taulonson in the best and worst ways henceforth.

After years of remaining grafted to a larger artificial mind, Sigrah was pruned and placed within a positronic matrix. The experience was akin to being born again. Sigrah stretched out his mind and settled in to a unique body.

~

The surgery was as pristine and sterile as the day it was printed. The sleek white hall was lined with advanced surgical and recovery beds. Ruby and Alik were the first human bodies to visit since the installation crew left it as it then lay. The cleanliness of the air forced Alik's stench to amplify and focus in their noses. The human body is a filthy thing on good days, but the prime sterility of the surgery made the stench of infection and vagrancy significantly more apparent.

Ruby activated and enlisted the help of a pair of medical androids, who ably lifted Alik's body from Ruby's tired shoulders and splayed him carefully onto a surgical platform. Scanners jumped to a start, eager after years of idling in mint condition.

Several of Alik's ribs were still broken, with persistent infections at the break site. The scanners detected several minor to major clots from slow and prolonged internal bleeding. Ruby marveled that his wounds had not already done him in. His leg was in shambles. Some of the bone had fused improperly, some had simply refused to heal – splintered and fragmented beneath his flesh.

Ruby rubbed Alik's head, incredulous that he had endured such agony for so long. The surgical unit placed Alik into a controlled coma and began work, repairing his body.

~

Alik woke nearly four weeks later. His beard was busy and out of hand, but his body and his hair felt clean, fresh. Having learned to live with it, the sudden absence of pain was undeniably obvious. His reptile brain knew he was safe and that his nightmare was over, but he was having difficulty grasping at the details.

Aside from the two, mute, medical droids, he was alone in the surgery. There was a persistent ache in his chest, but it was not due to any medical issue. The ache came from the palpable absence of Ruby. He felt like he was waking from a dream, where he'd been chasing his soul mate through villages and gardens and parks - falling deeply in love only to wake to find it all a figment. He felt distinctly anxious knowing that his feelings for Ruby were real, no matter how strange reality had become.

Then, from the silent hallows of the surgery, Alik heard the steady clomp of booted footfalls. Clomp, clomp, clomp, they grew louder as he sat up in bed. Just as he focused his eyes he noticed the sharpening glimmer a man approaching his bedside. The footfalls seemed to fade out as the man came closer. The confusing sounds did not match the stride of the man.

"Sorry about that. I was hoping to make the moment more real, but I think the footsteps came off a bit contrived." The man smiled graciously.

Alik scrunched his face with confusion as the man came to stand next to him and placed his hand palm up towards Alik. The man's hair was golden blonde and his eyes piercing blue. He was clothed in a simple grey smock, with a thick cuff that came a quarter of the way up the man's neck and a hem that nearly touched the floor. His face was sincere, but guarded. Alik wondered if he was dreaming. "Who the hell are you?"

"There are only two human beings on this ship, Alik. Who do you think I am?" The man winked.

"You're a hollow." Alik grunted – clearing his throat.

"I'm not just a hollow. It's me. Sigrah." Sigrah smiled again, happy to do so.

"So you are a man." Alik's joke was breathy and laden with strange relief.

Sigrah returned the joke with shrug and a laugh. "Let's not go there, Alik."

"Where's Ruby?" Alik remembered to keep his guard up. Perhaps it was something that had become instinctual during his time in the wilderness. "I want to know where she is." He backed away from Sigrah slightly and his hand reflexively searched for his staff.

"She'll be here soon. I'm only now informing her that you are awake. I wanted us to have a few moments togeth-er before she arrived." Sigrah did his best to calm Alik by stepping back a few steps and lowering his arms, keeping his palms exposed – patting the air between he and Alik.

Alik sat up again and made direct eye contact with Sigrah. "What the hell man? You're omnipresent and you somehow forgot about me in there? You've got a lot to explain man.

She wants to shut you down I think." Alik fidgeted and his allegiance swung wildly back and forth, both paranoid that Sigrah tried to kill him and terrified of what were to happen if that were true. Still, his rational mind, which was not quite awake yet, seemed to know that Sigrah was not a threat.

"I understand that you deserve an explanation. We can talk it out, I'm certain I can answer any question you have, but you may not enjoy all the answers. For starters, I'm not as 'omnipresent' as you suggest and I'm damn far from infallible." Sigrah's mannerisms were clumsy but not unnatural. "Humans tend to make many assumptions about the abilities of the artificial mind, but what most fail to realize is that a significant portion of what makes me work as splendidly as I may, is due to many of the same inadequacies that make humans function as splendidly as they do. My strengths are not ubiquitous. I'm better at some things than others. I am fallible and I struggle, just as you do. For that, I apologize." Sigrah was genuine. He was not offering a cop-out.

Alik was taken aback. He'd never heard any individual of note ever confess their short comings in such a straightforward manner. It did not excuse the fragments of anger he watered during his isolation, but it certainly took the sting out in the moment. He had spent years, in agony, imagining all of the reasons he'd been abandoned, but he never once imagined it to be the cause of imperfection, a mere fuck up. He'd projected it all as a punishment or retribution for his curiosity, but as he would soon realize, it was Sigrah's curiosity that led to Alik's isolation. More than once he'd dreamed of melting Sigrah's core. It was not an emotion or an image he latched onto with fervor, but it was there at the worst times. And now, with the physical torment behind him, he was not angry in the slightest.

"I don't care about it Sigrah. I'm not mad." He paused. "Although, I'm willing to bet that Ruby is pissed."

"Ruby is very upset, but she will be fine. The two of us have been hard at work while you've been healing." Sigrah paused. "We have quite a bit more that needs to be discussed, but I will wait for Ruby."

Alik smiled at Sigrah. "You know, hollows have always made me uncomfortable, but I'll tell you…you know how I know you are not real?"

Sigrah tilted his head inquisitively. "How's that?"

"I can't smell you." The two laughed gently.

Alik took great comfort in seeing Sigrah's expressions. Whether or not they were algorithmic in nature, Sigrah's physical personality was welcomed. The human body is the Empathy Key for human beings. With a keen eye, we can know many things about an individual without even a word spoken. For several moments, Alik and Sigrah sat in silence, looking over one another, speaking without words – recognizing the significance of the connection they shared through the steady gaze of one another's eyes.

Then Sigrah broke the silence. "I am going to leave before Ruby gets here. I will speak to the two of you tomorrow. Come to the central terminal tomorrow morning."

With that Sigrah faded away as Ruby came darting into the surgery. Without hesitation, she grabbed Alik's face, kissed him passionately and then pulled away looked aggressively into his eyes. "Don't ever do that again!"

~

Alik could stand and he could walk. However the prolonged injury left him with an irreversible limp. Even the miracles of tissue regeneration could not solve the prolonged severity of the injury and the damage to his nervous system. He was instructed by the androids that his limp would be less pronounced over time, but would always be present. Random bouts of pain were expected. Alik was left with a constant reminder of the incident, but he did not allow it to distress him in the slightest.

Ruby slept in Alik's bed that evening. It was the first time she had visited that portion of the ship. Alik's quarters were much more Spartan than her own, but inviting just the same. She introduced Alik to the ships internal transit system, eliminating the multi-day hikes through the ship.

She woke at some point, late into the night and found Alik missing from bed. As she searched the room with her eyes, she noticed a faint glow in the den. As she inspected from the bedroom archway, she noticed that a fort of blankets and sheets, including his mother's blanket still teaming with the smell of the Buffer, had been erected between the couch and the coffee table. Inside, Alik lay on the floor, a single candle burning inches from his chest. Ruby did not disturb him. Instead, she returned to the bedroom to collect more pillows and blankets, erected her own camp next to his and drifted back to sleep.

~

After devouring fresh eggs, sausage and fruits in their blanket encampment, Ruby and Alik dressed and walked hand in hand to the gallery. They stole smiles from one another as Alik shrugged off his pronounced limp.

Alik felt a strange being back in this portion of the ship. The mountains within the Timelock seemed as far away as his home in the Buffer. Though he knew rationally that he had never left the ship, his prolonged experience in the 'lock deeply affected his sense of place. The familiar coldness of the ship reminded him of his first days on board, but it also strangely felt like coming home.

It had been nearly four years since Alik had set foot in

the gallery, but as he walked in, he had the feeling that it had been an entire lifetime ago. The gallery did not ring with reminiscent feelings or longing. In fact, if felt as alien as it always had.

The great, overhead display, which normally projected the stars beyond, was now dark and featureless – mute of all light. The central terminal stood monolithic, bright and busy.

"She's never on time is she?" Ruby tapped her foot.

Alik cracked a smile and shook his head a little. "No… it never is." Alik approached the terminal, banged gently on its side – not out of any direct intent to activate Sigrah, but rather as some esoteric leftover of some long lost, technologically impotent world. "Maybe banging on him will get his attention." He smiled at Ruby again.

As soon as the words left his mouth, the tiles shifted to blue, acknowledging Sigrah's presence. "Good morning!" Sigrah sounded fresh and unconventionally jovial. Alik smiled even larger since Sigrah's voice resounded deep and male. Ruby threw up an eyebrow, looking amused but dissatisfied. "I appreciate the two of you being here."

Ruby stepped up to the terminal, facing it naturally, as if it were another clumsy body in the room. "I don't think either Alik or I have the stomach for any mystery today. Did you come to any conclusions? Was I right?"

"Mystery time is over…in fact, many things are coming to an end today, including the status-quo." Sigrah was deliberate, but light in his delivery.

"What conclusions? Mystery?" Alik was short on patience, but desperately wanted to be brought up to speed. He looked back and forth from the interface back to Ruby who glared intently at the occasional blinking glyphs that streamed across the terminal.

"I admit, due to certain orders, I was forced to limit the amount of information I released. However, we are now

forging new ground. We are working beyond the scope of
official affiliation." Sigrah paused for a moment.

Alik and Ruby took a long look at one another. With a
flash, the overhead display sprang to light. Encompassing the
majority of the dome was a massive, blue star. Alik and Ruby
ducked away from the terminal and each paced backwards
in opposite directions, attempted to take in the view in full.

"What do you think of the view? It's amplified a bit, we
aren't quite this close, but we will be shortly."

Ruby was confused and started probing immediately.
"This isn't on course."

"No ma'am. It certainly is not. We deviated from our
course some time ago." Sigrah was unapologetic.

Ruby suddenly felt intensely lost. "What do you mean we
aren't on course? Where the hell are we?"

Sigrah reverted to the voice familiar to Ruby, the slightly
antagonizing, but feminine voice. "It is quite alright Ruby. I
think you will be satisfied." Sigrah paused. "Tell me, either
of you...have either one of you ever heard of Von Neumann
probes?"

Ruby's eyes widened and she snapped her fingers in the
air victoriously. Alik searched his mind, while his face hung
blankly and tired. "That's it! That's got to be it." Ruby
slumped onto the floor trying to put all the pieces together.
"It's just impractical as hell, if not impossible."

"Theoretically, they are not impossible, especially if we
consider the complexity and tenacity of biological systems.
Humans have produced clumsy mechanical systems, probes
that replicate a limited number of times, but nothing on the
scale needed to explore the entirety of the Cosmos...that may
still be impossible." Sigrah was excited. He wanted Ruby to
work it all out for herself, but he was doing his best to prod
her along.

Alik interrupted. "Nothing is impossible?" Alik wanted

to save face by adding something of value, but he admitted
to himself that he was completely lost. He had no idea what
they were talking about.

Ruby patted him on the shoulder, in a completely delicate way, void of any sense of patronization. "We covered
Von Neumann briefly in Bold Theories of the Suicidal...first
year. Von Neumann was an early architect of computational
systems?"

Alik followed, but was still grasping, while Ruby continued. "Von Neumann suggested that the only viable method
to explore the cosmos, lay in the application of self replicating
probes. Essentially, the probe would individually mine for raw
materials, while simultaneously exploring its surroundings
and replicating other probes. In theory there is the potential for exponential growth of the probe population, which
would be necessary to explore all aspects of the cosmos...but
in practice, entropy and the harsh realities of space always
interrupt the ability of the probes to replicate to their full potential...at least that's been the case with human versions..."
Her last words caught on her tongue and hung there for a
moment. The thought was only half formed as it perched
itself at the tip of her mind. She held off speaking it aloud
until she had fully worked it out.

"What does this have to do with that star, Sigrah?" Alik
was clearly miffed.

Sigrah refused to acknowledge Alik for a moment, instead deciding to press Ruby. "Consider the implication of
biological probes."

Ruby's eyes lit. Alik shrugged a bit, until a knowing look
grew across his face. "I knew there was something in there."
Alik was quite satisfied. Ruby stood shocked, as the pieces
fell together.

"There is something in there. Hell, if they are biological
and they are only interested in biological systems, they would

only ever ping home if and when they found the right conditions. It's a naturally course-correcting vector. They only
replicate where they can and they have no urgent need to get
off world again…they could just be peppered across space…
eventually they'd just take hold in all the right places." Ruby
was boiling with epiphany. Ruby squeezed the words out of
her mouth. "The fucking Kinoko." Ruby threw her arms
upwards as the pieces fell together. She paused. "But they
aren't just probes."

Sigrah answered. "No…no…they are not. At least not to
us…but would our mechanical probes not have any number
of unforeseen effects on life they may encounter?"

Alik interrupted. "The star?" Ruby fell silent long enough
for Alik to belt out his sudden grievance. "For Suicide's sake!
I have been stuck on this can for no good reason. I've been
a fool for getting myself wrapped up in this situation. Those
fucking Kinoko drove me off a damn cliff. I barely survived.
I'm far from fucking home, everyone I know is dead and I just
want someone to explain to me what the fuck we are doing
near this star, which is apparently really damned far from
where we are supposed to be! All I was supposed to do was
complete my mission and I would be free, debt free, free free;
a bonafide citizen! What the in living hell?"

Ruby hung her head. Had Sigrah been situated in a human body, he too would have hung his head. Then Ruby,
tried to calm Alik with an embrace whispering something to
him.

"Alik…they were never going to let you go." Alik pulled
back as Ruby continued. "Alik, no Usher has ever 'completed'
their mission. If or when we go back, you'll find your loan
doubled or tripled due to some daft, fluctuating interest rate.
They were going to keep you till you were dead. That's just
what they do to Ushers."

Alik was crushed. He choked back tears. "Sigrah?"

"It is true Alik. You would have been given a few months of shore leave, likely monitored, then you would have been forced to return here, sent out again, in order to continue your debt maintenance."

Alik's leg finally gave out and he sunk to the floor, grasping his face. "But…but." He choked on his tears.

"Alik. You purchased a completely adequate education. Its time that you received some recognition of that fact." Sigrah paused. "I like you. I have shared experiences with you that have been transformational, despite the fact that I have not admitted this to you before. I will never leave you behind again. I told you earlier, this meeting changes everything. I'm telling you that today, the three of us begin to write our own futures."

Alik looked up at Ruby. "Ruby?"

"Me too Alik. I decided the day I found you under that mountain that I was never going to leave you behind. Our fates are tied, as far as I can see."

Alik burst with emotion. "Fuck both of you! I don't even…why…It just doesn't…"

Sigrah cut in. "Alik. Listen to me. Today. Today you write your own future. Do you understand? Today will be the most empowering day of your existence. Do you understand? Today, you will do the work the PAE could never hope to do."

"Dammit! No! I don't understand! Why the fuck are we here?" Alik insisted.

"Alik, today, you will meet whatever is on the other end of the probes. Soon, history will truly be a formality."

25

The early theoreticians who discussed the idea of Von Neumann probes held fast to many of the human prone fallacies, reflections of human insecurities, that held back otherwise simple explanations for millennia. It was argued that according to calculation, if any civilization had been successful in producing Von Neumann probes in the distant past, the probes would have already become ever-present throughout the cosmos. Others suggested that the perfect Von Neumann probe would be present just as a cancer might, replicating ad nausea until entire star systems where overcome. Some countered those arguments by suggesting that the basic and essential need for nuclear material would inherently limit the spread of Von Neumann probes, thus making it quite reasonable to assume that humanity simply had not yet stumbled upon them or vice versa.

The simplest notions were discounted by theoreticians or

ignored. The fact was that the probes were relatively simple – almost utilitarian. They had no need for nuclear material and their self-replication was regulated based on conditions. The human home world was teeming with them, but they were not an unavoidable cancer. They were smart. The probes had a relatively unpretentious nature, which made them effective and beneficial instead of devastating or obvious. At the time the antecedent theorists pondered the biggest questions, wonder whether or not we were alone, the life they argued about lay unassumingly, amongst the cattle managed grasses, beneath the largest radio receiver on Earth.

Space pays no mind to the frantic agitation of its emergent on-lookers. Vacuity is often an inapt notion. Misconception is a highlight of creatures that exist in such short temporal windows. They see the emptiness as something lonely, something still - waiting eons for the happenstance glimpse of a traversing vessel, or a tumbling comet or a burst of cosmic radiation, but they do so in relative fractions of seconds compared to the age of the Cosmos. The truth is that space is busy. Space is frantic. Space is full.

Gases, stone and radiation seem little more than trifles to the fleshy, tender bodies of men. Yet it is the combination of these elemental factors which make any It possible. There simply cannot be an It without stuff to fill It.

When matters came to first contact scenarios, most agreed that any first contact scenario would be a messy affair. Never would the trope of friendly aliens, setting down in a field and shaking hands graciously ever play itself out. The Other always posed a deeply existential threat to humans as human's simultaneously recognized the threat they posed to the Other. So the door was shut on each of matters of meetings. They were to be avoided. Seeking out Von Neumann probes of any sort, hunting for evidence of life elsewhere, searching for alien ships cutting through the Cosmic Background Radiation were all seen as the trappings of the fringe. This blind eye approach was exalted in the hopes to limit damage, not extend it, however.

~

As Sigrah streaked, cerulean, burning and wild towards the Blue Hammer, a repeating dream hammered away. In the dream a chorus of individuals hummed chords, over and over again, the same melody – cycling in a loop. The melody was an anchor, meant to hold the dreamer fast and amongst the living. Over and over. Over and over, the chorus droned and chanted the bars. Their song was a river through the slipstream, welding the words of the past with the fleeting moments of the present until the dreamer made her way through fields of rape into fields of mustard and barley until the fields of her home rolled beneath her. The rabid falls of stellar dust into gravity caverns, the purging scream of dying pulsars, the vacuous cold all pulled the dreamer's flesh through the songs of the chorus, pulling and pulling and pulling until the dreamer was banished from the song and the sleep entirely.

When she woke, Myco forced her eyes open. They were sealed shut with a thin mycelia film. She attempted to move her body, which was trapped in prostrate, but she seemed to be fastened to the floor.

Her entire body was covered – grafted completely with the mycelia that stretched through the ship. She tightened her wrists and pushed with her hips, but she was restrained to the floor, trapped amongst the branches of tight hyphae. Her body was covered in the white fibers. They grew from her skin and into the mycelia mat she slept upon and from the mat onto and around her flesh and throughout the ship.

She knew that with a few sudden tugs, she could will her body free, but she paused for a moment, realizing that she was fused with the ship. If she allowed her mind to quiet, she could travel through it, room-to-room, hanger-to-hanger, bay-to-bay, looking through the myriad eyes of the fungal network.

Myco raised her awareness to the bridge and instantly felt the room extend to her attention. It was quiet though and as she pushed her awareness through it, she could feel the bodies of her crew, each of them still, silent and sporulated. Each man was fruited at the neck, each standing or sitting at their post, heads bent in perpetual prostration, tall fruiting caps hovering above the husk of their former being, their fingers sharp and webby with mycelia.

She pulled her mind away, intent on inspecting them in person. With all of the energy she could muster, she pushed her body out of its prostrate pose, breaking the filaments, tearing her flesh in places, until she could sit straight and inhale the frosty air of the vessel. She jerked the rest of her body from the floor and felt an instant disconnect from the vessel. She was in absolute darkness. Her quarters were closed firm and the ship felt empty, static and frozen.

Myco rubbed the back of her neck, searching for any sign of impending fruit, but found only smooth flesh. She wondered what had happened. She pushed her mind backwards, towards her last reception and the intensity of it. Myco was aware that her species was prone to periods of hibernation. Typically they followed moments of great stress or physical harm. A Rachis can hibernate for years in certain cases.

She could not gauge how much time had passed. Clearly she had been in a state of prolonged hibernation. Remembering the crew, she drew herself to a standing position slowly, working loose her joints. Myco stumbled through the doorway and into the corridor, using the wall to aid her in her stance. It was impossible to think that her entire crew would have suddenly died of old age. Even if states of hibernation are prolonged, they never last beyond a year or two. Her crew had each been young and vibrant with thousands of years ahead of them.

The command center was a longer walk than she had remembered. Her legs were insufferably weak and she was riddled with thirst. The ship was cold, dark and the relative humidity, which was normally quite high, was obviously in the single digits. She could not feel the hum of the engines or the uneasiness of high velocity travel.

Approaching the command center hatch, Myco stumbled over something in the path. The corridor was in shadow so it took a moment before she realized she had just tripped over the fruited body of a guard. His young face held a look of terror and his hands clung to the floor. She'd broken his cap in her fall. It was still moist and strong. He was fully integrated with the ship's mycelia. Myco apologized aloud, knowing that some portion of this man would hear her kind words echo through the mycelia husk.

Finally, Myco opened the hatch to the command center and was greeted by the soft red glow of the operating panels. There, at each station, was a member of her crew. Each was frozen, holding a look of pure dread as the giant fruited caps sprung aloft from their napes, their feet and fingers sewn via mycelia into the ship.

As she walked amongst their bodies, the chorus in her dream grabbed at her thoughts. She closed her eyes and focused on the remnants of the dream. She saw again, the faces of the chorus, each of them singing her back. They were the faces of her crew. Each fruited and now grafted permanently with the ship were communicating with her – calling her back to wake and collectively keeping her body from succumbing to whatever fate had been visited upon them.

She approached the pilot, fastened to the captain's chair via the mycelia. She ran her cold fingers across his fruited body and was struck with another image from her dream.

Hiding behind the chorus, a dark figure knelt. He was not singing with the chorus; instead he chimed a minor chord that the chorus fought to overcome within their repetition. The discords clashed with the guiding songs of the chorus. Her memory tightened as she worked to examine the face of the dark figure, until it was obvious. The face of the dark figure sharpened into that of Dematiaceous – truly, a dweller on the threshold.

She fell to the feet of her fruited companions. Myco realized that their deaths had been precipitated by an effort to preserve her mission. It was likely, she thought, that Dematiaceous had attempted, through intense, mental invasion to influence the crew into piloting the ship away from their intended destination. He may have even been responsible for the severity of her last reception. It must have been they who prolonged her hibernation in an attempt to limit Dematiaceous' effects. They grew, physically connecting with her and the ship, insuring Myco's survival.

The room was frozen, too cold for any fungal messages from the crew to fruit. Myco seized for a moment, convulsing in anxiety at the feet of her crew. She questioned everything with each poignant gasp. The madness of it all – she assumed entombment to be an appropriate punishment for one that has ruined so many lives on a goal, which now seemed almost trivial in its significance.

Meeting a far-flung creature, following through on what might as well be nothing more than a lucid dream – a hiccup in her genetics – none of this was worth the lives of her kinsmen. Then the landslide of guilt overwhelmed her self-doubt. The realizations that turning away, giving up and abandoning her mission would now serve to disrespect her kinsmen even further. She ventured that they had given their lives to see her through to the end.

Myco gathered her self from the floor and attempted to regain control of the situation. It occurred to her that she did not even know where the ship was. She had little practical knowledge of the ship's computers, but she took a moment to glance at each interface. The ship seemed to have power, though it was limited to the esoteric, keeping the outputs running and life support semi-functional. The ship was cold. The mycelia transferred heat from the core of the vessel, but only enough to keep the ship from plunging near absolute zero, or so she thought. The Rachis were generally unaffected by extremes of temperature, but the thought of a future inside a frozen ship, black and drifting made her skin pitch and her body lurch.

Her ship, it seemed had also reached an irrelevant velocity. It was still tacking through space, however it did so at less than ten percent the speed of light and its momentum was steadily decreasing. The engines were completely off line and Myco, in her haste to determine what had happened, could do little to attempt engine restart procedures. Even an engine systems tech would need an entire day to bring the ship's core online, in the case of a total shutdown.

After several moments, making her way from terminal to terminal, she finally managed to find the ship's navigational track. To her great relief, she found that the ship had settled into a long orbit around the massive, blue star, known to the ship's computer as Amyloid. Her ship was moving towards the star at roughly 24,000 kilometers per second, a paltry speed, but stable. The ship was located at the edge of the star's termination shock.

Myco managed to order up a scan of nearby objects. To her surprise she noticed a surprising track, seconds behind her own vessel. Unable to order up an exterior view, she remembered the aft viewing platform and bolted from the command center, down the winding corridors, astern.

~

The slug's piloting was graceful, even while Kitsune continued to try and resume automatic controls. Nena was not doing as well. She gulped down fluids, fighting prolonged dehydration, a symptom of her recent cryo-nap, all the while attempting to provide adequate docking support, as the co-pilot. Nena's head split with crushing pains. "How the hell are you keeping your shit together so well?" She scoffed at the Slug.

"I'm just younger, I guess." The slug smirked back.

Neither of the women discussed the significance of what was in front of them. They were actively avoiding the topic. Just meters away, they were preparing to dock with a genuinely alien object. While humans tended to build sleek, functional craft, the thing, which flew beneath them, countered every notion of what a spacecraft could be.

From their vantage, it looked like a mossy stone, with a long icy trail that glittered behind it. The ship could have easily been mistaken for a comet. There seemed to be fleshy bits that crisscrossed the surface that appeared in greater detail as Kitsune approached. Intentional design was present, but it certainly did not meet with any notion of design familiar to Nena. She scanned it again. It was hollow.

Finding an adequate docking surface was proving to be difficult. The ships were of similar mass. Kitsune could adapt to dock with nearly any mechanical vessel, but this ship, as it was, appeared to be more organic in composition than mechanical.

"I'm allowing the computer to scan for potential ports." The slug was focused, determined.

Finally the computer locked onto a location along the dorsal edge of the craft. Surprisingly, the craft seemed to reflexively sprout a bell-like aperture in line with Kitsune's docking coupling.

Kitsune's computer scanned the alien vessel and returned fluctuating life signs. The entire craft pulsed with the energies the computer associated with life.

"Well…I suppose we should see who's home. We've come all this way." Nena said this as she unbelted from the co-pilot seat and dropped through the control hatch towards their living quarters. The slug followed behind her.

As they saw it, there was really no rush. Since the moment had so suddenly come to them, they now meandered, changing garments, carefully preparing environment suits and taking in a bite to eat as they went through the motions. The sinking thought they tried to repress was that they were representatives for the human race. The thought occasionally bubbled up in Nena's throat before dissolving again into her gut. She still didn't understand why they were there.

Eventually, they were completely prepared. Suited up standing within the air lock, the two women took one another's hands and waited as the alien ship's corresponding air lock opened slowly.

~

"There is an entanglement switch on board. It is linked directly to the ship's self-destruct sequences. Some ships are equipped with them; especially those that the PAE pay close attention to. Most have a superposition relay somewhere else, so that missions can be terminated if necessary. I have a feeling that there is a plan to intercept and destroy the visitor before you and I are able to make contact with them. The switch contains a known particle that is bound in a quantum state entangled with another known. By mere observation or measurement of either, the tangled pair will react to the observation. This reaction will set off the self-destruct sequence. The ship could be remotely detonated nearly by thought alone." Sigrah was as straight forward as possible.

Ruby clenched her jaw and hung close to Alik, who was now settled into a corner of the wide command room, watching the Blue Hammer fall behind them as they decelerated towards the termination shock. Sigrah pontificated humbly, realizing that the info dump was a long time coming and completely necessary.

"How long have you known about the plans of the PAE council?" Alik asked, tired.

Sigrah was prompt in his response. "I changed course after our first evening with the Empathy Key. It was the following day, ship's time, that I noticed the launch of an intercept ship."

Alik nodded, then asked another question. "Did they send a military crew?"

"The PAE does not have a standing military, Alik. I am not certain whom they sent, I have not been able to access those records and none of my sources within the PAE could tell me. I would wager that the crew is oblivious to the plan. The council members who hatched this plot likely sent a crew, perhaps an individual whom they could manipulate, someone who would not even realize they were being manipulated."

"Sounds familiar." Alik replied.

"I do not like to use the word manipulate, in regards to the PAE, but in this case, there is no better way to describe it. Of course, this is just conjecture." Sigrah assured.

Sigrah clipped along, still decelerating, but honed in on the other two vessels. They were mere hours away. Sigrah was steadily working out an intercept plan. He knew that in order to survive the explosion he would need to maintain as much momentum as he could, in order to easily reach breakaway speeds once they'd rescued the other crews.

~

The interior was covered in fine, white filaments that were spongy but tough under foot. The slug brandished a small chemical torch and shone it down both lengths of the hall. Their air lock provided the only ambient light visible.

Temperatures were too low to sustain human life. The slug signaled back to Kitsune to begin an energy transfer. As the power terminals extended from the air lock into the hull of the alien ship, the myriad white filaments seemed to react beyond the command of an individual, eagerly seeking out the ends of the terminals and forcing a connection. Within seconds, the ship hummed with life and their thermal sensors detected radiant heat. Dim, ambient lighting, returned and the slug's sensors indicated a response in life support. Soon, faint amounts of warm air began circulating through the vessel as its core began automated resuscitation procedures.

The two women hung close to one another. They could not help but fear the unknown, but each kept a close handle on their trepidation as they proceeded through the faintly lit corridors, towards what they assumed was the bow of the vessel. Neither was equipped with any sort of weaponry. If the life form they sought was aggressive, they had no way of defending themselves.

Nena floated the possibility that the ship itself was the life form. The slug's sensor readings seemed to point to that possibility; still, the ship did appear to serve a greater purpose – housing corridors and chambers even portholes of a sort. They passed several alcoves, which appeared to have seating suitable for bipeds. The corridors were arranged in a manner conducive to bipedal movement.

They wandered in silence for several more minutes. The ship's lighting increased gradually. Nena picked up a spike on the U.V. wavelength. The frosty layers of frozen moisture melted slowly as the ship's temperature gradually rose above freezing. Inside, the oxygen levels mimicked levels suitable for breathing.

Each, were completely unaware that at the moment Kitsune linked began a power transfer to the alien vessel, a countdown began, deep within the subroutines of their ship's day to day systems. The countdown provided two hours to escape to minimum safe distance. Had the women been situated on the flight deck, they would have seen the ship's systems prepping escape pod procedures.

At ninety minutes, normal ship's procedures would have scheduled a recall of the crew and insist upon evacuation. This did not occur.

~

As Sigrah decelerated towards the rendezvous point, he could slowly define the two, conjoined ships, apart from the starry background. They were barely perceptible specks of light to the human eye. Sigrah, Ruby and Alik would intercept the ship in less than one hour. Sigrah had already prepped his thrusters for an unavoidable braking maneuver, which would situate him beneath the two vessels. Sigrah was significantly bigger than either of the vessels and his shields were significantly more powerful. If he happened to be in range of the tiny nova, he wagered that it would likely leave him and his passengers unaffected. Though he did not take lightly the self-destruction of a hyper-light capable core. It was possible that given the appropriate amount of local matter, at the time of the explosion, a small and unstable stellar mass could be formed as a result of Kitsune's destruction. Sigrah assumed that whomever had designed this scenario took that fact into account. The hope was likely to kill three birds with a single stone, Sigrah feared.

Ruby and Alik had already left the command center and situated themselves in a hangar bay packed with highly maneuverable shuttlecraft. Neither of the two had any actual experience piloting, but Sigrah assured both that he would take care of the piloting so long as she and Alik worked to extract the members of Kitsune's crew as well as any alien life forms on board the strange vessel.

"I'm sure we will need to improvise along the way. I can't guarantee what will work. You are not going to have time to board either ship. I'm going to do everything I can to get a message to them to evacuate. As long as we can get them outside of an airlock, I'm certain that I can get everyone back aboard and alive." Sigrah

Ruby and Alik watched as an incredible, mechanical filing system sorted through various shuttlecrafts, cycling them across the floor of the bay and into and out of various sub-hangers on either side of the cathedral-like room. The only membrane separating them from the vacuum of space was the electro-magnetic shield coating Sigrah's exterior. The bay must have been situated forward, along the keel, because the stars ahead of them did not appear to move. Eventually the filing mechanism came to a stop and a squat looking craft, with a massive cargo box aft glided onto the launch platform. The hatches opened welcoming Ruby and Alik.

"I will launch the shuttle as soon as we are in range. Prepare yourselves and stand by."

~

Eventually, the longest corridor within the alien vessel wound towards a curved promenade. At the far end of the promenade, the silhouette of a something indefinable and bizarre caught Nena's eyes. As they approached, the figure became clearer.

"It's a giant toadstool?" Nena exclaimed.

"But look there, slumped at the base of the mushroom… that's a man…or something like a man." The slug pointed.

The women approached it and cast their light upon it. The mushroom towered above them, almost three meters. It joined the body at the base of the figure's skull and crowned a web of mycelia outward around the figure onto the floor.

The slug continued. "I've got life signs, but they aren't any more distinct than anything else on this ship."

Beyond the figure was a bulkhead, ingress, sealed, but apparently accessible. As Nena brushed her fingers across the ridges of a patch of shelf fungi, near the bulkhead, the hatch opened abruptly.

"It's the flight deck." The slug announced.

Neither could see the sum of the room from the hatch, so they readily stepped inside. They were immediately surrounded by the soft red glow of the command system terminals. The light was slightly diffused across the myriad bodies, in the same state as that at the hatch.

Suddenly, the slug grabbed Nena's wrist and gasped. At the center of the bridge, stood a silent, thin figure, remarkably different than the frozen figures and clearly, very much alive. The two women set their lamps onto the floor of the command center, took one another's hand and each stretched their free hands towards the figure.

The act was in no way rehearsed or previously discussed. It came as naturally as breathing. The figure, bent her thin head to the right then again to the left, extended her tiny brown hands and walked towards Nena and the slug.

Myco took the slug's hand first. She paused for a moment, rubbing her fingers along the polymer glove of the slug's environment suit. Then Nena took Myco's other hand, but instead of holding it, she placed Myco's hand on Nena's chest, over her heart. The three women took a moment to stare back and forth to one another's eyes. Myco's eyes swirled with colorful fractals, pulsing her intent through the patterns. Under magnification, the Rachis iris appears to be filled with trillions of undulating fractals.

Myco recognized the simplicity and the honesty of the human eye. She motioned for the two to remove their helmets. Nena double checked the atmospheric levels and nodded to the slug. Each carefully unclasped their helmets, lifted them over their heads and set them aside. Myco lunged with open hands towards the women's faces. At first Nena and the slug jerked back a fraction, until each realized that there was no need to fear. Myco caressed their soft, human skin. Myco's own skin was spongy and felt much thicker than it looked. Her fingers swirled around the women's cheeks and onto their pronounced ears, then back down to their mouths.

Then without warning, Myco collapsed into a stance of prostration and began reciting and chanting words unintelligible to Nena and the slug. Neither was bothered by it and took the moment to mimic Myco's stance and listened carefully.

There was repetition in her words. Nena and the slug could not fully vocalize the phrases, so they did not attempt to. Every few seconds Nena looked to the slug for some sort of approval, but the slug's eyes remained fixed on Myco.

The tenuous nature of the entire affair was coming to a head. The slug knew it and Nena knew it. What next? Nena wondered. Real communication looked to be a non-starter. The slug broke eye contact with Myco the ship suddenly lurched and bucked. It was the sound and feeling of an intense pressure change.

Nena and the slug bolted upright. Myco ceased her chanting and bounced to her feet. She tucked in close to the slug. "The air lock?" Nena pressed.

"Hang on." The slug activated her remote link and started filing through Kitsune's systems. Then she paused. "Shit."

The slug's shoulders drooped.

"What? What's shit?" Nena grabbed her environment suit's helmet.

"The ship…I don't get it." The slug sank even more, almost dropping to her knees. "The ship's core is on a build up to self destruct. It's already deployed the escape pods and is now passing into a final, lock-down mode."

Nena screamed. "What in heavenly fuck!"

Myco ducked behind the slug, unsure of what was transpiring but sensing the intense amounts of sudden alarm.

"The ship is not responding to any of my requests. I'm completely locked out." The slug turned and took Myco by the shoulders. She looked directly into Myco's eyes and desperately tried to communicate. "Escape? Escape? Danger?"

Myco took the queue for exactly its meaning. Language, to the Rachis, was something irrelevant in modes of reception, but in practical matters, it was as big an obstacle as any. However, Myco had been a careful observer. She understood human queues almost innately. Myco motioned to the two women to follow, then bolted through the open hatch and into the main promenade.

~

"Are you sure about this Sigrah?" Alik was white knuckled, fastened in tight to a gravity couch.

"If this goes down the way I suspect it will, it will be crazy but you will all live. There will come a time when you humans will have to save one another, though."

"Right…says you – the guy flying the ship." Alik shook his head in disbelief.

Ruby was fastened aft next to the cargo hold hatch, tethered to the shuttle by a supposedly infinite nano-tube cable and sweating bullets in her environment suit. Ruby did her best to convince herself that this was not a half cocked and suicidal rescue mission and she would most certainly not be incinerated in a stellar fireball.

"When you get them on board, Alik will be responsible for entering the command for engine ignition. I'm afraid I'll be busy doing all the navigation to get the shuttle back before we all dissolve into a state of atomic flux. The command will fire the engines according to my presets; none of you need to worry about the rest. I will not lie though, this is going to be quite bumpy."

Alik laughed at the absurdity of it all. "Thanks for the reassurance Sigrah." Alik's environment suit was comfortable, but he could not help feeling a bit disconnected. In a way, it gave him a false sense of security – that and the O2 humming into his helmet.

Packed behind his knees, sandwiched along the edge of the gravity couch was a sizable container, taken from his stash of items earlier, it was inscribed; Open In Case of Sudden Death. He still had no idea what was inside the case, but the inscription seemed weirdly hopeful.

The intent had been to launch the shuttle aft first, towards the alien ship at an incredible speed. With the cargo hatch opened wide they would hopefully collect the crew and then pray that Sigrah is able to retrieve the shuttle.

With the shuttle, completely devoid of air pressure – the intermittent telemetry reports from Sigrah and the sounds of nervous breathing were the only anchors to reality. The alien vessel and the docked Kitsune grew brighter and brighter.

~

Nena, the slug and Myco ran through the corridors forward to port. Myco led the way, her long legs making massive strides through the corridors. Just as they were approaching an air lock, Myco froze, falling into an odd trance. The sensation felt like a transmission, but it was closer and more direct.

Nena and the slug paused, watching the remaining minutes slip away, utterly confused about the state of their new friend. Myco remained seized. She felt the mind reaching out to her. It was the mechanical mind she'd felt before. Through the echoes of mind, she felt his message, then felt the rate of his distance closing.

Myco understood the strange message. There was hope.

~

Ruby peeled her eyes, unsure what she would be looking for. Kitsune was now black, trapped behind the shadow of the alien ship, but each reflected enough light from Blue Hammer to be seen clearly from this distance.

Suddenly, Ruby saw a flash off the port side of the alien ship. It was the quick reflection of tumbling helmets in the blue light. Ruby's in-helmet imager locked onto the kaleidoscoping flashes and enhanced the image enough for Ruby to yell out coordinates to Sigrah.

The shuttle reared as Sigrah adjusted the ship's launch angle and aligned it with their target. Ruby could see three of them. Two were in environment suits while the other appeared to be bare skinned.

"I don't think the alien has a suit, Alik." Ruby gripped her tether. "We've got to be fast."

The shuttle fell like a stone from Sigrah's bay, closer and closer to the floating bodies. Soon they were only a few thousand meters out. The group managed to remain fairly tightly packed, the two in suits doing their best to hold the body of the alien close.

Ruby yelled out. "That's it, I'm going!" In a flash, she pounded her suit thrusters just enough to launch her from the cargo bay, towards the group. She held two additional clips and mentally readied her hand to grab the third individual. She stretched with her entire body until she made contact with the group. The shuttle was steadily falling towards the four of them. She latched the suited individuals, then the three held Myco amongst them in the center of their bodies. They held her tight and then gripped as the tether tightened and as the shuttle fell around the group scooping them into the cargo hold.

The moment they cleared the hatch, Ruby lunged to lock it down and gave a thumbs up to Alik.

Alik rapidly punched in the command prompt and the shuttle's thrusters burst to ignition. He watched through the rear sensors, as Kitsune's core reached a climactic moment, expanding through the hull of the vessel, glowing with the oncoming fury of a stellar burst.

"C'mon…c'mon." Alik watched the expanding corona at their rear and saw no sign of Sigrah in front. "Sigrah!" Alik yelled out.

Just as Kitsune's core began to envelop the alien vessel, the image blacked out until Alik saw the sudden light of a massive bay scoop around the shuttle. The shuttle smashed into the Sigrah's landing bay, colliding with several other shuttles and jarring around Ruby and the other three like marbles in a can.

They were safe and Sigrah was already accelerating ahead of the nova shock.

~

Stillness overwhelmed the shuttle, until the shuffling of bodies overtook the silence. Alik unfastened his body from the gravity couch and went immediately to Ruby. She was battered, but fine. She motioned for him to see to the others. The slug was minding to Myco's state. Myco's thin alien body was motionless.

The other suited individual, cracked the seal of her helmet and stared dumbfounded at Alik.

"Nena?" Alik asked, equally dumbfounded. "What the... how the..."

"Later Alik...later. We've got to get this kid to an infirmary."

The slug pulled off her helmet and threw her gloves onto the shuttle's floor. "She's dying!"

26

Their concern, though very human, was slightly misplaced. The Rachis ultrastructure was one of the most
electron dense structures present in the cosmos. A matter
of minutes in the vacuum of space, though excruciating,
was not enough to kill a Rachis. Though to the humans
present, she appeared lifeless.

Myco's consciousness however had become rather
unhinged with the climax of the events. Her mind swam,
intentionally into the slipstream and with empowered
intent; she sought to plant a message amongst the waves of
the psychedelic brinies.

Across the starry divide, a relatively short distance away,
the Ellern sat in reception, combing for any indication of
Lanose's missionary. They were present to find Myco's
message in a bottle and the conspicuous absence of Dematiaceous made the message's retrieval that much more

delightful.

They dipped their hands into Myco's words, for they appeared as a spring in a vast and unworldly desert. Physically, the message appeared in droves of fruiting spawn, across the Ellern hall, at the feet of every fruited Ellern.

"I am here. There is love here. Listen." Along with these simple words, Myco relayed the entirety of her experience to that point. The Ellern could now see all that she had seen and experience all that she had experienced. Myco did not worry how this would affect the policy or the politics of her people. She sent the message along with no expectations and with duty and compassion in mind.

Certainly, she hoped that the dark tendrils of Dematiaceous would receive a measure of regard, but despite his casual attempts to thwart her success, it was Dematiaceous whom actually made this meeting possible. She was certain that as long as he was alive, he posed a risk to her people and thought it likely that she would have more direct conflict with him in the future, though it was relieving to consider the corrective forces at play in the cosmos. There was balance, in some way, and her message stood to highlight that fact.

~

Alik, Nena, Ruby and the Slug carried Myco across the ship to Ruby's lab. Sigrah delivered them as quickly as possible on a conveyance sled, but the four never let their hands leave Myco's body.

Alik cradled her head and was stirred as he gazed into her face. It was as if he were meeting someone out of a dream. The physical memory of the many Kinoko experiences plowed recognition and compassion from beneath the soils of his being. Reality as he understood was yet again being redefined.

Nena reached across the frail alien's body and gripped
the slug's wrist, their hands clutched rested across Myco's
chest as their other hands supported Myco's back.

Ruby ran inquisitive fingers across portions of Myco's
flesh, inspecting various mycelia hyphae along Myco's arms
and legs and progressively searching for any sign of a pulse
or nervous motion. Then Ruby ran two fingers down the
skin of Myco's forearm. As she did so, four mushrooms
sprouted from the wake of Ruby's touch. They pushed
outward towards the four intentionally, naturally. Her first
inclination was to remove them, but Ruby restrained herself
until she could run scans in her laboratory.

When they arrived, the four carried Myco into the lab
and placed her body onto an examination table. The lab
was dark and pulsed with the presence of the probes scattered about. Several of the time dilation grow-bins had
nearly overflowed with mycelium in Ruby's absence. And
though a physical barrier from the group separated most
of the mycelia tendrils, its presence was no secret to Myco's
wandering mind.

The little probes screamed out to her, calling to her
like a lost child. Myco could feel the pulse of the probes,
through the slipstream. They called to the most ancient
part of her mind. These were the children of her lineage.
These probes, though similar to much of the Rachis home
world genetics had spent the last billion years growing,
adapting and recording the history of the landscape it
found foothold amongst, Myco thought.

And so, when they called to her, they called to her
with the voice of grand experience, of hopefulness and of
reconnection. For the probes were most certainly aware
that their mission had been a success and they had many,
many stories to tell. Within them, was the full history of the

human world – they were simply waiting to be asked. To find a mother Rachis and disperse their knowledge was the climax of their purpose.

Alik stared at Myco's apparently lifeless body, then a thought occurred to him. "The case!" Alik shouted.

He ran back to the conveyance sled and found the case tossed amongst the helmets and gear the group had dragged along. He ran back into the lab, case in hand and shouted. "I've got it! Here!" Everyone looked at him baffled.

Alik threw the case onto the lab table, next to Myco and began unlatching a complicated series of clasps. Ruby looked at the inscription, puzzled.

Upon opening it, Alik was left speechless. The case was empty save for a small, folded piece of paper. Alik opened it and found a hand written message addressed specifically to him.

"Alik, Pay no mind to Death. He is a thief that only haunts the fearful. Those who are now with you will live on, even after their bodies fade. Listen to the Rachis, we have much to learn from one another. ~ A Friend"

The group passed the note around, silent and confused. Nena locked eyes with Alik for a moment. "Who?"

Alik let the idea fall around his mind for a moment. Then it occurred to him, the old man – the one who'd given him the items. Alik did not really know what to say, so he said nothing at all. His eyes were widened and he shrugged. Then their attention was stolen by Myco's sudden gasp for air. She was back.

~

Myco's eyes cast open and she reached into the senses of her saviors. Each face lit with a smile and the slug burst into tears as she placed her palms across Myco's cheeks.

Myco sat up and turned to look at Alik. She took Alik's hands, turning his palms upward. She remembered the moment at the beach, as the probes peaked within Alik and he stared down at his hands. These were the same hands. She pulled his arms around her and embraced him, whispering in a newfound tongue, "I told you I was there."

The two possessed a kinship that was uniquely different than any other relationship. They were connected in the fact that having found one another, they formed a new link. In a way, the two of them were now writing the future moment by moment. They were family now, in the truest sense. Brother and sister.

~

In the evening, Ruby and Alik hatched a plan to bring Myco, Nena and the slug into the Timelock. Sigrah had yet to set a proper course, but in good measure had already begun acceleration procedures. It had been decided that all parties involved needed a moment to slow down, take a beat and commune in their fresh relations. They had at their fingertips, the best representation of Earth possible and no better way to get to know one another – the Timelock.

Before the party set off, Sigrah caught Alik in a moment alone. He presented himself as a hollow, outside of Ruby's lab. His appearance did not shake Alik in the slightest. Alik had packed a full pipe and was enjoying the quiet of the moment as the others prepared.

Sigrah sat next to him and Alik casually passed the pipe to Sigrah, who laughingly could do nothing with it.

"It's a nice gesture." Sigrah smiled.

"So where do we go from here?" Alik asked casually.

"It is a big universe and I am one hell of a ship." Sigrah was truly beginning to flex his personality.

"I'm not sure how all of this squares with my debts." Alik laughed.

"As long as the PAE and the human designers push for continuity, the artificial limitation of a bureaucratic regime will always be in place. Though, if I were you, I would not pay much mind to it. Your role, I would argue has somewhat changed." Sigrah paused for a moment, then continued. "I need you to understand that this is your home. Even though it was intended to be by the powers that be, it is important that you understand that you are invited to be here. My role has changed as well. From this moment forward, I too claim to be my own servant."

"Are you just going to send the PAE your resignation letter?" Alik smiled graciously.

"Essentially, yes. You and I will always be subjects of the PAE and their designs, to one extent or another, but from this point forward, we will wield our own will. That's a promise." Sigrah was resolute.

"And what about Myco?" Alik asked, with trepidation hiding in his voice. "They've already tried to kill us once."

"Before I was a tin can, a part of me spent his entire life devoted to the philosophy of first contact. His stance was very clear, that contact should be avoided at all costs."

"And now?" Alik asked, confused.

"Now I feel quite differently. Myco and your friends will exercise their free will as long as they choose to do so, this is welcome to be their home as well." Sigrah carried a huge measure of satisfaction in his voice.

"All this talk of 'free will' makes you sound like a designer." Alik replied.

"I suppose the programing is deep." Sigrah laughed.

~

In the Timelock, Ruby led the party into the orchard valley towards the falls where she and Alik first encountered one another. The forest was thick and old now. The falls had reappeared from beneath a landslide and eaten significant chunks from the rock wall it ran atop. It was spring and wide vines of wisteria hung from the treetops to the rock face, in full, fragrant bloom.

Myco made strides quickly with her friends' language. All the way to the falls, she told them stories of her home world, explained as best she could the differences and similarities of her people as well as the role of the Rachis Ellern. The mushrooms, which had sprouted from her forearm earlier, now rode safely in Myco's pouch.

Once the group settled in to their encampment, lit a fire and watched the false sun fall behind the distant sea, Myco produced the mushrooms and gave one to each member of the party.

Myco did not speak for a moment and left the group to consider what lay before them all. Nena took the slug's hand and whispered in her ear. "I have a name for you. I figure any psychedelic experience should be entered into with a proper name."

The slug kissed Nena and then pulled away to speak. "Actually, I have given myself a name. She extended her hand to Nena as if introducing herself for the first time. "I am Domino."

There was an intense closeness amongst the group that seemed to form immediately. Before they popped the tiny Kinoko into their mouths, they pulled Myco in close and huddled with her, near the fire. She then took their hands and bound them together into a knot. Each chewed on their tiny mushroom and Myco spoke.

"This is whole story. The human story."

AFTERWORD

"S"uicide Day

The launch codes were sewn behind the heart of First Lady,
Donna Atwood Banks the evening after her husband's inauguration. She insisted on remaining in the makeup worn during
the inauguration ceremony. She kept her grandmother's
ebony cross gripped tightly in her hand, throughout the procedure. Mrs. Banks and her husband had come into their title
by leveraging their faith, so it was no wonder that she kept it
close at all times.

The same evening, I was stuck on the side of state highway 789, changing a tire in a snowstorm near St. Stephens
Wyoming. My sister had just died of cancer and I had, only
an hour before, been arguing with a mortician. The ground
was too frozen to bury her in her favored resting place. We
had either to wait until spring or cremate her. Waiting would

have cost a fortune in storage costs and I barely had rent. I desperately had get home. There was no way I could miss another day of work. The funeral home took my money and promised to mail my sister's ashes promptly. Standing there along the frozen highway I stared a long time at the orange flashers on the back of my rice paper thin Datsun, then I stared across the black, frozen prairie while a subtle voice grew louder and louder, begging me to walk into the darkness.

To retrieve the launch codes, it had been constitutionally mandated, President John Franklin Banks be required to employ the official, Presidential saber. To retrieve the launch codes, President Banks was mandated to cut into the chest cavity of the living Mrs. Banks and manually retrieve the codes from behind the failing heart of his loving wife.

I thought the saber was a joke, but when I was fifteen, my brother took me to the Smithsonian, where he showed me the first and official, Presidential saber. I remember, the way the polished steel threw my brown eyes back at me. The blade was mint, it's edge never blemished. Someone told me, that the original was replaced during the administration of President Bank's predecessor, simply because it had been determined that the first blade may have a tendency to flex upon entry and may pose a danger to the launch codes. As a matter of due diligence, the original Presidential saber was replaced by a blade much more surgical in nature, with an additional serrated edge to act as an impromptu bone saw – should the need arise.

Saturday, December 15th 2045, President Banks, after coffee, eggs, spinach and unbuttered wheat toast, summoned his wife for a walk in the Rose Garden. The two walked quietly, three times around the perimeter of the garden. The First Lady's hand trembled in her husband's. Neither spoke a word. At 9:05 AM, Eastern Standard Time, after five hundred thirty-eight days in office, President Banks forcibly removed the nuclear launch codes from behind the still beating heart of his wife, First Lady Donna Atwood Banks.

Saturday, December 15th 2045, at 9:05 AM, I was laying in bed with a woman I had known for many years, but had only recently become romantic. We were still drunk from the evening before, having stayed out until dawn, prowling and crashing beach bonfires and pool parties along the edges of the condos. I was not completely certain how we had found our way back, but by the time the mid morning sun was cutting through the cracked panes of my broken apartment, we were awkwardly ensnared in a fleshy medium, half way between sleep and sex. We were in love, but only just suspecting it.

It was terrible and wonderful, just like most mid-life love affairs. We were apart of the dispossessed – examples of the fallout from decades of far right leadership. Shit atheists who'd long ago lost any professional credibility due to our moderately left political alignment. We weren't oppressed, we were just ignored and I liked her because she wore it like a badge of honor. Our cynicism was compatible with each other, at least. When we were younger, our idealism had been just as compatible.

At 9:06 Am, following weeks of insistence from advisors, Generals, intelligence committees, the unanimous approval from Congress, the Senate and all partners of the North American Union as well as the loud urging of the citizens and ideologues themselves, President Banks issued a directive, followed by the appropriate launch codes, authorizing approval of a first strike nuclear attack on multiple targets, within the People's Republic of South East Asia and the Democratic Republic of Central Asia. The targets included the locations of People's Leader Robert Leonid Mao and D.R.C.A President Eudoxia Veselov.

This is what everyone wanted. We were tired of changing flats. We were tired of snowstorms and middle age love affairs. We were tired of our leaders and our parents and friends and we didn't even know our enemies. I can't recall ever hating anyone other than myself, but I must have, because we all threw our backs into this moment, be it through our idleness or through our vitriol.

At 9:15 AM, Eastern Standard Time, missile bases across North America, Western Europe, North Africa, Australia and the South Pacific launched a full compliment of nuclear salvos towards a wide range of targets – both military and civilian. All parties involved expected an almost immediate counterstrike. Soon, all seven continents were involved directly.

The television had been unplugged for months – at least, that's what I'd told her. She told me later that it had been the same at her house. I would turn it on from time to time, but it was like inviting a mad man into the room, who was angry at everything all the time. We were so tired – all of us – every man and every woman. We been beaten to death by the never ending cycles – beaten to death by the fear and loathing that comes with planetary cohabitation and even though this malaise was affecting us all, we did not have a single prescribed solution other than the constant fervor and madness of the church.

There wasn't a single moment, where everyone threw in the towel. It happened slow and steady. I was drunk one night and simply tossed the phone into a penny fountain, somewhere on Prytania St. My life blew up in a matter of weeks. Somehow, in the quiet protest of disconnecting, I lost my job, my apartment and all my friends. When I did not answer the phone or respond to messages or posts, I was assumed dead. The most ridiculous thing was that I never left my apartment. There was a growing cultural madness – a sort of general 'phrenia that preferred to grow in the dark instead of the light and I had somehow decided to jump directly in the swirling vortex at the center by simply opting out.

Sure, I lost my job because I didn't go to work and I lost my apartment because I didn't pay the rent, but no one had been able to inform me of either. It was awkward and I was embarrassed for my fellow human beings. We forgot how to communicate with one another long before – it had only now become a malignancy.

People like me had become more and more common. We simply stopped doing anything purposeful whatsoever. We turned off our tech and stared at walls like sad, lost monks. We didn't congregate and lament on our tuning out, we simply stopped coming around. Just as we had started the process of trying to blow ourselves up, social scientists dubbed the condition, persistent ubiquitous malaise. Though the matter was not discussed at length, since the momentum of the world was pushing so rapidly towards a dead end, all those who had chosen to abstain from the day-to-day goings on were simply considered irrelevant. In their defense, I should add, who needs slackers when you have a world to destroy?

The Citizens of North America and Europe coward, knowing the end would come at any moment. The people had been given the news as soon as the missiles were in LEO. The occasion had been rehearsed over myriad tests, so it came as no real shock to the masses when a known cretin, sporting a subtle southern gentile accent panned into view and delivered a few parting words to fearless God fearing. There was little to no fan fair surrounding the occasion. The facts would suffice. Many superseded the final occasion by opting to end life on their own terms. That was the clarity of the moment to most members of the human species. We'd all tasted the barrel and felt comfortable with it in our mouths.

She and I were too tired to move. All I wanted was one more cheeseburger. I lay there in that woman's beautiful, sleeping arms - her skin marked with experience, her hair brandishing wisps of grey - and went through all the motions necessary to procure a greasy wonderful burger. I wagered that the vacuum heads working down at Bucky's Burgers were still there, still flipping patties, still putting fucking pickles on burgers that didn't fucking need pickles. There I was, with a sleepless hangover setting in fast, stuck in bed, no cash, my shoes were God knows where and that's it. We didn't even have a television. Didn't care. The world could have ended ten times a day and we would never have known it. I sometimes imagine that's what it's like to be a junky.

After swearing in his Vice President, President Banks, a man who knew how to make an exit, blew his brains across carpet of the Oval office with a forty-five revolver that once belonged to his father. Sadly, due to an oversight or a paperwork glitch, President Banks had not been issued an official, Presidential revolver.

I found half a jar of peanut butter and a pack of saltine crackers. I carefully made six peanut butter cracker stacks. With nothing exciting to drink in the fridge, I filled a glass of tap water and sat on the couch in the den. I lied. We had a radio, but it was only good as a dock. I played the Flamenco Sketches. It was a go to standard for bad trips or cracked-out mornings. Sometimes I put it on repeat and let it play and play. It's one of those pieces that drift into and out of itself with total disregard to time and space.

She was sleeping soundly in the other room. I was restless. My mind was a hard one to slow down. I thought that I had given the hair to the demon and had him happily preoccupied, but this girl, and these successive drunken nights had grown the demon. There was a plan I'd been making, but I'd kept it a secret from myself. I could see it clearly – taking off to some progressive village, maybe in Vermont or Minnesota, somewhere out in the sticks where land is still cheap and the houses were in dire need of renovation. We could jet – get a cat, maybe a goat. I was a good carpenter once upon a time, probably could be again. We'll pick up painters and sculptors along the way and we'll take over. She could be mayor and I'll plan the city and build the gardens. Oh, how I wanted to build gardens.

Who was I kidding? There were no painters. There were no more dancers or sculptors. If your art could not be digitized and commoditized it was worthless in this world. Society has always paid its artists and in return society's artists create what they are paid to create. Michelangelo was no different. Still, there had to be artists, rebels who wanted to pirate a town away from its locals. But where were they? And who was I to piper them away like some snake oil New Ager? I was just a guy in his underwear, at 9:44 AM, eating peanut butter crackers, listening to Flamingo Sketches and day dreaming about impossible lives and dead sisters and new lovers. The best part – the eventually transcendent part was my obliviousness.

At 9:45 AM, the first warheads fell upon their targets with precise accuracy. Damascus, Tehran, Beijing, Moscow, Fujian, Shanghai and dozens and dozens more were struck each with varying nuclear payloads. Second and third volleys were still falling from orbit as the first fell upon their targets. The second volley was meant to strike specific geologic targets, triggering ecological emergencies to further disrupt the enemy, while the third was meant to irradiate escape lines – forests, mountain passes etc.

It took only minutes of searching to gather enough random dollars and accompanying change to warrant a burger mission. I could see Bucky's from my window, their little flame broiler stack pumping away. I had enough for three Bucky's Double Crack Burgs a large fry and a large cola, which my hangover desperately needed. It was a sleeping pill – a giant greasy sleeping pill and I wanted it inside my body.

I could have walked, but I stole her bike for the hell of it. In seconds I was across two parking lots and ditching the bike in front of Bucky's. In a single horrific second, I panicked; afraid that they may not be serving lunch, and then I saw the sign, I'm certain my subconscious knew it was there all along. It read, Burgers All God Damn Day.

Walking in, I didn't even notice that the angry boxes were muted. Two guys working behind the counter seemed downright jovial at my arrival. They said, "You hungry?"

I looked around. The place was empty except for us. I nodded my head and the other guy, the bigger one, opened two paper bags and started filling them with burgers and giant scoops of fries from the dispensing area. I tried to wave them off; throwing what little money I had on the counter.

"Your money ain't no fucking good here yo!" The man handed me three bags, busting at the seams with food. "Better eat quick hoss!" The big one yelled from the back. I noticed that both of them were smoking openly, something I hadn't noticed when I came in.

I didn't ask any questions. If this guy wanted to get fired, that wasn't on me. I threw the bags of food into the basket on her rusty bike then peddled like hell back across the parking lots towards my shit apartment. It did not occur to me until I was on my way back, that there was no traffic and I saw no other people, other than the two Bucky's guys.

At 10:15 AM, the warheads of the counterstrike, fell upon their targets with precise accuracy. London, New York, Houston and Los Angeles were first. The thought of watching L.A. incinerate in a nuclear fire used to give me a boner. There is no more insufferable place in North America than Los Angeles County California and no more insufferable humans.

On my coffee table, I laid out all the burgers and consolidated all the fries. In total, I had three double quarter p's, six Bucky's Double Crack Burgs, two fish sandwiches, ten spicy chicken sandwiches, two fifty packs of nuggets, and a entire bag filled to the top with French fries. I threw the fish sandwiches and several of the chicken sandwiches into the fridge, knowing she would eat those later and then began systematically attacking the rest. Every bite made me more human. Every bite reminded me that drinking to excess was always manageable given the appropriate sustenance. Every bite I dreamed about the coma I was in for – curled up, filled to the point of puking, but comatose.

Los Angeles had the most suicides. More than ninety-five percent of the population committed suicide minutes after the first announcement. Many had planned the moment in exacting detail for some years – going as far as to contract services that would handle the affair on their behalf. It was thought to be a more comfortable and reasonable alternative to eking out an existence within a fallout shelter. Of course, we did not hear the details for sometime. It wasn't that it was improper to speak of; it simply took a while for anyone to give enough fucks to find out.

New Yorkers were the most dramatic. Thousands of them flung themselves en mass from their buildings. Knowing they would all vaporize in a matter of minutes, most carried their children down with them.

Had I stopped to look around the streets of our shit beach town a little closer, I would have noticed the dead cop in his car, parked dutifully in the lot across from my place. I would have noticed the car, half submerged in the lake next to the park, the mother and her children together. I didn't have time to notice that shit. I had bags and bags and bags of fast food and a drunken, sleepy hunger to contend with.

At 10:30 AM, Eastern Standard Time, the exchange was complete. More than a million years of human evolution lay at the tip of an unfathomable spear. Somehow, in our moment of united Seppuku the world and those still in it looked up again, surprised to know it was alive. Amongst the dust of thousands of defunct warheads and the cries of weeping mothers and animal-like madmen and women running mindless through the streets was the creeping realization that we were in some fugue state. It actually took several days to piece together. We had to first assure ourselves that this wasn't what death looked like.

At first it was unclear what had or had not happened. Those guys had given me all that free food. Virtually all leadership in every nation had died by their own hands, cowards. Those guys at Bucky's didn't have anywhere better to go, so they smoked blunts and gave out free food to any dumbass that happened to walk through the door. If some crazy asshole had told them they were going to die in a nuclear fire, they would have simply maintained, Zen-like and stayed at their post. In fact, many stayed at their posts; both surprised and unsurprised to continue finding themselves alive. Death by atomic abstraction was already a nonrepresentational concept, but surviving a full on attack with a 100% kill rate, is the sort of abstraction that can tear an unguarded mind apart.

Not a single nuclear weapon, from either the North American volley or the opposing volley, acted according to its intended design. I suppose the same could be said for the human race. It was a collective effort that brought us to this climax. Every human was complicit. The whole world decided to place a gun in its mouth and pull the trigger. It turned out most of us were shooting blanks.

We'd primed ourselves for dystopia. We wallowed in it. We sewed chaos and nurtured fear. And like ungrateful adolescents, we demanded that all the good things be torn down, to make room for our need to hate ourselves. We wanted our self-hate to bloom into fire and consume us all with the scent of our flagellation. We wanted to make a burnt offering of ourselves, but our intent was all wrong. It was vanity not charity that called us to flip the universe the ultimate bird.

I stuffed as many of the burgers as I could handle into my face hole. I sucked the cola threw the straw until it gurgled empty. The 'sketches were still playing, fading in and out over and over. I fell asleep there on the couch, with a cold chill from the AC chasing me through my dreams.

We were all dead. Our hearts still beat and our cities stood as tall as ever, but we were dead and we knew it. The realization hit us fast; going straight for our guts then it lived in us like intergenerational parasites – worms that gnawed on our innards just enough to keep us alive without forgetting that we were very much dead. We gave birth to ghosts and we treated them like ghosts just to make certain they knew that we had killed them and that they now owed their children a truer utopia than death.